WEEKEND

COWBOY

A NOVEL BY

Maureen A. Maillet

Black Rose Writing

www.blackrosewriting.com

The final approval for this literary material is granted by the author.

First printing

All characters appearing in this work are fictitious. Any resemblance to real persons, living or dead, is purely coincidental.

ISBN: 978-1-61296-147-7

PUBLISHED BY BLACK ROSE WRITING

www.blackrosewriting.com

Printed in the United States of America

Weekend Cowboy is printed in Times New Roman

To Kyle
Thank you for always believing.

Acknowledgments

This has been a long journey and I want to thank all of the individuals who have inspired and supported me over the years: Mary Lou and Bill, Liam and Margot, Charles Repa, Fred Bressler, Beverly Ogden, Christa Forster, Julie Kemper, Robin Rosenberg, Jolie Sumbera, and Leach Edmundson. A special thank you to Tracey Hilfman, who will always be with me.

WEEKEND

COWBOY

Maurice A. Maillet

~Chapter 1

Kate Jones looked at her profile in the mirror one more time, smiling. She wasn't enormous, but definitely six months pregnant with a healthy baby girl. It had been a breeze being pregnant this time. No bed rest so far or any complications except the asthma, but even that wasn't bad she decided. Her face lit up when the door opened because Harlynn was going to break away from his meeting to be here today. If one thing hadn't been perfect it would be her husband, Harlynn Barrett, who was beyond famous now in business and legal circles. It seemed everyone wanted a piece of Harlynn these days.

She found her most pleasant smile when she saw Meg Grayden walk in the door sheepishly. Meg was married to Henry Grayden, Kate's Godfather. Henry was the only father figure she had known in her life. She sighed, thinking that Harlynn and Henry were trying to close the purchase of a company. She understood things happened at a closing, not long ago she had been sitting at the table doing corporate deals with Harlynn and Henry. Now she took more of a strategic planning part in her company, Moon Water. It was what she wanted she reminded herself. She wanted to be there for her son, daughter and for this unborn child.

Meg smiled, not saying anything for a minute as she took her seat in the corner like she had done numerous times in the past months with Kate. It made Kate happy to have Meg there and to have this child to share.

"I have a name," Kate announced carefully getting on the table, waiting for the doctor.

"Really?" Meg smiled in anticipation. "Let me hear it."

"Lane, Henry's middle name. We can call her Laney when she is little. Harlynn wants to call her Kate but that's just too confusing in my opinion. Ugh, people might call her Katie, I don't like that name. Anyway Harlynn put the names together, Lane Kate Jones Barrett. "

"It's lovely, Kateland. I know Henry will be honored." She paused. "Where did your name come from? After all these years I can't believe I've never asked you."

"I was named after my grandfather's castle in Scotland. Harlynn was named after his grandfather's ranch outside San Antonio."

"I never knew the origins of Harlynn's name. He said to tell you he was very sorry to miss another appointment. Henry is sorry too. It's really Henry's fault this time because he started making changes to the final draft ten minutes before the closing, which wasn't very nice. Did you see the picture of your husband on the cover of *Forbes*?"

"Yes." Kate waited. "What do you think of this feeding frenzy? I think Harlynn is being pulled awfully thin these days. Everyone wants a piece of him if you stop and think about it. It takes him hours to calm down at night. I know it's my fault because I created this company. I did the deal and bought the patents. Harlynn would have ended up where he is today anyway. I knew it from the beginning he would change the world. It's always been his path."

"Yes, it's his path, Kateland. Your path is to take care of Harlynn and the children. I know since the plane crash it's been difficult for you both. "

"It haunts us like you can't imagine. I can't tell you how many times Harlynn wakes up in a cold sweat after he has dreamt he got on the plane that day. He tells me he sees his funeral and. . ." She felt the tears come down her face as she tried smile.

Meg stood by her side, softly stroking her long brown hair, like a mother would do for her child. They had all had the same dream a hundred times: if Harlynn had gotten on that plane that morning six months ago he would be dead. He had chosen instead to come to Kate's doctor appointment to see this child inside of her. When the plane crashed it was reported to the world that Harlynn Barrett was in it. Everyone had thought he had perished that day, except Kate. The image of their house filled with people in shock, as they watched the plane in pieces on television, haunted her still.

"Let's go pick out the bedding for the nursery today?" Meg suggested. "It's time to get ready for the arrival of Laney."

"Yes, it is time to get ready for her. I was hoping to do it with

Harlynn, but perhaps that's wishful thinking at this point in time. With Levi we did everything together Meg, now we barely see each other. This is not how I envisioned my marriage when I agreed to spend my life with him." She watched as Meg's eyes filled with panic. "I'm thinking the nursery should be fuchsia pink. I already picked out the crib and an armoire. It's going to be contemporary and delicate."

"I'm thinking a white crib, round. How about a contemporary garden with giant flowers in pink and purple? A few little creatures added in like butterflies and bunnies."

"Yes." Kate felt relieved as Dr. Carr came in the room looking agitated. He slapped her folder on the counter. "Well, you're in a good mood." Kate giggled at him.

"I need to yell at your husband, where is he Kateland?" Carr snapped. "You lost a pound this week, again. This is getting dangerous, young lady. I will put your butt in the hospital if it doesn't change immediately."

"Your scales are off."

"Kateland, you lost a pound. This baby is going to be underweight if you don't gain weight. What do I have to do to make this happen?"

Kate concluded there was no point to answering his question. Dr. Carr would start yelling and she wasn't in the mood for this today. Yes, he was the best doctor around. Yes, she was under stress. Yes, she had two other children to chase around. This was her life and she was doing the best she could do at the moment.

There was silence as he did the ultra sound in the dimly lit room. She watched as Laney moved her right hand, finding her thumb to suck. The perfect fingers and toes in black and white stared back at her. What was she going to be like? What would her voice sound like some day? What color would her eyes be?

"Are you going to say anything?" Dr. Carr asked her sternly.

"No." Kate stared at him wanting to tell him to go to hell. She held her tongue, which took all her self-control.

"I want you back here in three days with that husband of yours and you better have gained some weight. The baby looks fine Kateland, but you better start taking it easy. I don't give a shit about Moon Water or your crazy families."

"I think you should call Harlynn and tell him that Dr. Carr." Kate watched as him as Carr picked up the phone and started dialing. She closed her eyes listening as Dr. Carr chewed out Harlynn up and down, then sideways. He didn't stop for fifteen minutes before he hung up the phone and smiled at her.

"Is that what you wanted?"

"Yes," Meg and Kateland said at the same time. They were ganging up on Harlynn, and he deserved it.

———

Two hours later the nursery was ordered and paint picked out. Kate had a sophisticated modern taste and it was reflected throughout their house and now in Laney's room. The fact Kate was a well known sculptor and painter was a plus when designing a nursery. It was pure enjoyment to bring this nursery together compared to dealing with her marriage.

Kate sat in the nursery sketching animals on the walls with giant flowers. Slowly she mixed paints getting the exact colors she wanted, the green that had a hint of lime in it contrasting the fuchsia pink along with chocolate brown. The large white walls were an endless palette for her imagination. Even if things were not perfect in her life she could make this nursery perfect. She would paint these walls with the love she had for this child.

The sound of his shoes coming down the hallway, a slide with a half step, didn't even cause her to pause anymore, although she did feel her heart race slightly. Harlynn Barrett had always done that to her since the first moment they met. He was a natural, with stunning cheekbones, beautiful golden brown eyes and thick dark brown hair. He stood at six' three and had played baseball in college. He had been drafted to the major leagues until he injured his shoulder and then went to law school. He had his own law firm and his own holding company. He was quoted weekly in the *Financial Times, New York Times,* and had a column in the *Wall Street Journal* that ran twice a month. He was a genius at mergers and acquisitions, but always humbled by his own success.

"Hi," he finally said after watching her paint for four minutes.

"Hi," she said, quietly, never turning towards him. What was the point of even saying what she felt at the moment because he would say he couldn't help it and she would get mad?

"I thought we were going to pick out the nursery together?"

"That was two weeks ago and it would probably be two weeks before you had time in your schedule." She slowly turned towards him putting down her paints and wiping off her hands. "This child is not going to wait on you, Harlynn. As it is the crib probably won't be here on time."

"Yes, it will. I will make sure it gets here on time. I still want to be part of what you are doing in the nursery or anything you do for our child." He reassured her with his smile. "Are you going to yell at me for missing today? I've already gotten chewed out by everyone else in the family."

"I only vented to Meg because it hurt you weren't there, Harlynn. It's not like I called everyone complaining, so don't make it sound like I did."

"No, you didn't have to call anyone. Meg called Henry, Henry called Keat, Keat called Nick and Sue and Sue called your father. That's what I have spent the last two hours on the phone dealing with instead of being home with you, Levi and Janey."

"Have you ever thought of letting the calls go into voice mail?" She suggested smiling back at him.

"No, because then they just show up at our house. What do you want Kateland? Why are you losing weight?" He watched as she got up, slowly, and walked over to him.

"I want you to be here with me and the children! I want you to be happy instead of stressed out all the time! I want you to show up at one damn appointment to see this beautiful child because you have missed the last six, Harlynn! I ask you for so little and it doesn't matter. You see your father more than you see me. You always have time for him. Shit, I don't want to discuss this because it's going to make my asthma flare up, then I have to call Dr. Carr and listen to his crap." She sat down in the rocking chair staring out the window, wondering what was going on in her world. Maybe having children back to back was not the brightest idea they ever conceived.

Harlynn sat on the ottoman in front of her taking her hands and he slowly kissed her. She could see his eyes move downward with fear.

"Kateland, I'm sorry for not being here for you the last couple of months." He closed his eyes taking in a deep breath. "My dad is going into heart failure. Someday he is going to have a heart attack and they won't be able to save him. I've spent the last six weeks getting all his financial affairs in order. He is only sixty-eight and I'm having a hard time with it, Kate." He looked out the window. "You know he has always been my best friend since I was a little boy. I can't believe that Levi isn't going to know him."

"I was wondering what was going on with you. Paul keeps coming by to see Levi everyday. I took some pictures of him the other day with Levi. He asked me for a copy of them." She waited. "This seems sudden, Harlynn? I don't know what to say to you, Babes. I know how much you love him. "

"He smoked forever, Kate. It's not a new thing. I could be wrong and maybe he has more time. When George told me that I needed to make sure things were in order for him, it hit me."

"Why don't you take some time off, and go away with him. Go to Utah to the house or go out to the ranch your family has outside San Antonio. You need that time with him, Harlynn."

"I think the ranch would be a better idea because it's closer to a hospital if anything happens. He wouldn't be able to handle the altitude in Deer Valley. Will you come with us? I want you and the children there."

"Is your mother going to come?" Kate asked with the most pleasant smile she could find.

"She hates the ranch. My father always loved going there, but she would never go."

"What other truths has your love been keeping from me?" She watched as he struggled for a moment confused by the statement. "Why have you been keeping this from me?"

"I tried to tell you a couple of times and the words wouldn't come out. I want you to enjoy this time and didn't want to burden you. Your pregnancy with Levi was hell on you, Kate." She smiled at him. He needed her to smile at him.

"Tell me," she whispered.

"I don't know where to begin, love," he whispered back. "I'm very excited to have this baby girl. I love her name. After Henry finished yelling at me today I told him we were naming her after him. He actually just stammered for two minutes before he left the room. He called me in the car telling me how honored he was that we would do that for him."

"Is that man I married still inside of you?" Kate questioned. "I miss him."

"Yes, he is there for you and our children, but you have to understand that I'm trying to protect you, and run this company that is bigger than anything we have ever done. I'm so scared of something happening to you or me. I want to know who tried to kill me, Kateland."

"I need more time with you Harlynn. You are cutting me out of your life and I can't take it." The tears came down her face, slowly. "And I'm fat. I'm tired. I just want to go to sleep in your arms and have you talk to me."

"I'm not cutting you out even if my father is ill. I can't stop thinking of that day I didn't get on the plane." He paused. "I have gone back to Dr. Brown to try to figure out a few things. We will get back to where we were before Moon Water and the plane crash. You were right when you told Meg I'm stretched too thin and everyone wants a piece of me."

"I knew you went back to Dr. Brown, even though you didn't mention it. I wonder why you think you can keep things from me like that, Babes."

"You usually know what I'm up to." He laughed. "I love you and you look beautiful sitting here in that light. I want a picture of you exactly like that, with that peaceful look in your eyes," he told her getting up and coming back with a camera.

"Why are you blushing? I've taken hundreds of pictures of you? And you aren't fat at all, Kateland. I can see I'm going to have to start making those protein shakes for you again. And you have a massage in an hour. In fact you are going to have a massage everyday from now on. I promise to be at the next doctor's appointment and all the ones after that one. I messed up and I'm sorry, Kateland."

"I don't know why I lost another pound. You know I'm trying to be very careful with what I eat and exercising. Your son keeps me on my feet all the time. Then throw Janey on top of it and we have a new form of chaos."

"Running a billion dollar holding company and a law firm is easier than our children." He confessed to her. "I wouldn't trade anything in the world for when I walk through the door and see them running towards me. You're the best mom in the world, Kate, but you need to slow down. I got us more help for the house to free up your time. I don't want you to worry about the house. I'm talking no wash or cooking or cleaning of any type."

"I think you're right. I need to focus on the children with this baby coming. I don't want to end up in the hospital on bed rest, which Carr is about to do."

"I won't let him. Okay?" He bent down kissing her for a moment. "You need some loving is what I think."

And that's how Harlynn could turn around her world in an instant. He could make her stop in her tracks and watch him. There was something so comforting about his voice. Yes, that man she had married was very much there.

"I'm going to go get Levi up, while you clean up in here." He kissed her again. "Then later on when the children are asleep we are going to go to bed early. I promise."

"Do you think sex at six months is such a brilliant idea?"

"Carr said it was good for you." Harlynn blushed. "That was a very interesting conversion of what we are allowed to do and not do."

"Oh, goodness, I'm glad I wasn't there for that one. Sorry everyone got on your case today. It wasn't my intention to rat you out."

"You know you could have come to me, Kate. I deserved it, but let's try to keep the family out of our love life. Sometimes I feel like I'm suffocating between the firm, Moon Water and dealing with the likes of Henry, Keat and Nick." His eyes went from soft to hard in an instant. "I don't need them all over me every time I screw up."

"I understand. I also understand that if you had been there or called it wouldn't have happened." She smiled weakly because he was gone again. He had slipped back into the new Harlynn from the old Harlynn that fast. She didn't like the word suffocating and family used in the same thought. It stung.

~Chapter 2

Kate sat at her desk looking at the pink orchid in front of her cascading with blossoms. She wondered what Harlynn was feeling guilty about that he sent her flowers out of the blue. Of course she had her list to pick from but decided not to pick from it. An hour ago she had tried to find Harlynn, the bodyguards couldn't locate him. Kate thought that was hypocritical since she couldn't go to the bathroom by herself.

This life was very different from what she expected when they got married two years ago. There were bodyguards because someone had tried to kill them both in the past year. She wondered if they would always require bodyguards to protect them. Their company Moon Water was on the verge of finding a cure with their first product. Moon Water held a serious of patents that contained a back door into cells using a group of unknown enzymes. These enzymes could travel only to the cells affected by a disease, destroying them one hundred percent. It was going to change how diseases were treated for all of mankind. It would take several years for testing and tweaking, but they had a drug going to the FDA within six months. Normally it might take ten to fifteen years of research and development. Harlynn and Kate ran the company together along with other family members, but it was Harlynn who was thrown to the wolves whether it was the media or the government.

Kate closed her eyes going over the last three years with Harlynn. Harlynn Barrett ran a law firm that was highly respected in Houston, Texas. The law firm was basically Harlynn and he was burned out. He offered Kate a job to be his right hand person, which she accepted immediately. Then it happened. He was getting divorced and they were falling in love. She was pregnant and then they were married. Then two years ago Kate purchased a group of patents to prevent Harlynn from being swindled in a deal. It was the Pandora's Box of biotech cell technology. These patents paired with a molecular technology that Henry Grayden owned, called Goo, had the potential to change the world. The Goo could transfer information or drugs in the body. For fifteen years it had never been successful until it was paired with the enzymes that Moon Water held. Overnight, Kate had changed the future of the world without realizing it.

Keaton Jones, Kate's older brother strolled into her office with a smile on his face. Keat was like no other brother she had ever met. He was her confidant, business partner and best friend. He lived with them in a lower level guest house. He was the best uncle in the world to her children. He always made time for them in his busy life.

"Hey, are up for going out tonight?" Keat inquired as he sat down putting his feet on her desk as he read a document on his iPad.

"What are you thinking?" She narrowed her eyes questioning him.

"A movie? You seem kind of down, so I thought it would be good for you to get away from your husband for some actual fun. It's not like you can get drunk at this point in your life. Your husband missed a conference call today. You wouldn't happen to know where I could find him so he doesn't miss the next one?"

"Don't ask. You know that his Dad is sick, so we have to be patient with him. Yes, a movie would be good to be honest. When should I expect the write up on JR6?"

"I want Danny to triple check these numbers because they are going to freak out the science community. We are going to have a cure for Janey's cancer in a year or two, at the most. I can't believe it, Kate. There is no stopping us if we can do this." He watched his sister smile taking in a deep breath.

"I know." Kate reflected on her oldest child who she had adopted when she was an infant with cancer. She shared custody with her biological father, Stan Rivers. Janey's mother had abandoned her when she was six months old and dying of a rare leukemia cancer. By some work of God, they got her through it. She was a healthy seven year old who was thriving and growing, cancer free. The fear was that the cancer would come back someday because that was what happened to every patient. Her progress was a miracle for the most part. Janey wasn't supposed to live this long. They had found a drug to treat her cancer with when it came back next time.

"Who are you meeting with this week?" Kate pulled back her emotions.

"I found this biotech company that could be a fit with what we are doing. They do data mining. It would speed up our research by twenty percent. Nick has a meeting with Merck."

"Interesting. I had an inquiry from some government official at the National Institute of Health (NIH). Why don't you give Blacky a call to see what this is about later? My understanding was anything with the government would come through him?"

"Done." Keat took the note from Kate, glancing at it. "I think you should call Elle because Nick and she are having major problems."

"What else is going on?" She could tell he wanted to tell her something. "Just tell me because I can't afford to spend any energy worrying about other relationships when my husband is being difficult."

"Again?" Keat immediately stood up and started ranting. "Kate what the hell is his problem? I know his dad is really sick. I know that he is trying to run this company and the law firm. And there is the plane crash," Keat said slowly and stopped. "I think Dad and Sue might be getting engaged."

"Really?" Kate asked slowly. Her best friend for the last fifteen years of her life was now dating her newly divorced father. Well, actually they had been dating for the last year. Kate was still getting use to the complete weirdness of seeing them together. "Go on."

"Harlynn thought you might not take it well. I reminded him last time he didn't tell you that our father was dating Sue what happened. Are you really going to the ranch again this weekend?"

"Yes. Please come," she pleaded. "I had a dream months ago that our father and Sue would get married. Thank you for telling me. There is no reason to dwell on the subject as far as I'm concerned. It is what is, dearest brother."

"I'm going to pick on her." Keat grinned for a moment. "Exactly what do you do on this ranch in the middle of nowhere?"

"At the ranch Harlynn feels better, which makes life easier. It's fun, sort of. You should see Levi ride his pony. You can pick from riding horses, swimming and drinking lots of booze. It's a very beautiful ranch in all fairness. There are endless subjects for your photography. Plus I will only be able to go one or two more times before the baby comes."

"I will come for you. Can Nick and Elle come?"

"Sure. It's a big place. It will give us time to hang out and relax. I think everyone could use some relaxation."

———

They drove in silence for the first hour to the ranch with Levi asleep in the back. Janey was spending the weekend with her father, which was good for her. Levi was exhausted from starting pre-school and it made Kate feel guilty. He loved going to the same school as his big sister. It was also going to help with baby Laney coming. And she reminded herself it was only for three hours in the morning. He was going to be fine she told herself.

Kate finished reading the document in front of her and put it in her briefcase still deep in thought. She often asked herself how she had gotten to this point. She really wanted to be doing her sculpting. The art she did irritated Harlynn even though he would never admit it. They were going through a rough period of time. She waited for him to explode because with each mile they got closer to the ranch she could see him tensing up.

"Can we talk?" he finally asked because he couldn't stand the silent treatment.

"It depends?" Kate answered him not opening her eyes. She had almost fallen asleep in hopes of avoiding the pending discussion. "I don't feel like being yelled at today."

"I don't yell at you Kate?" He looked surprised. "I yell, but it's not at you. I'm trying not to yell." He waited. "Why did you invite everyone up to the ranch this weekend without talking to me first?"

"I've been really nice about going to the ranch every weekend for the last four weeks without you asking me. I couldn't find you. You do your disappearing act like always and it's my fault?"

Silence filled the car for the next twenty miles. This was hard was all Kate could think as she watched him. It was hard to share him with the world and it was hard that he always wanted to decide what fit his needs instead of what she might want occasionally. What to do she wondered to herself? It wasn't like she had anyone to go to because even little comments seemed to blowup into mini wars.

"Are you having an affair?" Kate asked since she figured it was a point to start at in her life. Harlynn slammed on the breaks of the black SUV causing the other six cars to slam on their breaks.

"What? You think I'm having an affair? You are caring my child. We were together last night. It was beautiful. How could you think I would sleep with someone else?" They both jumped when one of the bodyguards knocked on the window. Harlynn rolled down the window.

"Is everything okay?" Charlie asked.

"Yes!" Harlynn snapped. "I dropped my phone."

"Yes, sir." Charlie went back to his car.

"I'm not having an affair," Harlynn said quietly. "I would never have an affair on you, Kateland. I can't believe you would think that for a second."

"I can count five times in the last two weeks that no one could find you. You have missed calls and meetings, Harlynn. I'm getting scared by your strange behavior. Are you doing drugs?"

"What kind of drugs?"

"I don't know? Pain killers for your shoulder? Pot? Are you smoking pot to deal with what is going on in our lives?"

"No, I'm not smoking pot. Keat and his side kick, Nick, would be the only people in our family smoking pot. I take pain medicine for my shoulder, but not that often," he said calmly. "Sometimes I'm with my Dad and I don't want to be disturbed. Other times I'm taking a break because I feel this enormous pressure on me."

"You need a break from us?" Kate asked slowly as she watched him.

"No, absolutely not Kate! You and our children are the only things that keep me sane. I feel like I'm leading this double life between our family and work. I want you and the children. Besides that I don't know what I want anymore."

"Well, this is a start, Harlynn. It can be lonely at the top. Have you thought about speaking with Henry?" She waited. "I invited Keat and he wanted Nick to come with Elle because they are having major issues. I was not trying to blindside you."

"It did blindside me. It's hard to be on all the time. There are times I only want to be with you and the children without everyone. It's not like I could tell Henry he can't come. Then Sue found out from Keat." Harlynn laughed at her because she had this way she could look at him and make him laugh like no else.

"Are we there?" Levi called as Claire sat with him in the back. His big green eyes stared at Harlynn in the review mirror. "I'm hungry."

"We have another hour, Levi. We'll stop for a snack at your favorite place."

"Okay, Dada." Levi giggled like his mother at times.

"I know you Harlynn and you need a break. You need to get a handle on what is going, and then you will find your path again."

"I hope so. I feel really lost, Kate. I can't stop the thoughts racing in my head between Moon Water and the firm. We need a vacation, but I know that Carr won't let you go anywhere. He told me this was your absolute last trip out here until after the baby."

"You're going to have to be in charge this weekend. I need to rest."

"I know you do. Meg and Sue have everything planned out for the entire weekend. You have been working too much. I think next week you need to wind down things at Moon Water. You need to stop micromanaging the company and focus on you and the baby, Kateland."

"Yes, I just realized that I'm dragging to be honest, Harlynn. God, that sounds weak and pathetic."

"Now those are two words I would never use to describe you, love." He laughed to himself. "We need to figure out how we are going to handle my mother and your mother when the baby comes." Harlynn glanced at Kate as she closed her eyes.

"Neither of them will ever come near Laney." She smiled to herself taking a cat nap.

—

The caravan stopped at a local restaurant as everyone stretched their legs. Levi had his favorite table and waited for his hotdog and fries, something he would never get at home. He was in heaven as he drank a Dr. Pepper and then burped like a man. Kate sat watching all the faces wondering how she had gotten here in the middle of Texas with this family of hers.

When they finally got to the ranch it was crazy as everyone settled in their rooms. It was a sprawling ranch house that was decorated in a modern rustic twist with a confusing color scheme. Kate loved some things like the photos of Harlynn as a boy roping. She would have to make the house one of her projects after Laney was born.

Kate was half asleep when Harlynn finally came to bed. She could smell the Patron on him with envy. She would feel much better with just one shot. Of course she would never do such a thing with being seven and a half months pregnant. It was nice to think of it as she tasted the tequila on his lips. The happiness was back in his eyes and Kate could see him unwinding.

"How many shots did you do?" She teased him.

"Three. One was for you," he told her as he kissed her softly. "Do you mind if I keep kissing your body?"

"That would be nice," she whispered back to him.

—

The sun bleed through the blinds in the room as Kate woke up forgetting where she was for a good ten seconds. Then it came back to her as she felt the baby moving inside of her. She was a very active girl, was all Kate could think. Laney was hungry Kate decided as she slowly rolled to her side feeling like a beached whale.

As she sat up she saw Harlynn come into the room. It was Harlynn, but not Harlynn in a way. He hadn't shaved or put gel in his hair. He had a worn work shirt on that was soft, old jeans and his scuffed black ropers. This was her weekend cowboy she smiled. He had breakfast for her on a tray. This was the old Harlynn showing up this morning.

"Hi," he spoke in a hush. "How are you feeling today?"

"I don't know yet. Laney is doing somersaults already. It might be a very long day."

"I think I'm going to take Levi out for a ride, if you don't mind? He has been up for hours. Our boy needs to be worn out. He already took apart Henry's phone."

"Yikes! Not too long? He needs sunscreen on. Make sure you take a drink with you for him."

"We're already packed to go." He waited. "I'm sorry about being cranky on the drive up here last night. It feels good to have everyone here. Henry and I had a good talk on the porch watching the sun come up." He took in a deep breath. "My dad should be here in about an hour. I think he is only staying for the day." Harlynn looked down. "It's really hard seeing him go downhill like this, Kate."

"I'm here for you." She sat up staring into his eyes. "I love you."

"Thank you." He leaned over kissing her. "Everyone is waiting for you when you feel like coming out."

"Tell them to go riding. I might sleep another hour since you kept me up late, mister." She watched as he blushed.

"I was only following the explicit instructions from your doctor. I think I know more about the female anatomy then I ever thought I would."

"I'm afraid." Kate giggled as Harlynn kissed her one more time.

The breakfast was perfect as Kate ate the omelet and drank the smoothie then inhaled one of Meg's blueberry muffins. There was something very calming about this house Kate decided. There were no telephones ringing or doorbells or dog barking. She realized she felt safe out here in the middle of the hills. The stress of having bodyguards or people staring at her when she went out in public was gone. No one cared who they were in this little sleepy town.

—

Sue was waiting in the vanity for Kate when she got out of the shower. They hadn't seen each other in days so it was nice. Kate knew that Sue was avoiding her and that was okay. Sue would confess that she was marrying Kate's father, then things would be better.

Kate sat staring in the mirror as silence filled the room. It was that moment again, where love came before the truth. These two women knew every secret in each other's lives. There was nothing they kept from each other until Sue and Sam became an item. It had torn the family apart, but now things were better. They had all moved on even though it was strange. Her best friend was technically going to be her step mother.

"I was sent to check on you." Sue informed Kate as she began to brush her hair. "You look exhausted, girl friend."

"It's going to be a long month ahead. Carr says the baby needs to come at 36 weeks because of what happened last time. I'm really nervous. He assures me that I will not be given the wrong medicine or get some obscure infection."

"Nothing is going to happen, I promise, Kate. Harlynn and Henry have been working nonstop with the hospital to make sure the background checks are done. The rooms are going to be ready weeks ahead of time. I will be there."

"Is there anything you want to tell me?" Kate asked staring at Sue in the mirror.

"We have been looking at rings. I know this is hard for you."

"Sue from the first time I saw you kissing my father I knew you both would end up together," Kate told her friend. Kate had these dreams about the future. It was common knowledge in the family even though they were never discussed.

"Are you mad?" Sue asked watching Kate as she dabbled with makeup.

"No, not at all. I'm happy for the both of you. I worry if my father is the best person for you. To be frank, I worry about the age difference. I know you really never wanted a child, but what if you change your mind?"

"I have your children to help raise for the next twenty years." Sue looked at Kate's reflection in the mirror. "I can't help that I love your father. He is good for me."

"Then I have one less thing to worry about today." Kate admitted to her. "Will you pick me out something to wear? I have no energy.

Oh, damn I forgot my asthma medicine." Kate realized looking through her bag.

"I bet Nick has something. I will call Dr. George and get you some. Anyway, George wanted to know how you were doing."

"Thank you and please don't tell Harlynn because he will flip out. He needs to relax while he is here." Kate watched as Sue nodded leaving the room. A couple minutes later Nick appeared with his bag of asthma supplies talking on the phone to George.

"Are you having some sort of attack gorgeous?" Nick inquired with a slight smile. "I was wondering why you weren't up this morning."

"No. It's hard to get air in. Inflammation." She watched as he listened in the phone. Nick handed her two inhalers telling her to use both of them.

"I'm going to get you some caffeine. I'll be back in a moment."

He looked a little concerned as he watched her. Then calmness came over her because she knew if there was one person she could count on it was Nicholas Black. He was her brother's best friend and part of her family. Nick was an investment banker like her brother and now helped to run Moon Water. She trusted him with her life any day of the week. Harlynn had finally gotten over Nick and her being close. There was an enormous amount of jealousy in the beginning and a few fist fights at one point; due to the fact Nick was gorgeous. He had crystal blue eyes and an incredible body from playing soccer. He was the person Kate could call day or night and he would be there.

She tried to rest in bed and stop her mind from racing. She didn't want all the drama. She knew that Harlynn would show up any moment. He would be stressed out and pack her up to go back to Houston.

"How are you doing?" Nick asked coming back with a Dr. Pepper, which she hadn't had in months due to the caffeine. Caffeine would help with the asthma.

"It's working." She drank it slowly. "What's going on with you and Elle?"

"We are struggling to be honest. I love her, Kate. I love that she is this stellar accountant, an accomplished swimmer who went to the Olympics and now designs wall hangings. I love that she travels all

25

over the world and is independent. She reminds me of you in so many ways."

"What's the problem?" Kate asked point blank. "Tell me."

"I want to get married and she doesn't want to rush into anything. And Shelly has been calling." He paused. "Shelly showed up at my place the other night."

"Are you talking to Shelly?" Kate asked because she was shocked. Nick's former girl friend was a complete drug addict and leech.

"No." He waited. "Okay, I haven't told anyone this, Kate. I trust you to not judge me. Before Elle and I were really dating, Shelly showed up at my place one night. She said she was sorry and wanted to talk. We had one drink and that's all I remember. I think she knocked me out with something."

"You need to tell your Dad." Kate said slowly. "Who knows what she is up to, Nick."

Nick's father was a high level spy for the government. He had saved Kate and Harlynn from being killed six months ago. Blacky oversaw the safety of everyone in this house. Kate and Blacky had a special bond going back years.

"I know. Elle knows. I'm not worried about that. George ran a whole range of test on me. I don't remember anything."

"Talk to your Dad, he will find out what's going on."

"How are you feeling?" He lay down on the bed next to her.

"Better. This is the first day in a long time I didn't want to get out of bed. I already know about my dad and Sue. What else is up?" Nick simply couldn't lie to her and they both knew it.

"My Dad wants to talk to you. He is actually flying out here this afternoon. I'm not sure what is going on. He said not to tell Harlynn. He only wants to talk to you." Nick waited. "Then there was a mess of calls between Stan and Harlynn this morning. Henry and Harlynn went into the office and closed the door."

"Is Janey okay?"

"She is fine because I talked to her for about twenty minutes. I heard Henry tell Harlynn 'I can't believe she finally called after all these years'."

"That's Janey's mother," Kate whispered.

"That's what I thought. She abandoned the child, Kateland." Nick's voice raced as he said each word.

"She is the biological mother." Kate closed her eyes. Her heart was racing. "Thank you for telling me, Nick."

"Well, I figured no one else would have the guts to tell you. How is the asthma?"

"Better." Her mind was spinning so fast she felt dizzy. "I just want to lay here for a moment, plus I know you already sent Harlynn a message. Go have fun with the boys and don't fall off your horse."

"Keat wants to explore the trails. This place is fantastic, Kateland. How come we have never been here before?"

"I have to admit that I love being out here away from the city. It lets me clear my head and relax."

"We need to come out here more often that's for sure. Rest sweet thing and your man will be here any minute." He kissed her on the head. "Be good baby girl."

~Chapter 3

In the distance Kate could see the two figures coming closer and closer as she sat in the kitchen while she finished her Dr. Pepper. Laney continued doing somersaults with the addition of the Dr. Pepper. Now the hiccups would come for the next hour. She smiled as she watched Harlynn and Henry hand off the horses to the ranch hands. They both walked toward the house drenched in sweat, still wearing their cowboy hats and chaps. It was a far cry from the Armani suits and Porsches they were seen in everyday.

Henry Grayden was her Godfather and just about everything else to her. She was much closer to Henry then her own father, Sam Jones, and Henry was closer to Kate then his own daughter, Jessica. Kate was finally at a place she could admit it to herself. It wasn't that Sam and Kate ever fought she realized. It was the idea they never bonded due to her mother and Sam's company.

Harlynn had been Henry's lawyer for fifteen years. He had been a huge influence on Harlynn's career and life. Henry Grayden had a holding company worth billions of dollars that everyone had benefited from. You would never know how successful the man had been at the age of fifty-two. Family always came first with Henry. Henry would walk out of a meeting if Kate or Keat needed him. Needless to say he had done it numerous times over the years.

"What's going on?" Harlynn said as he took off the chaps and kicked off his boots that were covered in mud.

"I'm doing better. Nicky took good care of me, so don't worry." Harlynn immediately got the steel eyed look.

"Stop it, both of you." Henry interjected. "George is coming."

"Why?" Kate asked confused as both men stopped staring at Kate. "What?"

Harlynn quickly grabbed a kitchen towel and gently tilted her head forward, catching the blood flowing from her nose. For the next fifteen minutes he stood there as Henry got more towels. Harlynn tried to cover up his concern as he told her not to worry.

As she lay on the couch Henry sat with her while Harlynn went to change his shirt because there was blood on it now. Her nose had finally stopped bleeding. It was just a bloody nose and those things happened she told herself over and over again.

"You will be okay, sweetheart. You're anemic. George called Harlynn to warn him that you might start having a few bloody noses. Then Nick sent a text telling us your asthma was acting up." He smiled. "You scared the hell out of us, but that's okay." Henry winked at her.

"Well you know I've done pretty awesome for the last seven months considering last time." She paused. "What do you know and don't lie?"

"Sam will propose to your very best friend in the world, Sue. I'm not even going to try to find a rational explanation for the events that will take place. Do you have any idea how weird this is for me Kateland? He wants me to be his best man. I felt like saying I was already your best man once. You know that I will do it because I love your father. Christ, I couldn't let your brother Keaton do it because he would start laughing like you do."

"Can I call Sue, step mommy?" Kate asked as Henry started laughing to the point his eyes watered. "You have no idea what I'm really thinking."

"Oh, yes I do because everyone is thinking the same thing." He looked her straight in the eyes. "I will tell you that under no circumstances will Amy Rivers ever get Janey. She has someone watching you and has filed a complaint. CPS will be coming to your house; it's not a big deal. I've already called a few judges to expedite the case. She wants something Kateland, they always do. It's going to be a big inconvenience, but we have a ton of evidence. We have the good doctor Danny Hill on our side. We have documented everything. Stan is rattled, which I understand considering what the hell that women put him through." He paused. "Your turn, what is going on, Kateland?"

"Apparently Blacky is going to pay me a visit this afternoon."

"What?" Henry sat up. "Why is Blacky coming here? What

happened that Blacky is coming here?" His concern mounted.

"No one told me?" Harlynn came in the room. "Why didn't he tell me he was coming?"

"He is coming to talk to me and no one else. Secret spy stuff, I would guess." Kate stared at Harlynn wondering what was going on. "I had the National Institute of Health (NIH) contact me the day before yesterday. It probably has to do with Moon Water. Moon Water is slowly becoming a pain in the ass if you want my opinion."

"Last time I checked our financial statement it had more zeros than I have ever seen on it." Harlynn causal commented.

"I always knew Kate would change the world in her own way. I knew she would beat me hands down one day." Henry confessed as Kate began to giggle.

"You better stop it. You'll start puking all over the place like your son does when he laughs too hard. " Harlynn poked at her as he walked over to the bar and fixed a tall glass of scotch. Then he poured another one as Henry nodded at him.

"When you two started seeing each other I knew it was only a matter of time before you did your own venture together." Henry admitted to the both of them.

"It's so incredibly unfair that you two are drinking in front of me. I'm going to bed and sleep for a long time." She got up off the couch slowly. "Who has our child?"

"He is with Keaton," Harlynn told her. "They should be home shortly, I would imagine. I had one of the hands drive out to get them. Levi loves riding his pony, Mama." Harlynn leaned over kissing her. "When Laney is here, then you need to coming riding with us. I love you. Sorry you had a bloody nose. I know it's no fun for you at the moment."

"Thanks for taking care of me." She kissed him back before going back to bed. It was only noon, as she shook her head frustrated. Out of the corner of her eye she could see Harlynn pick up the bloody towels off the floor and straighten up the house. His father would be here in the next hour, hopefully.

The next time Kate woke up she could hear the different voices as a murmur echoed through the house. There was blood on the pillowcase as she slowly sat up. It was a fraction of what had flowed out of her earlier. She felt better than she had earlier in the day. The tiredness was gone or maybe it was the stress. She needed more rest than she had been giving herself. There was a Pellegrino waiting for her and a protein bar. Harlynn. He did always think of her even though he may not show it.

"You look better." Harlynn watched her as she came into the dining room. Everyone was sitting around having a late lunch. "Here sit down, I will fix you a plate." Harlynn offered.

Meg came over to sit with her as well as Elle, Nick's girlfriend. Across the room she saw Blacky and Dr. George Nelly as they both came over to say hello to her. It was a family coming together to support Kate and Harlynn.

"How are you?" Meg asked warmly. "I had the most amazing morning with Elle. It was completely peaceful and therapeutic. All the stress rolled off my shoulders from the last six months. I told Henry he has to buy me a ranch close to here."

"No you don't, Meg." Harlynn's father interjected coming over to see Kate. He embraced her for a good minute. "Thank you for coming and bringing everyone with you," he whispered. He stood back, taking in the room and all the faces. "For the last year I have been redoing this ranch that Harlynn was named after when he was born. It belonged to my father." He paused clearing his throat. "This ranch is a gift to Harlynn and Kate for their family to use and their children to grow up coming here, like Harlynn did." The room became very quiet as Kate slowly turned towards Harlynn to see his expression. Kate watched him as he came over to his father, embarrassed and touched by the gesture.

"Dad." That's all he said before he embraced him. "You did this for me?"

"Yes, I did. You have made me a very proud man and filled my life with joy. You have a beautiful family standing here with you. I hope you know how much I love you, son. ''

"I do." Harlynn closed his eyes, hiding his tears. "I do."

———

George corned Kate after she put down Levi for the night. Dr. George Anelly was one of Henry's most trusted friends. Sam, George and Henry had all gone to Texas A&M University together. George's job was to keep everyone in the family healthy. It was a constant challenge to make sure they all stayed healthy to keep their impossible schedules. He made sure everyone got their stress test, annual checkups and managed the horrible allergies they all seemed to have.

"Let me listen to you breathe and check you out. You really had me worried when Nick called," he told her flatly.

"It wasn't that bad. Let's try hard not to over react like the rest of the world," Kate told him flatly. "I know you are here to check on Paul so don't push this visit on to me."

"He's not doing well, Kateland. I don't think your husband is doing that great either to be honest. He looks like hell and it's not from his allergies."

"He looks better than he did yesterday. Getting out of Houston seems to help. At least he isn't sneezing and coughing half the day." She frowned at George. "What the hell do you want me to do with him? He won't sleep and works twenty hours a day. It's not like he came with instructions."

"I gave him a new antihistamine to take that he needs to try. Cutting back on the booze might be a good idea," George said slowly. "I don't know if you have noticed how much he is drinking."

"Really?" Kate sat back thinking. "He usually doesn't drink that much in front of me to be honest, George."

"He is a pretty cleaver guy at hiding it. Blood tests don't lie. If you would like to see them I can arrange it. This is becoming a serious problem, Kateland." Silence filled the room as he listened to her chest.

"Do you even know that you are full out wheezing? Do you know I have to call Carr now. Do you think I want to speak to Carr and explain what is going on with you?"

"Shit George, it's not like I'm doing it on purpose!" Kate yelled back at him.

"I know. I'm sorry for taking this out on you. It's hard watching Harlynn going through this. I really like his Dad." She watched as George paced the room three times.

"It's just where we are all at right now, George. I want to believe things will get better. I will call Carr. Give me the chart."

"No. I will do it." He smiled at her. "I'm glad I came because I would have worried about you. You'll be fine, but I don't want this asthma getting out of control. You need to take these inhalers exactly on time and in the order I'm writing down. You are under too much stress, Kate. We need to try to minimize the stress in your life."

—

After dinner Kate was sitting outside on her favorite swing. She needed time to go over the day's events. She couldn't internalize anything she told herself over and over again. Harlynn drank, he used to drink a lot and apparently he was now drinking a lot again if it was affecting his blood work. He still ran and biked, but his moods. This would explain why he was all over the place at times. Did he have a drinking problem?

"Hi," Blacky said quietly sitting down with her. "Julia is so mad she isn't here tonight." Julia was Blacky's wife, who was a surgeon. Nick's parents were both amazing in their own way and did have the best marriage Kate had ever seen.

"Well, apparently we have a new place for the family to meet up at now. Wow, that shocked the hell out of me, Blacky. I mean, this place is beautiful and tranquil. There must be twenty thousand acres at least."

"Actually, it's thirty thousand. I think it's a complete act of love by Harlynn's father. You bet that we will take you up on coming here anytime. I could spend a month here by myself."

"You can have your month anytime you want it. I'm very serious that I want you and Julia to use it when you have time." She sighed. "What did you come to tell me, Blacky? I can handle it, don't worry. I can tell you are trying to size me up to see how I will react."

"You are very much like my wife in the way you can always read me." He sat down on the swing next to her. "This is going to sting a bit, Kate. We have to put a stop to what's going on." He sat back in the swing. "Apparently, Harlynn has been checking into a suite at the Four Seasons two or three times a week for the last month. Sometimes Sue shows up."

"I already asked him if he was having an affair and he said no. Was he lying?"

"My gut tells me Harlynn wouldn't be unfaithful to you." Blacky admitted. "I've thought about this for a long time. I think you need to handle this because it's your marriage. I don't think you want anyone else involved in what may or may not be going on."

She wiped away her tears, the tears that came rapidly before she could wipe them away again. Blacky put his arm around her and held her. They sat there in the dark for the next twenty minutes in silence.

"I have a plane waiting for me to go to Washington. I'll call you tomorrow, the day after and the day after that, honey. I will help you with Harlynn."

"Thank you, Blacky. You are our guardian angel, Mr. Jack Black, secret spy." She gave him a long hug. "It's actually a relief to understand what is going on with him. At least I have a point to begin with him."

"I want you to take care and if it gets too crazy, I will be here. Harlynn is a good man with way too much on his plate right now. I think he needs to choose between Moon Water and the law firm. No man could do both of those jobs without going off the deep end."

"It sounds like a simple choice, but it's not, Blacky." Kate blinked several times still processing the situation. "Thank you for caring about me and my family."

"Always." He smiled, and then left her sitting on the swing as he walked to the car that was waiting for him. She didn't have the faintest idea how the man managed to do what he did. She was very thankful for Mr. Jack Black.

—

After Blacky left Kate decided to go to bed. Physically she felt much better, but emotionally she felt like she had been run over by a truck. She went to Harlynn's briefcase and got out the Bible that she had given him. She needed to find those words that would provide the comfort she was lacking. And there in the briefcase she found an envelope that contained what she needed. It was the receipts from the hotel neatly placed in order. Why would he keep them? Her hands were shaking as she looked at each one and the dates.

—

The next morning, as she sat eating breakfast, the house was quiet. Everyone was out hiking or horseback riding. Nick and Elle had gone into town, probably for some alone time. She admired the colorings done by her son this morning. She had been given kisses before they went out riding. It was a good feeling that Levi would have the memories of this ranch in his childhood.

"Hey beautiful, how are you doing today?" Paul asked as he came into the kitchen. "I've wanted to talk to you since I got here. In fact, I stayed longer just to have this time with you." He sat down next to her on the bar stool.

Kate could see his chest going up and down slowly as he took a moment to catch his breath. She had never noticed that Harlynn got his eyes from his father. They were exactly the same color. It was interesting how Harlynn so closely resembled his father and how Levi looked exactly like Harlynn except for her eyes.

"You are by far the best thing that has ever happened to my son. I want to thank you for all the happiness that you have given him. I want to thank you for these grandchildren. I never thought I would get to see Harlynn have children, let alone a son of his own. You have shown him what is important in life and I will always be grateful." He closed his eyes. "You are going to have to help him get through this, Kateland. It's going to be hard on him and he will fall to pieces. But he will get stronger and figure out things. He is going to need you.

Will you take care of him for me?"

"Yes. I will take care of your son, always. I'll make sure Levi and Janey know what a great man you were, Paul. You know I'm not so willing to give up on you." She looked down at the Bible in front of her. "Have you ever read the Bible?"

"I don't have a lot of faith these days," he confessed with a fear in his eyes.

"Do you believe in God?" Kate asked him slowly.

"I don't know." He looked her straight in the eye. "Are you going to save me?"

"That's not up to me, Paul. I'm going to read this Bible with you, if you don't mind. There have been times in my life when I lost my faith. In fact, your son had lost his faith and I was able to help him find his way."

"Well, I'm open to listening to you because I know that you saved him from a life that would have been treacherous. Everyone knows you saved him."

"You are my new project, Paul. We will find your faith together." For the next hour Kate read to Paul as he sat there listening to her. She talked about her belief that there was no luck or accidents in life. She believed God put people in our lives because they were supposed to be there for a reason. All we had to do was stop and look around ourselves.

—

Kate found herself alone on the swing on the back porch. The silence and the motion gave her the peace she needed. It was the rocking motion she always longed for as a child. She would sit in an old black rocking chair and rock back and forth for long periods of time. Kate would do anything to forget her own childhood with a mother who didn't love her. The words still played over and over in her head.

"You're so completely screwed, Kitty Kat. No one is going to want to leave this place tonight. It's too perfect." Keat admitted as he sat down on the swing across from her stretching out his legs. "Can I come next weekend?"

"You can come anytime you want my dear brother." She smiled

warmly. "I'm really glad you came this weekend, Keaton."

"Are you going to tell me why Blacky was here last night?" Keat asked quietly.

"I need to think things through, and then we can talk in a couple of days." She waited. "Tell me what we should do about Sue and Dad. Dad has hardly spoken to me. I'm not screwing his best friend."

"You did marry his lawyer. Sue said I'm not allowed to call her my stepmother. I told her I would call her what the hell I want since she was sleeping with our father. It still pisses me off if I think about it too long." Keat explained in a voice filled with distrust. "I suppose we shouldn't pick on her too much."

"Why not?" Kate asked with a wicked smile. "I don't know if this is good for Sue, Keaton. Twenty-two years is a lot of space."

"I mean of all the people in the world, why would she pick our father? I can see why dad would be attracted to her. She is athletic, independent and beautiful. He doesn't have to take care of her and she isn't crazy like our mother."

"Sue can be needy at times, Keaton. She has a very wild and unpredictable side to her that I doubt Sam has seen."

"Remember New Orleans when we couldn't find her. Or just going to Austin on Sixth Street if she has one too many. Then there was the problem in New York last year when she almost got everyone arrested because she mouthed off to a cop for no reason, I might add."

"I can't understand the emotional attachment she has to our father. What does she see in him?"

"I don't think it matters what she sees in Sam. We can't understand it since he will always be our biological father. Why did he let Henry play such a big part in our lives? Did Dad want us at all? Do you know if he wanted children? I was going through some old letters from Henry. It was like Henry had joint custody of us when we were younger." Keaton tried to cover the pain.

"I don't know. Our mother was crazy and he had his company to run. He just didn't have time for us, Keat."

They both sat there swinging, trying not to think of anything at all. It was easier not to think about their lives or try to remember. It was a puzzle they would never understand, which was best.

~Chapter 4

Kate was sitting in her art studio working on a painting for the nursery. It had come together perfectly in her mind. She was getting very excited about Lane's arrival and getting to know this child. She was worried how Levi was going to get along with his sibling. He was so young, but he understood perfectly that there would be a baby soon. Levi had always understood whatever she had said to him.

Harlynn came into the art studio, cautiously, glancing at the painting. He waited for Kate to put down her paint brush as he cleared his throat to make sure she knew he was behind her. She smiled softly at him without saying anything. That's what Kate had done for the last several days since they got back from the ranch.

"Dennis Kavel was trying to track you down today. Did he give you a call at the house?"

"Yes. Wireless Email (WE) is buying a company and he wants me to look at it. Plus, we were trying to figure out what to do about the board meeting next month."

"Well, the only option is to do it by teleconference or have it in Houston. You aren't traveling to San Francisco while you're eight months pregnant. It's too dangerous, Kate."

"They are having the meeting in Houston to accommodate my situation." This was the most they had said in days to each other.

"Do you want to talk about what Blacky said to you at the ranch? I feel like you are angry at me. I don't want us having problems with everything going on at work and the baby coming. You're shutting me out."

"Not really," she told him with the same smile.

"If I ask you what you talked about, would you tell me?" She could see the frustration building in his eyes.

"I would tell you to have faith in me." Silence filled the room as they locked eyes.

"Did you happen to see an envelope in my briefcase? I think I left it at the ranch."

"What kind of envelope?" Kate asked knowing exactly what he was asking because she had shredded it.

"It had receipts in it that I need?" His voice was agitated. He couldn't stand when Kate played mind games with him.

"Are you referring to the receipts for your thirteen visits to the Four Seasons penthouse?" Kate asked. "Leezann can look them up on the American Express bill for you. Just tell her what dates you would like and she will print them out." She slowly got up walking past him, looking down at the ground. Even though she wouldn't admit it, she felt betrayed by him. She couldn't bring herself to even ask what Sue had to do with it all. It was all too painful.

He reached out for her arm, gently stopping her. As they stood there Kate raised her eyes and stared at him. She waited for him to speak or try to explain what was going on.

"It's not what you think?" He told her quietly. "I would never be unfaithful to you, Kateland Jones. That's like saying you would be unfaithful to me. You would never do that in a million years."

"Then explain it to me, Harlynn! Explain what the hell you are doing and why is Sue showing up there?"

"How do you know that? Sue told you?" he questioned.

"No. My so called best friend, who is going to get engaged to my father and apparently hanging out with my husband in the middle of the afternoon at the Four Seasons pent house, didn't tell me anything! Blacky told me!"

"Son of a bitch! Who else knows?" He looked up shaking his head.

"No one. How could I even utter this to anyone? I don't have anyone to turn to when it comes to you!" In a way she felt like she had been overtaken by Harlynn Barrett. He consumed all that surrounded her.

"I didn't want you know." Harlynn admitted.

"Say it Harlynn!" Kate demanded.

"I didn't want you know that I'm drinking more than I should."

"What does Dr. Brown say?" she asked. "Has she told you to go to AA?"

"We have discussed it at length. I think I'm having trouble adjusting to all the changes in our lives. I need things to calm down."

"You don't have to go to a hotel room to drink, Harlynn. I have never given you a hard time about your drinking."

"I didn't want to upset you, Kateland. I didn't want you to see how I'm struggling with work and my father. I didn't think it was fair to burden you with all of this."

"Well, it's a little late for that one. You have Janey, you have a son and a daughter on the way. You are scaring me," she whispered trying not to cry.

"I know. I'm very sorry."

"Are you doing pain pills for your shoulder with the alcohol? Don't you dare lie to my face!"

"I have, not very often." Harlynn walked away from her looking out the window. "No one else knows Kate and I don't want them to know."

Kate didn't respond because she was wondering what amount of truth her love would give up. She didn't know if she could help Harlynn was the problem. She wasn't sure if he wanted to change his ways today or in the future. She refrained from asking him one of the hundred questions that continued to spin in her head. She didn't know how she had gotten to this point in her life. She felt as though she knew nothing and was risking everything again. It was history repeating itself she realized. When they first started dating Kate had risked her career and her relationships with Keaton and Henry. She was doing the same thing again, except now there were soon to be three children she had to raise. Was she going to have raise these children by herself? Eventually Harlynn would make a mistake. Eventually he would go after her when he had been drinking or make a complete ass out of himself in front of everyone.

"Are you going to tell Henry and Keaton?" he asked her in voice that was somewhat mocking.

"I don't know what I'm going to do. I'm almost eight months pregnant with two other children to think about, Harlynn. I have a company that has both our names on it and I have a law firm that has both our names on it. I have a husband that has a drinking problem. I have a husband who has been deceptive."

"I never lied about it, Kateland!"

"When I asked where you were and you tell me you're in a meeting or with your Father, that's a lie, Harlynn. We both know that the reason you were at the Four Season's drinking is because you are under extreme pressure and you're trying to escape. That's how people with addictions behave. They lie to cover up what is going on."

"What if I say I will cut back starting right now?" Harlynn offered up to her.

"I think that would be a good start to facing what is going on in our marriage." She waited. "You will have a bodyguard with you all the time and you will only drink in this house."

"Or what?" Harlynn asked her slowly.

"Or I go to Henry." she whispered. "And the kids and I will move in with Henry and Meg until after the baby is born."

"Will you go to Dr. Brown with me?" Harlynn asked her as Kate closed her eyes because she hated going to shrinks. "I know it's asking a lot of you to go. We won't discuss your childhood or mother, I promise.

"I will consider it after the baby comes. I can't take on anymore at this juncture in time. I need to rest." Kate could feel Harlynn's eyes on her as she walked out of the room.

When life got tough she sought out Janey to calm her nervous. She found her playing in the downstairs playroom. She pulled up a chair and sat with her daughter.

"Hi honey. What's going on?" Kate asked as the child dressed her American Girl Dolls. Kate picked up a doll putting a party dress on her with matching shoes. Then put her in the chair to style her hair. "Are they having a tea party today?"

"No, they are giving a charity gala for the Pediatric Cancer Fund. They are raising money like you do for cancer research." She smiled.

Kate went back to that night she had seen Janey's mother walk out of the ICU unit at Texas Children's Hospital. She was a volunteer and tried to put in a couple hours a week. A volunteer had called her to cover because it was the holidays and they were short handed. There was Janey screaming her lungs out in pain. She was so tiny and sick. Janey's father was a mess torn between going after his wife and a screaming child. He asked her to rock the baby while he stepped out. Every night Kate came back and rocked her. The only time that Janey didn't cry was when she was sleeping or Kate was rocking her.

"How do you feel about your new sister Laney coming?" Kate asked holding the American Girl Doll named Lanie but spelled different. The stress started to leave her body as the baby girl kicked her again and Kate patted her stomach.

"God gave me a brother and now he is giving me a sister. I have this family that I never thought I would have, Mama. I love her nursery. I made a picture of a butterfly for it. Would you like to see the butterfly? I worked hard on it for Laney. It's a love butterfly."

"Yes." She watched as Janey scampered off to get her backpack then returned with her masterpiece.

Kate's eyes followed the lines and colors that formed a beautiful butterfly with shades of pink and purple. It really looked as though it might come off the paper and fly away. Again she was stunned by her daughter's talent at the age of seven. It appeared lifelike and the detail in it was completely accurate.

"Janey this is the most beautiful butterfly I have ever set eyes on. Can I frame it for the nursery?" Kate watched as Janey giggled and nodded her head yes. "Tomorrow we will go have a frame made for it."

"Like your artwork? You're going to frame my artwork like you frame yours?"

"Yes. That's how good you are at drawing." Janey showed her the other artwork she had been working on.

"Can I show Papa?" Her eyes sparkled with excitement.

"Sure. On second thought let's do that later. Papa's had a long day." Since Janey had two dads she called Stan her Dad and Harlynn her Papa. Kate wasn't sure what Harlynn was up to and didn't know if she wanted to know. Levi would be up soon, so she wanted this time with Janey. She wanted to just watch her and listen to her voice.

"Everyone at school keeps asking me why Papa is on magazines all the time."

"What do you tell them?" Kate was surprised at Janey's comment.

"Because he works hard and wants to help people. I'm very

proud of my Papa. I love him so much it makes my heart ache."

"Me too." Kate felt the tears come to her eyes but she held them back behind her smile. That is one thing she would never deny, how she loved Harlynn. "We are blessed to have Harlynn in our lives, love bug. God takes good care of us Janey." As she hugged her Harlynn stood in the doorway watching them.

She could tell by the look in his eyes he had heard every word. It made her think of how from the beginning Harlynn and Janey had this instant bond between. He did love Janey just as much as Levi.

"Janey, do you want to go for a bike ride?" Harlynn asked her as he smiled at Kate. His smile had gotten them through all their dark moments in the past.

"Yes!" She screeched, running by him to get ready.

"I was going to take Levi with us, if that's okay with you." Harlynn waited for her response.

"Yes, I think that would be nice if you took them for a ride. I'm going to take a nap before I pass out. Could you order dinner from Auntie Pasta's? Pizza sounds good to me for some reason."

"I'll take care of dinner. Charlie can go pick it up. After the children go to sleep can we finish talking later tonight?"

"Yes." She waited. "I would never give up on you, Harlynn."

"Thank you. I know you are very upset and I'm sorry for not telling you. I promise I will get a handle on the drinking and stop the pain pills."

"I need to go take a rest and get off my feet because they are throbbing on top of not being able to breathe."

"Do I need to call Carr?" Harlynn questioned immediately.

"Let me rest and I'll decide. It's going to be a long month ahead."

As she walked through the house that was fifteen thousand square feet she longed to be back in her other house that was much smaller. The need to not be pulled emotionally in every direction came upon her suddenly. The pressure to hold all the pieces together was enormous as she changed into one of Harlynn's t-shirts and slid between the sheets.

—

Hours later, Kate woke up with her phone vibrating next to the bed. There were twenty emails ranging from Levi's teacher wanting a conference to Nick telling her he needed to talk to her about business and Elle. She answered the phone not looking at it.

"Kateland, its Roger Carr."

"Yes?" She sat up in bed fully awake now because Dr. Carr usually didn't call her.

"My asthma is better and the ankles are less swollen."

"Your blood pressure is climbing, Kateland. What are you doing right now?"

"I was sleeping since I'm trying to be careful."

"Well, I want you to stay in bed and come in tomorrow morning first thing."

"Sure." Her phone went dead as she looked at it and put it down. Harlynn came in the room looking better after an afternoon with the children.

"What's wrong?" He stopped and waited. "Who were you talking to on the phone?" So she told him what Carr had said, and watched the look of fear come back to his eyes mixed with guilt. "Would you like me to run a bath for you?" he asked as he sat on the edge of the bed. "I'm sorry I made you upset. You really can't have any more stress in your life. I don't want anything happening to you or this baby. Do you need to go to the hospital?"

"I feel better. Harlynn, I will tell you if I have the headaches or get dizzy. The baby is moving fine. She keeps kicking the hell out of my diaphragm. Laney will let me know if she's unhappy. A bath would help. I got a very strange email from Nick that needs to be dealt with tonight."

"Elle is really pissed off about Shelly showing up all the time." Harlynn told her as he took off his riding shirt. He still had really nice abs was all Kate could think.

"They will end up married some day. It's business. He said he had a conference call with the head of the NIH. They suggested we slow down our research for a year. They basically told him to stop

44

what we are working on."

"What?" Harlynn walked over to her reading the email. "They can't tell us to halt our research when we haven't even gone into clinical trials. From what Danny said we are roughly six months from starting to design the project. They are interviewing families for the next two weeks. It's going to be hard because the patient population is so small. JR6 will be the only hope for these families."

"Do you think the pharmaceutical sector pulling back has anything to do with us? I shorted the industry two weeks ago. The charts look like a double dip pull back to me and Keat. Every time you are on a cover of a magazine or interviewed the stocks pull back more and we haven't even released the positive data."

"I agree with the pull back. I will call Nick and get the details. You need to rest for this evening. We have a conference at school for Levi on Thursday. Apparently he is running the classroom and the teacher is overwhelmed by him." Harlynn rolled his eyes. "He isn't even two yet? I'm going to take a shower and run a bath for you. The food should be here shortly. Could you text Nick that I will call him?"

"Yes." She smiled because it was the old Harlynn back again. The man who wasn't dark and depressed or drank too much stood in front of her. The man who loved his family and was her hero was slowly coming back.

—

After dinner, Kate watched as Harlynn and Henry were building Legos with the children. Janey was building a pink castle that they had designed on the Lego website. Levi was sorting the Legos for a giant car he was building while giving directions to Henry just how he wanted it done. Levi was one of the few individuals in the world that could order the Great Henry Grayden around.

They had only lived next door to Henry and Meg for six months and it was wonderful. Henry had decided he wanted Kate and Harlynn to live closer to them so he bought the house for them as a surprise. It made Kate feel good that Levi and Janey had these people in their lives that loved them so dearly. Henry and Meg would stop by for dinner or just to say hi. It was a family she never thought in a million years she would be fortunate enough to have.

Kate decided to go upstairs to lie back down since the children were being spoiled. Twenty minutes later she could hear Harlynn playing on the piano with Levi and Janey. She smiled waiting for Henry to check on her before he left.

"Do you need anything before I go?" Henry asked her coming in the room stretching out on the chaise lounge. He picked up a book from Kate's reading basket, glancing at it. "Is this one better than the last one?" Henry inquired.

"No, but it has four chapters in it that will make you laugh pretty hard." She took a sip of her water. "When does Meg get back from her trip to Utah?"

"Tonight." Henry smiled. "You won't believe who called me today. Harlynn's father, Paul."

"Really? Why?"

"He said he wanted to talk to me about finding his faith again. He mentioned that he had been talking to you last weekend. We are going to meet tomorrow afternoon for a couple of hours."

"That makes me happy. I'm shocked he reached out to you, Henry. This is wonderful. I have to be honest, I don't know if he even believes in God. There is a Bible downstairs on my desk for him. I was trying to mark some passages for him, like you did for me."

"Well, I will take it home and work on it tonight for him. Perhaps together we can help him find his faith again." Henry waited. "How are you and Harlynn doing?"

"There is a lot of stress in our lives at the moment. He is trying to do his best, Henry." She smiled weakly, desperately wanting to tell Henry her fears, but she couldn't do that to Harlynn.

"Carr is very worried about the blood pressure. You can't afford any more stress at the moment, sweetheart. I talked to Keat and Nick tonight. They are on their own running the company until Laney gets here. Harlynn and I will help them, but you need to focus on you right now. You need to let go of all the crap going on. I don't want you in the hospital. That means, Sue and your dad, your crazy mother, work and problems in your marriage."

"What do you know about my marriage?" She lowered her eyes trying to cover up her doubts.

"Kate, everyone can see what is going on with Harlynn. Ever since the plane crash he has been drinking more than he needs." Silence filled the room. "I'm staying out of it, but if it gets worse, then I will get involved. Between Nick, Keat and I, we are keeping a close eye on him."

"He said he is going to try to cut back."

"There have been times in my life when I drank too much. Keaton has struggled and so does Nick at times. I think Harlynn will pull out of this, especially when he sees that baby girl."

"How do you always know exactly what I need to hear? You are the best dad in the world, Henry."

"Well, you happen to be the best daughter in the world. Thank you for naming this child after me."

"You are welcome. I will be okay, Henry. My dreams told me that I will be okay."

"That makes me feel better." He stood up taking the book with him and gave her a long hug. "We love you. I thank God everyday that we have you, Harlynn and these beautiful grandchildren in our lives."

She watched as he walked out of the room thinking she was the one who should be thanking God for Henry Lane Grayden. She would mostly likely be dead without him. He was the one who had saved her from her mother killing her.

~Chapter 5

Two weeks until baby Laney would arrive, Kate thought as she sat outside with her iPad going over what needed to be done before the child came. Schedules for the children were done, meals planned, shopping list for the grocery store and Targets, done. She had checked and tripled checked everything.

"Are you still not speaking to me?" Sue asked. Her arms were overloaded with gifts. It was a daily event for the past week. Kate didn't want a baby shower and couldn't have one for security reasons. Everyone who came to the house had to have a background check at this point. She wondered if she would ever be able to meet someone on the street or at a party and go to lunch with them.

"You should have told me he was drinking to the point you had to babysit him, Sue." It was the first time that Kate had responded to Sue. Usually they would sit there with Sue talking and Kate saying nothing. She didn't have anything nice to say.

"I thought you were mad that Sam proposed to me? Shit, Harlynn didn't tell me you knew about the drinking, what an ass." She sat back in the lounge chair completely flustered. "Look, the whole time the man sat there professing his love for you. I have never heard any man talk about loving someone like that, Kate. He is so freaked out about the plane crash. I finally got him to go back to Dr. Brown."

"Go on." Kate glared at her.

"I think if you weren't pregnant, he would talk to you more about what is going on with him. If you weren't pregnant, he wouldn't be here, Kateland. Do you realize how close we came to losing him?"

"You have no idea how I remember that day. I can't do anything until after Lane comes." She paused. "Then there will be hell to pay because I'm beginning to understand. We are getting a lot of threats against us. Even Meg is freaked out and she never gets scared. You should have seen the bodyguards with me at the board meeting for

WE, yesterday. I asked Dennis if he wanted me to resign, but he said not in a million years. He said he is watching my back so I didn't need to worry."

"I have a bodyguard now." Sue rolled her eyes. "You are going to change the world, Kateland. Moon Water is going to heal a whole lot of people."

"I talked to Danny and the results are better than he expected in the lab. We are months ahead of schedule." Kate tried to cover her concern. "Harlynn was upset after his meetings in Washington. There is something going on, Sue. I'm not sure what it could be."

"Danny said he was feeling a great deal of pressure. He wouldn't tell me from who or why." Sue added. "It will all work out. I think your father is going to help out Nick and Keat at Moon Water. Harlynn is trying to close three deals at the firm before the baby comes. He is stretched paper thin girl- friend."

"I know. He told me he is trying to wrap a few deals in order to take time off. He is worried how Levi is going to deal with the baby. I don't think Levi has a very good teacher at school. If they don't give us a new teacher he will be home with us."

"Meg was going up to observe his class today and I'm going tomorrow." Sue leaned forward. "I think we make his teacher nervous. He intimidates the hell out of his teacher. She doesn't know what to do with the two year old genius."

"They want to test him because he can talk in complete sentences and now, apparently is reading, thanks to my dear brother. Keaton has been doing *Baby's Can Read* with him and guess what? It worked." Sue started to laugh. "My fear is there might be something going on with him."

"Kate, he is fine and he is not Autistic. It's fascinating at times when you have this cute toddler who smiles and laughs at you. A moment later he starts talking about electricity and weather systems. He comes by it honestly through genetics. I wonder what Lane will be like? Henry is profoundly touched by giving her his name. I love that you did that for Henry."

"It's exciting in a calm way compared to what it was like last time. I'm getting to enjoy the experience compared to when I had Levi. Let me see your ring?" Kate took Sue's hand admiring the diamond that was several carats. "Have you set a wedding date?"

"We would like to get married at Thanksgiving if it works for everyone. I think your dad wants to make sure you aren't upset. What you think is very important to him."

"I'm not upset. I'm upset that no one told me what was going on with Harlynn. I don't want him crashing in his Lamborghini because he is drunk, do you understand me, Sue?"

"He never drinks and drives, Kateland. You know that he wouldn't do anything to hurt himself or anyone else. The man is not stupid."

"True, he always uses the car service or the bodyguards are with him if he is going out. Has he said anything about his Dad to you? No one will tell me anything due to my blood pressure?"

"I've been told to keep things light with you by seven different people." She caved as Kate gave her the look. "Paul is slowly deteriorating. Harlynn was telling me that for the first time his father asked him about his faith and for help. Paul gave you all the credit for the change."

"I keep thinking that it won't happen. I don't know how Harlynn will handle it, Sue. You know how close he is to his father," she whispered.

"Believe me, everyone is worried out of their minds. We will all be here for him. I have to believe that it's better to know. Harlynn and Paul have gotten to have conversations that would have never happened."

"It doesn't change the facts. Every time Harlynn has dinner with his father I can see the pain in his eyes when he gets home. It's like he is silently being tortured by the process."

"Well, he has you and the children to help him get through this, Kate. Think if he was still married to that witch?" Sue made her most sour face. "Doctors have been wrong before so who really knows what will happen or when it will happen. Just look at this baby girl in your body. You were never supposed to have a child, let alone two?"

"Let me see what you got Lane today." Kate didn't want to think of what was ahead of them. She didn't want to watch Harlynn fall apart in front of her eyes. Maybe she could help him for the moment and maybe Dr. Brown could, but inevitable, he would fall to pieces. It was like anticipating a hurricane to hit. You know when it might make landfall and you sort of know there will be damage of some magnitude, but there is no way to know the damage until it hits. You don't know until it's over. It takes a long time to rebuild after a hurricane.

Kate gazed at the beautiful delicate dresses and nightshirts for her daughter. There were tiny shoes and a monogrammed blanket that had a huge 'L' on it. There were socks and hats with matching sweaters. And of course a Tiffany rattle with Lane Kate Jones Barrett engraved on it. It seemed more real as she held the blanket and pressed it against her cheek. She was going to have a daughter to raise and teach about the world.

"Thank you." Kate smiled. "Thank you for trying to take care of Harlynn and protect me. And thank you for making up for my terrible mother."

"I can only imagine what you thought." Sue sighed. "Will you be my maid of honor? There is no one else I can imagine being there next to me."

"Yes. I will." Kate laughed thinking how weird was this going to be part of her father's wedding party.

———

The nursery had turned out beautiful as Kate rearranged the clothes and started to pack a bag for the hospital. She had ten days before she went in for her c-section, but decided when she got up today it was the thing to do.

"Hey, what are you doing?" Keaton asked coming in the nursery. "I don't feel like working anymore today. I seriously have no idea how you run Moon Water and take care of the house and all the other crap you do."

"I would love to be working today or tomorrow. Harlynn took my Blackberry when he caught me emailing you this morning. How unfair is that one?"

"He is worried about your blood pressure, Kitty Kat," Keat reminded her. "I have been sent to watch over you while he is in meetings this afternoon. He couldn't focus during the conference call this morning, it was really bad. Henry finally decided to reschedule the call because he couldn't take it. Between worrying about you, the baby and his father, the man can't take much more."

"How many nights did you stay up with him drinking?"

"Several. It helps him sleep and he needs to sleep. Everything is in check. Nick and I are taking turns, don't worry." She looked at him for a second, and then went back to packing. "Why are you packing?"

"I don't know exactly, it feels like I need to be packed. Did Harlynn give you my Blackberry back because I told him he better." She watched as Keat handed it to her.

"You need to relax or Carr said he is putting you in the hospital tomorrow."

"Not going." Kate smiled. "I hate hospitals."

"How about we watch a movie?"

"Yes. What I really need is Harlynn. I have hardly seen him this week and I don't know if he is working or sitting in a bar."

"You have to trust him, Kate. You are obsessing because you're about to have a baby. You never cared if he stopped at the State Bar after work before."

"There's more going on with him and we both know it. It's like dealing with someone with a split personality. I don't like it. I don't know who is coming through the door at night or who I am waking up next to, Keaton."

"I hear you, Kitty Kat." He stood up embracing his sister. "A month from now all this is going to seem silly."

"I hope so." She pulled away from her brother and handed an envelope to him from the bag she was packing. "Medical Power of Attorney for you, dear brother. I know I can count on you to make the decisions I would want to be made."

"Why don't you trust Harlynn to do this, Kateland?" he asked her slowly.

"I don't want to put him in that position on top of everything else he would have to deal with if something goes wrong again."

"You're right." Keat admitted taking it from her.

—

As they sat in the media room watching a new James Bond movie that somehow Keaton had gotten a copy of, Kate felt her eyes close. It startled her when her bodyguard, Charlie, appeared and the lights came on in the room.

"What's up, Charlie?" Keat asked with concern.

"We have a situation concerning Janey," Charlie said slowly. "A person by the name of Amy Rivers tried to pick her up from school."

"What?" Kate went into pure panic. "Where is she?"

"Kate, calm down," Keat said glaring at Charlie.

"Janey and Meg are on their way to the house. They stopped at *Sprinkles* to give us time to deal with what is going on. Amy Rivers is at the front gate demanding to see Kate. I have already told her I will call the police, but she refuses to go until she sees Kate. It's out of hand and I don't want the media showing up."

—

An hour later Kate, Keaton, Meg, and Henry sat at the dining room table with Amy Rivers. Stan was flying back to Houston and no one could get a hold of Harlynn. He was somewhere at the Moon Water Labs in the Woodlands about an hour away. Nick was looking for him.

Janey had been taken over to Meg and Henry's house with Claire to make sure she didn't walk into the room. Three bodyguards stood in the room glaring at Amy Rivers.

"We have just filed a restraining order against you, Amy. This is our last meeting and if you ever go near Janey again you are in jail."

"Well, I will go to the papers, Henry." Amy replied not flinching.

"You abandoned her when she was six months old and you show up now?" Keaton questioned.

"I made a mistake." Amy answered him. "I am Janey's mother on her birth certificate. I do have a right to change my mind to see my daughter. I will fight for her."

"What do you want?" Kate asked slowly. "What do you want

after six and half years? You are remarried and have a child. What do you want?"

"I want Janey back is what I want. I want to share custody with her father."

"She doesn't even know who you are, Amy. You have never even asked for a picture of her and you show up at her school to take her? You have no legal right to her anymore. You gave her up when you walked out of that hospital room and left her to die. Now I'm going to ask you why you have shown up at my daughter's school and tried to kidnap her or I will call the police and have you arrested. One phone call in six years does not give you parental rights in the state of Texas. This is an act of desperation."

The room filled with silence as Kate waited. She picked up the phone and pressed one key putting it to her ear. "Wait." Amy looked at the people at the table. "My child has the same cancer as Janey. I need Janey's medical records and a sample of her blood. I need to see if she is a match for a bone marrow transplant."

"What!" Henry yelled at her. "You get the hell out of this house and don't you dare come back! I told you before what would happen if you ever did something like this, Amy. I told you I wouldn't stand for it. The police will be waiting to arrest you when you get to the gate." The bodyguards escorted her from the room in a split second.

Kate felt Keat reach over for her hand and squeeze it. What would have happened if she had gotten Janey? What would she have put Janey through? She didn't care about Janey she just wanted her to test her blood. It was her worst nightmare that was coming true.

"Kate, I promise you that she will never come near this house or Janey again." Henry stated firmly. "Where the hell is Harlynn?" Henry began to pace the room then glanced at Kate. "You don't look good, sweetheart?"

"I'm going upstairs to lie down. Can someone go get Janey? I need to see her."

"I'll go get her," Keat offered. "She is not going to get custody of Janey."

"We have a huge problem and I think everyone in this room knows it. But the real question is how did she find Janey and is the story true? Is there someone else behind this because it would seem someone of her intelligence wouldn't do something as stupid as trying to take a child? We need Blacky here now." Her hands were shaking as she left the room. Kate wasn't sure if it was because she was upset or hungry or there was another problem.

Meg came upstairs with a snack and juice for her. Kate was going through a photo album of Janey wiping away the tears. Everyone knew that one day Amy would show up and want to see Janey, but not this. Not for her blood and bone marrow. How desperate was she that Amy would do this?

"Harlynn is on his way back to the house. He was on a bike ride on a trail in the Woodlands. His bodyguard was with him. Harlynn didn't realize there was no reception on his phone until they stopped for a break. Everyone is working on it, Kate. They will figure out what to do about Janey's mother." Meg embraced her, and then wiped her tears away. She stayed with her until Janey came.

Janey curled up next to Kate like a cat. She closed her eyes, smiling because that is what she wanted. She wanted her mother to hold her. Did she even know what was going on Kate wondered as she closed her eyes.

The next time she opened her eyes Harlynn was on the balcony on his phone, drinking a glass of scotch. He had showered because his hair was wet. He was dressed in a dress shirt and slacks, most likely going back to work she guessed. He looked completely handsome as the clothes hung on his body, outlining his broad shoulders and narrow waist. People at times would stop and stare at him because he had this magnetism that radiated off him. She watched Janey asleep next to her, smelling the strawberry shampoo that still lingered in her hair. She sat up thinking of Levi. Then she saw Harlynn talking to him as he played with some blocks on the balcony. One of Levi's favorite things to do was dump his blocks off the balcony and watch one of the bodyguards pick them up.

"Gravity, Dada." He smiled then pointed at Kate. "Mama's up!"

She watched as he called Claire to come get the kids. He gently picked up Levi whispering to him. He brought the child over to Kate as she reached out for him.

"Hey little man, how are you doing?"

"Great!" Levi told her with a big smile. "Mama, Levi loves you."

He gave her a big kiss then hugged her as Harlynn gently picked up Janey to take to her room. He paused holding her, then closed his eyes taking in a deep breath. He didn't have to say what he was thinking as he kissed her head. Kate knew he was rattled by the look in his eyes and the way he held his jaw.

"Where's the baby?" Levi asked poking at Kate's stomach. "Wake up? Levi loves the baby too." He smiled, and then he stopped. "No more school."

"Why?" Kate smiled warmly at her son. "Bad day?"

"Bad teacher." He told her firmly.

"How about a new teacher?" Kate asked as she watched him thinking.

"Yes." He kissed her again jumping on the bed. Then he jumped into Claire's arms when the nanny appeared.

"Why don't you take him to the play room? I think he has some extra energy."

"I think that's a marvelous idea." Claire nodded at Kate. "Are you feeling better?"

"I'm probably going to the hospital to have baby Lane," she told Claire.

"Don't you worry about your angels, Ms. Kate. I will take good care of them for you."

"Thank you. I couldn't do it without you Claire. I deeply appreciate how you love my children. At least it won't be as crazy as it was last time."

"I will say a prayer for you."

—

The water in the shower felt good on her face while she stood there. She just needed to get through the next twenty-four hours then life would be better. Her head was pounding and she knew her blood pressure had kicked up another notch. She felt a slight twinge across her belly.

Harlynn was waiting for her when she came out of the shower. He had a smoothie and her robe. As she sat down in front of the mirror he dried her hair with a towel. He knelt down turning the chair towards him as he looked into her eyes.

"Look at me, love. No one is going to take Janey from us, do you understand me? I will fight like you can't imagine in order to protect our daughter." She nodded her head as the tears came down her face.

"I'm sorry I was on a bike ride and no one could find me. I will make sure I text you next time. You are going to know where I'm at all the time, Kateland."

"It scared me when no one could find you, Harlynn. I didn't know if something had happened to you and I can't stand the idea of anything happening to you." She wrapped her arms around him his neck and held on to him crying as he held her. He held her tight while she sobbed and gently rubbed her back.

"We are going to be fine." He smiled as she sat up.

"I think baby Lane is coming tonight. The contractions have started and my head is pounding hard. She is not happy." Her voice quivered.

"That's the best news I've had in a long time." He kissed her, "why don't you get dressed and we are out of here." She was frightened Harlynn realized as he peered into her eyes. "Don't be scared, Kateland."

"I need you to be here, by my side, Harlynn."

"I'm not going anywhere."

~Chapter 6

As he held their daughter, Kate watched as the tears came down Harlynn's face with such force that he didn't even wipe them. It was one of those moments that Kate knew she would never forget because it was so real and beautiful. She watched as Harlynn stared into her face. This child had saved her father once again, unknowing, just by the way she stared back into his eyes with calmness. Although Laney had only been in this world for a few hours, she already had her father in the palm of her tiny hand.

"She looks exactly like your baby pictures," Harlynn whispered as her eyes closed slowly. He held the child watching her sleep. "She is powerful, like you." Harlynn smiled at Kate after he placed the child in the bassinet next to her bed.

"How do you feel? Be honest. If you need more pain medicine Carr said he had written an order." He raised his eyebrows studying her.

"I'm good. A little tired from having my insides moved around, but it's not like last time. Perhaps they gave me more morphine this time because I'm still a little fuzzy on the edges. And I can breathe, the asthma is gone. I want two more children in a couple of years. I think my body would like a break."

"Sounds like a plan to me." He couldn't help it as he smiled at her. Harlynn gently took her hand and slid a beautiful pink diamond on it. "Do you like it?"

"Yes. I do. You remembered I showed you a pink diamond when we were in Utah last time," she whispered as she admired it. "We did it again, Babes. We have these beautiful children and we are so blessed."

"Yes, we are very blessed. I can't believe that Laney is so observant. It's like she knew exactly who I was, Kate. I loved the way she kept looking around the delivery room as though she was studying people's faces."

"I like this time with you Harlynn. It's as if time stops for a moment. It's us again with the world outside of that door like it was in the beginning."

"You are my world, Kate." He leaned over kissing her slowly. "Thank you for our daughter and for putting up with me. I know that it's been very hard on you and unfair."

"How about we leave the past behind us and look forward. Let's try to do our best to be there for each other going forward." She watched as he nodded. "We are so lucky."

"Thank you for forgiving me for not being there."

"You are welcome." Kate watched as Harlynn climbed into the tiny hospital bed with her. "How much longer do we have alone?" She giggled.

"Twenty minutes. I don't think Keat and Henry will last any longer."

"Good." Kate closed her eyes feeling Harlynn's heart beating strong and steady.

—

Kate stared at her son who was standing with the black Sharpie marker in front of the white wall in the entry hall to their contemporary home. Levi took ownership of the master piece that was six feet long and three feet high. The lines told Kate that he was very upset with her for leaving him for four days. The green eyes stared at her waiting. Everyone stood watching what was going to happen. Kate glanced at Harlynn holding a glass of champagne as he blinked his eyes several times and nodded at her to handle it.

"Did you do this for me?" Kate asked kneeling down at his eye level.

"Yes." He pouted staring her down.

"I like it." She smiled at her son as she held out her hand for the marker. "Is this your welcome home sign for baby Laney?"

"Yes." He told her handing the marker to her.

"Let's sign your name to it." Kate suggested. "I think next time we need to use a canvas from Mama's art studio. Since you broke the rule of not writing on walls tomorrow you will help Mama paint the wall. First we will take a picture of your art work and frame it for Laney's room."

He smiled at his mother as he leaped into her arms giggling. He watched as she signed his name to the wall in large letters. Then everyone clapped as Levi continued giggling as ran to his father, embarrassed.

"I wish I had you for a mother growing up. I would be a much different person." Nick admitted, handing Kate a glass of champagne. "You have the most beautiful children. I love that she looks like you and has Harlynn's dimple on her chin."

"Wow, can you believe she is here?" Kate asked him as they walked into the living room. "It's all such a miracle to have her. Would you like to be her Godfather also?"

"I'm incredibly honored, again. You can't imagine how much this means to me to be the Godfather of both your children."

"Well, Godfather Nick, I'm going to need your help with these two children as you can see by my son's latest creation. All the books said he would be acting out. I'm sure he felt like I abandoned him."

"He was asking me where you were the last two days," Nick admitted. "Have you spoken with my father today?" Nick asked slowly.

"Briefly. Why?" Kate asked. "Blacky has been so good to me over the last months calling me each day to check in."

"He called me late last night, and . . . he said I may not hear from him for a while. He asked me if I had heard from my brother Max and to call him immediately if I do. I can't find Max anywhere."

"I don't understand?" Kate responded slowly.

"You know I can't tell anyone else." Nick looked out the window. "There is a lot going on, Kateland." Nick pulled a small velvet box from his jacket. "Here." He held out a gift for Kate as she took it from him. "I thought you would like these."

Kate opened the black velvet box to two gold crosses, one for her and one for Laney that matched. The crosses were both delicate and beautiful. It was his love for her and this new child she saw in the crosses.

"I love them." She smiled as Elle came to sit with them in her elegant way.

"How are you feeling?" Elle asked in her silky voice. "You make everything look so easy, Kate. How do you manage?"

"Patron." She smiled as everyone laughed. "I have all these people who love me is how I manage. No matter how impossible I am or what crazy ideas I come up with, they are always there." She got up slowly going to check on Harlynn. As she came in the den off the kitchen she saw Harlynn gently place the baby in his father's arms as Henry took pictures of what was happening. Everyone in the room watched with their hearts aching as Paul sat there holding this child who would never know him. She was grateful Paul had gotten the opportunity to at least meet her.

"Why don't you relax for a while?" Meg suggested, "Do you need anything?"

"What do I need?" Kate smiled. "I need to sit down and do nothing for five minutes before it gets too crazy. How is Janey doing?"

"She is doing well. She and Stan are at our lake house in Austin. Henry thought it would be good for them to get away for a couple of days. They will be back here in about two hours. Henry has the best lawyers working on this Kateland, so don't give it another thought."

"My children have bodyguards, Meg." She fought back the tears turning away. "Is it true that Amy's daughter has the same cancer that Janey had when she was sick?"

"Yes. Blacky could verify that she does. Danny wants to meet with you and Harlynn in a few days to talk."

"Do we help this child?"

"I think we need to talk to Danny and think of what Janey has already been through. We need to decide if Janey would want to know she has a sister, Kateland. It's not always easy to do what is right."

"My job is to protect Janey from being hurt again by this person. It's only been six months since Janey finally stopped asking why her mother left her and then she shows up. I'm scared of losing Janey. I'm scared Janey is going to want this woman who was a heartless bitch."

"Well, we haven't agreed to anything yet, Kate. Henry thinks we can pay her off by offering to cover all the medical bills."

"She must know something about JR6 is my bet. I can't let Janey be hurt by this person again, Meg. I won't do it."

"Henry wouldn't let that happen or Harlynn for that matter. I don't think I've ever seen Harlynn so furious, Kateland. As soon as Laney is old enough, he wants to take you and the children to the ranch for awhile."

"It actually sounds perfect to me. Will you come?"

"Yes, I think we all need to get out of this city for a break from all these problems that keep surfacing."

Kate could always count on Meg to support and be honest with her.

—

A week later, Kate sat at her dining room table with a worker from Child Protection Services (CPS). The evaluation was to see if Janey was being taken care of in a loving home. It really pissed her off as the woman continued to ask questions.

"You have a lovely home, Ms. Jones."

"Thank you."

"I'm sorry to be bothering you with all these questions. Will your husband be joining us?"

"Harlynn's father is terminally ill with heart failure. He said he would do his best to be here." Kate lied through her teeth. It was the best she could come up with as a reasonable explanation for his absence.

"How many nannies do you employ to take care of Janey?"

"I would say that we use our nanny for the younger children. If we have an engagement, we go after the children have been put to bed. We have extended family that helps out."

"Do you work?" The woman asked as she glanced at Kate's wedding ring.

"I work from home for the most part. I do occasionally go into the office when the children are in school. I have complete flexibility if Janey has a doctor's appointment. It helps to be the CEO of your own company when you have young children." Kate joked as the woman smiled at her.

"How is Janey doing in school?"

"She has straight A's and one of the highest grade point averages at her school. We bring in tutors to give her more exposure to subjects not taught at this age. She plays soccer, tennis and the piano." Kate paused. "I have everything you should need documented in the packet.

The packet was five inches thick as social worker opened it to a well organized binder that showed Janey's school report cards, healthcare, after school activities and schedules right down to a list of books that Janey had been reading with Harlynn and independently.

Kate looked up as Harlynn came in the front door. She knew instantly that he had been drinking and was depressed. He locked eyes with Kate, and then she could see it hit him that he was supposed to be here.

He walked over to the table greeting the social worker and kissing Kate. Then he sat down at the table with them. He held Kate's hand while they waited for her to finish going through the documents and medical records.

"I'm going to be honest with you since you have both been so gracious and helpful. I have spoken with Judge Gold. He has given me permission to speak with you openly and honestly because of the circumstances. I think you have more than enough to dispute the claims by the biological mother. I can see you have done everything for Janey and beyond. I will present my report to the Judge Gold. I think it would be harmful for Janey to have Ms. Rivers suddenly come into her life and the idea she would take Janey shows complete instability in my view."

"Can she go to court and force us to give Janey's blood sample."

"Janey cannot go through a bone marrow transplant." The social worker commented looking at Dr. Danny's report.

"Would you like to see Janey's room and the play rooms?" Harlynn offered. "And Janey has her own garden in the back that you should take a picture of, she is so proud of it."

"Yes." The social worker responded mesmerized by Harlynn.

Kate half smiled as she watched Harlynn pour on the charm making this woman feel like she was the only person in the world that mattered. It was so subtle that the woman had no idea what was happening to her.

——

When Janey came home Kate's nervousness finally calmed down. It was that way every morning she left for school until she came back. She was so scared of losing this child who had taught her about unconditional love and hope. Janey had taught Kate to never give up on herself or anyone in her life.

"How was your day?" Kate asked as Laney slept in her arms. Laney loved to be held and did her best sleeping on Kate's or Harlynn's chest. Then it hit Kate, the child had acid reflux and couldn't sleep lying down. Another mystery solved, Kate sighed.

"Are you going to tennis today? Meg wants to take you if that's okay. I have to stay with Laney right now. When Laney is a little older I promise I will take you again. I know it's been a really long time and I'm sorry."

"I like getting to be with Meg by myself. Meg really loves me. I know that when Laney is older things will be better. Papa explained to me how it's hard because Laney doesn't sleep a lot at night." She stopped. "There is this woman who keeps watching me at tennis."

"Really?" Kate's heart began to race. "Maybe she just likes watching you play, Janey." Kate smiled gently putting down Laney in the bassinet and going through Janey's backpack.

"I love this drawing." Kate looked at the angles and lines of the house almost like an architect had drawn it. "Who taught you to set back these lines like this?" Kate asked slowly. Janey's mother, Amy, was an architect.

"My art teacher at school talks about lines and angles, I guess." Kate watched as she bounced off to change her clothes.

Then it came to her again, do they punish a child for what her mother did? Do they help this other child? Could a person really change over time?

—

A week later Kate laughed to herself when the children were all asleep, finally. It was a long day with a newborn and two year old. Levi seemed to be adjusting to the baby, but only because of Meg taking the time to make him feel special. It was all working out and in another week she could start exercising again. She glanced at the clock thinking Harlynn should have been home an hour ago.

She checked her email and text to see if he had tried to contact her. He didn't have a dinner tonight from what her schedule said. For the next hour she went over letters and emails for Moon Water trying to focus. Laney would be up in an hour to eat so there was no point in resting. She was tired from the little sleep she was getting.

She heard the front door open, but it wasn't Harlynn it was her bodyguard, Charlie, which meant only one thing: there was trouble and it was probably Harlynn. She walked out to the living room where Charlie was waiting for her. They both stared at each other for a moment.

"Just tell me." Kate waited.

"We need to go pull Harlynn out of the State Bar. I'm hoping he might go calmly if you are there."

"Who is he with?" Kate asked because Harlynn usually went with someone to drink.

"No one. He ditched his bodyguard and went by himself. Luckily, I have a payment plan with the bartender to call me when Harlynn shows up there. Steve called me. He said he was going to have to cut him off and that Harlynn was acting very strange. He said it wasn't Harlynn and wondered if he was on drugs."

Kate sighed because Nick and Keat were out of town. Henry was at an important dinner this evening and she didn't want to bother him. The night nurse was still there, so she would have someone to watch the children. There must have been something that happened, was all Kate could think as she got dressed quickly. Harlynn was still drinking, although he had cut way back to the point it didn't bother her. She didn't like that he drank at lunch. As long as he didn't drink until he got home again, it was okay for now, sort of.

65

—

"Hey," Kate said sheepishly as she sat down at the bar next to Harlynn. She kissed him for a moment. "I've been thinking about you for the last four hours."

"I was thinking of calling you. It's basically a no win situation from where I'm sitting."

"Why don't you tell me what is going on with you, Harlynn? I kind of thought we were turning the corner on this one." He didn't respond. "You were covering it up again?" She noticed how bad his allergies were tonight. His eyes were red, he was congested and his voice was scratchy. He was a complete mess in her opinion.

"Blacky." He waited. "Blacky said I need to start carrying a gun on me at all times."

"Why?" Kate was so confused.

"There is a contract out on all of us, Kateland, right down to our infant daughter. Someone wants to kill us, our children and the rest of the people we love." Harlynn looked into her eyes.

"Then we deal with it. We do whatever we have to in order to stay alive. We don't sit at a bar getting drunk, Harlynn."

"I didn't know how to tell you." He sighed. "My dad's cardiologist and George called me today. Apparently he only has a month or so left if we are lucky."

"What are you going to do when he dies, Harlynn?" She asked him as she signed the bar tab surprised at how much he had drunk. No wonder Charlie was afraid to come by himself. She could see Charlie standing by the door letting her know they needed to get him out.

"I don't know, Kate. It's not when he dies I'm worried about to be honest. There will be the funeral and all sorts of things I have to do. It's when it's over, when I'm sitting in my office and I pick up the phone to call him to talk. Or when Levi has his first ball game or when I take our son fishing or all the little things that probably no one will notice."

"Let's go home." Kate suggested, softly.

"What if I say no I want to sit here alone?"

"Then three body guards are going to drag you out of this bar,

Harlynn. Do you want that in the papers?"

"I've been angry with you, Kateland. You haven't even noticed." He looked at her like she was nothing to him. There was no love in his voice or the way he spoke.

"Really?" Kate sat up. "What did I do?"

Harlynn didn't answer her as he got up and walked out the front door. Kate sat there dumbfounded, not having any idea what she had done. She had never had Harlynn say he was angry with her.

~Chapter 7

The next morning, Kate sat at the table in the kitchen getting Janey ready for school trying to smile as she tried not to think of last night. When they got home things had gone from bad to worse immediately with Harlynn yelling at her for things she didn't understand. It was almost like he was on the verge of saying he wished he never met her. Finally one of the bodyguards decided Harlynn was going to sleep at his old place that was a loft not far away. It was beyond ugly.

"Mama why are you sad?" Janey asked quietly. "Is Granddad okay?"

"He is doing okay, Janey. Laney was up all night crying again. I'm sleepy is all, love bug."

"Levi is still asleep. Do you want me to go get him?" Janey asked.

"No, let him sleep, love bug. I think he needs a break from his teacher for today. They don't seem to get along very well."

"Everyone knows she doesn't like boys. It's not Levi's fault." Janey told her in a matter of fact tone.

"Okay, I think he's done with that teacher, Janey. Do you mind if Levi goes to a new school? I know that you like him with you at school."

"Could we both go to a new school because I don't want to leave Levi?" She frowned for a good minute.

"I think I will call First Steps to see if they can take you both."

"Who is taking me to school today?" Janey asked noticing Harlynn nor Keat were around.

"Do you mind if Claire takes you with the driver, just for this one day, so I don't have to wake up Laney or Levi?"

"That's good." She gave Kate a long hug gathering her lunch box and backpack. Kate looked at the clock on the wall. If she hurried, she could get in a shower. She put the dishes in the sink, something a person with OCD would never do. She didn't have time to clean up the kitchen. Then she remembered the maid would be here soon.

She had a meeting with Dr. Danny Hill this morning to go over the research for JR6 and other issues in the lab. It would be good to see Danny she smiled. She needed something to look forward to today. Danny couldn't be swayed by Harlynn or anyone else.

As she stood in the shower, it all came back to her even when she tried to block it out. As soon as she came in the door last night Harlynn was yelling because she had come to the bar. He told her he didn't need her to take care of him. At one point he told her he was going to leave her. He didn't want to live in Houston anymore or do deals or be part of this family she had created. He wanted to be left alone.

The tears came down her face as she sobbed in the shower for at least ten minutes. Never in her life could she have imagined Harlynn could have been so terrible to her. It hurt so deeply she thought she was going to be sick.

—

Mid morning, Levi finally got up with a smile on his face. He came in to see Kate in her office because he just wanted to be held by her. They sat in the window bench snuggled together under his blanket. She remembered this was a blanket her and Harlynn had picked out in Austin at this quaint little baby shop that was her favorite store for children. She remembered how excited they were to be having Levi and starting this life together.

"Why are you crying?" Levi asked curious.

"Happy thoughts." She promised her son as they watched a robin outside the window.

She saw Harlynn's Porsche pull up in front and took a deep breath in because she didn't want to talk to him. Laney was crying as Claire brought her in to be fed in exchange she took Levi who wanted to eat and go play outside. By the look in Claire's eye she knew that there was a problem or maybe she could look at Kate and see the pain. For a moment, Kate wondered if she could ever be happy again. There were moments in life that one couldn't take away. There were words that saying sorry for never really took them away. No matter how many times she told herself that she forgave Harlynn, it didn't take away the pain of his words or how frightened she had felt. For the first time she had been afraid of the man she loved.

After she feed Laney, she rocked her in the rocking chair. She heard this person sobbing and didn't realize it was her. She was sobbing uncontrollable as Laney peered into her eyes and wrinkled her brow. It made Kate try to at least smile through her tears. And then Laney smiled at her almost laughing. As if to say, I love you Mama. Don't cry on me.

"I love you too, sweetie pie. You're my wonderful baby girl. You're my sunshine, Laney." She held her and kept rocking. Even when he came in the office she just kept rocking her.

"Why is Levi home?" Harlynn asked, with a tired voice.

"I'm not sending him back to be in a class another day with that teacher. The teacher doesn't like our son and she can go to hell."

"That's not the most rational analysis I've ever heard come from your mouth." Harlynn raised his eyebrows waiting. "Where do you want him to go?"

"First Steps. Actually, Janey wants to go with him," she said quietly.

"That should be easy I know a lot of people on the board. I think we need to get the testing done on him to make sure he is okay."

"Fine." Kate told him never looking at him because she didn't want him to see the pain and despair in her eyes.

"Can I hold Laney?" He came towards her. "What's wrong, Kate?" Silence filled the room. "I'm sorry I fell asleep at the loft and didn't call. I guess I needed to sleep because I didn't wake up until nine."

Kate slowly turned to look up at him with her tear swollen eyes and he saw it in her eyes. The pain, the distrust and sadness so deep it stopped him in his tracks.

"Wait." Harlynn ran his hand through his hair slowly.

She didn't say a word as she rocked back and forth trying to decide what she was going to do. When Danny was here later she would have to ask him when she could travel with Laney. Perhaps a couple weeks apart would help her figure out life. She and the children could go to Utah or Jackson Hole.

"I don't remember how I got to the loft last night? The last thing I remember is you coming to the State Bar and sitting down next to me."

"Why don't you go ask Charlie what went on in this house last night." Her voice was cold as ice filled with anger.

"Why don't you tell me, Kateland?" Harlynn countered to her, walking closer.

"No. I'm not going to, Harlynn." She wiped away the tears as she felt the sobbing come back. Harlynn gently took Laney from her and left her in the rocking chair, alone. She wasn't crazy. He had said those words to her and been mean. It was hard to know what was true or why he wanted to hurt her like he did.

There was no way she was up for a meeting with Danny today, she finally admitted to herself, as she sent him a text. He immediately text her back saying sooner would be better than later.

———

A walk sounded good as she put on her running shoes and went out the back door to find one of the trails on the property. The sun felt warm on her face and with each step she felt stronger. In her mind she told herself for the next thirty minutes she wasn't going to think about children, work, art or family and especially not Harlynn. It was the loneliness that got to her because she was very much alone in what was going on. There was no one to bring into her world. Everyone said not to worry, he would get through this. How was she going to get through it? How was she going to stay whole when Harlynn was taking a chisel to her heart? The reality was there was no way she would subject any of her children to this behavior. And the reality was also this could affect whether she got to keep Janey. Harlynn might be able to charm a social worker, but there was no way he was going to charm a judge.

She sat on a bench off the path next to the bayou because her side hurt. Maybe this wasn't her best idea after a c-section. Wow, it stung so she lay down on the bench looking up at the sky thinking of all the shit she needed to get done, but she couldn't move emotionally. She was frozen in this state of emotionally denial. This was not good she concluded.

The footsteps coming down the trial made her jump. She smiled as she saw Charlie, her favorite bodyguard run by her.

"Charlie?" She called out to him as he stopped. Part of her wanted to stay hidden, but she knew that if they thought something happened to her this place would be turned upside down in five minutes. Plus, she didn't have her phone on her so they couldn't track her through the GPS.

"What's wrong?" Kate asked as he sat down out of breath staring at her.

"No one could find you." He stopped calling Harlynn telling her where they were at on the property.

"Did you tell him what happened last night?"

"Yes, I did. Then he yelled at me for involving you in getting him out of the bar and you know what Kate, I yelled back at him. I don't know if I have a job, but somebody needed to ask him what the hell his problem is that he would go after you. You are one of the most caring people I know, Kateland. I wanted to beat the hell out of him last night." He watched as Kate smiled.

"I might have had to fire you if you beat up my husband, Charlie. I'm glad that you didn't. There is a part of me that would have enjoyed it to be honest. You will always have a job with me for as long as I'm alive, Charlie. If they kill me you will probably be dead also." They both laughed. It felt so good to laugh. It had been days since she laughed at anything or anyone.

"I told him you wouldn't fire me." Charlie admitted. "He is a good man Kate and I care deeply about you both and your family. Harlynn shouldn't be drinking with what is going on with his father and work."

"You're right. He is very powerful and not use to taking advice from other people."

"Kate, you are much more powerful than Harlynn Barrett. You are going to have put your foot down about his drinking. Do you understand me?"

"Yes, I do understand. Here he comes, so take off super bodyguard."

"Text me and tell me what happens." Charlie took off before Harlynn could see him or maybe he could see him because Charlie didn't care.

The stone bench felt cold as her laid back down on the bench trying to let her side rest. The pain was going away. The problem was that in a moment she would have to climb back up to the house. Again, she reminded herself she needed to give her body more time to heal. Harlynn walked by the sitting cove. She didn't call out to him because he would circle back in a moment and find her. Three minutes later he appeared, staring at her stretched out on the bench with her eyes closed.

"Did you see me walk by here?" he asked her irritated.

"Yes." She opened her eyes.

"What's wrong?" He asked slowly. "I mean, why are you lying down?"

"I did too much walking and my side hurts a little. I wasn't thinking when I decided to go for a walk because I am completely and utterly shattered by what you did last night. I'm not okay and I don't know if I will ever be okay. I was truly afraid of you last night, Harlynn." She sat up slowly as the tears came down her face, again.

She watched as Harlynn sat down next to her and buried his face in shame in his hands. The silence hung in the air for a long time. What could he say that could ever make her feel right again? What could he say that would take away her humiliation at being yelled at and berated by him? What if one of the children would have woken up from all the yelling? What did she do to deserve this?

"Apparently I blacked out last night. I don't remember what happened, Kateland. I'm ashamed that I treated you with such disrespect. I can't believe that I've hurt you so deeply. I love you and our children with all my heart. I don't know what is wrong with me that I would do this to you. I hope that someday you can forgive me. I promise this will never happen again."

"If you ever come home like that again I will move out with the children. You better sober up real fast Harlynn and if you can't, then don't come back. You have a drinking problem and it just spilled over on top of me and the children. You were mean last night Harlynn, really awful."

"Can you tell me what I said to you?"

"You mean what you yelled at me?"

"Yes." He waited. Finally she told him word for word then looked him in the eye waiting. "Apparently Charlie left out a few things." He dug the toe of his boot into the ground. "I don't know what to say to make this better, Kateland. I'm sorry a thousand times over. I'm sorry to the bottom of my heart. What do you want me to do?"

"You can't, Harlynn. Last night can't be undone." She sighed. "I don't know what to do from here. I don't know how I begin to trust you again."

"What are you thinking?" Harlynn asked peering into her eyes.

"I guess, I'm thinking what I could have done differently last night." Kate peered back into his eyes. "I miss the old Harlynn who was in control of his life."

"I'll find him for you." He leaned over to kiss her as she pulled back, shaking him off. "That bad?"

"Yes." She closed her eyes nodding her head. "I think I need to go lie down for a while. Could you please check on Levi to see what he is up to?"

"Yes. I already canceled my day today and tomorrow. I'm going to see Dr. Brown later this afternoon. Do you want to come?"

"Not today but another day I will go." She slowly got up from the bench and started to walk back to the house. With each step she felt a pull in her side. Finally she stopped, waiting for it to settle down.

"Here." Harlynn carefully picked her up and carried her back to the house, and then put her down. "Why don't you lie down on the couch while I check on Levi? I will take you upstairs after I get him settled."

"Okay." She smiled weakly at him. "Thank you."

When she came in the door of course Henry was standing there, lock jawed and furious. She smiled because it was nice that in her heart she felt like Henry was her father. Henry was holding Laney feeding her a bottle as Kate went into the office. She was hoping she would fall asleep before Henry came in. No such luck.

"Your daughter wants to see you, sweetheart. Then we are going to have a talk."

"Did she smile for you?" Kate watched as her baby girl smiled at seeing her mother. "Laney is the best baby in the world?" The baby laughed again, which made Kate smile. It seemed to help the pain go away. She could see by the look in Henry's eyes that he knew. He knew exactly what had happened last night: he was pissed and about to explode. One drawback to having family live next door and the same bodyguards, everyone knew everything.

Kate watched as Laney started to close her eyes and her little head began to wobble back and forth. Kate let her fall asleep on her chest. There was nothing that felt as good as having this baby sleep on top of her for one of her cat naps.

"Kateland, why didn't you call me last night when this all started? You just had major surgery and you don't need to be pulling Harlynn out of a bar."

"You were at an important dinner," Kate said softly fighting back the tears.

"You are more important than any dinner or business meeting!" He stared at her. "What happened when you got back to the house?"

"I don't know Henry," she whispered. "It wasn't Harlynn, is all I can tell you. He started in on me and I didn't know what to do. I stood there for awhile. I tried to go upstairs to get away from him, but he wouldn't let me. It was crazy."

"Did he hit you?" Kate shook her head no. "Did he try to hit you?"

"He grabbed my arm." She waited. "It's sore and bruised. He is so strong he probably didn't realize what he was doing." She slowly turned her head towards him. "He doesn't remember any of it, Henry."

"None of it?" Henry was perplexed. "Explain?"

"He had to ask Charlie what happened last night. He couldn't remember how he got to the loft."

"What are you going to do?"

"I can't do anything right now with this little angel here. I told him he better never come in our home drunk like that again."

"Do you want to stay with us until things calm down?"

75

"I think I would like Janey and Levi to spend the day at your house and maybe the night"

"We can do that, Kate. Do you feel safe staying here?" Henry asked her quietly.

"Yes." She waited. "Do Keat and Nick know?" Henry nodded.

"Apparently Keat got upset when he couldn't find you last night. He asked me what was going on since you hadn't called him all day. You might want to call him." Henry gave her his look. "I'm only concerned that you are okay. This should be a happy time, not a struggle. Meg and I are here for you and the children. I'm also here for Harlynn."

"I don't know what to do, Henry? I forgive him. It really hurts."

"You will figure it out in time. I'm going to go talk to Harlynn, calmly I might add. We all need to try to help him figure this out."

"That would be good. Do you mind taking Laney to the nursery?"

"I'll do it." Harlynn offered as he came in the room. "Levi was asking for you, Henry. He is in the playroom building with his Lego blocks." Harlynn added as he gently took the baby kissing her on the head. "Sweetie pie, you need to sleep in your bed."

Kate stared at this tall, athletic man with this tiny baby in his arms and smiled. Tomorrow would be better she promised herself. Tomorrow everything would be clearer. She closed her eyes too tired to climb the stairs to their bedroom.

—

The next time she opened her eyes Keaton was standing over her looking haggard and like he hadn't slept in a while. She didn't know if he was going to yell at her or hug her. He was on the verge of complete breakdown.

"Thanks for not calling me back," he snapped at her. It would seem that he had a Patron or two on the plane as he sat down across from her in the office. "I'm so pissed off, Kateland, you have no idea," he admitted to her. "I just want to kick his ass."

"Please don't, Keaton." She loved that her brother loved her that much. "It was frightening, but I'm sure in a day or two it will be better."

"What do you want me to do? You know that I would do anything for you, Kateland?" Keaton pleaded with her. "I've never seen Nick as angry as he was when I told him."

"Just be here for the both of us and the children. Anything you can do to help with Janey would be good. She thought Harlynn's father had passed away." Kate's voice quivered. "I have to believe things will get better because the alternative is terrible, Keaton." Keaton went to his sister as she buried her head in his shoulder embarrassed and relieved that he was there.

"I'm always here for you, Kitty Kat," he promised her softly. "We are all here."

~Chapter 8

Somehow everyone made it through dinner, with no one saying anything harsh to Harlynn or bringing up the events in the last twenty-four hours. Harlynn had one glass of wine with dinner that he barely touched. The star of the evening was Janey reciting a poem she had written in class and Levi playing the piano with his father,

"Do you want me to sleep in the other room?" Harlynn asked Kate when he came in the room getting ready for bed.

"No," Kate told him flatly. "You might get more sleep though. Laney was up every two hours last night. I think she has acid reflux. Danny called in some medicine to try. Let's keep our fingers crossed because I don't know if I can go with no sleep for more than two days."

"I woke up every night at least three times until I was three." Harlynn admitted to her. "She has to be the sweetest baby in the world, Kate. I will help you tonight with her."

"You seem better," Kate watched him as her eyes got heavy.

"Henry helped me, to be honest. We talked for over an hour. I thought he was going to tear into me, but he was firm and kind, like a father would be when his son royal screws up." Harlynn waited. "I'm sorry, Kateland."

"I know that you are, Babes. It was frightening to see you out of control."

"It frightens me that I don't remember what happened. Is your arm okay?"

She pulled up the long sleeve shirt to show him the bruise. It was there for the world to see so she would be wearing long sleeves for several weeks. Harlynn closed his eyes again, as though someone had just punched him in the back.

Carefully, Kate moved over to lie on his chest and hear his heart beating. It was so solid and strong was all she could think. It was good to be in his arms again. She couldn't imagine being any place else in the world or with another man. She could hear him fighting back the tears as they came. Kate looked up at him watching him.

"Tell me?" She asked softly.

"Today when you looked at me, I didn't know if I would ever get to hold you like this again. I thought you were done with me. Because of who you are you forgave me. I don't know if I deserve that, Kateland. Thank you." He closed his eyes as she placed her head on his chest again.

—

When she came down to the kitchen the next morning, Kate saw Henry and Keat with smirks on their face, sipping on coffee, staring out the window at the pool.

"I told him he can only hit him once," Keat whispered to Henry not realizing Kate could hear.

"Harlynn's a lot tougher than he used to be, I told him to be careful. Knowing Harlynn, he will take it like a man." Henry responded.

She watched as Harlynn was getting out of the pool and Nick walked over to him. She sighed because Nick was going after him. Harlynn nodded his head and she could see him standing his ground, then it happened. Nick hit Harlynn, but then Harlynn had Nick on the ground in a head lock. It was juvenile, was all Kate could think.

"Since you mastered minded it, you better go stop it before someone gets hurt, Keaton," Kate snapped as the two men jumped.

"Nope." Keaton shook his head at her. "He deserves to get his ass kicked for being such a bastard to you."

"I'm not worried about Harlynn because he doesn't have his face shoved into the cement by the pool. If you want to spend the next six hours in the emergency room with Nick getting his face sewn up, that's your choice." Kate blinked several times at the two men as Henry took a deep breath putting down his coffee and heading for the door.

"Why are you defending him, Kateland?" Keat asked pissed off.

"I'm not defending him and he will pay in spades for what he said to me." Kate reassured Keaton. "You three need to step back for a moment. If I can't handle it I will have to make some very difficult choices in the near future. Let me figure out how to make this work. I do love the man and there are three children included in the family, not to mention what is going on with the custody of Janey."

They both were still watching what was going on as Harlynn released Nick. As soon as Nick stood up Harlynn pushed him in the pool, Blackberry and all. Harlynn looked mad as hell as he yelled at Nick, then turned grabbing his towel and walking towards the house.

"Shit." Kate got some towels and headed out the door. She really didn't want to do this today.

"Are you okay?" Kate asked Harlynn when they passed on the porch.

"He is still in love with you!" Harlynn told her. "I thought we were through that phase."

"Harlynn, you're being insecure and that's way more than I can deal with today. You kicked his ass, what else do you want, Babes? Blood?"

"I need you to tell me that you love me?" He searched her eyes for the truth.

"Yes I love you! What the hell is the problem?"

"How long am I going to be admonished by everyone for what I did? A month? Two?"

"You did this, Harlynn." She walked away from him furious. This was not how she wanted to spend her day, she thought, as she threw the towels at Nick.

"Gorgeous, I know that you're mad at me. He needed to know that he doesn't speak to you that way ever again."

"Thank you, Nick. See, if there is one person I can depend on in my life, it would be you." She sat down leaning back in the chair letting her hair fall back. "Do you think that Harlynn would ever hurt me?"

"No. " He paused. "I'm sorry I hit him. No, I'm not." Nick smiled at her for a split second.

"I wish I could smoke or have a drink. How do I even get through this?"

"Well, you need to get off your ass, go upstairs and talk to him. It doesn't matter what you talk about, but you have to go do it. That's what my parents always do when they have a disagreement with each other, and they have a pretty damn amazing marriage all the way around. Believe me, my father is flawed to a degree like the rest of us."

"Thank you, Nicky. Thank you for loving me and my completely crazy family. I'm having lunch with Elle tomorrow. I will see what I can do for you."

"You would think after your second child, the man wouldn't be so insecure."

"Yeah, I know. You make him feel insecure." Kate shook her head giggling.

—

Harlynn was in the nursery playing with Laney on the floor. Meg had taken Levi to the park and to the Lego store. He smiled when Kate walked into the room, and then looked back at their daughter.

"I'm not trying to punish you Harlynn," she told him as she slowly sat down on the floor with them still sore. Hopefully next week she would feel better. She let her head fall back into the giant stuffed animals as Laney smiled at her. They were having a party in her little mind. "Do you promise to behave?"

"I already told you that I would behave. That doesn't mean I'm going to take any shit from Keat and Nick. I'm sorry for being short with you and defensive." He put the silver rattle in front of Laney as she reached for it with all her might. "I will try to behave going forward."

"How are you going to behave?" Kate persisted, which Harlynn didn't like. Kate was determined they were going to talk it through.

"I'm not going to drink for a while. I'm only going to drink around you when I do drink. When I do drink, my limit is two drinks. Henry asked me if I might be depressed when I came inside. I think I am depressed, Kateland. Dr. Brown thinks I'm depressed, but I don't want to go on medication."

"I'm listening to you, Babes."

"I'm going to meet with Dr. Brown three times a week for now.

She says I can try some over the counter vitamins, herbal stuff. I started taking them yesterday. I'm going to be biking and running. I really slacked off since my Dad hasn't been feeling well."

"What can I do, Harlynn?" Kate asked as Harlynn handed her Laney to be feed since she wouldn't take a bottle from him. He got a blanket to help support Kate's arm while she held the baby.

"I think I'm jealous of our daughter right now." He poked at her. "Love me. Let me inside that head of yours once in a while, Kateland. There is so much going on and we aren't talking about any of it."

"Why don't you pick a time that we can talk everyday without children or anyone else?"

"We can make it lunch? I can come home and bring lunch, or when you are more recovered we can out for lunch."

"I would like to have a grownup conversation with you in the middle of the day. Three weeks of children twenty-four-seven is killing my brain cells. I feel like I have to be focused on the children right now and getting everyone used to having Laney."

"It will happen, Kate. You are doing great, love. I need to get my act together."

Kate wanted to hold on to this moment. It crossed her mind that perhaps Harlynn was acting out to get her attention like her son had been doing. Did he simply need to know he was special and could have attention also? How was she going to bring balance to this family?

"It makes me feel good that Nick, Keat and Henry care about us to the degree that they do," he told her slowly. "It's nice to know that we have people like that in our lives."

"They do mean well, although it doesn't always appear that way. They love me, but they also love you, Harlynn."

"Do you mind if I go see my Dad for an hour?" Harlynn asked Kate as he took Laney to burp her. "You know, I think you're right, she has acid reflux because she really slept last night."

"I want you to go see your father, Harlynn. The other night you said a few things we need to discuss when you get back."

"Like what?" He looked at her confused. "I was drunk out of my mind, Kateland."

"You said that you didn't want to live in Houston anymore." She waited. "You said you didn't want to do deals anymore. You said there was a contract out on our lives."

She watched him pacing with Laney as her eyes closed slowly. He was singing to her in a whisper until he put her down. He slowly went and sat down next to Kate in the giant stuffed animal pile.

"I want to spend more time at the ranch and in Utah. I do want to get out of the city more. I need a break from work to be honest, Kate. I think we both know it, but I'm not sure what or how I'm going to do it. I don't want to miss out on the children or this time with my father." He paused. "Yes, Blacky found evidence that someone was looking to hire to put a contract out on our family or anyone connected with Moon Water."

"What are we doing about this?" Kate asked biting her lower lip because she didn't understand how finding a cure for a certain cancer or any other disease could cause such problems for the people she loved.

"Blacky should be here late tomorrow to go through security with us. I'm sure that he will also chew me out for getting drunk on you."

"Yeah, that will happen, Harlynn. We're lucky we have Mr. Jack Black to protect us Harlynn."

"I got the feeling he is under a tremendous amount pressure the last time we spoke. He was extremely careful how he chose each word. Kate, it's going to be okay if we can get through this. I really believe it will all work out in time." He leaned over and kissed her.

It was a long kiss and made Kate feel good. She closed her eyes remembering all the times this man had kissed her, from the first time to their wedding day and each night. It made her blush how he could kiss her and make her world completely stop. When she opened her eyes, she froze because one of the bodyguards was watching them. How long had he been there?

Harlynn stood up immediately wiping Kate's lip gloss off his mouth. He raised his eyebrows. "Who are you and why are you up here?"

"I'm Derrick Smith, sir." The bodyguard stammered. "I was doing a sweep of the house and I couldn't find Ms. Jones."

"Derrick, you know who I am right?"

"Yes sir, Mr. Barrett."

"This is part of the house the bodyguards don't come into. You should have been briefed already by Charlie and Burt."

"Yes sir, Mr. Barrett."

"Where is Charlie?" Kate asked thinking it was strange that Charlie would let this happen. She hadn't seen Charlie at all today.

"He was in a car accident last night driving home," Derrick told them. "He will call you when he feels up to it, Ms. Jones. Apparently it was a bad accident. He needs to rest for several days." The bodyguard nodded his head. "Burt has the flu. Blacky didn't want Burt in the house with your daughter being only a couple of weeks old. We have been scrambling to cover everything with both of them out."

"No one told me." Harlynn folded his arms across his chest.

"I'm a back up on the list. I'm very sorry for the intrusion, sir. Mr. Black is flying back from Europe this evening. I'm sure he will call you when he lands."

"You need to find Ethan and he will brief you on the procedures and schedules." Harlynn snapped.

"Yes sir, Mr. Barrett." Derrick turned and exited the room as Kate stared at Harlynn.

"Have you checked your email in the last two days? Or voice mail?" Kate asked still thinking of Charlie.

"No." Harlynn smiled. "Leezann said my work email is full. I told her to go through it and let me know tomorrow what has to be done."

"Harlynn, you can't do the law firm and run Moon Water."

"I know. Hopefully things will settle down at the law firm in the next two months. I'm trying to help Ed gear up to take over the firm. When you are ready, I need your help at the firm. I'm not talking now, but in a couple of weeks?"

"Send me the names of the deals so I can get up to speed on them." She waited.

"First Steps called this morning. Apparently they have room for both of our children starting next week."

"Thank you."

"No problem. Dr. Forrester is going to do the developmental test on Levi tomorrow. She likes First Steps and thinks it's a good fit for

Levi," Harlynn told her calmly trying to leave the urgency out of his voice. It made Harlynn and Kate very nervous how fast Levi was learning and retaining complex ideas.

"He will always be our beautiful challenge, Babes."

"I know he will be. What are you doing this afternoon?" Harlynn asked as they left the nursery.

"Nothing. I'm going to watch a movie and wait for Janey to get home from school and do nothing."

"When I get back we can do nothing together." He kissed her going to take a shower as Kate went to the family room, curling up on the couch. Her mind drifted all over the place, wondering if Harlynn had charmed his way out of what had happened. Was she being naïve about his problem? Did he have a problem?

Nick and Keat came in the room with wet hair, which meant they had both ended up in the pool somehow. Kate smiled at them. She didn't bother to ask what happened.

"I guess no one is working today?" Kate glanced at them.

"Mental health day, Keat announced taking the clicker from her. "We are watching movies all afternoon."

In some ways everything was different in each of their lives, but at this moment, everything was the same. She was hanging out with her brother and his best friend for the afternoon watching a movie. Moon Water didn't matter nor did the success they all had gained from it.

~Chapter 9

It was amazing at what having five hours of sleep without being woken up could do for a new mother. Kate's eyes were brighter and she had energy for the first time in months. Her mind darted from one problem to another as she sat trying to focus on her daughter while bathing her. Laney loved to have her bath when she woke up.

"I'm taking off with Levi to do his block designs. Danny also thinks it's a good idea before we switch schools. He said he needs to meet with you today." Harlynn leaned over kissing his baby girl and then Kate. "I will see you in a while and I love you, always."

"Sounds good and I love you too." Kate watched as Harlynn turned and walked away looking better than he had in a long time. Maybe all the alcohol was doing a lot of harm to him physically. "Your Dada is a good man, Laney, misguided at times, but he is really a good man."

"Well, it sounds like things might be getting better." Meg smiled coming into the room. "I needed to see my girls." She had a beautiful little purple jumper for Laney. "Do you like it?" Meg asked the child as she smiled and splashed. "Why don't you let me finish her bath?"

"Really? I have a list of calls to return starting with Henry. Did he send you over here?"

"He mentioned he needed to discuss a few problems with you. Your Dad and Sue went to Las Vegas and got married the day before yesterday. They will be back around lunch time."

"You've got to be kidding me? Ugh." She sighed. Sue was now officially her stepmother and her father was still her father. "I can tell today is going to be just brilliant. I knew they would get married. I was thinking we had a few months before we crossed this bridge. Does Keaton know? He will not handle this well, Meg. We still can't figure out why Henry and Gems basically raised us."

"Henry is calling him as we speak. You could think of it as one less thing that will turn into a drama. You and Henry don't have to stand up for them while they say their vows."

"No, there is going to much more drama. Baby makes three?" Kate warned Meg. "Sue will eventually decide she wants her own child."

"Henry told him he needs to get a vasectomy." Meg smiled as Kate tried not to laugh. "Go call your father and I'm not talking about Sam."

"I really only have ever had one father and that is Henry."

—

Three hours later she had all the information she could handle from Henry and Keat. She was on overload when she finally made it into her office. It was then that Levi appeared with ice cream all over him and Harlynn looked perplexed. Claire came to get Levi and change him before taking him outside.

"Well?" Kate waited to see what Dr. Forrester had to say.

Harlynn sat down in the chair in front of her desk reflecting on his morning with his son. "He explained everything in the room to the tester that used electricity and who had invented it. They have never seen a child with a vocabulary this large at this age or who is already trying to sound out words. She said they can't measure his IQ yet. She guessed it was in the top one percent. Apparently our biggest challenge will not be Moon Water; it will be educating our son. She didn't know if there was a school that could meet his needs in Houston. He might need to be home schooled with tutors one day. At the same time she stressed not letting him take over and socializing with other children. He needs play dates."

"No signs of autism?"

"Nope. He is perfectly fine. He needs a different school and a couple tutors."

"That's easy. I will see what Jill can come up with at Rice University, maybe a couple of graduate students in math and science. He is learning Spanish. I put him in a music class. And he is taking a swim class also. I'm on top of it, or at least trying."

"I need to go run an errand. It's a surprise for you," Harlynn told her as he gazed at her.

"You already got me the ring, Harlynn?" Kate protested.

"I know." He looked like a little boy with his eyes dancing.

"Am I going to have put you on a budget?" He completely laughed at out loud. "I will see you in an hour, Babes."

"Most likely sooner. I will get lunch while I'm out." He stopped. "You look like you are feeling better today."

"I'm much better." Kate assured him. "I can't wait to start exercising again or sex." She watched the surprise look in Harlynn's eyes. "Yeah, I do think about sex with you believe it or not."

"You always know how to make me feel good." He blushed completely embarrassed and caught off guard by her comment.

She leaned back in her chair closing her eyes, thinking this could work out. They could get through what had happened and his drinking. He needed to be loved, Kate reminded herself. He needed to feel wanted and respected like all men did.

She opened her lap top begrudgingly, not wanting to, but knowing that she had to do it. The screen was on, which made her stop in her tracks. She hadn't touched this computer in two days. She started looking at documents that were opened. They were all highly confidential about Moon Water's patents. Why didn't they just take the computer? Who had been in the house? They were here all the time as she searched the times. It was in the middle of the night while they were sleeping. No one was in the house except the bodyguards. Something was wrong, she told herself. Very wrong. The phone ringing broke her concentration.

"Hey George." Kate had missed seeing her good friend Dr. George the last couple of weeks. He stopped by to see Laney and check on her, but it wasn't the same as talking to him every day. "I really miss you."

"Kate." He paused. "Harlynn's father was just taken to St. Luke's."

"How bad?" She closed her eyes wondering why Harlynn couldn't catch a break lately.

"This is it, I'm sorry. I can't find Harlynn."

"Did you try his phone? He stepped out for an hour. I know he would answer your call, George."

"I've called twenty times. Can you meet me at the hospital?"

"Yes. I can do that George."

———

Meg and Henry appeared instantly, taking the children from her, as she dressed quickly. And then she was weaving in and out of traffic with Henry by her side. All the faces appeared except Harlynn's. It didn't make sense, she kept telling herself. She could feel it in her heart there was more going on.

"Gorgeous, what's going on?" Nick tried as she sat by herself. "I emailed Harlynn with an update. We really need to find him, Kate." He used his raspy voice on her. "Do you have any ideas in that brilliant mind of yours?"

"If I tell you, you will think I'm crazy," she whispered.

"Tell me." Nick's crystal blue eyes waited patiently.

"I don't know, there is this new bodyguard and he walked into the nursery when Harlynn and I were with Laney. He had this look in his eye like he wanted to hurt to me. Now that I think about it he had a gun on him. You know we don't have the guns near the children and only Harlynn has a gun upstairs. Anyway, my favorite bodyguard was in an accident and he hasn't called me. Charlie would die for me in a second." She paused. "Burt has the flu, which is strange because I know all the bodyguards had flu shots. Someone had been on my computer in my office and I know it wasn't Harlynn. Shit, I was going to call your father, but then this happened. And now Harlynn can't be found."

"Oh, my God! They got him! Find Jack Black now! Find my father!" Nick yelled as he went sprinting down the hallway.

"What's wrong?" Keaton asked out of breath.

"They got Harlynn, Keat! They have got him," Kate whispered. Her head fell into her hands as she tried to breath.

Keat wrapped his arms around his sister, cradling her for a good minute. Even though there were people all around them yelling orders he just kept holding on to her. Every bone in her body ached with a pain she had never known. It was like she couldn't move and had turned to stone.

"Keaton, check on the children." She pleaded. "Please check on them." She didn't even notice that all the agents in suits had suddenly appeared in the room, until she looked up and saw him. He didn't take his eyes off her.

"Let's go talk," Blacky said to her slowly. He had come straight from the airport. His flight had been delayed coming through Newark. "Keaton, why don't you come with us?"

"Who is Derrick? We don't have anyone on our list named Derrick. Draw me a sketch of him, Kateland." Someone handed a sketch pad and pencil as she drew those eyes that had stared at her. Before she was done Blacky took in a deep breath. He knew who it was.

"Did he get anything off your computer?" Blacky asked next.

"The files that were opened, he couldn't break the encryption to download them."

"Harlynn picked up a bracelet from a jewelry store for you. He stopped at Beck's Prime to pick up lunch." He paused. "As soon as I landed I had an email from him asking about Derrick. I tried to call him."

"Then what?" Kate asked slowly.

"When he answered his phone he used the code word he has that he felt he was in danger." He waited. "Why don't you go in and see Harlynn's father."

"Tell me." Kate pleaded with Blacky.

"He has multiple devices on him to be tracked. I am talking boots, belt buckle, and in his arm. We have located him," Blacky told her quietly, waiting for the next question.

"Is he alive?" Keaton asked.

"We think he is still alive," Blacky said looking at the floor. "I'm waiting on confirmation. That's the best I can do for now." He stared at Kate blinking several times.

"How the fuck did this happen, Blacky!" Keat yelled at him.

"There'll be time to figure that out later. Are my children safe? Is Meg safe?" Kate questioned.

"Yes, you have my word, Kateland. I think you need to go see his father. He is stable at the moment, but we don't know how much longer. Can you do this because Paul is asking to see Harlynn?"

"Yes." Kate wiped her eyes, and then turned walking towards the room. Out of the corner of her eye she saw Henry on his phone. She saw Sue and Sam coming down the hall, almost running. There were federal agents with semi-auto machine guns. Other patients had been taken out of the vicinity.

The room was quiet with machines beeping. A doctor and nurse were watching the readout. She went to Paul taking his hand as he opened his eyes, he half smiled.

"Can you hear me?" Kate smiled trying not to cry even though she wanted to because she could tell that Paul was in pain.

"Sure can. Where's my boy?" He searched Kate's eyes.

"He should be here soon, don't worry." She waited. "You know how he loves you, Paul? I remember the first time he told me that you were his best friend. He said you had always been there for him. I hope he has that kind of relationship with Levi."

"I always did my best by him, Kate. I'm so proud of my son for all that he has accomplished in his forty years. It has been a pleasure being his father. I could not ask for a finer man to be my son." He stopped. "I'm most proud of the family he has with you and all the children you have together. I'm thankful I got to meet Laney."

"Thank you, Paul." Kate tried not to cry with all her strength. "What can I do for you?"

"Talk to me." Paul smiled closing his eyes. "Your voice makes me feel calm. Harlynn always told me how you made him calm inside, darling."

"I love him. I have traveled the world and I have never met anyone that compares to your son. What is one thing I can tell him when he misses you?"

"Tell him I love him and he was the best son in the world. Tell him I want him to always take care of his family. Tell him I will be watching him." Paul waited. "You made me believe in God. You showed me the way. Thank you." He closed his eyes as Kate held his hand. She could feel him squeezing her hand back. Every once in awhile he would squeeze it again to make sure she was still there with him. Levi would do that to her when he was sleeping.

Kate heard someone come in the room as she turned slowly to see Henry motioning for her to come out.

"I will be right back Paul," Kate promised him as he opened his eyes and looked at her. "It won't be long."

She watched as Keaton came in the room to be with Paul. It made her smile that her brother would do that for her. Henry took Kate's hand guiding her back to the room that she had been in before.

"This is the deal." Henry looked her in the eye. "They found Charlie. He is alive and he is not part of what is going on. He is pretty bad off. Charlie helped Harlynn escape. That's all they got out of him before they took him into surgery."

"Did they find Harlynn?" Kate asked slowly.

"Not yet. They thought they knew where he was, but when they got there he was gone. Blacky isn't sure what is going on. He has the very best people looking for him and we should know some news any minute. This would be the time to pray like you have never prayed before, Kateland. You must have faith, do you understand me?"

"Yes. I know in my heart that Harlynn will be okay. I know that man would fight like no one can imagine for his family."

"Yes, he will. Did you see the way he handled Nick the other morning?"

"I did," Kate whispered. "I need you to be by my side, Henry."

"I'm here." Henry held her for a minute. "We'll get through this, sweetheart."

As Kate came out the door of the room she turned her head toward the doors coming into the emergency room that had guards stationed there. She stared in disbelief because it was Harlynn. His forehead and mouth had blood running from them. His shirt was torn and had dirt and blood on it. He was holding one arm close to his chest. When he saw Kate he started running towards her and he didn't stop until he was holding her. He held her tight as she cried in his arms.

"Harlynn?" Blacky stood stunned with his mouth opened. "Where is Derrick?"

"He and his partner are in the suburban outside." He held out the key. "They aren't breathing."

"Your dad is waiting to see you, Harlynn. Let me clean you up first. " George showed him into a room. Harlynn followed, still holding Kate's hand.

Kate watched as two nurses cut off his shirt and cleaned off his face quickly. George did a once over him quickly, then handed him a scrub shirt. Harlynn shook his head no because he didn't want his father to see him in a scrub shirt. It would be too confusing. George took off his shirt and gave it to Harlynn to put on. The sleeves were a little small so he rolled them up.

"Look at me, Harlynn." George told him. "You are going to spend some time with your father then you need those cuts cleaned up and you probably have a broken rib, so we need an x-ray."

"Sure." Harlynn nodded his head as he took Kate's hand again. They walked into his father's room together.

Kate watched Harlynn's father's face light up at seeing his son. He had made it to the hospital because that was Harlynn, Kate told herself. He was her hero, she thought as she watched him with his father.

—

Three days later Paul passed away in his sleep with Harlynn by his side. It was painful to watch Harlynn waiting for this to be over, but also not wanting to let his father go. Kate's job had turned into helping plan the funeral and making sure everything was organized. It was better than sitting around waiting and watching her husband struggle. And then there was the law firm and trying to get all the things done Harlynn did in day. She had slept three hours in the last forty-eight hours.

She looked up from her desk seeing Henry and Keat coming into her office. As she glanced at the document in front of her she noticed it was going on midnight. She put her pen down, rubbing her eyes slowly. Tomorrow was the funeral and then they would go to the ranch for a couple of days. She had checked everything twice to make sure it was done for the service. Harlynn's new suit was ready, the children's clothes were done and hers. She was wearing a black Chanel suit that was sexy and sophisticated. Harlynn had told her he wanted her to wear it. She sighed, wondering if he had finished his father's eulogy tonight. It was beyond her understanding on how he could get through it.

The other problem they had was that they had to make it a private funeral for security reasons. Blacky was in town still handling the list, which was absurd to a degree. They hadn't talked about Harlynn being kidnapped or what had happened. He said he would tell her, later.

"You have to go to sleep, Kateland." Henry told her sternly. "You haven't even had a chance to completely recover from the c-section yet." The two men took a sit in front of her.

"You have no idea what I have had to deal with at the firm. It's sort of like the old days."

"Are you doing okay?" Keat asked slowly. "Can you handle tomorrow?"

"I don't have a choice, Keaton. What do you need to tell me? Make it quick because I need to check on Laney since the night nurse has the night off? Don't ask." She rolled her eyes slowly.

"Blacky is taking a temporary leave of absence from his job at the National Security Agency. He will be staying here with you and Harlynn."

"Well, I don't know what to say?" She paused. "He can have the guest room downstairs." She became very somber. "I want to know the details, but not right now if you can understand."

"Okay." Henry agreed. "I'm going home to go to sleep with my beautiful wife. Don't you two stay up getting drunk."

—

As the light bleed through the blinds, Kate opened her eyes. She had slept for six hours. Immediately she sat up thinking of Laney only to see her in a bassinet at the foot of the bed.

"She just went back to sleep after having a bottle," Harlynn whispered as he rolled over kissing her. "When we get to the ranch I want to make love to you if you think you're ready. Carr said it was okay." He kissed her, and then fell back on his back because of the broken rib. The pain was sharp as he held his breath.

Kate moved closer to him pushing the hair out of his eyes. "I need to trim your hair for you. How are you holding up, mister? Don't play the hero, today."

"I profoundly miss my father. It's a feeling of sadness so deep that it takes away any hope."

"This feeling won't stay forever. I'm here for you."

"I hate today," he admitted closing his eyes.

"Your Dad loves you. He is so proud of you."

"I got drunk of my ass and was horrible to you a week ago or did you forget? I sure as hell haven't forgotten."

Kate took in a deep breath thinking she needed to tell him even though Blacky wanted the blood test completed. She didn't want him doubting himself on today of all days.

"It's possible that you were drugged, Harlynn." Kate told him in an even keyed voice. "You were completely out of your mind and the fact you still don't remember any of it supports the findings."

"That makes me feel better on one level, but not on another. Do you believe that I was drugged or drunk?"

"I have never seen you be nasty like that since I've known you, Harlynn. I think you were drunk and the interaction with the drug made you react in a complete rage."

"I need your help to get through today," Harlynn whispered. "I need you to be by my side and to hold my hand. I need the children with us. I don't care if Laney cries the whole time; I want them there where I can see them."

"I will be there with you, Harlynn. Everyone will be there for you today as we honor your father."

"I don't want to deal with my mother and sister." He admitted. "They are leaving for some spa tomorrow. My dad specifically said not to feel responsible for my mother, that it was my sister's problem to deal with her and that I had to maintain control of the money so they didn't spend it all." It made Harlynn laugh thinking of it. "He was still mad at my mother for what she had done to Levi when she dropped him. He always loved her, but said he couldn't forgive her for that one."

"Yeah, I know exactly how he feels so don't get me started." Kate watched as Harlynn laughed harder.

—

Every seat was filled in the church as Harlynn stood at the podium talking about the man his father was throughout his life. People had flown in from all over the world to be there. Everything was perfect was all Kate could think. From the flowers to the music to the eulogy his son had given that was poetic and a tribute to him. And then it was done.

By the time friends and family left their house it was too late to go to the ranch. Meg and Henry stayed along with everyone else to help get the children down for bed. Kate found Harlynn out on the balcony by himself having some scotch.

She kissed him slowly, and then stared into his eyes wondering what he was thinking. He seemed at peace with himself as he smiled.

"How do you think I did?" he asked her looking down at the grounds.

"I have never seen you give a more eloquent and passionate speech. I love how you intertwined his success as an oilman with being your father. I love that you gave him credit for the person you are Harlynn." In the distance echoes of the crickets from the bayou could be heard in the dark of night.

"I miss him. I felt him there in the church standing next to me putting his hand on my shoulder." He smiled. "I have had everyone ask to come to the ranch and I said yes."

"You need these people around you."

"I do. Thank you for being next to me for the last several days. Thank you for taking care of everything so I could focus on my father."

"I think I'm going to bed, Babes. I'm tired." He wrapped his arms around Kate holding her tight.

"I will be up soon because I just want to be with you." He whispered to her. "Thank you for loving me."

"If you can manage I would appreciate it." she whispered back to him. Kate wanted to be alone with Harlynn. They had barely had a conversation alone without someone being there with them the last couple of days.

As Kate climbed the stairs she reflected on the past week. How were things going to be going forward? Even though Harlynn had said all those things under the influence of drugs and alcohol she wasn't sure if there was a lot of truth to them. She could see that things were different with Harlynn now. He was different. She didn't know if it was from losing his dad or the plane crash or now the kidnapping. It was more than any one man could handle.

~Chapter 10

It had been an extremely long ride to the ranch as Kate watched Levi and Laney sleeping with those angelic faces staring back at her. It had been an hourly meltdown with each child taking turns, which was nice of them. Harlynn didn't seem bothered by the whole drama. Usually he would have gotten annoyed, but today he didn't.

Stan, Janey's other father, was taking off a few days to spend with his daughter and was bringing Janey up to the ranch on Saturday. Then they would all get together and discuss what was going to happen with Janey's biological mother. The judge had determined that Amy had no rights to see Janey or ask for any medical assistance for her baby. Kate couldn't stand the idea of this woman becoming a part of her daughter's life when she hadn't bothered to take an interest in the last six years. Then there was the problem of this other child. Did they punish this child for what her mother had done? Kate didn't want to think of what she had to decide. Did Janey want to meet her biological mother?

As Kate came out to the kitchen, she smiled to herself thinking only Henry would bring two chefs from *Marks*, two maids and his favorite massage therapist with him. Meg had taken care of every detail from diapers to champagne. One of the chefs set down a glass of raspberry tea for her along with a plate of roasted garlic and sourdough bread.

She carefully took it out to her favorite swing reflecting on the last week. It would all work out she told herself slowly. The creaking of the swing seemed to calm her insides along with the soft hot breeze across her face. The bluebonnets were just coming out as she gazed at them off in the distance. The specs of purple dotted the hill side with Indian paint flowers mixed in that were bright orange. It made her want to paint was all she could think.

"Have you had your massage yet? It was the best massage I have ever had in my life," Sue exclaimed sitting down on the swing with her as she took a sip of Kate's drink and indulged in the roasted garlic. "I think we need to utilize this place as much as possible. It's fantastic. Henry said there is an airport about ten miles away. He is going to see if the runway is long enough for his plane." Sue waited. "What are you thinking about, Kate?"

"Laney. I love her so much it hurts. There is something about that child that takes my breath away when I look at her. What if Harlynn had gotten on that plane instead of coming to see her first ultra-sound picture?"

"But he came to see you and Laney." She put her arm around Kate giving her a hug. "I think the fact Laney looks like you is what gets everyone. Your dad said he can't believe that she looks exactly like you except for her dimple on her chin. He said that she even smiles the way you did when you were a baby. He feels like he has a second chance with you and baby Laney."

"Sam does come by to see her and Levi pretty often. Things are getting better with him I think. I'm trying just to accept Sam as part of my life and move forward with the situation, Sue. I would say it would be better to let Sam and I figure this out. You know you can't really be absent as a father for thirty years and then decide one day that you want to be a father. I always thought of Sam as my career and business mentor. I didn't expect any support from him in any other aspect of my life. Henry was the one who was my father figure. Henry will always be that, but I'm open to Sam and I being closer."

"I was there, Kateland, I do understand. I remember how Henry called everyday in boarding school and came up several times a month to see you. I remember spending Spring Break with Henry and Gems. Your parents never showed up for anything. You and Keat have been on your own for a very long time. We did have the best summers with Henry traveling. Don't you remember the car accident freshman year? Henry was there in hours while your parents showed up a week later. Henry was the one who called to see how your test went or dealt with that one professor who was harassing you."

"Yes. I know. Don't get me wrong, I do love Sam too, but we all know that Henry and I are much closer than Sam and I will ever be." Kate said with compassion.

"And that's okay with your Dad. I think Sam wants to be part of your life and the children's lives. He is willing to take whatever you will give him."

"And I want that too Sue. I will try to speak to him while he is here. I know the man loves me and I know if I called him now, he would be there for me." Kate waited. "How is married life with my father? Do I get to call you mother now?" Kate started laughing as Sue hit her. "Don't hit me! I didn't marry your biological father, did I? I should be the one kicking your ass." Kate was at the point she was giggling while she cried. What else could she do besides tell Sue off, which had already happened in the beginning.

"You and Keat cannot call me any form of the word mother," she snapped.

"You are my fourth mother when you think about it, Sue. I have Jackie who is unstable and tried to kill me as a child. I had Gems, Henry's first wife who passed away. Sometimes I think what life would be like if Gems was still here with us. Then I was blessed by Meg. I'm so lucky that Henry married Meg and she came into my life like this clean breeze bringing life into everyone. Meg always tells me she can see my soul and I believe her. And now you, my best friend of fifteen years, has married my father." Silence hung between the two women. There was this history between them that neither of them was willing to deny.

"Who would have thought that you and Harlynn would own a group of patents worth billions of dollars and I would marry your father a year ago?"

"I don't know if we are going to keep those patents if people keep trying to kill us," Kate admitted getting quiet. "I don't think losing Harlynn is worth that technology."

"Harlynn talked to Sam about taking over the Woodland's research labs for six months. Your dad has the perfect background and he wants to be part of Moon Water. How do you feel about it?"

"I need to have a talk with Harlynn. He needs to get out of the law firm is all I know. He needs a break from it all."

"Blacky has the evidence to go after the pharmaceutical company, Star. They are the one that ordered the hit on Harlynn and the rest of you. Apparently Derrick was able to tell him that before he died. Plus they got Derrick's Blackberry which had everything documented in it."

"It's not worth it Sue," Kate stated firmly.

"It's worth it to save all those children who have cancer like Janey did, Kate. Since when do you give up like this? You go after that company and take a stand. You short the shit out of that stock and let it be known what happened! You have to ruin that company and its CEO, Kateland!"

"I have to think about it. I'm really tired from this life I've been leading since Harlynn and I got married." Kate smiled as she saw Nick and Keat walking out to the pool.

"Hi mommy." They both said to Sue with a grin. "Hey Kitty Kat." Nick leaned over giving Kate a hug.

"You better watch it or Harlynn may kick your ass again." Keat told him without a smile. "I can't believe you let Harlynn kick your ass like that man."

"You both can go to hell. I'll never claim either of you as my children."

The two men continued walking away flipping her off. Kate thought they looked a little stoned, which wouldn't surprise her at this point. Silence hung in the air between the two women as Kate glanced at her Blackberry.

"So why did Nick go after Harlynn the other day?" Sue asked slowly. "That must have been weird."

"Don't know and don't want to know." Kate responded slowly still reading emails. "I think I will go get that massage after all. I will catch up with you later to go riding." Kate didn't wait for anymore questions. She didn't know if what Harlynn said to her was true or whether he was on drugs or drunk or both. Did it matter was all she wondered. Would he ever tell her what he was thinking?

—

The soft sensual music playing in the background of the room allowed Kate to actually breathe for the first time in days. She was trying to stop the chatter in her head and just be present. The lights were turned down in the room and the blinds were drawn, blocking out the sunlight. There was a fire going in the fireplace and she could feel the heat of the flames on her shoulders as she closed her eyes.

Slowly the masseuse began working, trying to loosen the knots that were prevalent in her back. It felt good to have someone touching her and caressing her body. Of course it made her think of Harlynn because he was the only one who ever touched her back in a certain manner. She waited as the masseuse stopped for a moment, which was a bit annoying, and then he began again, in the same methodical manner. It was the lightest and strongest touch as he moved to working on her neck. Then with no warning Kate felt the man kiss the back of her neck. She jumped straight up in shock, the masseuse was good looking, but this was out of line. As soon as she looked up she saw Harlynn standing there in a towel with a smile on his face.

"You scared the hell out of me, mister." She saw the black and blue ribs that made her cringe. There were some bruises around his wrist and on his arms. She closed her eyes as the evidence of what was happening in their lives stared back at her.

"I'm sorry." He kissed her holding her face with both hands. "I wanted to surprise you, not scare the hell out of you."

Kate lied back down on the table feeling Harlynn's hands working on her neck then down her back and legs. Finally, she couldn't take it anymore as she sat up.

"I want to love you," Harlynn spoke slowly. "Are you up for it?"

Harlynn kept massaging her right arm down to her fingers.

"I want you to talk to me first," Kate whispered as he came close to her. "I want you to tell me what is going on in your head and in your heart." Harlynn closed his eyes slowly leaning his head against her shoulder for a moment.

"I don't know what I want except to be with you, the children and the rest of our family. I don't know how I'm going to get through the next day or week. I need to get out of the law firm, but Moon Water, I'm not sure. I want to be here on the ranch as much as we can. I don't know if you want that, Kateland. I'm afraid is all I can tell you."

"Do you love me?" Kate asked him slowly.

"Yes, with all my heart."

"Are you angry at me?"

"For what?" Harlynn asked confused.

"The other night you told me you were angry at me. I thought you might be angry at me for creating Moon Water? This company has brought us a lot of grief, Harlynn."

"I've never been angry with you. I'm going to take down that CEO and board." Harlynn promised Kate as he kissed her.

"And I'm going to help you. Are you sure you aren't angry with me?"

"I get worried that you want a different life than I do."

"I want to be with you. I don't want you getting drunk out of your mind. And I think we can spend time on this ranch and maybe at our house in Utah."

"I don't know what is going on in our lives at times. I need you to tell me what you are thinking or feeling, Kate. Usually Meg or Sue tells me when I'm desperate. If I press Keat, he tells me a small piece in hopes of driving me crazy."

"This has been a very difficult six months, Harlynn. I try to filter out the white noise for you." He ran his fingers across her nipples slowly. Kate could feel her whole body shutter as he leaned over kissing her. "What about the children?"

"Meg and the nanny have them covered. Meg arranged this important business meeting in the middle of the afternoon." Harlynn pulled Kate over to the bed with him in the darkness with the only sound in the room being the fire crackling. "I promise I'm not angry with you in anyway. I promise we will work through these changes together so both of us can be happy."

"How much time do you need here?" Kate asked slowly.

"A week? Can we do that, Kate?"

"Yes." She smiled back getting between the sheets. And then she felt this man who she loved begin to kiss her and touch her body. No one had ever touched her body the way Harlynn Barrett did was all Kate could think. He smelled like her ginger soap and tasted good. He tasted like a little tequila when she kissed him. There were so many things running through her mind. She kept kissing him like she had never kissed him before in her entire life.

It had been months since they had been so uninhibited in making love. It was emotional and physical with nothing held back for a moment. When they were done, Harlynn held her with a difference.

He held her like she was his whole world and nothing could come between them. It was beautiful, was all Kate could think. He was completely vulnerable and trusted her as they lay there in the dark.

"Are you happy?" Kate whispered.

"Yes," Harlynn whispered back. "I think I'm going to sleep if you don't mind. I'm exhausted from the last week." He pushed her hair out of her face. "Will you stay with me?"

"Yes." Kate closed her eyes thinking in a little while she would wake up and check on the children. They needed to stop and get off the rollercoaster they had been on.

—

The next time Kate woke up, she was alone in bed wondering what time it was as she looked for her Blackberry. She heard the shower running and guessed that Harlynn was in the shower. Things felt different between them she thought to herself as she found her robe and took the sheets off the bed. The almond oil was all over the sheets and she could never sleep on them now. It was eight at night and she was sure they had missed dinner. Was that rude they had stayed in their room sleeping? Ugh, what was she thinking when she closed her eyes, she had a house full of people. As she hurried making the bed up she went to get in the shower while Harlynn was coming out.

"Hey." She smiled sheepishly at him. "Why didn't you wake me up?"

"You are more exhausted than I am, love." He softly kissed her. "My Blackberry woke me up and I wanted you to sleep. Henry and Blacky need some assistance if you can imagine that one. Apparently the dynamic duo got stoned earlier and then hit the tequila hard. They have decided to go roping after dinner."

"I thought Keat was stoned earlier today when they were picking on Sue. It's always hard to tell with Nick. Do you want me to fix you some dinner since you have hardly eaten in a week, Harlynn?"

"My stomach has been killing me. I promise to speak to George."

"Here, take my acid reflux medicine." She offered as he took the bottle opening it up and taking two pills out. "You have to take care of yourself."

"Thank you. I haven't really thought much about me lately." He stopped. "I will have one of the chefs throw some steaks on the grill for us. That was so smooth of Henry to bring all these people."

"Henry is always smooth." Kate giggled. "Go take care of the boys and under no circumstances do you get in a fight with Nick. That little boy behavior has to stop."

"He started it," Harlynn smiled, "and I ended it." He stammered. "All that training that Blacky had me do prevented me from being killed. I want you to start doing the same training."

"Yes, I think that's a good idea, mister. Are you ever going to tell me the details to what happened to you?" She gently touched his bruised ribs. "They hurt, don't they?"

"Soon. I need a little distance from what happened. I do promise I will tell you after some tequila one night. I need to check on the children and get the guys to behave somehow. Or maybe let them fall off the horse at least once."

—

Kate was giving Laney a bottle in the living room listening to Nora Jones. Nora Jones was baby magic. It was going on ten and her daughter's eyes were slowly closing. She was completely off schedule and overly stimulated from being held non-stop. Kate watched this little smile slowly form on her lips as she relaxed and fell asleep. It was almost like she was saying 'Mama, I can't go sleep without you, I need you'.

Kate sat there listening to the house that was quiet with only the music echoing throughout the high ceilings. She closed her eyes, slowly rocking to the beat of the music, with her angel asleep on her chest. It was a moment that was completely peaceful with no tension. This child who could look inside Kate and tell what she was feeling.

"Lane is just like you," Sam said slowly as he sat down with Kate. She watched as he picked up a camera and took a picture of them together. "Thank you for including me in this time with you and your family," her father told her with that smile that took away all the pain.

"You are part of this family, Dad. And you have married Sue, so you both are part of this family. I'm fortunate that I have two people who want to be my father. I need you to be part of our children's life. I need your support during this time because I am scared out of my wits, to be honest. You have no idea what it's like living with this kind of constant fear," Kate whispered staring at her daughter. "We have to get through this for these children, Dad."

"Kateland, the people who are here on this ranch all love you and Harlynn. We are here to help you anyway we can, honey. As a family we are going to stand our ground, do you understand me?"

"Yes. Would you like to know your wedding present?" Kate asked him slowly.

"Oh, I don't think you need to do anything for me marrying your best friend. Sue and I have a deal; I can't ask questions about your friendship."

"You now own five percent of Moon Water and you have a seat on the board," She watched how completely stunned her father was at what she had said. "I simply couldn't give it to you before the divorce because I'm not giving my mother millions of dollars. She should have been nicer to me." Kate laughed to herself.

"Kateland, I don't know what to say to you. I think you must have the most generous heart considering that I've never been there for you."

"You were there in some unconventional ways, Sam. There are a lot of good qualities I got from you like your work ethic and golf game." She watched as he smiled to himself, pleased he had done something right. "I think we should make a rule that we don't talk about the past." He nodded in agreement. "Are you okay with how close Henry and I have become? I don't want you to be hurt by that, Dad."

"Henry Grayden has taken care of you for many years. He has been my best friend for thirty-four years. Henry always kept me inform of what was going on with you, Kateland. I thank God that Henry was there for you and Keaton while I dealt with your mother and my company." He took a deep breath in. "The ironic part of this is I'm no longer married to your mother and I have sold that company. The best part is I now have you and Keaton back in my life and I have three grandchildren. I'm glad I wasn't too late to realize my mistakes.

It doesn't change what I did, Kateland."

"I forgave you a long time ago for what happened. I'm lucky you came around to be part of my life. There are a lot of positive relationships that have come out of these negative events. For instance, you are married to a very brilliant and vibrant person who adores you now."

"Yes. I'm married to a woman who I love and who loves me. I know you will never understand it, Kate." Kate nodded, but didn't say anything. "How are you and Harlynn doing?"

"We are making it or at least trying for the time being. He has a lot to figure out and I have to be patient. His father was his best friend. Can you imagine losing Henry?"

"Never. I'm worried about him, Kateland. Especially after Keat told me what happened last week."

"Well, I think we all need to help Harlynn through this the best we can. He knows that he has to watch the alcohol in the future. I'm tolerant of many things, but a raging drunk is not one of them."

"You need to tell me if he can't handle things. Harlynn is in a dangerous place and I will not let anything happen to you or the children."

"He feels terrible about the things he said." Kate confessed to her father. "I don't know what to think, was it the drugs or alcohol? I guess I need to speak with Blacky to get to the bottom of things."

"It was a mix of powerful narcotics that could have been lethal."

Kate kept rocking her daughter with tears coming down her face. Her father gently took Laney from her and disappeared to the nursery.

"Claire is changing her and putting her down." He smiled softly. "Has Harlynn ever lost his temper with you before, sober or not sober? Do you two fight a lot?"

"No, he has never done anything like the other night. We usually are pretty good about talking. When we have a disagreement it doesn't last long." The music drifted through the silence. "Is there something you need to tell me Dad?"

"Harlynn used to drink a lot, Kateland. All of it seemed to disappear when you came along. Henry and I are worried, honey."

"What do you want me to do?" Kate asked thinking she knew all this, but it was so out of character for Sam or Henry to be critical of

Harlynn she wasn't sure what was going on.

"I want you to communicate with Henry or me if anything else happens, no matter how big or small."

"I appreciate your concern and if things get out of hand I will let you know. I don't anticipate any more issues."

"It's easy to turn to drinking when life gets complicated. A perfect example would be the dynamic duo of Keaton and Nick at the moment. I hope Harlynn realizes how this group of people loves him and would do anything for him."

"I think he does." Kate smiled as one of the chefs bought in hot cocoa and warm ginger snaps. It was good that they were speaking to each other and it was nice that her father wanted to help. Even when things were awful there was hope Kate realized.

~Chapter 11

At two Harlynn came to bed after taking a shower because apparently there had been a mid-night rodeo. Luckily the bullring had lights and a well stocked bar. Kate slowly moved over to lay on Harlynn, feeling his heart race she looked up at him on the verge of breaking down.

"What's wrong?" Kate asked slowly. "Babes, I can tell you're really upset."

"I went to check on Levi and he was sitting straight up in his bed staring in the dark." He waited. "He asked me if I was going to leave him like Granddad did. He told me he didn't want me to leave him," his voice cracked with pain as he said each word.

Kate got up from their bed and went to get Levi. She came back with the child half asleep in her arms and put him in bed with them as Harlynn held on to both of them. Kate wasn't sure what Levi understood about the funeral. He seemed to understand that Paul wasn't coming back.

It took a long time for Kate and Harlynn to fall asleep, in the stillness of the house, with the wind hitting the trees limbs against the window above their bed. It was surreal that she was in this bed with Harlynn and their child with a baby in the other room. It was hard to put all the events of their lives together in the last two years. Tomorrow when she got up she was going to find Blacky. She wanted to know all the facts and why was he taking a leave of absence from the NSA to stay with them?

Kate had only been asleep two hours when the door to their room flew open. Harlynn very naturally extended his arm reaching behind the nightstand where he kept a gun. He stopped when he saw it was Blacky.

"You have Levi?" Blacky said in a low voice as Kate opened her eyes, confused and frightened. The child remained in a deep slumber as the three adults stared at one another.

"Yes." Harlynn said calmly pulling back his hand. "Is there a problem?"

"Why don't you get dressed and come out to the kitchen," he told him never taking his eyes off Levi. Then he turned and walked out of the room, closing the door.

"What is it Harlynn?" Kate asked as she pushed back Levi's hair while the child slept in her arms. He was so long like his father and looked exactly like him. She reflected on the way his head tilted to the left if he was in a deep sleep, just like Harlynn. This was her beautiful son and now Kate was wondering what had Blacky worried? Blacky usually didn't worry was all Kate could think. He was trained to be rational and calm in the middle of chaos and to take the emotion out of any situation.

"Let's say I made a few phones calls that I was going to short the hell out of Star Pharmaceuticals. I personal want the head of the CEO, Mr. Frank Waters."

"Well, I called a few people to let them know that if they knew anyone who had any connection to this company, they weren't going to be happy. It's only the beginning, Babes."

"You got that right. That son of bitch is going down along with that whole board."

—

Kate had Laney in the baby jogger going for her morning stroll around the ranch when Nick surprised her as she laughed. It felt good to laugh Kate thought to herself.

"You have been a bad boy, Nicholas Black," Kate told him sternly. "What were you two doing last night?"

"I guess you can't get stoned if you are breast feeding still?" Nick teased her.

"Nicky, stop it! What is going on with you?" Kate asked him slowly.

"I can't believe that Harlynn is still alive, Kateland. Those were some highly paid evil people that had him. They were professional hit men who have probably killed hundreds of people. Harlynn was able to take them down by some miracle."

"Go on." Kate said adjusting Laney's head and making sure her sun hat fit. "Now what is happening?"

"Walter Reed, yes that would be the head of the SEC, called Keaton at six this morning to inquire why overnight Star Pharmaceutical has completely tanked."

"Have no idea?" Kate smiled. "How much did you short?"

"I shorted every dime I could get my hands on. The stock is halted from trading still. What are you going to tell Dr. Reed?"

"I will tell him the truth, off the record. You know that Reed was Keaton's mentor at Harvard. I will probably have to work on a few cases for him, but I don't give a shit. What did Elle find on the company?"

"She is coming up tonight since I have been misbehaving. My father called her to ask for her help in getting me under control."

"Did you buy the ring yet?" Kate asked him as he nodded his head yes. "What happened?"

"Shelly claims that she is pregnant with my child." Nick looked like he was going to be sick.

"No wonder you have been freaking out. Did you tell anyone yet?"

"Only you, Kate. I think I need your help on this one, gorgeous. I don't want to lose Elle."

"We both know that Shelly is capable of anything. What was the date that this happened? Elle knows something is going on with you. I think we need to sit down with your father when we get back and figure this one out."

"Part was Shelly last night, but the other part is watching what Harlynn, Keat and you are going through right now. I love all of you. It hurts to watch Harlynn suffering, which makes you in pain. I can see you struggling to have a conversation. I hate this."

"I keep trying to separate out the different events, but everything is so connected. Some days I blame myself for starting Moon Water."

"I was there right beside you," He reminded her.

"Hmm. I never thought of blaming you?" She raised her eyebrows at him making him laugh. "Other days I blame that stupid law firm of Harlynn's or even Henry. Henry's Goo, a delivery system if paired with the right marker, would save mankind. The Goo molecule could transport anything. That's where it all started fifteen years ago. I remember Henry explaining it to me like it happened yesterday. He was so excited to own that company. I might have been brainwashed into finding the partner for the Goo at the age of fifteen."

"I think we are fortunate that Henry owns that company. In the wrong hands the technology could hurt people. I have a favor to ask you?"

"You want me to tell Blacky that Shelly is trying to blackmail you with the fictitious child she has created?"

"He won't go crazy on you because he loves you and thinks the world of you. He already chewed my ass out for getting stoned. Then he wanted my stash like I was in high school and I wouldn't give it to him. So he starts tearing apart my room while Keat and I are laughing on the floor because, well, we were completely stoned by that point in the day. As he put it, he loves me always at the same time he isn't too damn proud of me at the moment."

"This morning he came in our room freaked out looking for Levi. I thought he looked rattled. It most likely is a carryover from you, dear one."

"I can tell you have over done it, gorgeous. We are going back to the house and have the chefs cook us lunch. Will that make Harlynn upset?"

"I think I should see if he wants to join us because we don't need any Harlynn tantrums today." Kate smiled. "All my boys are acting out in different ways today." Her voice cracked as she tried to cover it up.

"What's wrong?" Nick asked softly as he took Laney out of the baby jogger.

"Levi asked Harlynn if he was going to go away like his Granddad did." Kate felt the tears come down. "That little boy shouldn't even know about things like that, Nick."

"Harlynn isn't going anywhere." Nick promised her. "I will talk to Levi to see what he heard. He tells me everything." Nick raised his eyebrows at her in his sneaky manner.

"Great you are teaching my son to spy on his parents."

"How did my little spy do on his testing?"

"He freaked them out and scored off the charts. It bothers

Harlynn because he wants him to play ball. No autism. "

"He will play ball. It's in his genes to be a ball player like his old man. I told you he was fine a long time ago. Shit the kid has the best gene pool I've ever seen."

"I just want him to be happy. I don't care what he does as long as he makes this world a better place in his own way."

—

After swimming with Levi and looking for lizards for his bug box, Kate was glad to hand off the child to his father, for a long ride that would hopefully tire him out. It was nice to see Levi exploring the ranch and the discoveries he made each day. Kate stood watching as Harlynn held Levi close to him as they slowly rode off down the trail. Levi was helping Harlynn heal from the pain.

Harlynn seemed distant to Kate as she walked back to the house. She wondered what had been the trigger to make him think of his father this time. When she walked into the living room it stared back at her. There was a large framed photograph of Harlynn, his father and Levi. It was beautiful and crisp as though you could reach through the frame and touch them. There was this content look in each of their faces. It was the same face looking back three times over as the two men leaned against the fence with Levi standing on the fence between them. The blue of the clear sky with the green grass swaying behind them was stunning. There were a couple other photos, not as large, of Harlynn with Kate and the children.

"They came today." Keat smiled at her as he wrapped his arms around her. "We need to talk in the very near future because Walter is not happy with all the trading going on. The stock never opened today as a result of the people in this house."

"Well, I didn't discuss anything with anyone so there is nothing to tell. You did these photographs, didn't you?" Keaton smiled at his sister. "I want you to take some of Laney?"

"Why don't we all go out to the bluebonnets later?"

"Thank you. That would be amazing to have a group photo of everyone in white shirts and jeans with the bluebonnets." She waited. "When are you telling Walter about the problem with Star?"

"He wants to meet with us tomorrow. He is willing to come here in person, off the record, because as he put it, 'he is afraid of what is going on'."

"Did you tell, Harlynn?" Kate asked slowly thinking this might be more than he wants to deal with tomorrow.

"He said he was surprised he wasn't here today because of the implications of what has happened. I hadn't intended to have him see the photographs yet. I feel awful about it, Kate. Please tell him."

"I understand. I think they are beautiful and I'm glad he saw them. They are powerful." She frowned. "What the hell were you doing getting stoned and drunk last night with Nick?"

"Well, I think things caught up with me. I thought Harlynn was dead, Kate. I can't imagine Harlynn not in our lives or seeing these children grow up."

"We need to find you a girlfriend, and then you can focus on your life." She waited, reflecting. "I knew he wouldn't let that happen. Harlynn has too many people who love him to leave us. I'm sure that back to back near death experiences is going to take a long time for him to deal with, Keaton. Can you behave and keep Nick under control? I don't want to ask you to go home early. I honestly don't know what Harlynn can tolerate without flipping out."

"Henry already told me I had used up my being a thoughtless bastard card for the week. He said he had almost blocked out all the trouble Nick and I used to get into in college and grad school."

"A true regression might I add. Where is the weed?"

"In the nursery, of course." Keat tried not to laugh as Kate hit him because Blacky wouldn't contemplate going into the nursery to find it. The dynamic duo had struck again.

"Go get it, now." Kate gave him the look. "Now."

A minute later she had the steel water bottle that was full of weed. She sighed shaking her head.

"It's really good stuff so don't flush it. Just put it away for an impossible day."

"I will put it in my room until I decide what I should do with it. If Blacky asks for it, then I will have to give it to him. You two were not very nice to Blacky last night, Keaton. You better apologize now, Keaton."

"You're right."

"After you apologize to Blacky can you tell him to meet me out on the swings in back?"

"Will do." Keat caved immediately. "Sorry. Will you tell Harlynn, Nick and I are truly sorry. "

"Yes. I need my boys to behave, do we understand each other?"

"Yes." He gave his sister a hug. "Are you pissed?"

"No, I'm grateful that I have a family that loves us to the end of the earth and back."

"Nick wants to go into town tonight for dinner? You want to come?"

"How about tomorrow night? I didn't sleep well last night nor did the children."

"Tomorrow and we will stay out of trouble."

"You will have a chaperon, dear brother. I won't let you two loose after last night." Keat rolled his eyes.

"I will invite Henry to come with us."

"Good idea."

———

Kate was lying in their bedroom with the shades drawn when Harlynn walked in. She could see the outline of his body and knew what he was thinking by the way he moved. He immediately went to change his clothes and get in the shower for one minute, and then he came out in clean clothes. Kate smiled thinking he was damn fast at getting ready. Her mind drifted between what Blacky had told her and what she wanted to believe when it came to her marriage.

Blacky had told her what Harlynn had said was most likely partially true when he was drunk and drugged out of his mind. He said they were very lucky he didn't die that night and by going to the bar she had saved his life. Blacky expected more bad behavior from Harlynn after talking to him. Supposedly it wasn't anything Harlynn could control. He suggested sedating him for a couple of days in hopes it would let him gain some perspective on what was going on. He warned Kate that she better be careful. It wouldn't take much to set Harlynn off.

For the last hour Kate had been throwing up. That is what happened to her when she hit her breaking point. She would get so upset she couldn't eat or drink. They never discussed all the other questions Kate had for him. The one answer had been more than she could handle, apparently. She still needed to understand why Blacky was stepping back from his job for the safety of these people in her house. It wasn't logically in her opinion.

"Meg went to go get the Zofran for you in town. She should be back in about thirty minutes. How many times did you get sick?" Harlynn asked as he watched Kate slowly get up and sit on the cool tile floor in the bathroom.

Kate held up four fingers then put them down. She sat on the bathroom floor with her eyes closed. She was mad at him because now she was falling apart and it was his fault. How much shit could she take she wondered.

"Do you think you caught a bug?" he finally asked perplexed. "You were fine at lunch, love."

"It's stress, Harlynn," she replied in a voice drained with energy. "It's happened before."

"Blacky is wrong, Kateland," he told her between his teeth, realizing he was the catalyst for her sudden illness.

"I hope so, Harlynn," she whispered. "Once I take the Zofran I will be fine, don't worry. With everything that's been going on it was bound to happen. I should have warned you so it wouldn't be shocking."

"Remember how you said we need to talk even when things seem impossible." Harlynn reminded her. "Nick is really pissed off you took his weed."

"It's under your sink in the water bottle."

"Good. I think I'll save it for another time when we are up here without Blacky. I could use some of that weed at the moment. I need to mellow out."

"Let's not add that to our list of problems. I think I might go riding when Meg gets back. Will you get one of the ranch hands to saddle up a horse for me in an hour?"

"I don't think that's what you need, Kate."

"You have no idea what I need!" She looked him straight in the eyes because he had consumed her again and she was tired. Yes, she did need time to be by herself away from the children and the mess that was her life. Every waking moment was consumed with Moon Water or Harlynn or the children. She needed a break was what she needed. She didn't want to talk to anyone or discuss if Harlynn was going to flip out or ponder her father's marriage or any of the other crap that was going on. And she especially didn't want to think about Janey's mother showing up.

"What is going on with you? You can't shut me out because Blacky thinks I'm going to freak out on you. That is not fair, Kateland!"

"Look at yourself in the mirror Harlynn! You look like hell. You are a walking zombie sleeping only two hours a night. You can't keep living like this!"

"That's funny, I thought you were on my side, Kateland. I thought you would stand by me no matter what was going on? Why are you being . . ."

"Don't you dare call me a bitch Harlynn Barrett, after what you have put me through these last six months. I will be gone."

Kate glared at him guessing that was the next word out of his mouth would be. That was one word she couldn't stand. Perhaps she had never explained that the word 'bitch' sent her packing. It was about as disrespectable as you could get in Kate's mind.

The room filled with silence as they stared each other down for a good minute. Harlynn was the first to turn away, which Kate thought was a sign of weakness to a degree.

"Just to let you know Harlynn there is a limit to the shit I will take from you. And if you ever want to stay married to me, don't ever and I mean ever call me a name, especially the word bitch. That might have worked with Joan, but it won't work with me. I have never called you a name. I would expect the same from you."

"In the next two days everyone leaves or I leave, Kate. I'm not going to have our marriage torn apart by people getting in your head. You let Blacky get in your head and that really, really pisses me off."

"Harlynn, I am so confused I don't know who to believe or not believe at this point. I'm trying to do the best I can, considering everything that has happened. You haven't talked to me. I get bits and pieces from everyone. All I can do is keep guessing what everyone is keeping from me?"

He started to walk away, then turned around and sat down on the floor next to her. He took her hand pulling her close to him. Slowly she rested her head on his lap as he gently ran his fingers through her hair while she closed her eyes. Then he told her what happened to him when he was kidnapped. How he did what he had learned from all the self-defense classes he had taken. And there was such clarity what he had to do to protect himself that he really felt God was with him telling him what to do. He didn't know where his strength came from or how he could be hit so hard and still stand his ground. He didn't know why he put an extra knife in his boot that morning. It was almost like his subconscious took over and he seized the very second when these two hit man were not paying attention. He could anticipate their next move perfectly and counter automatically. He had seen the texts from George and knew his father was in the hospital. He knew in his heart she would figure out what was happening and be frightened. The worst part was the idea of never seeing her again or the children.

"This is your bracelet, love." He took out a beautiful gold link bracelet that had one large blue topaz in the center with two large pink diamonds next to it. It was absolutely gorgeous was all Kate could think as Harlynn put it on her wrist. "I designed it for you."

"That makes it even more beautiful, Harlynn." It still stunned Kate when Harlynn would buy her expensive jewelry out of the blue.

"It was supposed to be done when Laney was born, but I didn't like the stones that they were going to use. And I did get you a new car because if you have all three kids with you, there needs to be more room."

"The new Mercedes? What color?"

"Black. It's nice." She smiled because that is what Harlynn was really good at: buying jewelry and cars.

"I need some alone time, Harlynn. I feel like I might be going crazy. I'm so worried about you I'm making myself sick. How crazy is that one?"

"I understand needing time to be alone and feeling like the world is on top of you. There is no way I'm letting you take off riding by yourself. You take me or Henry with you."

"Are you going to be sweet to me?" Kate asked slowly.

"I apologize for being ugly and defensive. I won't call you names and I wasn't going to use the word bitch. You know that I have never called you a name before Kateland. It really hurt when you said I didn't know what you needed. It was like you were saying fuck off in a nice way."

"I was." She admitted as she smiled at him. "We need to decide if we let Janey's mother see her. We need to decide what we are going to tell Reed when he gets here."

"I have no problem if Danny can help design the treatment plan for this baby. I don't want Janey becoming attached to this child who we both know has about a twenty percent chance of surviving. Henry wants to pay for this child's medical expenses. Amy is pretty damn successful architect so I don't think it will work. What do you think?"

"I'm still thinking on it. I don't really know what Janey wants and she may change her mind. I hate to put her in a position of choosing. I want to protect her from getting hurt again. I have to protect her from this person who damaged her, Harlynn. She has wanted to know this woman for years. I do agree to help this child, but not at any cost to Janey."

She closed her eyes still feeling Harlynn running his hands through her hair again. They stayed there on the bathroom floor for a long time in complete silence. It was the idea they were together in spite of all that continued to be unfairly thrown at them. Their love was stronger than the truth that stared at them.

~Chapter 12

As they rode up to the house some of the stress and fear was gone from Kate. She felt stronger than she had in the last six months and she didn't know why. She glanced at Harlynn and he also looked better. The stress was gone from his eyes and maybe some of the pain. He had shown Kate all the trails that he explored as a child and his secret hiding place. There was an old Indian that had lived on the property. Chief had taught Harlynn how to know this land and track animals. It was this other dimension to Harlynn that created this weekend cowboy. He loved this land and it was part of him.

Henry came out to meet them looking rather perturbed as they walked up to the house. Harlynn took Kate's hand and smiled.

"Walter Reed has been sitting in the kitchen for the last hour waiting for you two." Henry didn't like the SEC. In fact, Henry hated the SEC because the SEC liked to do audits on his holding company.

"Yes, I knew he would be waiting." Harlynn commented nonchalantly. "Henry relax."

"Harlynn, please don't tell me to relax when I've been sitting with the head of the Security and Exchange Commission chit chatting while eating baked brie cheese and drinking wine."

"It will be fine because Walter is on our side, Henry." He paused. "He is here to see how he can help us and see what Elle has found. Did Elle arrive?"

"Yes. She has found fraud going back two years from what she showed me. Elle wouldn't go out on a limb like this without something concrete."

"Good. I needed Elle to find the support for what I was thinking." He stopped, still holding Kate's hand. "Henry, I appreciate your concern for our marriage and family. Kate and I can't have everyone undermining us."

At first Henry didn't respond as he stared into Harlynn's eyes, searching them. Kate remembered that look, that one that said she is my daughter and don't you dare forget it. Then Henry looked at Kate with the look that said you are the most important to me and don't forget it.

"Would it help you if I spoke with Blacky?" Henry asked. "I'm always here for both of you, do you understand me?"

"I think it would be good if you spoke to Blacky, Henry. I need you on my side and to be there for us and the children. We both know that you are Kate's father and I'm going to need you to help me get over losing my father. I want to do what is right for Kate and the children."

It made her smile because this is what she wanted to happen. She wanted Harlynn to turn to Henry. She wanted Harlynn to let Henry know that he was Kate's real father in all the ways that counted in his opinion. Even when they were in a rocky phase Harlynn knew how to make her world less rocky. Kate also knew that she needed to get Dr. Walter Reed out of the house as fast as possible.

—

After an amazing dinner of beef brisket, fresh corn on the cob and salad, Kate sat outside eating brownies with the Walrus as Kate called Walter. He sat smoking a cigar and having cognac. It was a beautiful night with the sky covered with a blanket of stars that Kate could never see in the city. The Walrus had asked for a word with her alone, which didn't make any of the men happy in the room. Kate knew this would only last maybe five minutes or less.

"Off the record Kateland, tell me what the hell has prompted such extreme aggression from the powerful individuals on this ranch. I need to understand why this company is purposely being destroyed."

"Tell me what you know?" Kate asked slowly.

"People are dumping the stock as fast as possible. The stock has had the hell shorted out of it and I was already investigating it for fraud due to how they were booking sales."

"Moon Water has made a breakthrough in how to treat a certain type of cancer." Kate paused. "Frank Waters, CEO of Star Pharmaceuticals hired two hit men to try to kill my family. Ten days ago they kidnapped Harlynn . . ."

"What?" The Walrus began to pace. "What else?"

"Jack Black is trying to figure out the best approach to protecting us. We are going to destroy this company, Frank Waters and the board." Kate sat back in her chair waiting for a reaction.

"What happens after you have turned it into a penny stock?"

"We will find new management, and then turn it into a growth story. With the right management team it will be a great company, but not with that ass Waters running it."

"I saw the work Elle Hunt did on Star. She really has an incredible mind, Kateland. I will send in a team and seize the accounting department tomorrow and freeze the assets. What else can I do to help you?"

"Help find out if there is anyone else going after us?"

"Sure." The Walrus smiled. "I need to leave Kate. Don't be a stranger. I will leave the situation at hand alone. I will need your help on an upcoming case in the Fall."

"Expected. Thank you for your concern and taking time out of your schedule to come in person."

"I always love some good Texas barbeque." He confessed before leaving.

Kate watched as the Walrus stared at her, but didn't move his lips. It was there in his eyes was all she could think to herself. He knew something he wasn't able to tell her. What was he waiting for, Kate wondered as she saw him walk away?

"What did he want?" Henry asked her sitting down with a bottle of wine and two glasses.

"Nothing really. He wanted to know why we're doing this so I told him the truth; someone was trying to kill us. I get the feeling there might be more for us to worry about than anyone knows except Blacky."

"Like what?" Henry watched her and waited.

"I don't know, Henry, but it's not good. Do you know why Blacky is stepping back from his work?"

"You mean why would one of the top intelligent officers for the United States government walk away from everything? Maybe he is tired of the stress in his life, Kate. This man and his family have made a tremendous sacrifice for our country."

"I have a question for you, Henry. What would be the economic fallout for finding a cure for a type cancer or anyone of the other costly diseases?"

"What do you mean? Why would you ask that question, Kateland?"

"I ask the question only on the bases of what you have taught me. If Moon Water can jeopardize a company, with a market cap of say five hundred million to the point the CEO and board will hire killers, who else is willing to do the same? Think of all that goes into treating cancer or arthritis? What would happen if suddenly people only needed to be diagnosed with a disease and have one treatment? Healthcare is a business of human lives, Henry. There are so many hands trying to make a profit from these diseases you can't even count them: from the drug companies to the people who make the MRI machines to that glass tube and plastic needle they stick in your arm."

"Yes, but we are years from having a product," Henry questioned slowly. "Or are we?"

"Danny has a cure for the leukemia that Janey had, Henry. The results are better and more conclusive than anything on the market. Within six months we have developed a viable cure for a disease that kills thousands of children each year. What happens if we try to go after something really big?"

"Your question would be who or what is Blacky trying to protect us from."

"My feeling is that we need to go public as soon as possible with how Frank Waters paid to have Harlynn killed. I think we should be open about what we want and why. It might be the only way to protect us. It might keep us live."

Henry slowly finished his glass of wine and poured another one.

—

For the last two days Harlynn had slept with the help of a large dose of Tylenol PM prescribed by George. Kate stayed by his side in their room never leaving for more than a moment, because that is what he had asked her to do. He wanted her by his side; he knew that she wouldn't let anything happen to him. Kate was playing blocks with Levi while Laney slept in the swing, with that faint little smile on her face. She was the best baby in the world Kate had decided as she gazed at her daughter. Levi built a huge building for his father so they could play when he got up.

Kate kept trying to pinpoint what the tipping point was days ago and the only thing she could think of was when she told Harlynn he had no idea what she needed. It was harsh, but she was tired of worrying about everything for everyone. From that point on things had started to smooth out. Harlynn seemed more rational and could handle the pain he was in.

Things were moving at lightning speed, which seemed to happen with Harlynn. Tomorrow there was to be an interview at the ranch with one reporter from Fox News to discuss what was going on. It was a show of force with the entire family there to back up Harlynn and Kate as they told the world that Frank Waters and six members of the board of Star Pharmaceutical had put out a contract for their lives. The fact that company funds had been used to pay the hit men only added to the furor of the people in the house. Kate was thankful to have Henry and Sam there along with Nick and Keaton to handle what they were being inundated with for the last two days.

Kate and Blacky had kept their distance the last two days. Kate would smile when she saw him and he would smile back at her. No one seemed to notice what was going on except Henry. Henry noticed everything that was going on no matter how small or large, especially how individuals interacted with each other.

"Would you like me to take Levi swimming?" Nick asked as Levi looked up at him and smiled.

"Levi?" Kate asked quietly, waiting for the child to respond.

"Dada?" He pointed shaking his head no.

"Dada will be here sleeping when you get back?" Kate whispered to him in his ear. She smiled letting him know everything was going to be okay.

He went to Nick as Nick picked him embracing the little boy. Levi was use to hanging out with his father non-stop for the last week. Kate kept telling him that Dada just needed a long nap and he would be better and maybe not so sad.

Kate crawled into bed next to Harlynn wrapping her arms around him. For a moment she thought she might fall asleep. When she saw the bruises on his arms it made her heart stop, thinking of the what ifs. She was so tired of the 'what ifs' in her life that she couldn't stand it.

It was as though Harlynn could feel or sense what she was thinking as he opened his eyes. They stared at each other for a couple of moments until Laney stirred and Kate got her out of the swing and brought her back to bed with them. Harlynn reached out for his daughter placing her on his chest as she looked at him smiling then curled into a ball going back to sleep listening to her father's heart beat. The heart beat that could calm your mind and ease your soul was all Kate could think.

"You look good, Babes," Kate whispered to him thinking he did look better. Could two days of sleep do that much healing? When she did the math it was as though Harlynn slept for twenty days because he was barely sleeping two hours a day. Forty-eight hours gave his body a chance to calm down and rejuvenate like he hadn't done in months. Blacky was right, it was what Harlynn needed.

"Thank you for staying here with me. I promise things are going to be better. I love our baby girl. She is my angel and always will be."

"I hope you will be close to her like you are to Levi."

"I will. I need to take a shower and have some food because I'm starving. Then I need to go over what is happening tomorrow. And finally after the children are in bed I need to be with my beautiful wife."

"I don't know if I can wait that long to be with you, Harlynn. I have spent the last two days watching you sleep in this bed thinking of every conversation we ever had together. And all the time I wondered if you knew how much I love you."

"I do. How about you take my angel to her nanny and get me a protein shake, then we can spend some time together and take a shower."

"That sounds better." Again Kate felt this physical attraction to him that words couldn't describe. She needed to lie next to him and have the world on the other side of the door, if only for a moment.

"I want Janey to be here tomorrow?" He told her watching her.

"She will be here for tomorrow and I already had Henry handle it with the judge so it won't have any bearing on our case going forward."

"Why don't you leave Laney here while you get the protein shake? I need to hold her for a while. I didn't think I could love another child as much as I love Janey and Levi. She reminds me of you the way she looks at me with those eyes. It's the best feeling."

Kate smiled as she walked into the kitchen thinking that things were slowly calming down, finally. Laney was a month old today. How was that possible that her daughter was a month old in blink of an eye?

She slowly put different fruits and protein powder into the blender as one of the chefs watched her with curiosity. It was nice to be doing the simple act of making a protein shake after all the chaos in her life. What would life be like a year from now she pondered as the shake mixed in the white noise of the blender?

"You look better today Ms. Jones." He said with a warm smile. "I have warm chocolate chip cookies or perhaps fettuccine Alfredo with grilled chicken and a salad?"

"That does sound good. Will it be good in an hour?"

"Yes. For dinner I'm doing peppered filets with garlic mashed potatoes and asparagus."

"Perfect Fred. Thank you for all your help over this last week."

"I will be glad to cook for you any time you need me in Houston or to come to the ranch or Utah."

"I will speak with Harlynn and get you on our calendar."

As she finished making the shake and a couple of peanut butter and jelly sandwiches she laughed out loud thinking of how life still was very much like peanut butter with all its ridges. If she would just let the problems sit like peanut better, they would smooth out.

"I like seeing you happy," Blacky told her sitting down across from on a bar stool. "That smile would mean that Harlynn is awake and feeling better?"

"Yes. Thank you." She glanced at him for a minute.

"Kate, I was not trying to interfere in your marriage. I would hope that you know how much Julia and I love the both of you, and your children." He had that worried look mixed with hurt in his eyes. "I think what you are doing tomorrow is the right thing."

"I realize there are only certain pieces of information you can tell us. Are you going back to your job?"

"No. I can do consulting work for our government and other clients. My son and Keaton have made me a tremendous amount of money over the last several years in the stock market."

Kate slowly took out a check from her back pocket of her jeans and slid it over to Blacky. She watched as he opened the check closing his eyes and shaking his head.

"No, absolutely not Kateland." He handed it back to her. "I'm here because you are family and Nick wants me here. Nick has never asked me for my help before. Kateland, if I can't help the people I love than what I do has no meaning."

"Moon Water is paying you from now on. I want you to protect my family and I will not freeload off you. This is going to be so complicated for months. I have to know that you are watching out for Harlynn and I don't give a damn if you have to be by his side every waking second of the day. A million dollars may seem like a lot of money, but honesty I would pay you so much more to keep my husband and family safe because there are about five people I trust in the world at this second." She placed the check on the counter and slid it back to him.

"Can Julia come to visit me?" He paused. "I haven't seen her in three weeks, which is a long time for us."

"Of course, it would be lovely to have Julia here with us. She is welcomed anytime and you let me know who you want to hire because you will need a break at times and Burt can't cover us every night."

"I have three people who I want to help me. We need to build out the staff over the next month. Thank you, Kateland."

"You are one of my favorite people in the world Blacky and I consider you part of the family. You know there is no reason for you to stay in Washington all the time. Julia could have her pick of hospitals to work at in Houston?"

"We have been discussing it. Can you tell me what is going on with my son because he is completely stressed out and it's not Moon Water? Are he and Elle having problems? It really bothers me when he won't talk to me. It must be pretty bad."

127

Kate handed a peanut butter and jelly sandwich to Blacky and a protein shake. Then she smiled as silence hung in the air. She could see how worried he was in his eyes. She didn't want to cause him pain unfortunately there was no choice.

"Shelly. Shelly claims to be pregnant with Nick's child and is trying to blackmail him. There was one night she said she wanted to talk and came by. The next morning Nick remembered nothing. George ran some test, give him a call. I don't think it's true, okay. He is scared to death of losing Elle."

"Damn. This would be my worst nightmare coming true at this very second. I told him to cut off all contact with her." Blacky closed his eyes slowly, shaking his head back and forth.

"Your son needs your support, Blacky. He didn't know how to tell you. All of his family will get him through this. He needs you and he needs to know you love him no matter what."

"I know you aren't supposed to have favorites in your children, but Nick will always be the most to me. There is something about Nicky that I can't explain to you, Kate."

"I do understand, Blacky. He loves you the most too. He won the lottery with you and Julia. Try to calm down and focus on the good. Even in the middle of all this chaos, we are all closer. There is this bond here. We are going to change the world, Blacky. Nick loves that you are here with him. Nick loves you more than you will ever realize."

When Kate got back to the room Harlynn was showered along with Laney. He was giving her a bottle as he walked her back and forth in his robe. She gently took the child from him taking her over to the rocking chair to breast feed. The child closed her eyes latching on to Kate with full force of tiny jaw muscles.

"Still acting like her father." Kate smiled taking in a deep breath. "Blacky is now working for us and paid up for a little while."

Harlynn didn't say anything as he inhaled his sandwich and drank the protein shake in a few minutes. She gave him a rundown of the last two days while trying to burp Laney. Then Kate put the baby down on a playmate as she played with the mobile over her head. She was strong, was all Kate could think. Strong and determined to tackle the world in front of her, like her father.

She watched as Harlynn watched them for a couple of minutes. Then she saw the look in Harlynn's eyes that said I want you and nobody else in this world, except you. She smiled at him as she picked up Laney taking her to the nursery where Claire was waiting for the baby to come back after two days. Kate had given the nanny a break for the last two days to rest and relax.

Harlynn was on the phone with Henry when Kate came in the room. He smiled at Kate as she locked the door and took off her clothes slowly. Harlynn cut off Henry and hung up the phone.

"Are you back?" Kate asked him slowly.

"Yes. I'm better, but I'm different now. You, the children and the people in this house come way before work. It's complete war for anyone or anything that messes with the people I love." She waited. "Come get in this bed with me please."

"You know that thing that you do that makes me completely dizzy."

"I think I do," he whispered to her as he started to kiss her. Kate closed her eyes feeling him touch her slowly and trying to breathe. She could feel his body move across hers and she could feel his tongue as he kissed her softly. For a moment there was no one in the world with her except Harlynn as time completely stopped. It was perfect. It had been a long time since anything was perfect in her life.

~Chapter 13

It was a controlled chaos Kate had decided an hour ago. Today was the day the interview was to take place and the world would know. They would get a glimpse of what it was like to have someone try to kill your husband or wife because of a business deal. Blacky was perfectly calm which Kate found rather odd. Everyone seemed okay with the interview. It would start with Kate and Harlynn then the rest of the family would come in and finally the children. Kate didn't like including the children, but Blacky and Harlynn thought it was important for the world to understand in most ways they were like everyone else and they would do anything for their children and family.

Kate watched as Janey came into the house running into Harlynn's arms. It was almost like she understood what he had been going through as she hung on.

"Papa, I've missed you," she whispered in his ear as everyone smiled. "You look better. I'm here to help take care of you."

"Would you like to be on television with me to tell everyone we have a cure for your cancer? We don't know if it will work for everyone. We will keep on trying until it does."

"Oh, yes!" Janey hung on Harlynn as everyone tried not to get choked up, including Stan. Janey had always believed in Harlynn even when he didn't believe in himself.

—

For the next twenty minutes the family posed for pictures in the bluebonnets. Keaton choreographed it smoothly, working from a list of exactly what each picture should look like. Fox News filmed this group of people together that didn't seem like a bunch of individuals worth billions of dollars. It was an intimate glimpse of a very private family that the world had never seen.

Then Kate and Harlynn sat down on the patio with the reporter, Mike Smith, who Harlynn had worked with over the years. It was a friendly meeting as they went over a few questions before the tape started to roll.

Kate felt Harlynn reach over for her hand as she saw the red light go on and the tape started to roll. She smiled watching Harlynn as he leaned back in his chair rocking slowly, wearing a white starched western shirt, jeans and scuffed ropers. He looked healthy and happy. Harlynn undid his cuffs, rolling up his sleeves, revealing his black and blue wrists, and then reached back for her hand. This was the first day he could wear the watch that Kate had given him when they first started dating. The watch held special meaning because it has been Henry's.

"Harlynn Barrett and his lovely wife, Kate Jones, are with us today on their ranch in Texas to answer a few questions on the recent downward turn in Star Pharmaceuticals. Let me begin by saying that I am sorry at the recent passing of your father, Harlynn."

"Thank you." Harlynn squeezed Kate's hand glancing at her for a moment. There was a silence that filled the air as Kate stepped in.

"Paul will be greatly missed by family, friends and everyone who knew him. It's a great loss to our family and the business community." Kate paused. "There has been a great deal of speculation why Star Pharmaceuticals has the short interest on it that it does today. Our family has remained silent because we weren't ready to release the information that we will today." Again she waited as Harlynn nodded at her to go ahead because he simply couldn't do it.

"About eight months ago, the individuals who you see along with Harlynn and me formed Moon Water. The philosophy behind this company was to find a cure for diseases that were not being addressed in the scientific community. We are funding this research by doing very broad licensing of the patents that Moon Water holds. Our technology along with the 'Goo' that Henry Grayden has held for many years has created a new method for drug discovery and drug delivery that is more economical and a fraction of the time compared to standard methods. By combining these two technologies we have found a possible cure for one cancer in the matter of six months. Now, it still has to go through FDA approval and trials, but the initial research indicates a much higher rate of success than most drugs going in front of the FDA in the last ten years."

"If you have this success, what bearing could this mid-cap pharmaceutical company have on what you are doing?" Mike asked as camera two zoomed in on him.

"We have conclusive evidence that the CEO and Chairman of the board along with six of the twelve board members put a contract out on our lives in order to stop our research. They used company funds to hire people to kill us. Two weeks ago Harlynn was kidnapped and held at gun point. We are lucky he is sitting here with us today." Kate paused unable to go on as her throat became very tight and she could hardly get air in and out.

"Last time I checked we lived in a country that didn't permit these acts of terrorism. I am determined to destroy Frank Waters and bring this company to its knees. I would ask shareholders and members of the business community to take a stand against what has happened to me and my family." Harlynn looked directly into the camera. "We want to help children like our daughter who survived cancer and all the families faced with diseases that cripple and kill. This is very personal what has happened to me, but it transcends the people here. This is not how our country was built or what we stand for as Americans. And I will be blunt to anyone involved in what has happened, if you threatened to kill me or my family you better be prepared to die yourself one way or another. I believe in our justice system and I'm positive that the authorities will step forward and do something as the result of the evidence that has been given to them." There was dead silence as Mike Smith sat back speechless.

"Harlynn, what do you intend to do with Star when the CEO and board have been forced out because I can assure you after the statement that you two have just made that they will be gone."

"My hope would be to bring in a talented management company that will revamp the atmosphere and possibly partnership with Moon Water. I am hopeful that in the next year or two it could be a nice turnaround story. Until then, I will continue to short the company and do everything in my power to protect my family. The reasons for my shorting have to do with what happened to me, but also because there is evidence of accounting fraud that goes back at least two years."

"The SEC sealed the office of Star three days ago." Mike interjected still overwhelmed by what was being said. "What can we expect Harlynn Barrett in the next coming months?"

"I think I will be cutting back on my work hours and spending more time with my children." Kate smiled as Levi crawled up into Harlynn's lap and Laney was handed to Kate by Henry. Janey came behind Harlynn, giving him a kiss on the cheek as she wrapped her arms around his neck. Then Keaton and Nick joined the picture with the others.

"I think I can speak for all us here who are involved in Moon Water. We want to help find cures and give hope to those who don't have hope." Henry stated firmly.

"And I have no doubt you will." The reporter nodded slowly. "And because I know each of you standing before me, the business community and the world is going to stand in unison behind you. As a reporter I have known these people who sit before me for my entire career. I'm stunned to learn what has happened to Harlynn Barrett in the last two weeks and although he has never spoken about the plane that crashed earlier this year that he was supposed to be on, I have a feeling that wasn't an accident. Before me is a group of individuals, who have the highest ethics in business, and who will make this world a better place. I know that as a reporter I will do everything I can to support them."

—

It was late as Kate sat in bed watching a rerun of the interview with Laney asleep on her chest and Levi asleep next to her. Janey was asleep at the foot of the bed because she wanted to stay near Kate. It was painful to watch Harlynn in the interview. It was all there: the determination, the fear and the pain mixed together. He was still standing in spite of it all. It was so like him to roll up his cuffs before a big meeting, not realizing the world would see those bruises on his wrist and forearms. Everyone would think the same thought, at the same second: how was he still alive?

"By the grace of God," Kate whispered to herself. "Only by the grace of God was he still standing."

The phone hadn't stopped ringing, everyone's email boxes were filled and they could only imagine what would happen tomorrow. Kate was hiding with the children because there were enough people to help with the calls and questions. And it frightened her completely was all Kate could think. Her hope was that in a week or two this would all be over.

"Who do you want me to take back to their room first?" Meg asked softly.

"Levi can go back to his bed and Janey. I'm not sure what my sweetie pie is doing yet. Why don't you ask Claire to come get her in ten minutes? I'll be in trouble if I don't get some sleep tonight."

"Yes. I'll send Henry in for Janey. You did well today, Kateland." Meg gave her a long hug. "I would like to stay a couple more days to help you with the children since Harlynn will be busy."

"Is Harlynn going somewhere?" Kate asked slowly.

"I think some F.B.I. agents have a few questions for him. Henry and Blacky are going with him, no worries Kate. The meeting is in Austin, which if they leave first thing will get them back by lunch. It's amazing the support that you and Harlynn have gotten since this morning from across the country and around the world. The law firm is shut down from calls trying to find Harlynn or wanting a statement. I don't think anyone expected this when we went on television this morning."

"I did." Kate admitted. "Everybody respects and loves Harlynn. Everyone of those executives keep looking at photos of their families thinking this could be them. I think the fact that I ended up talking got to people. From what Elle said, the way Harlynn looked at me made her cry. Elle never cries."

"I believe anyone who watches that interview, even if they didn't know either of you, would stop and listen. The President has made a statement concerning the matter and also called both Henry and Harlynn."

"My Blackberry is full, I've cleared my email twice and it just fills up again. Do you think it will slow down, Meg. I need it to slow down?" Kate stared at her daughter. "I can't believe Laney is mine."

"Do you know how beautiful she is, Kateland?"

"Yes." She gently picked up the baby who smiled at her. "You were faking sleeping my little angel." The baby kicked with glee as her mother covered her with kisses. "You are going to sleep in your crib tonight, for a little while."

Kate watched as Meg took Levi to his bed and Henry appeared taking Janey. Then Claire came taking Laney to the nursery. The room was quiet as she picked up toys and blankets along with books, placing them in the large colorful baskets. The room slowly turned back into a room for her and Harlynn verses another playroom. It was a good day as she looked around the room before going out to the living room.

Harlynn was in the office on the phone as he smiled at her through the glass door, she waved and half smiled back. She was trying not to feel overwhelmed, but she was completely overwhelmed by letting the outside world into her world. There didn't seem to be enough air in the house as she grabbed her jacket to go for a walk and watch the stars.

"Hey, can I go with you?" Elle asked with fear in her eyes. "I need to talk."

"Let's go star gaze." Kate waited as Elle got her jacket and they went out the door, down to a sitting area where a fire pit was already going. There were marshmallows to roast as the cool night air breeze blew both women's hair.

"This is the first time I've had five minutes with you since you got here. How are you and Nick?" She twirled the marshmallow in the flame wondering what was up with them.

"There is no one who I can trust the way I trust you, Kateland." Elle confessed. "I'm pregnant."

"Really?" Kate tried to calm her heart down as it began to race. "Does Nick know this?"

"No. Do you think Shelly's baby is Nick's?" Elle blurted out. "I love Nick, but the Shelly problem is hard to deal with, Kate. I know he doesn't love her and I know he wouldn't cheat on me."

"I talked to Blacky yesterday. He retained all of her medical records that exist to see if there was an ounce of truth to what Shelly claims. It helps to have a father who is one of the top intelligence officers in the world. He has conformation she had an abortion six weeks ago and the baby was not Nick's baby. Shelly was only trying to get money from Nick, again. She is not a good person."

"That makes me feel better. Thank you, Kateland!" She gave Kate the biggest bear hug. "I love Nick. Even if Shelly was having his baby, I still love him. And to defend Nick, it's more my fault because we were always so careful, except once. To make a long story short I was all over him after Blacky's birthday bash in Utah." Elle blew on her marshmallow that was on fire. "Can you blame me? The man has a perfect body and those eyes? I'm glad that I'm pregnant. I hope he will happy about it. His mother is going to hate me I have a feeling."

"How far along are you?" Kate asked wishing for a glass of Patron.

"Almost nine weeks." Elle whispered. "Any advice?"

"You need to tell Nick and you both need to tell Blacky before Julia gets here. Wow, I mean this is wonderful news when you think about it, Elle. I think God wanted you two together and now you will be together. Babies are fun and hard, but gosh, think how amazing this child will be with two parents like you and Nick."

"See, I knew you could make me feel better." Elle wiped away a tear.

"What kind of wedding do you want?" Kate inquired. "I will help you plan everything and yes, your family is going to freak out, but who cares."

"I was wondering if we could have the wedding at your house in the gardens." Elle looked into her eyes. "It would mean a lot to us."

"Yes! It would be wonderful to have it at our house in Houston. Or we could do it here on the ranch?" Kate laughed to herself. "Thank you Elle for telling me about this child. Thank you for helping with finding the fraud in Star. It helps knowing that you are there through all these crises going on. You are a very important person in my life."

"I promise not to sleep with your father." Elle watched as Kate busted out laughing. "I love Sue, but her marrying your father is about as fucked up as things can get."

"I know. Thank you for not sleeping with my father, you have no idea how I appreciate it." Kate watched as she saw Nick coming out to join them with champagne and glasses.

He set down the bottle and glasses on a table and went over to

Elle. Kate tried not to cry as he got down on one knee, putting a ring on Elle's hand.

"Ellison Mary Hunt, will you marry me?" Nick waited in anticipation for her answer.

"Yes," she said with no hesitation and then started to cry.

Kate watched as the two of them kissed and hugged each other. It was a beautiful night with the stars in the sky twinkling. It made Kate happy to see Nick finally find the right person for himself.

"Did Elle tell you we are going to be having a baby?"

"I better be the Godmother," Kate told him with no hesitation.

"I couldn't think of anyone else besides you and Keaton to be the Godparents." Nick told her slowly as Elle nodded her head in agreement.

"How did you know?" Elle asked as Nick poured the champagne.

"I found the four pregnancy tests when I was looking for dental floss yesterday. I had my suspensions for a while."

"You only did four? I usually do at least twelve to make sure," Kate commented as she got up to go inside. "I think I'm checking in until Laney wakes up." She gave them each a hug and left them to gaze into the fire thinking of the life before them. Everything was turning out good was all Kate could think.

When she was half asleep, Harlynn finally came into their room looking exhausted from the events of the day. He didn't even take a shower before he got into bed with her.

"Are you awake?" he whispered to her as he held her in his arms slowly kissing her. "I don't feel like sleeping."

"Will you take care of Laney?"

"Yes." He promised her as she took off his t-shirt she was wearing. Kate usually slept in one of his undershirts, but they never seemed to stay on very long.

"I want you to hold me all night long because I'm getting scared again."

"Don't be, Kate." He kissed her neck, and then stopped. "I don't know if Nick was drunk when he said he appreciated us letting them use our house for their wedding next month? Did I miss something when I was sleeping?"

"There's more."

"Like what?"

"They are having a baby?" Kate watched as Harlynn sat up in bed.

"You're kidding me?" he asked again. "Did you know?"

"Not until this evening. They will have very beautiful children."

"Speaking of beautiful children, Levi needs more attention from you. He told me today that Laney was taking up too much of your time."

"I see." Kate half smiled. "I'm doing the best I can with the three of them." Kate could feel herself getting defensive.

"You need to take him tomorrow afternoon and I will take the girls." Harlynn offered to her with a smile. "I understand how he feels at times and I understand you have this bond with our angel."

"You think I'm playing favorites?" Kate was thinking he may not be getting anything tonight because it hurt that Harlynn would say she played favorites with one of their children.

"I'm saying that Levi is going to have needs just like Janey or our angel. We have to do our best because we don't want a jealous two year old who's I.Q. is off the charts."

"I'm paying attention to the little man and I will find more time, somehow." She felt like he was being unfair. It felt like he was saying she wasn't being a good mother and it hurt.

"Kateland." He took in a deep breath like he could read her mind. "I don't want to argue with you tonight. Why shouldn't I be able to point out something so simple to you without you getting that look in your eyes?"

Kate laid back in her pillow, closing her eyes trying to make sure the tears wouldn't come down her cheeks. She was on the verge of a major meltdown, worse than anything her two years old could do. Slowly she rolled over, turning away from Harlynn because this was not the life she wanted. Couldn't he see she was doing the best she could on this ranch in the middle of nowhere with a house full of people and trying to avoid being killed?

"Please don't shut me out, Kateland?" Harlynn tried again with his voice wavering. "I want Levi and Laney to love each other and that love starts now. We have to show him how to love Laney. I want them to be close like you and Keaton." Silence filled the room as Kate got out of bed and put on her robe. Then she left.

When Kate walked into the kitchen she didn't expect to find Keaton and their father there eating Rice Chex cereal. It was a family affair as both men stared at Kate and then started laughing at her.

"You owe me a hundred," Keaton told his father. "What did you two get in a fight about tonight? The phase of the moon?"

"He told me I was ignoring Levi for Laney? You know I almost told him to go to hell." She watched as her father poured her a bowl of cereal and Keat put in chocolate milk.

"What a shit," Keaton told her as her father only laughed. "Do you want me to be mean to him?"

"Yes." She narrowed her eyes at him. "Am I a bad mother?"

"You're a wonderful mother to all your children and to defend Harlynn, I know he thinks you are, Kateland. You are stressed out from today. You're overwhelmed like the rest of us and you haven't really been eating. You are going into your hyper sensitive mode, honey. Eat and things will seem better in five minutes." Sam smiled.

"Are you going to tell her how Sue is pissed off over Elle's wedding?" Keaton asked then stuffed his mouth with more Rice Chexs.

"No, can this wait for tomorrow, son?" Sam slowly raised his eyebrows at Keaton as if to say lets deal with one issue at a time.

"Absolutely not. Sue was yelling at Dad because she feels like we didn't do anything, but sabotage their relationship."

"If I wanted to truly sabotage their marriage, they wouldn't be married." Kate interjected amused by Sue's statement. "She should be more appreciative that I have so damn nice."

"I can see her point," Sam defended his new wife. "Do you think you two could throw a little something together when we get back to Houston?"

"You're kidding?" Both Keat and his sister said at the same time.

"I'm serious."

"What do we get in return?" Keaton bartered with his father. "This is asking a lot, Sam."

"I have two of the new Ipads in my briefcase?" He offered.

"More?" Kate demanded. "I'm in a bad mood."

"You both can pick out new custom boots in town tomorrow."

The brother and sister locked eyes and nodded their heads.

"Get me a guest list as soon as possible, navy and white invitations, white orchids, lemon curd cake and food catered by Jackson. And Evin for pictures. I will send Ann an email in the morning."

"Thank you," Kate got up from the table, feeling better.

When she came in the room Harlynn was still lying in the same place with his eyes open, waiting for her. She slowly took off the robe and climbed into bed, waiting as he rolled over to her.

"I'm sorry that I upset you, Kateland. You're not being unfair to Levi and I do think you are an amazing mother with our children. I marvel at how organized and loving you are to them."

"I was hungry. I didn't like today and I don't want to do this again."

"I understand. Please don't be upset with me because I need you more than I have ever needed you before. You have dropped a lot of weight since having Lane. I think you weigh less than before you got pregnant. I will help you with your eating like I use to. You know, I like taking care of you, Kate. You are my sexy beautiful wife, forever." Slowly he began to kiss without stopping for a long time.

~Chapter 14

It was early, as Kate soaked in the bathtub before the children were up and the chaos was back with Moon Water. She closed her eyes, thinking she needed to start running again and doing her yoga. And eating, yes eating was going to have to become a priority before she got sick.

"How come you are up this early?" Harlynn asked coming in from his run drenched in sweat. It was five a.m. and the house was silent for the moment. "I should be back by lunch from Austin." He sat down taking off his shoes.

"Why are you going to Austin?" Kate asked slowly. "I would prefer not to hear your schedule from Meg or anyone else from now on."

"I'm going to Austin to meet with the F.B.I., Kateland." She rolled her eyes giving her best go to hell look that she had been saving up for the appropriate time. "Look, what is the problem? I don't like to start my day with you pissed off at me."

"When are we going back to Houston?" She snapped back at him.

"I don't know. Is that what you want, to go back to Houston?" He asked. "I thought you agreed to give me a week here? It's been six days since the funeral, Kateland. Two and half of those days I was sedated and the other day was a media circus. You can't give me a couple more days here?"

"I don't want to live on this ranch full time, Harlynn, and I can see you want to live out here." She stared at him.

"I have never said anything about living on the ranch full time. I do want to spend time here on the ranch with the family. I never said we were moving here, Kate. You think I would move everyone out here without talking to you about it?" Silence filled the space. "You don't want me going to Austin because you're scared something will happen?"

"Harlynn you killed two men?" She waited. "I want you to explain what is happening today and the day after, not Meg or Henry or anyone else. I feel like you are avoiding talking to me except when it comes to the children."

"Yesterday was crazy and I'm trying to figure a few things out. I'll tell you if I'm making plans to go anywhere else." He waited for her to respond as she got out of the tub putting on a robe. "It was self-defense, Kate. I'm not going to be charged with anything when they kidnapped me."

"I'm not sure who is on our side anymore. I would be very careful in that interview today. They are going to ask a lot of questions concerning the research we are doing. They don't care about the hit men, Harlynn. They want to know what we are going to do with this company."

"Did you ask Danny Hills to come out to the ranch?" Harlynn asked her slowly as he started the shower.

"Yes. I need to understand what is going on with JR6. Stan and I have to decide about Janey's mother today and treatment for this other child."

"Does my input count for anything when it comes to Janey?" Harlynn barked at her before he got in the shower.

"It did," Kate whispered to herself. She tried her best to get ready before he came out of the shower because he was fast. Finally, she decided to take her time and be calm if possible. She watched Harlynn in the mirror as he got out, drying himself off. His ribs looked worse by the day. She imagined it was very painful even though he never said a word or let on how much pain he was in. It hadn't been a week since Harlynn's dad was buried, even though it felt like forever.

"Don't you think I love Janey like I love Levi and Laney?" he asked when he was dressed.

"How can I include you when I didn't even know you were going to Austin?" Kate asked closing her eyes. "Why can't you cancel the meeting with the F.B.I. until next week or why can't they come here?"

"I will be back as soon as I can. Okay?"

"It will have to be okay, Harlynn." She needed to start running today because she was not good at mind reading still. As she put on her shoes she could feel Harlynn staring at her again. There was this anger in her that had taken over. Why couldn't they go back to when things were simple? A time when they didn't have bodyguards, people weren't trying to kill them and their lives were theirs and no one else's.

"Do you think running this soon is a good idea?" Harlynn asked trying to take the edge out of his voice. It was still there.

"I'll be careful. Hunter needs a good run since no one has been taking him out. Now there is someone who has been completely ignored, my dog."

"You're right. I should be taking him for a run in the mornings. I can do that, Kateland." Silence filled the room. "Did you have a dream about me going to Austin?" Kate had a dream about Harlynn and his plane crash. "You need to tell me? I'm not sure why you are attacking me at five in the morning."

"I'm very concerned who is supporting us. I know we have every CEO contact us that has any merit in business. I don't feel like we have a clear picture of what is going on, Harlynn. There are a lot more economic implications to what we are doing than any of us realize."

"Henry told me your concerns, which next time I would like to hear first. I have alterative motives in meeting with the F.B.I. We have to find out the information we need to win this game."

"Except it's not a game when we are talking about your life Harlynn. It's not a game anymore." She waited. "How do we get to the point where we can talk again and communicate? It's like you don't trust me anymore, Harlynn. All you want to do is protect me from the evils of the world."

"You're the only one who I completely trust in the world at the moment, Kateland. When I get back, we'll go for a ride for a couple of hours without anyone else. We can take Levi and Janey swimming while Laney sleeps this afternoon. It will only be us when I get back, I promise."

"That would be good." Kate half smiled thinking another ride in the country side was a nice gesture, but it didn't solve any problems.

—

Kate finally went into the kitchen hoping everyone had left. Please don't let anyone be there she told herself over and over again. This would be the down fall to having the world staying with you.

"You're the only one who can bring Harlynn Barrett to his knees." Nick whispered to Kate in the kitchen.

"I'm not a happy person at the moment, Nick. You probably don't want to speak with me unless you want me to start bitching about everything."

"I think you deserve to bitch about life at the moment." He smiled at her. "Keat said I can be mean to him if I feel like it." Kate continued eating her grits. "You aren't going running are you?"

"I'm resending my permission to attack, in other words don't be mean to him because his Dad just died. And yes, I'm going for a short run before I go insane. If I'm not back in thirty minutes then you can call a search party out. How are you and Elle doing?"

"Better. I'm going to tell my father tonight about the baby."

"Do you want me to be there because this is going to be tough? I don't know how Blacky is going to handle this after Shelly. Your mother is going to kill you, Nick."

"Please be there when I tell him. You are like magic with Blacky. My mother is going to come tomorrow for the day, and then I think Elle, Keat and I are heading back to Houston with my parents. Is that okay with you? Keat and I have some meetings to catch up on. Why is Harlynn pissed that Danny is coming out to the ranch?"

"Who the hell knows?" Kate said getting up. "I do need an update on Moon Water when you get back. I understand you signed two new clients last week before the funeral?" She felt better after eating and could be civil. Why did she go after Harlynn she wondered to herself?

"I have the contracts and write ups for you already." He stammered. "You didn't have to pay my father that kind of money, Kate. You and Keat are my family."

"I know I didn't have to Nick, but he deserves to be paid well. There is a tremendous amount being asked of him. Moon Water will always pay their people well. I refuse to take advantage of your father."

"I keep having inquires from Wall Street about going public with the company? I don't ever see us wanting to answer to the street,

Kate."

"Moon Water will always remain private as long as I am alive." She reassured him as he nodded with relief. "I need a date for your wedding and we need to have some sort wedding shower for you two. Elle needs to go see Dr. Carr because of her asthma when you get back. Plus are you two going to stay in the loft? You know there is a fabulous house for sale not too far away from us in Houston?"

"We were thinking June 11th, if it works for you and Harlynn? A wedding shower the first week of May. I already called Dr. Carr this morning. And we are going to see the house on Friday, Keat told me about it." Kate got up and gave Nick a long hug.

"I'm happy for you, Nicky. You are going to be the best father."

"I hope we can be half as good parents as you and Harlynn."

—

It was already hot outside as Kate started on her run down the path that leads to the west side of the property. The hills were pretty hilly Kate thought to herself as she climbed the second one and slowed down. Hunter, her faithful black lab was full of vigor as he pulled her along the path. The silence of the countryside soothed her mind as she tried to stop the chatter in her head. Sue had text her that they needed to talk. Kate sighed because she didn't feel like going at it with her. Elle had gotten sick twice this morning and wanted to know if Kate had any suggestions. Her father wanted to have lunch. An email from Harlynn said he was sorry for not making more of an effort to communicate with her. Kate turned off her Blackberry and kept going.

The snapping of a branch caused her to stop in her tracks as Hunter began to bark. She heard a loud sound like a pop, and then she saw Hunter fall to the ground slowly with a whimper. At the same instances something hit her neck, it was hard and stung.

—

The next time Kate opened her eyes she was sitting in a tepee that had a small fire burning in it. She sat up moving to the fire as an old man stared at her chewing on a leaf. He held out a wooden cup to her pointing at it.

"Am I dead?" she asked him.

"No. Drink the water. You are thirsty." He told her in a voice that was rough like sand paper moving over an old antique table. She gazed into his black eyes that reflected the fire, thinking who was this old man? Everything was hazy as her head was pounding and felt heavy. There was some dried blood covering her hand. Was this the Indian who had taught Harlynn when he was a boy about the land? How was it possible she was sitting in a tepee?

"You are the Dreamer who married the Little Shark." He waited. "What do your dreams tell you?"

"I don't know, exactly. At times they are happy, at other times they are dark. There is love in the dreams and family. There is darkness, like someone wants to hurt me."

"Why don't you sleep and listen to your dreams. Then you can find your way back to Little Shark, he will be worried. No harm will come to you and your children from now on. No harm will come to Little Shark. You must allow him to change. Change is good for him. He wants to leave the dark and find light."

"What does Little Shark need to find the light?"

"He needs you and this land to heal and find the light. Little Shark needs your love to heal."

Kate felt her eyes grow heavy as she lay down on a stack of blankets. She smiled, thinking the smells where different as her body finally began to relax. Was this real she wondered or what it a dream? Hopefully she wasn't dead.

The next time she opened her eyes she was back on the trail leaning against a tree. The sun was very high, she guessed around noon or later. Her head hurt as she stood up and began to walk, and then she stopped disoriented. Hunter? Where was her dog she wondered? She made a small pile of rocks in the middle of the path as a point of reference and slowly began to walk east because in theory she had taken the west path. She felt in her jacket for her Blackberry, but it wasn't there. Next she found a long stick to use as a walking stick and set forward. There was a stream on the property she remembered as she tried to find any reference point. Maybe she should just sit down and wait for someone to find her? Who knew where she was going? Nick knew. Harlynn knew. She wondered why she wasn't afraid of being out here alone.

Kate looked at her watch an hour later as she kept walking. She sat down in some shade to rest. It was then she heard the sound of a horse and her name being called. As she stood up she saw Nick coming towards her. He immediately stopped the horse and ran towards her. He had the strangest look in his eyes.

"Hi." Kate was completely exhausted as she tried to keep her balance.

"Hi." He said sitting down on the ground with her. "Drink this?" He held out the water to her. "Eat some of this?" He gave her a protein bar. She watched as he took out the first aid box and started to clean off her arms and neck. Kate had forgotten about the dried blood on her arm.

"What the heck happened to you?" Nick asked her in a whisper. "How do you feel?

"I don't know. I was running with Hunter and heard a pop sound. It's all a blur."

"Kate, we've been looking for you for five hours. When you didn't come back from your run I went looking for you and found Hunter shot." His voice quivered as he tried to focus on her.

"I thought I might be dead. Is Hunter dead?" Kate asked with her head pounding. "I might have a concussion."

"We got him to a vet and they are working on him. It doesn't look good. I'm really sorry." He licked his lips. "I thought . . . I thought something awful happened to you." He closed his eyes and bowed his head for a moment. She watched as he took his phone calling his father. His hand was shaking as he held it to his ear. He looked pale to her as she tried to keep her eyes open.

"I got her." He managed to say.

"Is she hurt?" Blacky asked back.

"There is a gash in the back of her head at the base of her neck. Definitely has a concussion. She doesn't know what happened. I think I can ride with her back. I'm maybe ten minutes away."

"Nick, what is going on?" Kate asked confused.

"Did you kill a man? We found a man with his throat slit from ear to ear?"

"I haven't seen anyone on the trails out here. I had these weird dreams." She felt her head begin to sway back and forth. I want to lie down, Nick."

"You think you can get on that horse and ride back to the house with me? You would have made it there in another thirty minutes if you kept going. I saw that pile of rocks and I knew that you were alive."

As they road back to the house Nick held her close against his body as she tried to stay awake. She was very thirsty she realized and her lips were cracked and burned. Her scalp hurt from the sun blazing down on it. In spite of everything she was not scared or frightened. There was this calmness inside of her that made the chatter in her head stop. Was it a dream? Or was it real? Then she noticed the bracelet on her right wrist. It was real.

Harlynn sprinted out to meet them as they road up to the ranch. He helped her off the horse as she stumbled trying to stand up. He carefully picked her up, taking her inside to the coach where Danny was waiting for her.

"You are going to the hospital." Harlynn demanded for the third time.

"No." Kate yelled at him. "Danny can look at me." Then she decided she was going to sleep as everyone fought in the room.

"Kate, its Danny. You need to talk to me?"

"I'm thirsty? My head hurts. That's it."

"Can you tell me anything?" he asked as he started an I.V. on her then continued listening to her heart, taking her blood pressure and looking in her eyes with a light. "Tell me what happened here?" He asked as he cleaned the wound at the back of her skull. "Did you fall?"

"I remember a pop sound, Hunter fell down and then something hit the back of the head." She closed her eyes. "I'm very tired. Where is Harlynn?"

"I'm here." he whispered to her. "What is it Kate?"

"I'm sorry for yelling at you. Please don't take me to a hospital. Remember what happened last time?" The tears came down her face.

"As long as Danny says it's okay. If he thinks you need to go then we are going."

"Okay. He said we would be safe now." Kate held up her arm showing the finely braided bracelet to him. "He called me the Dreamer and you Little Shark." Then she fell into a deep sleep filled with dreams she didn't understand. She slept for sixteen hours while Harlynn stayed next to her waking her every couple of hours.

—

The next afternoon, Kate sat by the pool swimming with her son. Levi loved to go underwater to find his cars on the stairs. He was fearless was all Kate could think as she watched him. In her heart she wanted to believe that yesterday didn't happen. When Harlynn had gotten to Austin they told him there were other killers. The F.B.I. knew they were in Texas. Her lips still stung from being in the hot sun for so many hours.

There was a laceration at the back of her head that still stung. It could have been from a rock or fragments of the bullet that hit her dog. She thought of her three children and she didn't want to think of what could have happened. She knew that Meg and Henry would help Harlynn raise them. It was the idea of never seeing them grow up that brought her to tears instantly.

Stan came out to the pool with Janey carrying two beers. He sat down, handing one to Kate, as they watched Janey dive in the pool and swim to Levi. It was nice they had each other, was all Kate could think.

"How are you?" Stan asked slowly as he handed the beer to her. "You scared the shit out of me yesterday, Kate. We could barely keep Harlynn under control. I thought he was going to go insane as each hour went by."

"Can you believe I was never scared? I had faith in God that he would protect me." She smiled warmly at Stan. "This is Janey's family even if I'm not here, Stan. You will always be part of this family."

"After you went to bed last night we stayed up talking about what to do about Amy. I never told anyone, but Amy never wanted children or Janey." He waited. "I think that she doesn't care about Janey except for her own needs. I don't think she belongs in Janey's life. Everyone agreed last night and I hope you will agree also."

"I think when Janey is older we will have to cross that bridge. Right now she is thriving and I'm not willing to destroy what she has accomplished emotionally."

"Then we agree." Stan took several sips of his beer. "Danny explained to us that a bone marrow donation is not possible. He said he would be willing to look at the case to see if he could suggest a treatment plan for her baby. JR6 cannot be used on a child under one. It's possible that when the child is one, Danny could put her in the trial late."

"I want to help this child. What is the child's name?"

"Chloe," Stan said quietly as though it had meaning to him. "I can't believe she tried to take Janey out of school, Kate."

"Janey and Levi are starting at a new school when we get back. The school is well aware of the situation, plus we will have a bodyguard at the school. It might be over kill, but you know at this point I don't give a damn what anyone thinks. You'll need one for the next six months also."

"Blacky told me and I'm okay with it all. You're all making a tremendous sacrifice to develop this cure. If there is anything I can do, please let me know."

"Believe me, I will call you. Did Harlynn tell you that his father left property and stock for Janey in his will? He also paid off all her medical bills that you wouldn't let any of us help you with Stan. And there isn't a damn thing you can do about it because it's done." She smiled.

"No." He was stunned. "I can't believe he would do that, Kate?"

"Well, Paul really loved Janey. I think next week the Will should be probated. You don't have to do anything. I wanted you to know."

"I think you are the best thing that ever happened to Janey and I remember that night you walked into that hospital to volunteer." He finished his beer. "How are you doing?"

"I keep trying to get my feet on the ground, although nothing seems to work these days." She giggled. "I think I'm getting very drunk starting now. Don't tell Harlynn or the good doctor."

"Good for you. I'm going to tell the cooks to find a cooler and bring out some food. I think I'll get drunk with you."

—

The flames danced in the fire pit as Kate sat tuning her guitar. She had snuck away with her bodyguard for some alone time. Charlie was told not to leave her side for a minute. In the distance she could see more of the bodyguards when she was hoping for less. She hadn't spoken to anyone since yesterday. Harlynn had taken over the children today, which was what Kate needed. No one knew what to say to her. When they looked at her their eyes would tear up as they walked away. Even Blacky almost lost it this morning on her. It was as though they really thought she was dead.

Slowly she felt her finger tips go up and down the neck of the guitar with such ease and pleasure it brought a smile to her face. It made her feel strong and at peace, a peace no one could take away. She wanted to find that tepee again and lay on those soft blankets while drinking that honey water. She didn't know what was in that water, but it made her sleep like she hadn't slept in the last two years.

"How did you find that guitar? It was supposed to be a surprise for you." Harlynn informed her as he sat down with a six pack of Beck's.

"You must be thirsty?" She commented in a half whisper.

"I figured you would probably have a couple. I'm sure someone will join us out here. It seemed logical." He took several marshmallows and put them on the roasting sticks with the only sound being the crackle of the fire. She kept playing while he made them each a s 'more, then she stopped.

"Thank you." There was complete silence between them. "What do you want to tell me?"

"I'm sorry I went to Austin, Kate. I should have been here when this happened. I'm thankful that we are sitting here right now. I was terrified that someone had taken you." He immediately got choked up. "I would have done anything to get you back."

"I know that, Harlynn. I'm your world and you are mine." She felt her eyes tear up as she watched him. She imagined he felt the way she did when he was kidnapped and it crushed her that he would feel that pain.

"Yes." He closed his eyes knowing she did understand.

"What would make you happy?" Kate asked when she finished the s 'more and opened a beer. The flavors actually weren't bad together she thought to herself. She had managed to keep a nice buzz going for the last couple of hours. She was done breast feeding, apparently. She hoped Laney understood. Danny said he wasn't comfortable with her breastfeeding because of her neck. It all seemed to work out she thought as she finished her beer, waiting for Harlynn to answer the question.

"To hold you in my arms would make me the happiest person in the world at this very second, Kateland." He told her with tears stuck in his eyes.

"I can do that." She could handle sitting by the fire in the night sky filled with stars, staring into these flames. Slowly she put the guitar down and went to him.

Five minutes later, Keaton came out with Henry to check on them. Instantly Henry picked up the guitar and started to play. Kate closed her eyes listening to the music as Harlynn nuzzled her neck whispering to her how much he loved her. She wanted to stay in that moment for as long as she could.

~Chapter 15

There are points in life that you simply have to get through to move forward. As Kate lay in bed she prayed to make it through the day with everybody being well and getting along. Today she had to engage in the rest of her life, make decisions and take care of her children. She had to meet their needs and demands while not going backwards.

"Tonight Henry and Meg are going back along with Keaton and the rest. Do you want to go back to Houston?" Harlynn asked breaking the morning silence.

"I want a couple days without everyone here. You need more time, I think. Why don't we stay until Monday?" Kate rolled over watching Harlynn as he nodded. She knew if she said that she wanted to go home this second, it would have happened. There was nothing that Harlynn wouldn't do for her. It was the idea of going through life without her that still haunted him. She could see it in his eyes as he watched her.

"Are you sure?" Harlynn seemed surprised.

"Positive. I have a meeting with a designer today to redo some of the ranch."

"Really?" Harlynn repositioned himself so he wasn't leaning on his ribs. "What do you have in mind?"

"For the most part the interior design is there. It's the color scheme I can't live with, Harlynn. And I mean I really can't live with burnt red and orange at all. The children's room needs to be redone for children. We need to make that large room at the end of the hall into a play room. I don't like the couch in the den or the lighting. I don't like the bedding in here or the plates in the kitchen. The guest lodge needs different window treatments. I want wooden floors and get that awful carpeting taken out. Do you want me to go on?"

"Not really. It sounds like you want to make this our house, which I appreciate, Kate. Please don't erase my father from this ranch. This was his favorite place to come."

"I would never take Paul out of this house, Babes. Tell me what you don't want changed so we don't have any miscommunications?"

"His leather chair in the den stays. The gun cabinet is important because that was my grandfather's. New chairs for the kitchen table would be nice. I like the artwork in the hallway because I picked it out. New frames if you want." He tried not to smile. "I've always hated those plates. My sister picked them out and no one ever had the guts to throw them out. I don't like the wine glasses or water glasses. I hate the pots and pans. Please change them." He kissed her. "Thank you for taking the time to do this for us."

"Well, if we are going to be here two or three times a month I want it to be our home. I want to leave everything here so there is no packing or unpacking. I want Keaton, Meg and Henry to be able to leave their things here."

"That would be good. We need to hire a house manager to set up before we come, order food and arrange a chef for our visits. When we are here, I want it to be a time we can relax and enjoy the children." He pushed her hair out of her eyes. "Let me see the back of your head because you have been hiding it from me."

She pushed her hair out of the way, still being stubborn. Kate could feel him lightly push on it as it oozed. He got up and got a towel then did it again and again.

"Kate we may have to take you to the hospital after all. This doesn't look right to me at all. Let me go get Danny." Harlynn took off his undershirt he had on and threw it at Kate. "At least you won't be naked for the good doctor."

"I'm sure he has seen lots of naked bodies before, Babes." She laughed at him.

"Well, he's not seeing yours." Harlynn raised his eyebrows at her. "Have you been with Danny before us?"

"Oh, my God! He is my child's doctor, Harlynn." He watched her. "He asked me out once. It didn't matter since you were interested in me and I was already in love with you. It was when Janey was in the hospital."

He smiled to himself. "Henry told me I better get my act together if I didn't want to lose the opportunity to be with you. I was already in love with you." Harlynn kissed her. "Thank you for telling me."

A moment later Danny came in the room still in his pajamas and half asleep, which made Kate laugh because he had on more clothes than Harlynn and her put together. Harlynn showed him the towel then he opened up his bag of tricks. Poor Danny was never going to get to sleep.

"This is the deal, Kate." Danny told her as he put on rubber gloves and took out a scalpel. "You have a substantial infection in the wound, even though I cleaned the hell out of this thing. You'll feel a little prick, and then I'm going to take some cultures, clean it and put ointment on it. Julia needs to look at this when she gets up. I told her about it last night. You will take it easy today and tomorrow. To make myself clear that means no drinking, or swimming or horseback riding. And be careful when you're having sex." He glanced at Harlynn who became red.

"Can you talk and work?" Kate asked as she closed her eyes.

"Go ahead." Danny said slowly as Harlynn grimaced at what he was doing. "I really don't know what the hell happened to this except you went swimming. I know I told you not to go swimming or drink alcohol because of the concussion."

"I forgot and you said it was a minor concussion." Harlynn rolled his eyes at her. "Update me on JR6. I know I haven't made time for you Danny with all that has been going on."

"I know you haven't made time for me or you would know that it works. I'm not talking it might work, either. I have the completed raw data with me. In the lab, we got up to ninety-three percent results with no tweaking. It's the highest I've ever seen in this kind of treatment." He put on his serious demeanor as Kate waited. "I have an offer for five million to go work for a pharmaceutical company, not that I would take it. I need one of the bodyguards and a driver until life cools down. I would prefer not to be gunned down and I want this drug to be successful."

"Has anyone else had an offer? Do we need to meet with all the scientists?" Harlynn inquired.

"Yes and yes." Danny looked up at Harlynn. "Blacky needs to visit the lab and go over it thoroughly. We don't want anything walking out the door, if you understand what I'm saying."

"I'll take care of it today. I think Sam is going to be taking over running the lab because I don't have the time or expertise. Thank you for coming to us and we will see what we can do about a better compensation plan for you." Harlynn flashed a smile at Kate who didn't look happy. "I'm going to go fix you some breakfast, love. Would you like something Danny?"

"That would be great." Danny stopped working on Kate's neck for a moment. "I want to go horseback riding later if you could arrange it, Harlynn."

"No problem. Give me a call when you are up and ready to go."

Silence filled the room as Kate thought it was very strange to have Danny in her bed with her basically naked under the covers. She could feel him cleaning out the wound that was about the size of a dime, maybe a little larger. Then he finished placing a dressing on it.

"Julia needs to finish it. I don't want to cause more trauma to the area. "

"How are you doing, Danny?" Kate asked rolling over carefully as she pulled the sheet up. "Thanks for coming. I know it's hard to get away from the hospital."

"It's good to get away from the city. I'm worried about you, Kate."

"You know it's been very bumpy with the kidnapping and funeral." She stopped herself. "I'm sure life will get better in the next couple of weeks. This has changed Harlynn and our life is very different. I believe in what Moon Water is doing. I will be honest with you, Danny." Her face instantly became distraught. "I'm scared out of my mind if I think too long. I don't know what is going to happen second to second."

"You're right to feel that way. I'm getting calls from all sorts of people about what we are doing. People I haven't talked to in twenty years or met at a conference once have contacted me. Then I have the government breathing down my neck for information. People are very afraid of what Moon Water is doing. They are afraid of JR6. And they are afraid of you and Harlynn."

"Why?" Kate wanted to see what he would say.

"Kate, we are talking about their careers and livelihood. In ten years the life for a lot of these scientists could be very different. I have two hundred emails from the best and brightest researchers who want to work for Moon Water. We could challenge any research facility with what we have in the Woodlands."

"I think we can fund five more scientists. Send me your top people. Sam will be in charge of the Woodlands within the next two weeks. He used to have a semi-conductor company that made masks. He knows how to deal with organizing research and clean rooms." Kate waited. "What do you want Danny?"

"I want a bigger part in Moon Water," he told her. "I want to head up a division that deals with pediatric research."

"Do you have a proposal of what you need and what diseases you want to approach? How is Texas Children's going to feel about you working for me and taking care of children."

"I would still have clinic twice a week to review cases and follow treatment protocols. I'm tired of watching beautiful children like Janey die. I need a break for now. I think I can do both if I manage my time."

"Give me your proposals and progress notes to review before I approve it. Email me the best scientist you have and I will have look at them. We will get you what you need."

"I have to head back tonight with the gang. Can we talk when you get back in town?"

"Yes. Can you do me a favor and get Laney from the nursery since that hole in my neck is killing me."

"Sure. I still need to give you a shot of antibiotics. How about in your leg?" He winked at her. "And it will hurt like hell." Kate rolled her eyes at him as he gave the shot.

"Damn, you weren't kidding." She said afterwards.

When Danny left she got out of bed and put on a pink Nike warm up. At least she would be comfortable she told herself as she took the sheets off the bed and remade it. She even managed to brush her teeth and wash her face before Danny came back with Laney. She laughed because Danny had changed Laney, given her a sponge bath and dressed her, along with making her a bottle. Damn, he was good, was all Kate could think.

"Thank you." Kate took Laney from him as she did her kitty cat cry telling her mother she missed her. Instantly she stopped as Kate held her against her chest.

"I will take care of your children anytime. Laney is off the charts like Levi. Have you noticed?""We were waiting for you to notice, Uncle Danny," Kate told him. "You already know a lot of words, don't you, Laney?" She smiled at her mother like she understood what they were saying.

"I'm going to have breakfast and sleep for several hours." Danny yawned. "I will see you later."

As Danny left the room Harlynn walked in with a tray of food. Danny took his plate leaving them alone. Kate put Laney in her bouncy chair and put on music for her. Then she sat down with Harlynn eating.

"This is turning out to be a more productive day than I anticipated. I have had a business meeting and my neck cleaned out before six this morning. Plus we talked, which helps me." Kate smiled at Harlynn. "Tell me what's on your mind because you have that look in your eyes, Babes?"

"I'm worried about your neck. Julia will be in soon to finish cleaning it. She got in late last night after you went to bed." He waited. "Sometimes I get jealous of this relationship with Danny. I don't know why. He is such a great guy and I know that he saved Janey when she was very ill. It got to me when I saw you feeding Laney on the bed and he gazed at the two of you in complete awe. I guess the fact that you told me he asked you out startled me. What if you would have chosen to go out with him instead of me? Would we be together at this moment?"

"You always worry about how these other men love me." She leaned forward slowly. "They simply don't compare to you. I was waiting for you to come into my life. I didn't know who it was, I didn't know it would be you, I didn't have your name, but it was this dream of a man who could make me feel whole and accept me. This man, who no matter what loves me, I'm not talking about friendship or romance. I'm talking the love that will never end until time stops, even if then. A confident love, filled with hope and dreams. A love you can see. You have nothing to fear Mr. Barrett."

"Thank you." He closed his eyes reflecting on her words. "I

needed to be reminded."

"You've had a tremendous amount of heartache to deal with, Babes. You are starting to look tired again."

"You have that affect on me," Harlynn commented trying not to blush like a school boy. She had gotten to him with her honesty. "Why don't you think of what you want to do for Danny? We can talk later." Harlynn fed Kate a piece of French toast with strawberries. "I want you take it easy today until we see what is going on with your neck."

"Ask me?"

"Tell me every detail of seeing the Chief." His voice was filled with anticipation. Kate described the stitching on the blankets, the wooden cup with honey water and his voice that she could still hear. How the black eyes stared at her through the flames of the fire. Then she smiled at Harlynn as she saw his eyes dance with excitement.

"What do you think of what he said to you?" Harlynn asked.

"You're better when you come to this ranch and I don't exactly understand it. I've seen the change in you. I don't know what the darkness might be? Is that the law firm?"

"It might be. I don't think its Moon Water. When I go into the law firm I feel it come back to me. It's this weight that is heavy and suffocating me. I think I'm going to stop working at the law firm and remain a partner. I can try to handle once a month to oversee the business flow. If that doesn't work I will have to cut all ties to the firm."

Kate watched as he picked up Laney holding her up and covering her with kisses. There was this bond between Laney and her father that was so strong you could see it. You could see the love.

"You want to stay in here and rest, or come out to the family room?"

"I think I will stay here for a little while. You can leave Laney if you want?"

"Nope, I want to have time with her. And you need to rest as much as you can."

"After I deal with Sue, Elle, and my father." She protested with distress. "I love and care about each one of them. I don't feel like dealing with them when I'm still dealing with being shot at." Harlynn went to her, still holding Laney. He watched as she curled up to him.

"I'm going to tell them all you are sleeping. Try not to think what could have happened instead of what did happen. We are all still standing."

"Go act as my bodyguard against the world. I could use one." He kissed her before he left with Laney.

For the next hour Kate sat sketching what she had seen in the tepee with the Chief and made notes of her dreams. She never wrote down her dreams, but now she was going to keep a journal. Her writing lasted exactly forty-two minutes before there was a knock at her door. Most likely Keaton, because he would be up early with Levi, like he had done every morning this past week.

"Are you awake?" Keat stuck his head in the door. "I only have a second because Levi is busy eating and then we are going exploring and to feed the horses. Man he loves this place, Kate. I love it too."

"I'm doing some re-decorating, to put it nicely. What color do you want your room?"

"Gray with lime green accents would make me happy. I'll send you some pictures. Please get rid of those plates in the kitchen or I'm going to Targets to buy new ones today." He smiled. "Let me see the neck. Danny wanted my opinion on it."

Kate waited as he gently took off the dressing then took out a small flashlight looking at it. Keaton had a Masters in infectious diseases. He squeezed more of the ooze out of it, and then looked at it.

"This is really nasty and looks majorly infected. Can I poke at it? You said it stung when it hit you? I think I felt a fragment of some sort in it."

"Get it out. Danny left his bag over there." Keat was about to start digging in the wound when Julia came in the room. Blacky's wife was a surgeon as she gently moved Keaton aside.

"How are you doing?" Julia asked slowly.

"I might throw up if you don't hurry up." Kate mumbled under her breath.

For the next ten minutes Julia pulled out three fragments, and then sighed. She cleaned it and left it open.

"We'll probably have to get an x-ray of that neck to make sure we got them." She sat on the bed next to Kate. "Laney looks exactly like you. Levi has grown since I've seen him. I can't believe you gave

Blacky that check." She tried to cover up the emotions in her voice.

"We have missed you over the last two months. Your husband is the only one who can keep us safe, Julia. I am so grateful for his expertise." Now it was Kate's voice filled with emotions as she looked at the tiny fragments that had come out of her neck. "Thank you for coming to celebrate the engagement."

"Why don't we all sit down and talk about the wedding later?" Julia didn't smile or seem excited.

"One o'clock. I have to meet with someone at noon." Kate suggested as Keat stood guard at the foot of the bed. He wasn't leaving. They waited to talk until Julia left.

"Julia doesn't seem too pleased with the wedding. Wait until she finds out that Elle is pregnant." Keat commented getting on the bed next to her and flipping through the channels. "Why can't they be happy for Nick?"

"I don't know." Kate replied cautiously as she rested her head against her brother. "Can you keep Sue away from me today? My tipping point with her has been maxed out. " Kate glanced at her brother who seemed to be in a melancholy mood to her. "Are you down on the wedding too?"

"No way, I'm happy for them. Sometimes I wonder if I will ever have anyone to share my life with Kate."

"You have to ask God for help, Keaton. Let's pray together for someone who will fit in your life."

"God, please help me find a wonderful person to be my wife and the mother of my child and she must get along with Kateland. Amen." His voice was filled with love as he spoke. He winked at her. "We will see if the big guy comes through on this one."

"Never lose your faith, Keaton. If I can find someone who loves me, you can find someone who loves you. Did you think I was dead when I disappeared?"

"I didn't want you to be hurt, again. I would have known if you were in danger or hurt like I did the other times." He whispered taking her hand. They both looked up as Sue opened the door.

"Why are you two in bed together? I can always tell when Harlynn is lying his ass off." Sue came in the room as Kate sat up. "Did you really get shot yesterday? Or are you doing this to get attention from everyone?"

"Yes, she really had fragments in her neck that probably ricochet off when Hunter got shot so if you can't be nice get the hell out. In fact get the hell out since you are being a witch to her already." He was truly annoyed by the invasion of their new stepmother and by what she had said. "Kate doesn't need attention unlike you."

"Oh, go to hell Keaton. Why is everyone ignoring me! You haven't said a word to me in days, Kateland!" Sue protested. "What did I do now?"

"No one is ignoring you." Kate said bluntly looking out the window. "I'm on overload and I don't want to hear how I didn't do anything for your wedding when you ran off to Las Vegas. I have had to deal with a lot in the last two weeks. You said you were getting married in November when we last spoke. I can't handle doing funerals and wedding showers in one week. You better not ruin anything for Nick and Elle. Do you understand?"

"Why is Nick's wedding important to you? Why isn't my wedding as important?" Sue yelled at her as Kate stood up. "I matter! I'm your best friend or at least I used to be!"

"You married my father!" Kate yelled back at her loud enough that everyone heard her in the house. "Don't come into my bedroom, in my house, yelling at me at seven o'clock in the morning! We are giving you a shower what the hell else do you want from me!"

"I want you to stop ignoring me and treat me like your best friend! I should have been on that run with you yesterday. Every since you married Harlynn it's been one disaster after another. Look at yourself Kateland! We are all petrified of going to your funeral!"

Harlynn stood in the doorway behind Sue as everyone stared at Kate. There was a lot of truth in what Sue was saying. Harlynn was the problem. He had changed everything about Kate, but no one had the guts to tell her to her face until that moment. No one had stood face to face with Kate admitting how scared they were of losing her.

"I don't call having two beautiful children a disaster! I don't call having someone who loves me and supports me a disaster. Don't you dare speak that way about my husband or my marriage again or you can get the hell out of my life. Harlynn has always been on your side and you trash him?"

"Well, excuse me for not wanting to go your funeral or see your children raised by someone else for a mother!"

"Moon Water I did. You can't pin everything bad that happens on Harlynn. You can't blame him for what some greedy CEO chooses to do along with his board. You always tell me how Harlynn loves me. And now you hate him?"

"Why do you hate me now?" Sue asked slowly.

"No one hates you, Sue. I'm trying not to break into a thousand pieces. I can't take the constant bickering with you. Every time I turn around you are going after me and I don't want to do it. Why are you going after Harlynn? He is my husband and don't you forget it, Sue."

"Why don't we end this, now?" Harlynn suggested looking at Kate. "It's been a hell of a month for everyone and we all need to step back and relax." Everyone watched as Sue left the room in tears.

Kate felt the tears come down her face as Harlynn came over to her. Keat looked at his sister taking in a deep breath. He rubbed her back then watched as Harlynn took her in his arms.

"I got the kids," Keat offered as Harlynn nodded his head.

For the next hour she cried, unable to stop. It was the idea of Harlynn not being there that haunted her. In a way, she felt like she was losing him even though he was right next to her. What she was realizing was that she couldn't be there for everyone like she had always done in the past. She always thought of Harlynn being spread thin, but it was her too. Between marriage, children, family, friends, art business and Moon Water, there was no time to think. She felt like she was suffocating as her chest tightened up.

"You're wheezing, dear heat," Harlynn told her quietly. "Do you have an inhaler with you?"

Kate nodded as he went into their vanity and came back out. He watched her as she used it then sat back in the pillows. He tried to relax, waiting to see if she would get worse or calm down.

"What was this about, Kate? You can't react to every word that comes out of Sue's mouth. She is scared about being married to your father and being shunned by everyone in this house. Can't you see that she needs you and doesn't want to lose you?"

"I can't handle anyone going after you like that. How about for once I need the support of the people around."

"Because of me?" Harlynn asked her. "You've been spending all your time trying to fix me and support me." Kate didn't answer the question as she stared off in space. "I think it's time we go to a marriage counselor."

"I will think on it. How does my neck look?" She asked Harlynn changing the subject. "It finally stopped stinging."

"Actually it looks better. Julia was calling someone to take an x-ray of it. She said she couldn't believe how you let her dig in it because most people would have to be under a general to do that. Next time, we will go to the hospital, love."

"Whatever. I've been through worse in my life." She let the smile fade looking into Harlynn's eyes. "Life has not been a disaster with you, please don't listen to Sue. I always think of our life together as exciting and full of love. I feel loved by you and I've never truly felt that from anyone else."

"Do you think you are shutting everyone out? I've heard that concern from everyone in the last couple of days." Silence filled the room. "What are you afraid of, Kateland?

"I don't want anyone to think negatively of you. I know all these parts of you and I see you with our children and I feel you hold me in your arms. I remember that night and I don't know what to think."

"Do you want me to stop drinking?" Harlynn asked her.

"I don't know the answer, Harlynn. We are creating a way to change the world and I think I'm overwhelmed."

"Me too. I'm going to make you a smoothie, and then you need to rest. I think what happened to you the day before yesterday finally caught up with you. Life will get better."

—

Kate watched a humming bird outside their window trying to fight off the other humming birds invading the feeder. She marveled at how they moved so quickly while changing directions and hovering in mid air. The brightly colored red streak on the male made him stand out among the others. Their wings and heart beat with such speed it made her dizzy.

There staring at the humming birds she found her answer to why her mind and her heart beat so fast. She needed to stop changing directions all the time. Part of the day was for the children that flowed into her art that flowed into Moon Water that flowed into Harlynn. She needed to let things flow instead of diving and changing directions every other minute of the day. She needed desperately to find balance and stop this chaos.

Henry came in the room with her smoothie and sat down on the floor with her. He leaned back stretching out his legs watching the humming birds with her. He didn't try to tell her not to worry or that life would get easier because that wasn't Henry.

"I think Sue was way out of line this morning and everyone knows it. Sam took her outside to talk." Kate watched as Henry smiled at her. In code that meant Sam totally lost it and everyone heard. "Considering everything that has happened between Moon Water, losing Harlynn's dad and having another child, you are fine. Harlynn is fine. Everyone needs to make adjustments to the changes. It takes time, sweetheart."

"Will you and Meg come to the ranch with us when you can?" Kate asked slowly. "I know how busy you are these days, Henry. It would be nice to have time with you both here with us and the children.

"Anytime. I think we all finally found a place that we can slow down and relax. Meg likes coming here and it makes her happy. Do I need to say more?" Kate giggled at him. "I was thinking I need an office next to our bedroom if that's not too much to ask."

"The designer is coming today. There are several things that must be changed if I'm to stay here."

"New plates? I will gladly pay for them if I need to. I cannot eat off black and purple plates all the time. Who the hell picked those out?" He watched as Kate went into her giggles. "Meg said if I showed up with new plates it might offend Harlynn or I would have."

"Harlynn's sister? Can you believe they're related?" She managed to finally say.

"He got an ugly call from her today. This morning she got her copy of the Will and boy is she pissed off."

"We saw it coming and I'm sure it has a lot to do with Janey being in the Will. And the fact Harlynn got more from their father."

"Well, I'm glad his father gave you both this ranch," Henry admitted. "Why don't you take a nap and I will come get you in an hour. No one will come in here, I promise sweetheart."

"I want to check on the children first." Kate stated firmly. "Are you going back tonight?"

"Yes. You two need some time together with the children. Plus, I have a deal that needs to be closed by the end of the quarter."

"Thank you for bringing me my smoothie." She told him as she crawled back into bed.

~Chapter 16

Three hours later, Levi was putting together a giant fire truck puzzle while Kate watched him logically figure out the corners and lines. He smiled at Kate when he was done, then they both cheered and danced. This was the flow she was looking for in her life. These moments she could spend with Levi doing puzzles or building or collecting bugs. She wanted him to always know that he came first.

Janey came in from horseback riding with Stan and Nick. Her smile radiated from her like sunshine. Kate loved the pink cowboy boots that she had on. They had been one of her impulse buys on line one night when she couldn't sleep and shopped. It was a form of therapy she decided and that was okay.

Immediately Janey and Levi were playing with the new wooden toy ranch and barn. Meg thought they had to have it was all she told Kate. Henry and Meg watched with pure joy as the children played with it. They loved to spoil her children with their love.

Kate went over to Laney who was very quiet today, which Kate didn't like. She was in a bad mood and her baby girl was never in a bad mood.

"Did Danny get up yet?" Kate asked as she walked into the kitchen.

"He borrowed some clothes from Nick and should be out in a moment. He didn't pack any jeans, isn't that strange for someone who is completely brilliant? What's wrong with Laney?" Elle asked concerned as she watched the infant.

"Ear infection?" Kate guessed. "Levi had several ear infections at this age. I was hoping that she wouldn't have to experience it. I have an interior designer coming this afternoon and would love your input if you have any ideas for the ranch." She handed Elle her two page list that she had put together.

"You have it covered from what I can see. I want to do a wall hanging for your room. I can envision the way the master room should look. Let me sketch it out for the designer." Elle offered taking a piece of Janey's art paper off the table as Kate watched her. Elle had a fantastic mind whether it was forensic accounting, a top world swimmer or an artist. She was known all over the world for these beautiful wall hangings she created. Kate loved that she had that mix of business and art inside her head. "And I'm sorry that Sue freaked out and you guys got in a fight. I don't think Nick's parents like me." Elle fought back the tears. Laney started to cry when she saw Elle crying.

"What's wrong?" Danny asked as he came in the room trying to figure out the connection between Laney and Elle cry at the same split second.

"I think Laney has an ear infection." Kate repeated to him. "Could you look at her?"

"Sure." Laney screamed louder because she didn't want to leave her mother. "You should keep her and I will be back with my bag from the bedroom. She was due for an ear infection if I remember the problems that Levi had, Kate."

Elle managed to stop crying as she went back to finish the sketch between sniffles. Everyone watched as Blacky came in the kitchen. He opened a coke and drank it in one swig. He stopped, glancing at Kate with Laney screaming inconsolably as she tried to calm her down. The bad mood became more apparent as he opened a second coke and grabbed a blueberry muffin. Elle froze when he sat down at the table with them. He gently took Laney from Kate as the child stopped crying.

"She needs some Tylenol; she has two teeth coming in, which probably caused the ear infection. The same thing used to happen with Nick every time he got a new tooth." Blacky let the child gnaw on his finger as she stared at him as if to say 'thank you for your finger'. "Elle, Julia and I would like to understand why this wedding is being expedited at such speed. Why don't you see if you can find Nick? We have a lot to discuss if this wedding is going to happen in a month."

Kate watched as Elle left the room completely defeated. She started cleaning up the breakfast plates in hopes of escaping anymore conflicts for the morning.

"Can you please sit down?" Blacky asked her frustrated with life. "There were two people on this ranch. Charlie found your Blackberry on his run this morning. It hadn't been tampered with and actually still works."

"It's never going to be over, is it?"

"I think I'll be staying while you two are here. Julia wants to go to Houston to help with the wedding. My wife is not happy, which is a very bad thing, Kate. You can't imagine what it's like when Julia is pissed off and she is royally pissed off about his sudden wedding."

"First, we are talking about a thirty- four year old man. Why aren't you happy for the wedding?" Kate blasted him.

"It's too fast for a marriage that is going to last. They have been dating five months, Kateland. Nick needs to be focused on his responsibilities at Moon Water and give this relationship time. Elle is beautiful, smart and caring, that doesn't mean it will be successful. We are talking about my son and I don't give a shit how old he is because this is my family. You can't understand what it's like to watch your child make mistakes with his life that will hurt him."

"I don't think Nick is making a mistake and he had the best role models in the world for what a marriage should be as far as I'm concerned. He knows what he is doing with his life Blacky, don't undermine him. Nick is brilliant like you, Blacky. And if there was another reason, would you be angry or happy to have a grandchild? You had to think of that Blacky. You have to know."

"Surprised." Blacky said quietly. "Do you know how many times I've talked to him about being careful and using his brain when it comes to women? The guy has everything going for him, and now this?"

"Too much champagne one evening and it happened. Jack we've all been there before. What's the difference in age between your two sons?"

"Like you and Harlynn didn't do the same thing? And we were married. The key word being married before you have children because that is how Nick was raised. Do they really love each other Kateland?"

"I think so. Harlynn thinks so. You've seen them together, Blacky. You are the expert in human behavior. They are both such

Weekend Cowboy

good people, Jack. I think you should be thankful that Nick found Elle because it's not Shelly."

"And how far along is she? I know she stays at his place all the time."

"If it makes you feel better they didn't just jump in bed. They waited. I think if you count back to your birthday celebration, you will know." It had been a great party. "You have to be happy for them Blacky, Nick needs you to be happy for him. What you think means everything to him."

"I'm thrilled with Elle and she is good for him. This child is going to be beautiful and athletic, to say the least. You're right, we should be happy for our son." He finished his coke. "How are you?"

"I'm trying to find my way in the mist of being completely lost and confused. You know any good marriage counselors?"

"You don't need a marriage counselor, Kate. I think you need a break from everyone, including your friend, Sue. And Harlynn needs to find his way is all and he will. His father was someone who Harlynn had in his corner all his life. He is in tremendous pain that no one can fix. I only want to protect you, Kateland."

"I know. I'm glad you're staying because it helps me feel secure. We should discuss some numbers I ran tomorrow." She spoke with a wry smile.

"I have a report that came out of the President's Chief Councils office yesterday. We will go over it tomorrow and see what you think. Change is hard, Kateland."

As Blacky finished eating, Danny checked Laney's ears and yes, there was an ear infection. It was nice having Danny here to help take care of her children. Danny was becoming part of her family and she wondered if he knew.

—

There was something going on as both chefs were cooking up a storm in the kitchen and the housekeepers were setting a long table outside. There were flowers delivered and all she could think was Meg. Meg was up to something as she swung on the swing with Laney in her arms. She and Laney had taken another nap together. Things seemed clearer to her with the extra rest from this morning.

Harlynn came riding up to the house with the boys (Keaton, Nick, Blacky and Henry). They all looked so fearless in their chaps and work shirts with bandanas on. If only she had a camera to take a picture. It made her smile as they walked up to the house. She had sent him a text that she needed help with the designer showing up. There were only two people in the whole world that Laney would allow to hold her. It was either Kate or Harlynn and that was what her little princess demanded and got. It felt good to be needed by this child Kate, realized.

"You look better." Harlynn whispered to her as he leaned over. "How is she doing?"

"Better. I think the antibiotics are kicking in along with the ear drops. You want to change your shirt before you take her and say hello to the other two if they haven't fallen asleep watching 'Word Girl'? They are both exhausted from riding all morning."

"That's probably a good idea." He took one of the ice teas that the house keeper set down on the table. Kate watched as Nick and his father walked up together from riding. She watched as the two men smiled and laughed. They were happy was all Kate could think.

"Hey gorgeous, how is she?" Nick wrinkled his eye brows at her concerned as Blacky gently patted her on the back and went inside.

"We are doing better. How are things in your world?"

"We are doing better, also. Thank you for talking to my father this morning. It helped more than you realize." He waited. "You have a way to make people always see the good."

"Blacky doesn't like surprises. I think Elle and the baby were a surprise. He was caught off guard and didn't understand."

"He was worried I didn't love her. I love her so much I can't stand it," Nick confessed. "I'm nervous about going to see Carr? I'm making my mom come with me because you know he is going to give me hell. Do you think we should move the wedding up?"

"Yes. Why don't you talk to Elle and get back to me. We can make anything happen. Hell we could do it next weekend if you want to?" She smiled at him. "You know that I would do anything for you, Nicky. I'm very excited that this is working out with you and Elle. She is such a fabulous person. Freaky family, but we all have our flaws."

"I like her mom a lot and her brother. Her father is such a jerk, I can't stand him. Elle feels terrible, which is hard to watch. I've had the ring for a couple of weeks anyway." He peered into Kate's eyes. "I'm worried about this baby though, we both know there are at least a million things that can go wrong. You know we haven't done any genetic screening or blood work."

"You have to believe, Nick. You have to ask God for a healthy baby and pray like you've never prayed before." She looked at Laney and kissed her head.

"If it's a girl we are going to name her Kateland after you and call her Kat for short."

"Nick that is the sweetest thing I think I've ever had anyone do for me. I'm completely honored. And I will give you an out if you want to change your mind. A name is a very import thing."

"You are a very important person." Nick smiled walking away.

Kate closed her eyes imagining how wonderful it was going to be for Laney to have a little friend. In her heart, she wished it was her brother who was getting married and having a child. She wanted Keat to have someone in his life to share, well, everything. It must be lonely for him with her and Harlynn and now Nick with Elle. It made her heart ache in a way because he had such a wonderful soul. It made her feel guilty for all the things Keat had given up for her.

When Kate opened her eyes, Sue and her father were standing there. Kate wanted to laugh then decided it might be better to just sweetly smile, which everyone who knew her meant go straight to hell. She waited because she was not going to say one word without a big fat apology from Sue.

"I'm sorry for yelling at you this morning and making a scene." Sue apologized. "I will try to be more understanding of what is going on with you. You do not have to give us a wedding shower."

"I want to give you a wedding shower, Sue. It's already in the planning stages: the cake, invitations, and flowers are booked. We are waiting for conformation on the photographer. You need to understand it's strange for Keat and me to see my father with a new wife. I don't care if it was you or anyone else, it would be strange and I have to get used to it. I do appreciate you being there for me and the children.

You are still my best friend no matter who you are married to or who I'm married to."

"See, I told you." Her father put his arms around Sue much the way he would her mother at one point in time. It was strange to see him so affectionate with Sue. The love was there the way he touched her. "No more fighting." Sam lightly scolded both of them.

"Agreed." Kate watched as Laney wiggled on her. "She feels warm." Kate felt her head, again with her other hand. "Sue could you get me the Tylenol on the cupboard."

Kate's dad felt the baby's back and frowned at her, worried. Her father sat down on the swing, carefully taking the baby from his daughter, giving her arms a rest.

"I think both my arms are numb from holding her for the past three hours. You hold her for the next hour that will keep you from thinking of more children."

"I told Sue I would marry her in a second on one condition: we were not having children."

"I'll get off your case." Kate told him trying not to smile. "We need to have a meeting when everyone is back. We need you to take over the Woodlands lab, Dad. Are you up for that?"

"I told both you and Harlynn I'm happy to do whatever you want at Moon Water. You two need a break from this crazy life you have been living. I'm ready to get back in the action."

"This is a very different fear then I'm use to dealing with Dad. Janey's health or her mother showing up is one type of fear. Doing deals with Harlynn and Henry can be stressful. Now, there are moments I question everything and I wonder if the cost outweighs the benefits for this drug. We are creating this new model for research that will change the world, even though that was never my intention. Do I want to change the world at the risk of losing someone in this house?"

"If God gives you the chance to cure a form of pediatric cancer, Kateland, you damn well better do it with these technologies. You know what these families go through, honey. It's the bravest thing I've ever seen anyone do, Kateland."

"I don't want to die, Sam. I can't leave these children and Harlynn."

"Blacky is not going to let that happen, nor will Harlynn, Keaton,

Nick, Henry or I. If you let the fear consume you, you won't be able to move forward." He watched Laney. "Think of all the wonderful things that have happen to you, Kateland. Look at this child that I'm holding."

"As long as I know that you are there to help me. I do need you, Dad. You have always been the best sounding board for when I'm stuck. And I appreciate you being here with us during this time. I'm sorry for blowing up at Sue today."

"I think if I were you, I would have blown up also. Just because she is married to one of your fathers doesn't give her a free ticket. It's going to take time for everyone to get use to us being married, including Sue and I." He laughed. "I'm happy for the first time in my life, Kateland."

"And Harlynn and I want you to have happiness and I really hope that you have found it with Sue. You also have to understand that it's pretty damn weird for Keaton and I still. I wish you hadn't gone to Las Vegas to get married."

"I think it was easier on everyone," He told her quietly. "I never meant to hurt you or anyone else."

"I think we need to have a party to celebrate. I still need your list of names if you want this party to happen."

"You make me very proud, Kateland." He carefully gave Laney back to her. "I'm going to go find that Tylenol before she starts wailing and a bottle."

As Laney started to wail Harlynn appeared looking flustered as he gave her the Tylenol and then let her have the bottle. Kate closed her eyes listening to Harlynn talk to his daughter. He whispered to her in his enchanting voice.

"I remember when you would use that voice on me and I would melt." Kate watched as he blushed. "What do you remember?"

"I remember how every time you walked into my office my heart would race and my knees would get weak. It took every ounce of energy just to focus." He paced with the child slowly. "Sorry I took so long. This nurse from George's office called to increase my allergy medicine. She said her name was Gwen. I didn't realize George had someone new working for him."

"He is pretty busy with the family and his research these days. "

175

She closed her eyes listening to the silence of the afternoon. "Are you going to tell me what is going on?"

"I'm not allowed." Harlynn smiled at her. "Meg will kill me."

"I think it must be a surprise of some sort." Kate winked at him. "I guess I should get cleaned up for this designer who is coming. I'm sort of ticked since the person who was supposed to come had to cancel. They are sending 'Christa' who started today. Damn, I forgot to tell, Blacky. "

"I seriously doubt the interior designer is a security threat." Harlynn chuckled to himself. "Please hire her to work for us if she is any good. We have the houses to do in Utah and we have never gotten around to the house in Houston, plus if Nick buys this place on the next block he will need help. We could keep her busy for the next couple of years with projects. We need someone to manage all the places. I want to make one phone call to check on all the properties and get one email a week with updates. And I want one monthly statement on costs for all these places."

"Let's meet her first before we make her an offer." Kate suggested. As she walked by Harlynn he stood up in front of her and kissed her.

"Do you know how much I love you?" he asked her in his enchanting voice. "I can't stand seeing you like you were this morning? You are beautiful and I can't imagine spending my life with anyone else, no matter what happens, do you understand me? I appreciate you defending me like you did. I appreciate how you love me more than you will ever know."

"It's gonna be bumpy for a while?" She told him quietly. "Can you deal with it Mr. Barrett?"

"Yes." He told her as he kissed her again. "Can you handle that I want a different life?"

"You are my weekend cowboy, searching for a better life and escaping that city life."

"I feel better when I'm away from the city, especially when I'm with you and the children."

"Let's take it slow and see what happens." She searched his eyes seeing the pain that was there. He hadn't said one word about missing his father. This was the longest he had probably gone without talking to him in his whole life. "You know that I am here to talk about your father, Harlynn."

"I thought I heard him call my name when I was out riding today. I was looking at the fence on south part, seeing if we needed to replace it because Ray wants to. There was this dry wind and I heard him. Is that crazy?"

"No more crazy than waking up in a tepee with an eighty year old Indian staring at me."

"I keep getting this feeling he left something here for me. The last two days before he passed he kept trying to talk to me. I think he was telling me I need to write Levi."

"We will figure it out." She kissed Laney watching her smile as she drank her bottle. It was good to see her smile was all Kate could think. "Take care of our angel."

"I will." He promised. "Don't be shocked if Emma shows up. I've gotten several outrageous calls from her this morning."

"Expected. She is going to make an ass out of herself, Harlynn."

"Yep. Just like my father said she would. Expected."

~Chapter 17

As soon as Kate opened the door she was wowed by Christa Grant who stood five six' with a body that could model and long red hair pulled loosely into ponytail. She had navy blue eyes and a radiant smile. She was stunning and Kate guessed maybe thirty. Her long flowing navy Missoni dress and buff Via Spiga shoes told Kate a lot. She had an immaculate pedicure, light on the jewelry and the large aqua marine ring was amazing.

"Hi, I'm Christa," she announced with confidence and a graciousness that was inviting. "I hope you don't mind that I came today, but Alex quit. I could make up some story to cover for the owner. I don't like to lie to people. Apparently the owner of the place is impossible and I'm not sure if I will stay."

"Let's have a glass of champagne." Kate offered her as they walked into the living room. Christa's eyes went around the room as she smiled.

"I can see the problem with the colors in this room and the couch. There is no flow here for you." She sat down as one of the housekeepers brought in the champagne along with fruit and cheese. "This is exquisite champagne. As I was saying, I felt I should come out and see what you need. I believe in being honest, which can be a conflict in this business. If I don't like what you want to do, I will tell you. If I think the fabric looks like crap you are in love with, I will tell you. I'm not interested in running up my hours or overcharging you."

"How did you get into the business?" Kate asked intrigued by the character of this individual. It was completely refreshing to encounter a new person who was honest and sparkled. Christa sparkled much the way her brother did Kate decided.

"My father is an architect and my mother is an interior designer. I was brainwashed at an early age that this was my destiny. Actually, music would be my true calling if I had a true calling. This is my day job and I play in a band twice a week."

"What do you play?" Kate asked with a smile.

"I sing and play guitar," she said in a matter of fact way. "And the piano. And the drums."

As they chatted Levi came to visit as well as Janey then Laney and Harlynn. Elle came by with Nick to meet Christa. Elle wanted to show her thoughts on the room for Kate and Harlynn. As the two women chatted Nick leaned over to Kate.

"Keat needs to meet her," he whispered in her ear. "They are going to hit it off."

Kate nodded in agreement with the expression that resembled Christmas morning.

Basically everyone in the house came to ask Kate a question or if she needed anything.

"This is what I think, Christa. Would you like to work for my family?"

"I'm interested." She replied, trying to mask her excitement. "What would be the job description?"

"Decorating and managing several properties in Austin, New York, Utah and Houston. Of course I will have to do a background check on you for security reasons." Christa immediately pulled out a detailed resume of her work history and education, along with references that included family and friends. Kate glanced at it going over dates and places. "This is impressive." She immediately noticed a gap. Christa had taken a large amount of time off in the last year. Basically she was starting back to work from what it looked liked.

"That sounds like an interesting challenge." Christa paused. "I would like to understand exactly what you need. And meet everyone who I would be working in the family."

"Six figures and expenses paid." Kate waited as Christa considered it. "Phone and computers will be taken care of along with health insurance." Kate handed her a number as Christa agreed. She figured she could start her at a hundred and ten, and then give her a raise in a month when she understood how demanding the job was going to be.

"I'm very interested. Let's start with this ranch today." Christa took out her notepad ready to work with a broad smile on her face and a look of determination.

"Who is this?" Blacky asked surprised because he had spent the morning riding with Julia. Immediately he got the annoyed look in his eyes as he took a deep breath. Kate knew the look that meant you didn't tell me this person was coming to the ranch, Kateland.

"Christa Grant, Mr. Black." She introduced herself in the same confident manner. "My brother worked for you for five years until he was sent to Africa."

"Jeff . . . Jeff Grant? Of course he spoke about you, Christa." Blacky eyes darted around the room. "Is he still listed as missing?"

"He died in Africa or at least that's what they told us." She blinked several times. "He always spoke with such admiration about you. It's an honor to meet you. Thank you for being his mentor over the years. He always looked up to you."

"Thank you, it's very nice to finally meet you, Christa." Blacky walked out of the room already dialing his Blackberry.

Kate didn't know what to say and for a moment she was hit with pure panic at the person in front of her because she had seen it in Blacky's eyes. He was completely freaked out over this one.

"Was I out of line?" Christa asked slowly.

"Do you know who I am?" Kate asked slowly?

"Yes?" Christa said with the same confidence. "And I know who Harlynn Barrett, Henry Grayden and Nick Black are also."

"Why do you know this?" Kate asked slowly as they stood in a room that would be a playroom.

"You were on television and in the papers for the last week with your husband's father dying. How could someone with half a brain not know who you are, Kate?" She replied. "Do you know how famous you are, Kate?"

"I like to pretend that I'm not for my children's sake."

"Oh, that looked bad because I knew who Jack Black was, didn't it?"

"It was unexpected." Kate waited as they walked into the next room.

"My brother had a picture with Mr. Black from Quantico. He won an award and Mr. Black presented it to him. It's one of my favorite pictures of him. Anyway, he died for this country doing what he loved to do."

"Are you upset that he died doing what he loved to do? Are you angry?"

"I'm very proud of him for believing in what this country stands for, Kate. He saved people doing what he did. He prevented another terrorist attack in this country. He was a hero who saved thousands of people from being killed. It's an honor to meet Mr. Black for all the things he has done. My God, it's equivalent to meeting the President of the United States."

Kate smiled as they walked upstairs to Keat's room. Blacky was not going to like Christa working for them or maybe he would. Kate hoped that Blacky liked her since Kate was taken by this dynamic individual.

"This is my brother's room, Keaton. He wants shades of gray with lime green accents. He needs some office space in here, but nothing overwhelming. He will also require a place for his IPod and IPad." Kate turned slowly as Keaton came out of the bathroom with the music blaring and a towel barely wrapped around him exposing his near perfect abs and muscular legs along with his curly wet hair and the green eyes that matched Kate's. And finally there was the radiant smile that could melt any women's heart.

"Hi." Keaton walked over to his closet getting his clothes and went back into the bathroom. He didn't stumble over his words or pause as he kept moving in a way only her brother could do.

"He is gorgeous." Christa blurted out. "Is that your brother, Keaton? Of course it's your brother. I saw him on television with more clothes on. The nakedness threw me to a degree."

A moment later Keaton came out dressed with his hair slicked back. He had on black jeans that fit him nicely along with a white starched shirt. He walked over to the dresser picking up his watch and Blackberry glancing at the messages.

"You must be Christa?" He smiled slowly as he peered into her eyes. "I'm sure Kate has told you I'm her brother Keaton and I apologize for not being dressed earlier. We are about to have a late lunch if you would like to join us." Keat tried to be very cool and nonchalant with the invitation.

"No one told me we were having a lunch today." Kate

commented to her brother.

"It's for you." Keat confessed to his sister. "We always have one big meal together before everyone takes off. I think I might stay a couple more days."

"It would be wonderful to have that time with you."

They waited to see whether Christa would stay or not. Christa was busy making notes and measuring the room. She was oblivious to the brother and sister as they watched her.

"Yes." She finally looked up from her note pad. "I would like to join you for lunch on one condition."

"Name it?" Keat said leaning back on the dresser.

"I need a shot of tequila if I'm going to have dinner with the people who are going to be sitting at this table. This doesn't happen to normal people and I'm getting nervous."

"We have lots of Patron." Kate explained thinking what guts she had to be this open and honest.

"I like Patron." Christa smiled. "I have to ask, in order that I don't make a complete ass out of myself: do you have a girlfriend?" She turned towards Keaton.

"No, I'm not seeing anyone." Keat replied firmly. "Are you seeing anyone?"

"No. I'm completely single." Christa explained closing her eyes. "I've had a lot going on with losing my brother. I think it's time to start looking."

"I think it's time too," he told her staring into her eyes.

"Sounds like a date." Kate commented, walking ahead of them. She closed her eyes and said a prayer. If it was meant to be it would be.

—

When Kate got to their room to change there was a beautiful Tory Burch tunic waiting for her to put on that was fuchsia pink with matching sandals. She put on the bracelet that Harlynn had given her and it looked stunning with the pink diamond ring. She pulled her hair back in a large barrette and put on some makeup, something she hadn't done in days. She even put on some of Harlynn's favorite perfume.

The nursery was empty as Kate walked down the hall to the living room that was also empty and finally to the kitchen where she could see everyone outside as though they were waiting for her.

There were beautiful flowers in shades of every color of pink and white along with candles. The long table was covered with white linens and pink napkins. There were place cards that were delicately written by hand. Everyone looked at her slowly, watching her. It was Meg who spoke.

"Kateland, you mean so much to this family that we wanted to have a lunch in your honor. You seem to always be able to hold us altogether and you bring endless joy to all our lives. Thank you for being the daughter that Henry and I never had the chance to have and for sharing your children with us," Everyone raised their champagne glasses to her and it kept going whether it was Stan talking about how God had brought Kate into their lives and saved Janey or her father speaking about how proud he was to have her as a daughter or Keaton telling her that there were no words to describe how much she meant to him or any way to measure his love for her.

Blacky and Julia confessed that Kate and Keaton were really their children that they didn't have time to conceive because Blacky was never home. Everyone laughed as he waited to continue. "There is a pure love and strength that comes from Kate. I would like to be able to emulate her ways one day." Blacky concluded as his voice cracked. "We will always love you and your wonderful family. Thank you for letting us be a part of it."

And finally, Harlynn spoke in his eloquent manner as always. "As I stand before you I search for the words to describe what it's like to feel the love I share with Kateland. It is the most powerful thing I have ever experienced in my life. To have her as my wife, mother of our children and business partner makes me savior each day. I prayed for a long time before Kate came into my life and I thank God each day. She is my world." Kate wiped away the tears as Harlynn went to her.

The idea he would confess his love for her in front of all these people moved her as did it everyone else. The stoic side of him had disappeared for a brief moment. Again he was in pain because she knew that he wanted his father there to share this moment with him.

"Thank you." She whispered to him as he held her.

"Thank you." He smiled at her. "Can you hold Laney? I have to go take my allergy medicine, again. I swear this stuff is not working even though that nurse told me to take more. I'll be back in five minutes."

"Take some Benadryl with it. I will send George a text to see if he can see you when we get back. I can get him to call in something else in the mean time." She did feel bad for him because he didn't need to be outside all afternoon.

It was a perfect afternoon as everyone sat talking, eating and drinking. Not once did anyone look at their Blackberry or watches. They embraced this time together and knew how special it was to sit with one another. Kate watched as Laney slept in Harlynn's arms and Levi sat with Keaton. Janey hung on to Henry while they ate dessert and talked. She watched how all their lives had changed over the last two years and they were all good changes in spite of all the bad, it was good to be sitting here with these people she loved. She watched how Christa was talking to Elle and they were sketching things on one of Janey's drawing pads.

"How are you doing?" Blacky smiled at her pulling up a chair next to her.

"I don't want to forget moments like this. I call them spots. These spots are what get us through life I think."

Blacky closed his eyes slowly reflecting on Kate's words and smiled a real smile. He leaned closer to her so no one could hear what they were saying to each other.

"Jeff Grant was one of the most outstanding individuals I have ever trained and worked with in my career. I know you saw how startled I was today by her being here. Christa is fine and I think if you want to hire her that will be good." He waited. "I think if Keaton and her want to spend time together that's good too." He smiled glancing at Keaton and Christa playing with Levi. "Keaton looks very smitten, which is good. I don't want you to worry, okay."

"For a moment I was completely panicked and expected you to pull out a gun or something. I figured when you didn't boot her ass out of here after two minutes it would be okay. I'm sorry I didn't tell you that she was coming. I know we have to be careful with anyone who comes into the house. Perhaps I was being rebellious, again." She watched as Blacky laughed at her for a good while. "How are you doing?"

"Better. Julia and I spent a long time talking today about what you said to me. Henry always talks about how wise you are Kateland, and he is right. I think you're rocky childhood with your mother gives you a very different view on people and relationships. Nick is very happy with Elle. I guess after Shelly I was afraid he didn't know what he was doing with his life. Thank God you got him away from her." He calmly looked around the table. "How is Harlynn doing?"

"Well, his allergies are killing him even though he is taking all sorts of medication. The poor guy cannot catch a break. My gut tells me he is putting on an act for everyone. And I'm worried because today I found these boxes of letters that his father wrote him since the day he was born. It's stunning, Blacky."

" Kate, that's incredible. And Harlynn has no idea?"

"No. I'm going to give them to him tomorrow. I didn't want everyone to be around in case . . . he loses it. I can see him with a bottle of scotch when he starts reading them. It's good you and Keaton will be here."

"We'll get him through this, Kate." Blacky leaned over and gave her a hug. It was very unlike him to be affectionate as Nick stared at them.

"I think we need some music." Blacky announced as he looked over at Henry and Keaton who followed him in the house and came out with Kate's guitar and four others. Kate watched as the five men sat down and started to play. For the next thirty minutes they sat there playing different songs that had special meaning to her. It was like each of them had picked out a couple songs to play for her. She was completely touched by the gesture. This party had been planned for a while, apparently. Meg came over and cradled Kate while she held Laney. Levi and Janey danced up a storm.

"Thank you for doing this for me Meg. I truly don't know if I deserve to be treated this way."

"You do. I don't know if you will ever understand how you touch the lives of the people here Kateland. We would do anything for you."

She gave Kate one more hug before going to dance with Janey and Levi.

When they took a break Christa walked over and picked up a guitar. She strummed a few chords.

"Why don't you play?" Kate asked her with a warm smile.

"I think this is a family affair." She whispered back embarrassed. "This is your party."

"I want to hear you play." Kate requested. "Then you will see how well you fit in this group and I believe that nothing happens by accident, Christa. This morning Keat and I were talking, we asked God to bring someone into his life that would bring him happiness. As crazy as this may sound, I think you might be that person."

"I have been asking for the same thing, for a person to love and a family to be loved by. I don't know anyone else looking for the same thing."

"I always say that it doesn't matter what you have done in your life if you don't have anyone to share it with."

Kate went inside to give Laney some Tylenol and see if she would sleep in her bed since she had been held for nine hours straight. As she changed her and put a soft sleeper on her, Danny came in to check on her.

"How is she doing?" Danny asked over Kate's shoulder.

"I don't know? It's a bit of a puzzle to be honest," Kate told him. "I thought she was improving."

"I didn't want to tell you before Kate, there is a lot of fluid in her ears. She might need tubes if it won't clear up. We need to keep a close eye on her."

"This is very bad." Kate whispered. "Should we go back to Houston?"

"No. I think you need to try the antibiotics until Monday unless she gets worse. I will come by the house when you get home to see what she needs." He promised in a voice that was hypnotic. "What's going on with you and Harlynn? You two have hardly said a word to each other all afternoon since he made that beautiful speech. Are you two in a fight?"

"I don't know." She responded, hoping no one else noticed. "Why do you ask?"

"Harlynn doesn't seem himself. I know his father died and all the other problems with Moon Water are weighing on him. This isn't the first time I've seen mood swings in the last couple of months." Danny stammered, hesitating to go on.

"What happened?" Kate could feel her heart begin to race.

"Is he taking drugs? I talked to him five minutes ago and he was acting very strange? He said he knew I wanted to date you." Kate was mortified as she stared at Danny shaking her head.

"I appreciate you asking me, Danny. I need a friend to be honest with you. It's very complicated what is going on and I don't understand it. Why don't we go to lunch on Tuesday? Please ignore what he said to you. I apologize."

"Tuesday works for me." Danny forced a weak smile. "Why don't you go back out and I will stay with her for a while. If I remember correctly, she can be rocked to sleep?" Kate nodded her head.

Christa had this beautiful blues voice as she played with such passion everyone stared in awe. She was playing songs that no one had heard that she must have written herself. They were country songs with a little twang and rock-n-roll mixed together.

Keat came over and sat down next to Kate as Christa played another song. He looked truly happy was all she could think. He had hope again, Kate decided.

"Don't sleep with her tonight." Kate suggested.

"How about I won't have sex with her tonight, but I will make out with her all night long?" Keat responded. "How could this person walk into my life that I have been looking for years?" He was completely baffled by what had transpired.

"God doesn't work on our time line, dear brother. He works on his. Just take it slow with her. How is this going to work if she is working for us and you are dating her? I don't want some sexually harassment suit, brother dearest."

"Henry already spoke to me about it. He said I had that look in my eye that I was going to marry her." Kate nodded in agreement. "She has to work for you and Harlynn, but not me." He peered into her eyes. "What are you worried about Kitty Kat?"

She told him about the letters waiting to see what he thought. Now Keaton had the same worried look in his eyes.

"Where are they?" Keat asked slowly.

"In the room next to yours. I don't even know why I went in there to be honest. I want to turn it into a play room so we don't have toys all over the place and I opened the closet, which is like a secret room. I noticed all these boxes with Harlynn's name on them. You know this is going to be more than he can handle."

"After everyone leaves we are taking him up there and giving them to him. Kate, you have to give them to him as soon as possible."

"He is going to be upset I waited to tell him." She explained with fear.

"Or he could be grateful that you found them. Maybe it will help him heal to read his father's words." Keat smiled as Christa stopped playing and put the guitar down. She had put the men to shame and no one cared.

—

Around nine everyone left for Houston except half the bodyguards, one chef, the house keepers, Keat and Blacky. Kate walked through the house thinking how strange it was that it had been so busy for days, but now it was quiet and peaceful. She laughed at the guitars that were now hung up on the wall in the den to keep them out of Levi's hands. They were a gift from Henry and Meg, of course.

Harlynn was in the office when Kate found him. He was reading over an article he had written for the *Wall Street Journal*. It was a follow up to the information that had been released on Star with a more detailed explanation of the events. He handed it to Kate to look over as she made a grimace.

"What's wrong?" Harlynn asked leaning back in his chair looking tired from the party.

"Nothing. It's great." She didn't want to explain to him that it would just bring more attention to them, which she didn't want right now. "Danny said that Laney may need tubes for her ears when we get back to Houston."

"You didn't mention that this morning. Why didn't you tell me?"

He seemed surprised.

"He told me the infection is substantial after the party. He is keeping an eye on her."

"What else?" That was Harlynn's way of nicely saying that he had work to do and didn't have time for chit chatting. They would talk later when he had time.

"Why didn't you talk to me all afternoon at the party?"

"I talked to you at the party." She was agitating him.

"What are upset about, Harlynn."

"I feel like every damn time I turn around you are talking to Henry or Blacky or Sam about me. I hate all these people involved in our relationship. I have asked you not to discuss me with them." His voice was razor sharp and his eyes were filled with fury.

"Blacky asked how you were doing at lunch. They care about you, Harlynn." Kate snapped back at him. "They love you. Your father just died and everyone is worried sick about you because they know how much he meant to you."

"I think at times they don't want me married to you." Harlynn said with the same sharpness. She looked at the glass of scotch on his desk.

"Well, it's a little late for that, isn't it?" Then she threw a stack of letters at him.

"What else?" He asked as he glanced at the letters and stopped.

"Nothing. Absolutely nothing." She got up and left the office slamming the door. She didn't work for him anymore. She was not his associate or partner at the law firm.

—

After Kate checked on the children she changed into her soft jeans. She needed a lot of Patron and her guitar. Blacky looked up from the book he was reading on the couch as she walked by.

"You want some company?" He asked as she went by.

"Nope. I'm good." Kate mumbled as she went out the door. As she started the fire in the fire pit she saw her favorite bodyguard walk up with a smile.

"I was told to keep you company and out of trouble," Charlie confessed, quietly.

"You are off duty." Kate reminded him. "Go get some sleep before you pass out."

"Actually, I got to sleep all afternoon. Blacky is giving me extra time off to recover from getting the hell beat out of me. I know I haven't told you Kateland, but I'm so thankful you and Harlynn are alive. I deeply appreciate this opportunity to work for you and your family." He watched as she picked up the guitar and started to play. "There is only one person who can hurt you that I know. You want to talk?"

"I'm trying to be understanding." Kate stopped taking a long sip of Patron. "You know I keep trying to figure out what I did wrong today."

"You didn't do anything wrong, Kateland." Charlie whispered to her as he sent a text to Blacky to find Harlynn.

"Well if you saw how he looked at me ten minutes ago you would think I had been horrible. Probably waiting to redecorate the ranch would have been a good idea I suppose. I'm only trying to make it more livable. Is that a crime?"

"I hate those plates. They are the ugliest plates I have ever seen in my life," Charlie told her as Kate almost fell off the bench.

"And the couch?" He nodded in agreement.

"Please, I had a better couch in college."

Kate started to play the guitar and sing. Maybe it was the tequila or maybe she figured that Charlie had seen her at her best and worst, so it didn't matter. She was singing *Summer Time* when suddenly Harlynn appeared and he was furious. Kate stopped playing.

"What the hell is going on out here?" Harlynn yelled at both of them as Charlie stood up immediately.

Kate had heard that tone in his voice once before. The tone like that night he went after her at their house. It was apparently about to happen again, on a ranch in the middle of nowhere. Kate put down the guitar wondering if she should run.

"Kateland I said what the hell is going on?" When she didn't answer Harlynn picked up the guitar and smashed it.

Slowly, Kate moved her eyes to Charlie for help. Her heart was racing and she could feel her lungs tighten up. She watched as Charlie stood in front of her, which would give her a head start. Where could she run that Harlynn couldn't find her?

"Kate, get out of here, now!" Charlie told her.

"Are you sleeping with Charlie? Do you have a thing for him? I thought it was only Nick and the good doctor?" Harlynn yelled at her.

"Stop it, Harlynn." Kate stared him down.

"You want a divorce? You get the house in Houston and I take the ranch. You can have Laney and I get Levi! We are done. I'm not going to be looking over my shoulder, always wondering who the fuck you have been with, Kateland. I will not do it again!"

"Back off Harlynn!" Blacky yelled at him. "I don't know what the hell is going on with you. We both know that Kate would never screw around on you!"

As Kate tried to walk away Harlynn grabbed her by the arm as she fell to the ground hitting her head. Finally Kate got off the ground and started running. She could still hear Blacky in the background.

"What are you on Harlynn?" Blacky asked as he pinned him to the ground. "What did you take?" Harlynn continued to try to get up as Blacky pinned him down harder with all his weight. "Harlynn if you keep fighting me I'm going to press on this artery in your neck and you will pass out. Then I'm going to handcuff your ass, do you understand me!" Blacky yelled at him. "Charlie go look in the office and their bedroom to see if you can find out what he took because this is not the Harlynn Barrett that I know."

She wasn't going to cry anymore because it wouldn't do any good. What if Blacky hadn't stayed she thought to herself? What would he have done to her?

"Kate, what is going on?" Keaton asked her in a panic. "You are bleeding! What the hell happened to you?"

"Harlynn," was all she said as she pointed in the direction the yelling was coming from. "I can't do this. I love him, but I can't do this."

—

The silence filled the room as Charlie cleaned off the wound on the side of her head above her ear while Keat got the first aid box. There was nothing to say that could change what had happened. There was no way to erase the events that occurred seventeen minutes ago.

"You need stitches." Keat finally told her.

"No kidding." She was in a daze as she looked in the mirror. It had been such a perfect afternoon, but now her life was a mess, a complete and utter mess.

"I'm going to check on the children and try to explain what the fuck just happened to Christa. Then we will get you to a hospital," Keat told her.

"I need to pack," she told him slowly.

Kate was still packing upstairs when Blacky came in the room and closed the door. She kept moving because she would never come back to this ranch. Everyone knew how strong Harlynn was, he could break Kate in half without trying.

"Let me see your head," he told as she sat down on the bed. "Yep, Keat was right about the stitches." He waited. "Do you know why Harlynn was taking these pills?" Blacky asked Kate as she looked at them.

"Allergies. He has really bad sinus problems this time of year with elm pollen. George's nurse, Gwen, called him this morning and told him to double the dosage. I know he took them at least twice today during the party. He started taking them about a month before Lane was born."

"George doesn't have anyone who works for him by the name of Gwen." Blacky told her slowly. "I didn't see Harlynn drink at all during the afternoon."

"He was drinking scotch in the office tonight." She stopped packing. "I don't want him at the house in Houston, do you understand me?"

"Kate he is having an allergic reaction to this stuff. We have to get him to the hospital, now! His heart rate is so high I'm afraid of him having a heart attack. He could die. This could be the same stuff that he took last time."

"You do whatever you have to do to help him." Kate told him. "No one is to know what is going on except, Keaton. I have to finish packing and get the kids out of here, and then I will come to the hospital." She stopped. "Blacky, can you see what I'm seeing right now?"

"Yes. I can see that you are afraid one day he is going to kill you when this happens and you don't know what to do." He watched her as the dazed look came back to her. It was the realization that her marriage was over that she couldn't handle. "I think you need to forget about packing and come with me."

"What about the children?" She questioned as her hands were shaking.

"Keaton and Christa can take care of them. We will leave several bodyguards. We need to go."

~Chapter 18

For four days there had been no sleep for Kate, Blacky or Keaton. Kate watched as Laney slept after being terribly sick from the anesthesia the doctors had given her to put in her tubes. Kate hated hospital rooms and she still had a headache. Hopefully she could take the child home later today.

Slowly he put his arms on her shoulders like he had done for the last four days. It was nice that he was there for her because she needed him. The ear infection had gotten worse and when Kate checked on Laney two nights ago there was blood coming out of her ears. There was no time to get a second opinion when they took her into surgery. She watched the I.V. thinking of Janey. She was so thankful that Janey and Stan had gone home from the ranch before everything had gone wrong.

"Do you need anything?" Danny asked her slowly. "I picked up your clothes that Meg packed. Although I have to say, I do like the scrub look on you. I need to clean your stitches and make sure there is no infection."

For the next ten minutes Kate sat there as Danny carefully cleaned off the side of head that had eight stitches in it. With her hair pulled up it covered them up. When she fell her head had hit the edge of the fire pit.

"Thank you." Kate sighed still not wanting to talk to anyone.

"George said Harlynn had a good night and should be awake today." Danny told her as she watched Laney.

"Do you think this will affect her hearing or speech?"

"I would expect her to be fine. We will watch her, she should be okay. It was very painful for her. No swimming for the time being and be very careful when you bath her." Kate looked at him as if to say, do I look like an idiot. "Sorry. I'm hoping when she wakes up she will be herself again. The anesthesia should be completely gone by now."

"Can I take her home?" Kate asked wondering what the word home meant now.

"She has to be eating and not vomiting before she goes home. Are you going to see him?" Danny asked almost reading her mind.

"When I go they still have him sedated and he tries to wake up. I don't understand anything he is saying. It doesn't even look like him because of the reaction he had to the drugs. I will go when Keaton gets here with Henry. I don't even know what to say to him if he is awake."

"Are you going to tell me what happened?" Danny asked for the third time. "You know it was the drugs, Kateland. He was given a very powerful narcotic that would make anyone violent when mixed with alcohol. I'm telling you it could have happen to me, Keaton or Blacky. He could have died Kateland. We are talking about Harlynn being dead."

"I know. I know. I also don't want to end up dead. Danny, I don't want to be killed by him. I have three children and I don't want to die next time."

"What do you want Kateland? You need to talk to me," Danny asked her.

"I don't want to be afraid anymore," she whispered back then began to sob. She managed to keep it inside of her until that second. Slowly Danny put his arms around her and held her. He was still holding her when Keaton and Henry walked into the room.

"How is Laney doing?" Keat asked causing Kate to pull away from Danny. "What did the doctor say when he checked on her this morning?"

Kate locked eyes with Henry and went in the bathroom. Slowly she ran the cold water washing off her face three times. Under no terms was she going to talk about her marriage with anyone. When she came out Keaton and Henry were waiting for her. She wished that Danny had stayed. Knowing Danny, all it took was the look from Henry that said back off and he was gone.

"We need to talk, Kateland." Henry started slowly.

"I'm listening." She stared back at him.

"Please think about what you are doing. What I saw when I came in the room is not the first time I've seen how close you and Danny

195

Hills have become over the years. You're still married to Harlynn Barrett." Silence filled the room. "Harlynn woke up and wants to see you. This whole situation needs to be resolved because I know exactly what you are thinking. You are thinking that this is over." Henry spoke in his boardroom voice.

"I want a divorce. I will not be a statistic for domestic violence."

"You know Blacky won't tell me what the hell happened at the ranch Kateland, because you said not to, which I think is verging on bullshit. The bodyguards won't tell me what the hell happened. When the hell is someone going to tell me what happened!" He paced the room running his hand through his hair as Keaton waited.

"Have your lawyers start going through the prenuptial agreement. I want a clean split of all the assets. I want custody of the children and he can see them when he wants to, but there has to be someone else there."

"No! Not until you see him and you two talk." Henry was an inch away from her face. "You love him, Kateland."

"If you don't help me Henry I will get my own lawyers."

Keat didn't even try to talk her out of it. There was nothing anyone could say to change her mind. If Henry couldn't convince her to stay married, then what was going to happen?

"Kateland, I'm begging you to tell me what happened because this is absurd. You need to slow down and get some perspective." She slowly rolled up the sleeve on her arm showing the two men the large bruise in the shape of a handprint. Then she took down her hair. Both men blinked several times at the eight stitches on the side of her head before she put her hair back up.

"That is what happened to me with Blacky and Charlie standing there. What would have happened to me if they weren't there? The first time I didn't show the bruise on my arm to anyone. I'm showing you this time."

Keat walked over looking at the black and blue arm that was swollen. He tried to raise her arm up, but she pulled back and rolled her sleeve down. She pushed back her tears with her sleeve trying to turn away from Keaton, embarrassed.

"I'm so sorry, Kateland," he told her. "We need to have someone look at your shoulder later." Kate nodded pulling away from him to face Henry. "You didn't tell me you got that many stitches. Did the headaches go away?"

"Not yet. I've been up for two days with Laney."

"Kate, he had an allergic reaction? I know Harlynn Barrett and he would never hurt you like this. He loves you and the children with his soul. He'll do whatever you want him to do, Kateland," Henry told her in protest as Keat stood there shaking his head because this was going to tear everyone apart. It would tear apart Meg and Henry. It would tear apart Sue and Sam.

"What did George say?" Kate asked.

"There was a temp there eight weeks ago named Gwen. Blacky is trying to locate her as we speak," Keat told her calmly. "He was psychotic on this stuff that night. You didn't do anything to cause this. It wasn't about you at all."

"Tell me exactly what happened, sweetheart." Henry took her hand and pulled her over to the couch. "Tell me what happened from the time we left. I want every detail and word that you can remember," she told him word for word what she remembered.

The room fell quiet as Henry swallowed, looking defeated. Kate waited for him to speak fighting back the tears because in her heart she didn't want this. She did love Harlynn and knew she could never love another man.

"I'll do whatever you want as long as you talk to him first. You and the children are the most important thing to me. I wish I had never left the ranch, I'm sorry, Kateland. Everyone turned as they heard Laney move around.

"Laney?" Kate said quietly as the baby began to scream at the top of her lungs because this was not her crib and she was hungry. Kate went to her, picking her up gently, like a china doll. The child wailed as Kate sang to her trying to calm her down. It was painful to hold the child, but she didn't care.

Kate was still singing to her twenty minutes later when Harlynn walked in the room with Blacky. He was wearing scrubs and looked pale, like he might pass out. He watched Kate with the most helpless look, and then his eyes drifted towards Laney.

The room filled with silence as Keaton stared at Harlynn as though he might kill him. Kate didn't look at anyone because she wanted them all to leave. She wanted to hold her daughter and feed her. How did she get to this point that she couldn't even look at the man she loved. She felt covered in a shame that she didn't understand.

"Let's go get a Starbucks," Blacky suggested to Henry and Keaton. Henry went slowly and Keat more slowly. "Kate, we will bring you back a Dr. Pepper." She nodded her head. "Harlynn?"

"Orange juice." He managed to say.

The nurse came in the room with a bottle, as Kate smiled, relieved. Her voice was gone from singing to the baby. Slowly she gave the ravenous child the bottle, stopping every ounce, with Laney yelling at her until Kate let her have more. Finally, Laney looked at Harlynn smiling.

"There's my angel." Harlynn gently took her and sat on the couch burping her. "I bet you feel better now." He kissed the child as he held her against his chest with his eyes closed. He wiped away a single tear that he couldn't hold back.

Kate took the baby as he leaned forward putting his head between his knees as though he might get sick. She sat with Laney in the rocking chair, rocking her back to sleep. Again the silence filled the room as Kate focused on the baby. She could feel his eyes watching her as she sat there. He was obviously in bad shape as he lay down on the couch unable to sit up anymore.

"Is her hearing going to be damaged?" he asked.

"Probably not." Kate told him.

"Do you believe me when I tell you I would never hurt you?"

"I don't know what to believe, Harlynn. You scared the hell out of me again," she told herself she would not cry. Never let them see you cry her father told her as a child. You can cry all you want, but don't let anyone see you.

"I'm never drinking again," he told her. "I don't want to lose you, Kateland. I know you have every right to leave me, but I'm asking you not to because I didn't know what I was taking. I took two before the luncheon and two more later. I felt so strange I didn't understand it. When I had the Scotch sitting in the office I felt like my head was going to explode. The last thing I remember is me being really ugly to you. I was thinking what the hell am I saying? I don't remember breaking the guitar or any of it." He watched the way she held Laney trying to support her left arm that was injured at the same time. "Did I hurt your arm?"

"And eight stitches in my head." She waited. "I figured you wouldn't remember, Harlynn. I want someone to explain to me what it means. What does it mean when you say these terrible things to me? Is this how you feel about me inside? Harlynn, my arm is so bruised I'm surprised you didn't break it."

"No, it's more the opposite of what I feel mixed with my greatest fears. You really believe I think you would sleep with Charlie? Or that I would want to hurt you like I have? Your love is the only thing I have ever been sure of in my entire life, Kateland. How can I make you understand I would do anything to change what I did?" Kate could see the sweat dripping down the side of his face. He was in no condition to be out of bed or talking to her.

"I shouldn't have started making changes to the ranch so soon. It was thoughtless of me," Kate told herself out loud.

"No, Kateland! You aren't listening to me. There is nothing you did to make this happen. This goes back to those guys trying to kill us or mostly me. You can do whatever you want to the ranch except what I asked you not to change. I saw you ordered new plates."

"I would have thrown up if I had to eat off those purple and black plates again. Is your sister color blind?" He smiled at her curled up on the couch and she knew. She couldn't leave him because it wasn't his fault that he was given the drugs. As she looked into her daughters eyes she knew she couldn't leave him.

"I feel like hell still." Harlynn confessed closing his eyes. "I thought I was going to die and never see you again."

"You look pretty bad. Why don't you go to sleep?" She finally made eye contact with him. "How did you end up here?"

"I woke up and you weren't there. I knew there had to be something really wrong that you weren't in that room. I looked at Blacky who had the scrubs waiting for me. When he told me about Laney I couldn't believe it. I don't know if I will ever forgive myself for not being there."

"They couldn't wait for you Harlynn. I was very afraid." Kate put the baby back in the crib and put up the gate. She didn't know what to do as she stood there completely depleted and devastated. It was like there was this invisible force pulling her towards Harlynn and those golden brown eyes, but she resisted getting back in the rocking chair waiting for her Dr. Pepper.

"Please come over here for one minute." Harlynn pleaded with her. "If I wasn't about to pass out I would come over to you."

Kate got up walking past him, and out the door. Harlynn lay there devastated covering his eyes with his arm until the door opened and he looked up.

"Drink this." She handed him a Gatorade. "And don't you dare puke because I have been puked on every hour for the last twenty-four hours. Apparently, Laney doesn't handle anesthesia too well." He sat up drinking the Gatorade slowly. Then she handed him a granola bar next since he hadn't puked yet. When he was finished he laid back down.

"Thank you." He stared at Kate. "Did you file divorce papers yet?" He smiled at her joking, but not really joking.

"No, I haven't had time." She smiled back at him. "That's what Henry and I were discussing when you came in. You're lucky that so many people care about you even when you act like a complete lunatic. Henry fought for you like you were his son. "

"Good. You know that you love me." He reminded her closing his eyes.

"Yes. And you know that I will get whatever I want going forward." She squished in close to him.

"Kateland, you have to know that you will always have whatever you want," he whispered as his eyes closed. "I can't love anyone else."

"I know. I can't love anyone else either."

Kate lay there in his arms unable to sleep. Quietly, she got up checking on Laney once again. From the rocking chair she tried to keep her eyes open, fighting off her exhaustion from the last four days. She watched as a different nurse came into the room. The nurse pulled out a syringe quickly going towards Laney. She didn't look at the chart or scan it in. She hadn't cleaned off the port she was going to stick it in.

"What are you giving her?" Kate yelled standing up immediately as Harlynn jumped up. She stood in front of Laney blocking the nurse who held the syringe up with determination. "What is your name? You aren't following protocol." Kate noticed she didn't have a badge on her. "Get away from my daughter!" Kate yelled as loud as she could.

Blacky barged into the room upon hearing Kate yelling. Harlynn grabbed the nurse's hand with the syringe in it and twisted it behind her back. As the woman fought back the syringe went into her back instantly. She immediately fell to the floor as everyone stared.

"What were you going to do to my daughter?" Harlynn demanded. "Who are you working for?" Kate wondered where Harlynn had gotten the energy from to even stand up as she watched him lean against the wall for support and slide to the floor covering his face as he closed his eyes trying to breathe.

It wouldn't stop was all Kate could think as the chaos went on in the room and the woman was taken out. Henry stood there staring at Kate as she finally sat down. He gave her the Dr. Pepper and she took it as her hand shook. Slowly, she tried to drink it, fighting back her emotions.

"We are going to destroy anyone with that company." Black told everyone in the room.

"Yes." Henry responded furiously.

Danny came in the room still in his calm demeanor. He went straight to Laney as Kate pointed at Harlynn.

"Let me see where you ripped out the I.V.?" Danny cleaned off his arm. "Next time, hopefully there won't be a next time, pull out and straight back. You could use a stitch here Harlynn. I'm going to butterfly it."

"Why do I feel like hell still?" Harlynn asked him.

"Harlynn you have no idea what they did to save your life. If Blacky hadn't life flight you here, we would be at your funeral. You're going to feel like hell for a couple of days, Harlynn. It might be weeks before you are a hundred percent." He waited. "I can start another I.V. or give you a couple shots to help you."

"Shots."

"You need to drink fluids." Harlynn nodded his head. "I think we need to get everyone out of this hospital this afternoon. I'll stay at the house tonight in case Laney or you need anything on one condition?"

"What?" Kate asked slowly.

"I get to go to the ranch again because that was a fantastic time before all this crap happened. And the next time any beautiful woman shows up, I get a chance at her."

"Yes, we do need to find you someone, Danny." Kate laughed. It felt good to laugh after all the impossible moments. She smiled at Henry because he knew. He knew if he could get Kate in the same room with Harlynn she would remember all the good things. Henry walked over to her and put her arms around her.

"See, I told you."

"I know." Kate smiled to herself.

—

It was late as Kate sat reading her emails in the office. She had two interviews this week, which she would never do but it was war in a way. The CEO of Star was denying everything. Like anyone could make up this story she thought to herself.

As she walked through the house she found Harlynn watching television. He hadn't gotten up from the couch since they got home. Danny couldn't find anything wrong with him. He turned slowly staring at Kate.

"Can you come here and talk to me?" He asked her. "I don't want to be alone and I need you." He turned off the television. "How is Laney?"

"She is better and very angry." Kate smiled at him. "I was telling her how the doctors fixed her ears and she made this little pouty face. It took every ounce of energy not to laugh at her. I think she was happy to be in her own bed with her blanket. And Levi did another master piece on the wall for the world to see. I can't say I blame him. His whole world disappeared, especially you."

"And you. You're his world, Kateland." He reminded her. "I can't explain to you how terrible I feel about what I did." He reached over and pulled up the sleeve to her shirt, staring in horror at her arm. Then he took her hair down to see the stitches. "And Laney. You had to be by yourself while Laney was going into surgery? I know that Keaton was there and Henry."

"They aren't you, Harlynn," Kate whispered to him as he laid his head in her arms. Slowly she traced his eyebrows. "I thought you didn't love me."

"No. It was never about you. I keep remembering bits and pieces. I think I was going outside to tell you I was sorry. I saw you playing the guitar for Charlie, which you never do for anyone including me. I was crushed and afraid." He closed his eyes. "I can't believe I smashed your guitar or did this to your arm and head."

"The important thing Harlynn is that you are okay and Laney is okay. It's going to take a while to work through this one. We will do it somehow."

"I can see it in your eyes? This changed you in a bad way, Kate."

"No. I have faith in you. Are you really going to stop drinking? Do you want me to stop?"

"I'm scared what it will do to me. I might have a sip of something, but at the moment I can't see myself drinking again. You can drink, I don't care. I don't care if people drink around me. I never want to go through what I've been through the last couple of days."

"I keep thinking of that woman trying to kill Laney." Kate whispered. "What would make a person kill an innocent child?

"I don't know. You were incredible the way you stopped her, Kateland."

"You were my hero today, Harlynn. You saved me and your daughter even though you won't admit it."

"I don't feel like anyone's hero if you want to know the truth."

"Harlynn, you are your own worst critic." She reminded him. "I have loved you for a very long time and that will not change. It was never about if I loved you."

"How do we get beyond this point? How do I forgive myself and how do you forgive me?" He asked confused and overwhelmed.

"By not getting divorced." Kate responded with a new confidence in her voice. "I already forgave you when I saw you walk in that hospital room so depleted and in pain. You should have been in bed for another week, but nothing was going to stop you from seeing your daughter."

"Or you." He gazed at her. "I really need your help."

"I'm here. I'm not going anywhere. We have to get you healthy and things will get better. You have to find your faith again, Harlynn. I have to believe that God is on our side or we wouldn't be here."

"Can you keep talking to me? I want to hear your voice." He closed his eyes.

As they sat there talking, in her mind, she wondered what this had done to Harlynn. What had these last several weeks done to him because he was broken, physically and emotionally? She wondered if she would ever get him back, if it was even possible to get his smile back or his laugh.

~Chapter 19

Time had slowed down and things were inverted in many ways, Kate reflected as she finished her yoga. It was her favorite moment because her mind and body were one as she lay in the darkness of the room at complete peace and there was no chatter in her mind. She basked in the space almost feeling as though her body was going to rise from the floor and levitate. Slowly she inhaled, knowing it was a fleeting attempt, as she rolled to her side and sat up feeling the blood rush from her head. The feeling was gone, but she felt better as she sat in the meditation room.

Levi would be up soon, and then Janey and finally her sleepy angel would call out to her. Harlynn would get up to get the children to school or he wouldn't. She liked when he was part of the morning and missed him. It was Kate who was dealing with the press and government now. She was overseeing Moon Water and dealing with the law firm. Meg was helping with the children and getting them different places. Kate was grateful for how Christa had come into their lives helping out. She was most grateful to see Keaton happy and in a real relationship that was healthy. She turned off the music grabbing her towel and turning on the lights. She jumped when the door flew open and a frightened Harlynn stood in front of her.

"There you are!" Harlynn said out of breath as he leaned against the wall. "No one could find you. You can't do that, Kateland."

"Babes, I have been coming in here at 4:45 every morning for the past two weeks. You're usually asleep when I get up." She reminded him, feeling bad. "I'm fine. What are you doing up?"

"I'm going for a bike ride," Harlynn told her questioning himself. "I'm sure how far I go will be pathetic, at least it's a start. Would you like an omelet?"

"Yes. I would like one of your fabulous omelets because I haven't had one in a long time." She leaned up on the tips of her toes kissing him as her body pressed against him. He kissed her back with a slow passionate kiss.

"Tonight I want to slowly kiss your whole body," he whispered in her ear as he kissed her again. "It's been a long time since we were together."

"Yes, it has been a long time since you made me crazy, mister. I don't think it will take much to make me go crazy, kissing you, well . . ." She giggled.

"Well, what?" Harlynn's eyes sparkled. "Tell me."

"Makes me want you this very second," she confessed.

"We could go into the mediation room? And lock the door." He pulled her gently by the hand into the meditation room and turned off the lights. He watched as Kate put some blankets on the floor, lit two candles and put soft music on.

Kate walked over to Harlynn taking off his shirt and then he was taking off her clothes. His touch was gentle and soft, which made Kate want him more. She wanted to feel his hands all over her body and the way he kissed her took her breath away. He never once took his eyes off her in the dark. It was about her and she liked it just being about her.

"Was that good?" He asked watching her as she nodded. "You have no idea how much I needed to make love to you."

"You have no idea how I needed for you to make love to me." She giggled. They watched the sun coming up wrapped in blankets and each other's arm. Harlynn laughed when there was a knock at the door.

"What are you two doing in there?" Keat yelled. "I'm cooking breakfast!"

"We are doing yoga," Harlynn yelled as Kate giggled.

"You know when we walk into breakfast everyone is going to know we just had sex in here."

"I don't care," he told her with his smile. "Let's jump in the shower, then that will keep them waiting even longer."

"We haven't taken a shower together in a really long time. I miss when we used to take showers together."

"What else do you miss?" Harlynn asked her as they stood in the shower.

"I miss seeing you in the mornings these last weeks. I know that you are still recovering and it's good that you are sleeping."

"I'll see what I can do about getting up with you and doing yoga."

Kate felt him kiss her as the water hit her face and his hands moved lightly across her body. They were going to be very late to breakfast was all she could think.

—

When they finally got to breakfast, Keat had already done the cooking with a grin on his face. Henry was reading the Wall Street Journal with the same grin on his face. Meg was making a list to see what was needed in the pantry because she was going shopping and always picked up what they needed.

"Where's Levi?" Kate inquired slowly.

"I checked on him and he is sleeping. Laney was also sleeping still." Henry glanced at Harlynn. "Your shirt is on inside, son. Who are you riding with this morning?"

"No one. You want to go?" Harlynn asked him.

"That sounds good to me. I'll go home and change."

"I want to go?" Keat said putting down their breakfast in front of Kate and Harlynn. He had made breakfast tacos with bacon and fruit. "I'm sure you both are very hungry after your long yoga secession." Keat raised his eyebrows as Henry smacked him with the paper.

"I told you not to do what you are doing." Henry glared at him.

"Don't hit me. You might want to tell Blacky to turn off the camera in the yoga room, Harlynn."

"It's our house and I would expect people to act as professionals. Did you ask Kate about Christa moving in Keaton?" Harlynn poked at him.

"No one asked me about Christa moving into the house. I have to think on this one, Keaton. How does this work exactly?" Kate tilted her head to one side, thinking it wasn't even seven A.M. yet.

"It's not all the time, but when she is in town I would like her to stay here." He paused putting on the charm with his green eyes. "I would like her to get to know everyone." Henry looked at Kate. "We do have common sense that there are three children who live in the house."

"How about we try it, but let her use one of the guest rooms downstairs for appearance sakes. I really like Christa and I want her to feel welcomed in this house always. We will figure it out and I appreciate you talking to us about it." Keaton leaned over giving her a hug.

"Thank you." He went back to fixing breakfast for the kids and whoever else would show up.

Blacky came in the room for breakfast next, still in his running clothes, with a smile on his face. He leaned over showing Kate and Harlynn a picture of the ultra sound on his Blackberry.

"A girl?" Kate asked very excited.

"Twelve weeks. Laney is going to have a little playmate. Why is your shirt on inside out Harlynn?" Blacky asked pouring everyone orange juice.

"Yoga." Harlynn winked at Kate, and then went back to eating. "Where's Nick?"

"He should be by soon. He is flying to New York today, I think." Blacky sat down, joining everyone.

"Yep." Kate drank half her orange juice. "He has a meeting with Sloane-Kettering about doing an internship with two of their fellows. And then he is going to meet with the FDA about when we can start the drug trials."

"And you are going on CNN business report today?" Blacky asked Kate going over everyone's meetings for the day on his iPad. "I will go with you on that interview."

"I'm going to go get our children up or they will never sleep tonight." Kate announced because she didn't know what to say to Blacky about the interview. She was going to fight against this CEO every way she could. Henry nodded at her with a smile as he went out the back door.

"Julia has an interview at St. Luke's in Houston next week," Blacky told Harlynn excited. "Apparently we are moving to Houston in the very near future."

"That is the best news I've heard in a long time." Kate yelled from the other room. As she climbed the stairs life seemed better today she thought. Even though things were different in their lives, they were still good.

Laney was already rolling over and wiggling around her crib. Kate watched as she looked back at her laughing, as though she was telling her one day I will find a way out of this place. As she changed Laney, Levi came in not looking like himself. He had his father's allergies Kate concluded as she looked at this child with puffy red eyes and a runny nose. It was just another day, Kate smiled to herself.

———

An hour later, Claire was there, which allowed Kate to sit in her office preparing for her interview on top of the other pending fires to put out. She had a call with her father who was overseeing the labs now. Danny would also be in the interview today and he was nervous. He was there for the science end of the business, which took enormous pressure off Kate.

Harlynn came in the office and sat down waiting for her to look up. Now this was a role reversal as she smiled at him. He looked good, was all Kate could think as he smiled back at her. They were finding their way back to each other, slowly.

"Levi doesn't look right to me, I called George and he is setting up an appointment with an allergist since Danny has the interview this morning. After that I think I'll take him to the zoo." Kate focused on him. "Are you ready?"

"Yes, I'm ready." She took in a deep breath. "Is Emma coming by today?" Kate asked because his sister had been bugging the heck out of her with emails and texts. She wished she could block them, but thought that might look bad.

"I don't know. I don't care." Harlynn admitted coldly. "I'm not listening to her crap about the Will. I did exactly what my father asked me to do and it's all documented. She is the last person I want to deal with today."

"I will take care of it. How was your bike ride with the boys?"

"Good. I'm going to have lunch with Henry tomorrow and talk about what I want to do."

"Why don't you give yourself six months? You've earned a

break, Harlynn." Kate suggested leaning back in her chair.

"I don't know what I want, which is strange, because I've always known what I wanted."

"We will figure it out." She reassured him.

"Thank you for being patient with me, Kateland. I deeply appreciate that you are picking up the slack. I couldn't take this time off if I didn't have you here to take over. I always said you could run that law firm. And we know you can run Moon Water."

"Well, I'm sure there are a few partners pissed off after they saw their quarterly bonus. I'm meeting up with Ed after the interview. Is there anything you want me to tell Ed?"

"Tell him what we talked about last night over dinner. I'm keeping my ownership of the firm and voting rights. I'm not taking on any legal work for the time being. He is in charge and to take over my clients. I still get the origination fees. You have the document we drew up last night. They can notarize them at the firm."

"I think it's a good choice. I know it's hard, Harlynn."

"I'm wondering if I built that law firm for me or my father. I always felt like I had to prove to him I could be successful. I don't want our children to feel they have to prove anything to anyone. I want them to be happy and find their own passion in life."

"They will have choices because we will make sure they have that opportunity. Have you thought about playing golf?"

"No. Cycling is what I want to do for the time being. I want to spend time going over the letters my father left. How many letters do you think there were in the closet?"

"Harlynn, there were boxes of them in that closet with your name on them. Hundreds. I was thinking we should put them all in a book of some sort after you've read them."

"Do you think we could go to the ranch in the near future?" Harlynn asked slowly as Kate looked away. "Just for a day or two? I want to get some of the letters. I guess I want to show you that you can trust me again. I need to face what I did there or I won't be able to move forward in my life."

"How about Friday night and come back Sunday? I need to check on what Christa's been doing up there. I want Keaton to come." Kate locked eyes with him never saying what she really thought.

"Yes. I'm sure Henry will be there and Blacky. I understand." He got up and kissed her. "I'm taking up yoga for real."

"You want sex." Kate laughed at him.

"Well, yeah of course I want lots of sex with you. Your body was so relaxed, Kateland. It was a very different experience for me. I like to go in the meditation room when I'm reading our Bible."

"Are you reading the Bible, again?" Kate asked because she had seen the Bible she gave him under their bed along with his car magazines. Some habits were harder to break when you got married later in life.

"The five of us are meeting one morning a week. Blacky has a study guide from a class he used to take that we are using."

"I think that's amazing." He was changing was all Kate could think. He was lost for these last weeks and was trying to find his path again with the help of the people around him. She watched as Levi came in the office with his latest Lego creation. He was very proud of the multi-colored plane he had crafted.

"What do you think?" Levi showed her as Harlynn watched them. "That's the engine."

"I'm so impressed my little man!" Kate told him as she marveled at what he had done by himself. It looked like it could have come from a Lego kit. She watched as he climbed into her lap wanting to be held. He wanted her love, if only for five minutes.

"When I get home later I have a surprise for you. Will you be a good boy for Dada?" Levi nodded his head as he snuggled with his mother for a couple more minutes. With no warning he popped out of her lap running out of the room.

"I will call you later." Harlynn kissed her again. "Don't take any shit from that reporter."

"I won't."

———

The morning was going fine as Kate got ready for her interview. She looked at herself in the mirror wondering how she had gotten to this point. She was going to be interviewed by CNN and she wasn't nervous. The idea she wasn't nervous bothered her. Why wasn't she nervous?

"Do you need help getting ready?" Meg came in the vanity. "How are you holding up?" she asked in that warm fuzzy voice.

"I don't know if I have even said thank you for all that you and Henry are doing for us?" Kate whispered. "Am I crazy for taking all this on?"

Meg took the flat iron going over the back of Kate's hair. Next she made the eye makeup heavier and lightened the lipstick a bit. Finally she picked out a different pair of earrings. "You need to wear the larger diamonds because you want to throw it in their face, but not too much. I think you are sending a message that you are powerful." She stopped. "You don't have to thank us, Kateland." She became very solemn. "We will always be here for you and the children no matter what. We both feel bad we left you at the ranch, I didn't want to leave. I'm so sorry that all this has happened to you. I honestly don't know how you do it."

"I have you, Henry and Keaton there to help me. And everyone else," Kate whispered. "Do you think Harlynn and I are going to make it?"

"Two months ago I would have said not a chance. No relationship could survive the events that have occurred in the last year. Now I see the forgiveness, love and a stronger relationship. I don't know how you got through what happened and I don't know how you forgave Harlynn. I know logical that it wasn't his fault. It doesn't charge the fact it happened."

"Yes, that's true." Kate smiled softly at her.

—

Blacky was waiting for her when she came downstairs, dressed like Nick dressed him with a stunning tie and his hair slicked backed. He looked embarrassed at how Kate and Meg stopped staring at him.

"You and your son could model for GQ." Kate whispered to him as she walked by.

"I don't work for the government anymore and I can dress like I want." He tried to defend himself as he smiled.

They all looked up when there was a knock at the front door.

Kate ignored the voices because she had gotten use to never answering their front door between the bodyguards and Blacky.

It was this surreal part of her life she had learned to ignore. They knew all the bodyguards and feed them. She always made sure everyone got cupcakes to celebrate the birthdays. The staff was part of their home, and knew if they had a problem they could come to her.

Blacky walked into the kitchen with Emma, he didn't look particular happy. Kate looked at her watch because they had to think of traffic and didn't want to be late. She hated to be late, especially for an interview.

"Why don't we sit down?" Kate suggested walking over to the dining room table. Kate knew exactly why Emma was there and if this was going to happen, it was going to happen now without Harlynn in the house.

Emma placed the Will on the table with red tabs sticking out of it. Kate took the Will from her going through each tab then handed it back to Emma and waited as she looked at her watch.

"I only have five minutes," Kate said calmly. "Harlynn isn't here."

"If Harlynn doesn't make the changes I want to the Will then you both will find yourself in court."

"First, the Will is a legal document and it can't be changed unless it was done illegally, which I can assure that there wasn't anything illegal about it. Second, you can take us to court and tie up the estate for years if you like. The estate will not pay the legal bills and you will not have access to any funds from the estate nor will your mother because we will request that the judge freeze all assets."

"You can't do that!" Emma yelled at Kate.

"You've never had to pay a legal bill, have you? Harlynn has always taken care of everything for you? You have never paid for your girl's school or clothes or tennis lessons because Harlynn takes care of it. You have never paid your mortgage because your father paid it. I would be grateful for the large sum of money you've been given."

"Why did Harlynn get the ranch and more stock than I did?"

"Because your father wanted it that way."

"Why do your children get more damn money than mine?" She

yelled at Kate again with no reaction from Kate.

"Your father wanted it that way." She watched as Emma stood up.

"Why the hell should Janey get a damn cent of my family's money? She isn't even related to Harlynn! She is a cancer charity case you picked out to make yourself feel better!"

Kate looked at her because she knew it was coming. Everyone in the room knew it was coming as Kate stood up slowly and walked over to Emma.

"You need to get the hell out of my house and don't bother coming back, ever! We are done. You have been cut out of our lives Emma! If you want to talk to Harlynn or me again, get yourself a lawyer. Now get out before I kick your ass across the room!"

"You need to go," Keaton told her, which Kate didn't even know he was in the room. Keat stepped between the two women as Kate grabbed her briefcase and headed out the back door where the car was waiting for them. There was only so much shit that she was willing to take from Emma.

"I guess I should have handled that better," Kate mumbled to Blacky in the back of the car. She thought about calling Harlynn for a moment. Keat and Blacky would tell him what happened.

"Actually it went better than I anticipated. If she had half a brain she would have taken what she got and been grateful."

"Well, apparently Harlynn got all the brains in that family." She waited. "Why are you coming on this interview with me?"

"I thought you were going to be nervous for some reason. And we need to talk after the interview. I needed to get you away from the house where we could relax."

Kate nodded, thinking there was always something she didn't know. As the black SUV wove in and out of traffic she gazed out the window. And always, she wondered how she had gotten to this exact point in life. She questioned if she wanted to be here.

~Chapter 20

Dr. Danny Hills, world renowned pediatric oncologist, had puked his guts out forty minutes before the interview. Kate didn't know if he had the flu or it was nerves. Blacky sat in the waiting room watching the scene. When the door opened Kate smiled as the dynamic duo stood in front of her. Keaton and Nick glided into the room calmly and looked at Danny.

"Danny boy, what's up?" Nick asked slowly as he felt his head. "Man you are burning up. Why don't you go have George check you out?" Danny nodded his head.

"I'll walk you down." Blacky offered, helping him up. "Your driver will take you to George's and home afterwards. I will send an extra bodyguard over to your place in case you need anything else."

The room was silent for a moment as Kate got her puzzled look. She watched as Nick and Keat went over to the bar and poured three shots of Patron, then handed one to her. She knew what they were thinking. "How the hell did we get here?"

"Guess you didn't make that plane this morning?" Kate inquired.

"I got what we wanted from Slone-Kettering. And I want you to put the screws to the FDA, do you understand me? They cancelled my meeting and it really pisses me off. Plus, Elle is sort of freaked out and she won't tell me what is going on. Do you know anything?"

"She got the job for the White House and didn't want to tell you." Kate smiled as she drank her shot of Patron. "Who's going on with me?"

"He is." Keat and Nick pointed at each other.

"Then you both go on with me," Kate told them in voice that said I'm not screwing around boys, this is the big time and you better act like it.

Kate was in the zone as the interviewer threw question after question at her. She would slightly smile and answer it, waiting for the next one. Blacky stood behind the camera pacing slowly, as he listened intently.

"Ms. Jones, do you plan on rewriting the business model for the pharmaceutical industry?"

"I plan on offering an alternative model that is focused on the end result and not the end profit margin. We estimate we will only charge ten percent over the cost of making the drugs. We are only interested in helping individuals. With the patent portfolio we are able to absorb a great deal of the research and development cost while condensing the time table."

"Who makes the decision of what diseases you will be targeting and why did you choose this one?"

"We do. My daughter is in remission from this cancer." Kate paused trying to rein in her emotions. "After seeing what she has gone through over the years along with the families we have met, I wanted to find a cure. With the help of brilliant scientists and the grace of God, I believe we have it. I think there is a range of diseases that we will hopefully be able to tackle."

"Can we expect your husband to be running the company in the future?"

"Harlynn is always involved in what is going on with Moon Water. Just because he isn't in the office doesn't mean he isn't on a conference call or reading emails."

"Where is he today then?"

"Harlynn is at the allergist with our son. Perhaps one day we will tackle finding a cure for allergies for my son and husband." Kate smiled to herself. "Speaking of children, it would be wonderful if your viewers would take a moment to contact the FDA concerning our drug trial. We need to let the FDA know that children's diseases must be addressed. If you are a mother or father or grandparent please contact the FDA by email or call them to let them know how you feel. It's very important we address these children's needs. The FDA needs to make children a priority in the future and we hope to help facilitate that change."

"Can you understand that what you are doing will cause people to lose their jobs?"

"The industry will have to be more efficient in what it does and cut the waste. We are not remotely interested in taking over any pharma company or the industry. We are going to prompt change in how these businesses are run. It's basic competition from economics 101. If I can make a better widget for less money and I'm willing to charge less for the end product, I will take market share. The markets we have targeted for the next year are small markets. We are taking a large amount of waste and profit out of our business model that has been the industry standard. Another problem is the waste that goes on in research. There are lab teams working on the same disease, but unwilling to share technology or actually try to work together. That's one thing about our labs, the teams share their findings."

"And if you could tell Mr. Frank Waters anything what would you tell him?"

"You will go to jail and your board members will go to jail for what you tried to do to my family. Put it another way, we will find you."

"Do you think that you and your family are safe?" Kate looked at Blacky and smiled.

"Emphatically yes, we have the best security analyst in the world working for us. We will remain safe." She turned to Keaton to answer questions about the science part of Moon Water and the new drug JR6. It was nice to see him being noticed for his accomplishments as he stated his credentials. He was confident and elegant as he spoke thoroughly explaining the process in layman terms. He reminded her of Henry being interviewed with his body language. Next Nick talked about future acquisitions and plans for expanding. Nick was charming and smooth as glass. The camera loved him and the reporter was stumped.

"Ms. Jones, why are you doing this?" The reporter asked closing the interview. "Each individual in this privately owned corporation has achieved a level of success most people wouldn't dream of in a life time. You could sell Moon Water tomorrow and walk away from all the threats and problems."

"My father once told me that I should make the world a better place, that we all had a responsibility to do our part. This is my part. Moon Water is not for sale. It will remain private for as long as it exist."

It had gone well, was all Kate could think, when it was over. They had done it and yes, it would turn up the heat as the world saw who she was and that she didn't deserve to have her family attacked and killed.

"You were stunning," Blacky told her proudly. "You handled them like a pro, Kateland."

"I had good mentors." She smiled, hoping that Henry had seen it. He was the one who told her to make the world a better place.

"You're the one who decided to actually use what you have observed. You could have done nothing and we would all love you just the same."

"I need to have a chat with Keat before we take off. Do you mind having a coffee with your favorite son? Don't forget to tell him how proud you are of him."

"I won't. I need to check on Danny. Harlynn called me a couple of times trying to get a hold of you."

"I turned my phone off. If he calls while I'm talking to Keat, tell him I will call him as soon as possible." Kate went to find her brother who was having another shot of tequila with Nick.

"Gorgeous, you were amazing and decimated that reporter. You took away his manhood." Nick gave her a kiss. "Thank you for giving me this opportunity, Kateland."

"Always. I need to talk to Keaton while you have a coffee with your old man." Nick took his order like a man and didn't argue or ask questions.

"What's up?" Keaton asked sitting down on the couch as Kate watched him. "What did I do?"

"Tell me what's going on with you?" Kate asked softly. "I've been so busy the last several weeks I haven't checked in with you. I'm sorry, you obviously needed to talk."

"You had enough to deal with these last weeks without me adding to it." Keat responded as the room became still. "I feel like this relationship with Christa is moving too fast. I feel like if I don't marry her tomorrow I will lose her." There was pure panic in his voice.

"What happened?" Kate leaned back into the sofa watching him. He was a complete mess and she couldn't believe she hadn't seen it. Keat was beginning to freak out as he stood up and started pacing.

"I love her. I'm not ready for marriage. I'm not ready for us to move in together. I want to know her and that takes time. Christa is exactly like you, very complex to say the least."

"Keaton you don't have to do anything if you aren't ready. If Christa is putting pressure on then slow it down. I personally think you need more time before you start thinking about getting married. Eight weeks is not that long, Keat. What can I do to help you?"

"Will you talk to Christa and tell her that I need more time? Tell her how our parents had a crappy marriage and the idea of marriage makes me have anxiety attacks. I tried to tell her and she got mad at me."

"I think we are going to the ranch this weekend and I need you to come in case Harlynn flips out again." Kate admitted in a matter of fact tone.

"If Harlynn flips out again, Nick and I are going to take turns kicking his ass this time." He took in a deep breath and smiled. "Thank you for taking the time to talk to me because I know you are beyond overwhelmed. You were like this rock star in that interview, damn, Kateland."

"I know, wasn't that weird. I wasn't even nervous, which is crazy, Keaton. Millions of people are going to see that interview and I don't care."

"No, it's you, is all. Someone tried to kill your family and you will never let them win. You have finally adjusted to being married to Harlynn and having this family. You are very powerful and you handle it like Harlynn does. Very quietly."

"I don't know if Harlynn is coming back to Moon Water." Kate admitted. "It may be you and Nick running it with Henry and me helping."

"Are you okay with that Kateland?"

"It's weird for me to think he is walking away from his career, but considering people keep trying to kill him, I do understand it. My strategy is to support him and be kind. He needs to be loved to heal from all this trauma."

"The bike ride this morning was good for him. Henry, Nick and I are trying to be there for him because he is struggling. It's weird to see Harlynn like this. It's like he can hardly cope with all of it."

"Do you think I should talk to his shrink?"

"She won't tell you anything, Kate. I think you should talk to Harlynn and make sure he is okay." Keat suggested. "It's like he has lost his confidence in himself. How are the two of you doing and I'm not talking about your sex life either." Keat didn't smile when he said the words.

"I don't know. I would say everything is slowly going back in place. If he has really changed, then I don't know who he is anymore, Keaton." She turned wiping the tears away because she didn't want him to see it. The pain and fear came to the surface again with no warning.

"Hey Kate," he whispered. "I'm here, okay. You're not alone." He hugged her for a while.

"Thank you for always being here for me, Keaton." She pulled herself together, fixing her eye makeup. "Don't say anything to anyone? Promise?"

"Yes, I promise." He glanced at his watch. "You have a meeting with Ed Quarter at the law firm that you are late for and I will check on Danny."

"Really check him out because he told me he had people following him. I think he is a target now, so I need you and Blacky to take care of this."

"Nick was going over to his place." Keat stopped and gave her one more hug. "I will call you in a while."

—

In the car on the way to the law firm Kate dialed Harlynn who answered immediately. She smiled to herself thinking what Keaton had said because he was right, she had to understand what was going on with Harlynn and it needed to start now.

"Why didn't you take my call?" She could tell his feelings were really hurt. "Are you mad over Emma?"

"I'm mad at her. I love you and if I'm mad at you, I will tell you straight to your face. Emma went after Janey. She called Janey my cancer charity project."

"I'm glad I wasn't there because I would have gone ballistic and told her what I thought of her. I'm glad you got in her face, Kateland."

"I feel bad because she is your sister and you need to have her and the girls be part of our lives. Why did she go after Janey?"

"Kate, you know I have always thought of Janey as my daughter. I told Emma's husband that Emma will not be allowed back in the house. She is not allowed to go after any of my children or question what my father decided to do. It's done."

"I'm sorry. I should have handled it better for you, Harlynn." Kate admitted. "Are you mad at me?"

"No, please don't think that, love. The reason my father did what he did is because Emma never accomplished anything in her life. We were always bailing her out. Paul hated it, but he never told her once. It was his way of letting her know that he didn't like the choices she had made in her life. I told my father that I was okay with him giving it all to Emma and he said never. He wanted my family to have the ranch and the other stocks."

"I can't have her attacking Janey. For her to say that after everything she has been through. What a complete bitch, Harlynn."

"I agree." Silence filled the line. "Levi has a sinus infection and allergies like his old man. He has to go on antibiotics, which I know that you don't like."

"Well, I don't think we have an option at this point. I should have taken him in last week, ugh. What did you do all afternoon?"

"We spent an hour watching the giraffes and got to feed them."

"Don't tell Janey."

"Levi already did when we picked her up from school. I really like the new school. Kate, that was a good call." He paused. "I saw the interview."

"Say what you are thinking, Babes."

"You were captivating. I have three dozen calls from people wanting to talk with us. You were a natural in front of the camera besides looking beautiful as always. The camera loves you, Kate"

"How do you feel about it?"

"I like that you are accomplished and can handle anything. I also know that you don't really want to be in front of the camera. Guilty. I feel like I let you down in a big way."

"No, you haven't let me down, Harlynn. You have never let me down willfully as long as I have known you aside from the drugs you took. I think this is what I need to do for us until you have time to get back on your feet. I don't want do this for the next ten years, but I will do it for the next six months. I've already spoken to Keaton that he and Nick may be taking over with Henry and me as back up."

"I'm feeling overwhelmed." He waited. "What are you thinking?"

"I don't want to meet with Ed in ten minutes. I want you back somehow, but I don't know what it means. This morning it was really good to make love to you again. I love this father that you have become and how you take care of Levi and the way you picked up Janey from school. I'm scared of going to the ranch at the same time I know we face what happened. I wish I knew it would never happen again. I wish we could erase the last eight weeks because they are painful." She stopped.

"It won't happen again. Kateland, do you understand that I don't want to be that man who lived at his law firm? I'm tired."

"What does that mean? Are you tired of me?"

"Absolutely not, Kateland. I'm talking about the insane life I have been living for the last seventeen years."

"What does the shrink say?" Kate asked slowly. "What do you talk with her about when you go there?"

"How many shots of Patron did the three of you do?"

"We did one before and one after the interview, like normal. Considering I was with the dynamic duo that wasn't a lot. I haven't eaten since breakfast, which I know is dumb."

"Kateland!" His voice immediately went into the worry stage. "I'm emailing Ann to make sure she gets you lunch. We talk about what I have accomplished and why."

"Why do you have to analyze the hell out of what you have done with your life? It doesn't sound like you, Harlynn. It sounds like this shrink has you thinking backwards."

"Can we finish this later? Janey just came outside to go for a swim and I need to check on Levi and Laney?"

"Yes, I will see you later." Kate hung up the phone wondering if you had to go back to figure out the future? What was he trying to deal with that he had to spend hours talking about it?

—

For the last thirty minutes Harlynn's best friend and managing partner at the law firm had been berating Kate about what was going on with Harlynn. She sat there eating and drinking wine listening to his complaints.

"He is not coming back?" Ed questioned as he read the document and reluctantly signed it. "For real?"

"For real, Ed. You had to know that this was coming, eventually. We have been talking about it for a year. He can't run Moon Water, oversee a holding company and run a law firm."

"I miss him." Ed admitted to her with regret. "Can I consult with him on cases?"

"I will have to discuss it with him. I'm here to offer my help if you would like it. I know that I'm not Harlynn, but I learned a great deal from working with him, Ed."

"I'll take it. You were the best the lawyer in this firm next to Harlynn and if I could use you as a sounding board that would be very helpful. Also, if I could have your input for new hires and the business side, I would be grateful."

"Done." She finished her wine and leaned forward. "I need your help. I'm not willing to watch him become Mr. Mom."

"You have it." Ed poured more wine into both glasses. "Let's look at what was the catalyst for what's happened. His father dying has destroyed him for a moment. He talks about Henry a lot and their relationship has evolved from business to one of Henry's confidants. He is part of Henry's most inner circle now."

"True. Harlynn has become family to Henry."

"If you want me to talk to Harlynn I need to spend time with him. I miss him, Kateland. I spent the last twenty years with him almost every day. He is my best friend."

"Yes, you are one of his best friends, Ed. He values your friendship and your trust." She paused and smiled. "Can you come to the ranch this weekend?"

"Sure. I haven't been there in years."

"Are you upset about my father and Sue getting married?"

"No. She didn't want to help raise my children. I couldn't give her what she wanted in a million years. I'm seeing someone who adores my children and understands that I work and when I'm not working I'm with her and my kids. Life is turning out the way it should."

"I felt terrible how Sue treated you."

"Our relationship ended Kateland, and it wasn't ugly. Sue and I still talk about once a week. I would say we are good friends."

"I don't think they'll be at the ranch, but I can't guarantee it," Kate told him getting up from the conference table. "I will email you later to let you know. There are a lot of bodyguards that travel with us."

"I've heard." He smiled. "It's good to see you, Kate."

———

An hour later she sat with Blacky at *Grappino's* on the terrace. Blacky looked so different and so much like Nick now, it was funny. His hair was longer and curly like Nick's. He wore a pair of Oakley sunglasses that fit his face perfectly. She giggled at him and he smiled.

"You clean up well." Kate teased him again because she couldn't resist.

"Thanks." He winked at her. "Where did you think Nick got his good looks from?"

"It's interesting. This is what Nick is going to look like in twenty years."

"He is my boy." Blacky smiled. "Thank you for giving Nick this opportunity, Kate. And thank you for what you said about me today."

"It's true. You know that Nick is one of my brother's now. That's what family does for each other. That's what Henry taught me a long time ago."

"You want a drink? I feel like a granita and some of that roasted garlic you like."

Kate closed her eyes thinking she wished she could have had parents like Blacky and Julia. Nick had won the lottery in many ways. Then again she had Henry and Meg, which made her a lottery winner also.

"I've seen the report," Kate told Blacky slowly as he stared at her. "Walter Reed sent it to me yesterday. I'm not sure what it means that the government is doing a cost analysis if we find a cure for one type of cancer that affects five thousand children a year. I think the analysis is way too aggressive and boarders on pure fiction. The idea Moon Water will put a band aid company out of business is sensationalism."

"Kateland, you with the help of Harlynn, Henry and the boys are changing how drugs will be developed from here on out. People are completely freaking out, honey. I can't even tell you how many calls I get daily from agencies inquiring what is going on. "

"Do they know that you are being paid by Moon Water?"

"Yes. And at some point we need to have an agreement in place."

"Six hundred a month. And I need to know what kind of budget you need to do what you do with projections going forward. I'm sure you will need several groups to alternate. I want the entire family included in the projections."

"Kateland I will do it for a fraction of what you have offered."

"We feel it's fair considering what comes with the job. If you can keep us safe and all the people around us safe, then it's worth every cent. We both know that you are the best at what you do Jack. We feel extremely fortunate to have you on our side and part of this family." She watched as Mr. Jack Black became very somber and reflected on her comments, and then smiled at her nodding. It was done and they didn't need to discuss it again.

"How do you want to handle this report?"

"I want to leak parts of it to the public and counter with a real analysis. Can you do it?"

"Yep. I think the spin should be the profit from cancer. I have a person who can work up real numbers for us. I should have the information on Monday."

"This is what I'm supposed to do Blacky and I can't change it. People may lose their job, but children will live. I have to believe after what we have been through with Janey this is my path."

"Kate it's going to be the hardest challenge you've ever have to face. There will be days you want to walk away."

"This report makes me think we are dealing with someone in the government. The crap the FDA is making us do seems extreme. We are dealing with someone who is powerful and has connections to someone who is very powerful. How do we make sure that the government will back off?"

"I think we have to find the source and cut off its head. When we find this individual I think we are going to be shocked. It's someone who we think is on our side or at least appears to be."

"We are in more danger than you have admitted to me?"

"Yes. This is what you pay me to do. You can't be alone or the children. I'm not trying to scare you. I respect you enough to be honest with you."

"It's not even close to being over, is it? Do you think we can win without anyone getting killed?"

"There's a large amount of chatter on Moon Water, Kateland. If it gets more intense we will have to go underground." He waited. "Statistically speaking, someone is going to get hurt. I will do my best is all I can tell you."

—

Kate sat outside by the pool avoiding everyone. At some point she would have to go in the house. She glanced at her watch, Laney would need a bottle in ten minutes, and she was never late for ten o'clock feeding to go to sleep.

"Why are you sitting out here by yourself?" Harlynn asked bringing her out some lime sherbet ice cream.

"It was a really long day and I wanted to relax before feeding the baby and going to bed. How are you?"

"I have a new found respect for what you do with these children each day. I don't think I've taken all three for the day, even with a nanny." He watched her. "I've been thinking of what you asked me today, about what I'm doing in therapy."

"I'm not trying to be critical of Dr. Brown or maybe I am. There are times I wonder if she is still helping you, Harlynn. For the last several months you have been spending countless hours with her. I don't see anything positive coming out of it. I see you more tormented after each visit and it's killing me."

"Before when I went to therapy, it was for the divorce or trying to find balance in my life between work and our family. I'm trying to learn how to grieve for my father, which is important. Then about three weeks ago she started asking me questions about my career. I think you're right that I don't need to dig through every event in my life. I need to focus on one career and my family with you. I'm going to take a break from tearing apart every decision I've made in my life. After spending the day with our children it made me realize everything we have Kateland." Silence hung between them as Kate waited.

"Is that what you want or what I want."

"It's what I need." He smiled at her. "I will get the baby. She has been asking for you. Then you are going to bed since you have been drinking all afternoon and you need to sleep it off." He laughed at her. It was a total role reversal.

~Chapter 21

There was tension in the room as Kate got out of bed to go do her yoga. Today they were going to the ranch, which she didn't want to do. Today she was not dealing with anything concerning Moon Water or the law firm or Harlynn's sister or Sue. As she walked downstairs she went through the past several days and concluded the conflicts that existed and what she really could do without. Levi stood before his mother with chocolate on his face.

"What have you been doing?" Kate smiled picking him up because he was Houdini. He had escaped once again so they were going to have to come up with a different plan.

When she came into the kitchen there was another surprise. The colorful marker writing all over the table and chocolate chip cookies randomly half eaten left all over the place was a clear message from the two year old. He stared at his mother with his large green eyes that were bloodshot from not sleeping.

"You left me," he told her. "I missed you."

"I didn't leave you Levi, I was working." In no time she cleaned up the kitchen and was making breakfast. There would be no yoga this morning and that was fine because her son needed her. It was six-thirty when Elle came in the back door with swollen bloodshot eyes and went to lie down on the couch.

Sue appeared next waiting for attention from Kate as she read to Levi ignoring her. When she was finished with the third book they moved on to painting. She found the largest canvas she could in the art studio and let Levi do finger painting on it. She helped him make different animals with his hands and feet. It was a master piece to be hung in the playroom. Slowly she saw the frustration leave her sons face because his cup had been empty and now it was full. He wanted to make sure that he got to be with his mother.

"Little man you look tired. Would you like to go sleep in Mama's bed?" He smiled with delight because it was a big deal to sleep in Mama's bed. She walked him upstairs and tucked him in. She imagined he had been up a long time before she came downstairs. They would have to come to some agreement.

Harlynn came out dressed in his riding clothes as they locked eyes. He immediately noticed the paint on Kate's shirt and the chocolate on Levi's face. He tried not to laugh as he left the room without saying a word. She sang to Levi until his eyes closed. Before she went downstairs she sent a text to Nick inquiring why Elle was sleeping on her couch.

"Why can't I come to the ranch?" Sue pounced on Kate as soon as she came in the kitchen.

"Ed is coming to the ranch." Harlynn glared at Kate because she didn't tell him that one as she smiled. "It would be weird to have my dad and Ed there don't you think?"

"Sam doesn't care about Ed and Ed doesn't care about Sam. Your dad has been working his butt off Kateland and he needs a break."

"Fine, come! So help you if there is one awkward moment, do you understand me?" Harlynn stood watching Kate because she had that look in her eyes that said I have reached my breaking point with you.

"Can we go talk, alone?" Harlynn asked her.

"No." She took his smoothie off the cupboard that he had made for himself and drank half of it. "I'll be in the art studio if anyone needs me and it better only be one of my children or a real dam emergency."

Two hours later she put down her paint brush standing back from the painting. It was an abstract of the tepee she had been in. Perhaps she would go look for the Chief when she was at the ranch. He could help her understand Little Shark because she didn't understand him anymore.

Kate didn't realize that Harlynn was standing behind her. She had completely blocked out everyone and everything. Janey had come in for a couple of minutes before school and Kate was going up to school to have lunch with her. She wondered if being shuffled between her and Stan was affecting her. At least she loved the new school.

"I'm not leaving until we talk?" Harlynn told her sitting down on a bar stool glancing at the sketches of her dreams and the ranch.

The strokes of the paint brush moved across the canvas as Harlynn waited. If he wanted her attention he was going to wait. They both looked up when Blacky walked in the art studio.

"Why is Elle asleep on the couch?"

"Nick and her father got in an argument again because Nick didn't like her father making fun of her for only getting a gold medal in a relay in the Olympics. Words were exchanged. Her father said he won't come to the wedding or walk her down the aisle. In Nick's defense, her Dad can be a real jerk like you wouldn't believe. I think it would be nice if you told her you would walk her down the aisle, Blacky."

"Good for Nick for not taking anymore shit from her father. I will gladly walk her down the aisle. What time are we leaving for the ranch?"

"Three." Harlynn said without looking up. "I want to pick Janey up from school and take her to Stan's since we won't see her all weekend."

"Kate, have you decided if you will be going to the ranch this weekend? I need to figure out the bodyguards if you are staying in Houston."

Kate felt both men stare at her as she breathed in, and then slowly turned to give Blacky her go to hell smile. Then she looked at Harlynn who was waiting for her answer because usually Kate would be completely blunt, but not this time.

"I'm going, I guess. I don't really want to go. I'll let you know if I change my mind."

"Could you clarify the ambiguous nature of that answer? A simple no or yes would suffice." Blacky requested trying not to laugh at her.

"Yes. I will go to the ranch in the middle of nowhere." She sighed throwing down her paint brush.

She watched as Harlynn raised his eyebrows at Blacky, which meant can you please leave. The room became quiet when the door closed. Kate cleaned off her paint brushes waiting for him to fire away.

"I hate when you do that to me." He snapped. "I know that I made you upset two days ago. I'm sorry. I don't like how you've been behaving to be honest."

"I don't have a drinking problem. You have a drinking problem," she stated firmly. "I shouldn't have to stop drinking because you stop drinking."

"For the last three days I have watched you drink starting at noon and ending at midnight."

"You make it sound like I'm fall down drunk, Harlynn? Are you having an epiphany about how you have lived and it scares you? Are you projecting onto me?"

"I've never seen you drink at lunch every day, when did you start doing that?" Harlynn asked not backing down.

"Well, I've never been stretched this thin before, Harlynn. What time is appropriate for me to start drinking alcohol? Please be very precise so we don't have any miscommunications."

"Why are you being impossible? There is something going on you're not telling me? What aren't you telling me? Why are you acting strange?"

"I have been shot at, my husband has been kidnapped, my daughter's life has been threatened, I have almost two billion dollars not invested for Moon Water, I have a law firm to deal with, my brother who is my best friend is having a hard time, my best friend has married my father and is more needy then my three month old, Elle and Nick are just making it, you and you are a mess."

"You forgot the report that you didn't give me about the economic affect of Moon Water on the health care industry."

"Yes. The report I didn't show you because I don't know what you want or who you are anymore."

"Why didn't you come to me? Why are you leaving me out of a major strategy, Kateland?"

"Are you back? Do you want to deal with what we are facing? Can you face what we are facing?"

"I would prefer that you don't use alcohol to solve problems like I have done for the last ten years. I don't want you making the same mistakes I have, Kateland. I'm not asking you to stop drinking. That is your choice."

"I promise it's under control." Kate frowned. "It's a lot right now."

"Yes, it is Kateland. We are going to have to come to an agreement about going to the ranch. I want to go twice a month and for some holidays like Thanksgiving. Once a month I want it to be just us and Keaton. And maybe Henry and Meg, but Sue and your dad or Nick and Elle or Ed or whoever else doesn't have to be with us every waking moment. I want to be with you and not worry about a house full of people."

"What do I get to demand?" Kate asked.

"What do you want to demand, demand away? We will spend part of the summer in Utah and ski during the holidays. I want to travel more than we have in the last year."

"I want to have a weekend where it's just us without the children or anyone else sometimes." She looked down. "The report made me sick as it talked about how curing these children would take incomes out of communities and people would lose their jobs. It was sick."

"Blacky showed me the report last night. I know that it stirs up some horrible times with Janey. We need to do this."

"I know." She waited. He walked over to her and held her in his arms. For the first time in a long time she felt safe in Harlynn's arms. There was a difference in him today.

"Are you taking the day off today?" Harlynn asked in his soft voice filled with love.

"Yes. Where is Laney?" Kate leaned into him closing her eyes.

"I already took care of her and Claire has her. She only wants you. And I only want you." He kissed her. "Maybe we can find a moment before we leave for the ranch."

"Find a moment for what, Mr. Barrett?" Kate inquired.

"I want a moment to kiss and a few other things." He whispered in her ear as he kissed it. "That would make me feel better. I can't stand when we aren't getting along. We could go by the loft after we have lunch with Janey at school?"

"I will think about it." Kate smiled. She wanted to ask him if he was back but didn't want to know if the answer was no. Maybe there would be times when he felt better and maybe there would be times when he couldn't cope.

A moment later Elle came in the art studio with a smile on her face. Harlynn took his arms from around Kate. Their thirty minutes of alone time was gone until later. It was invaded as Kate watched the confidence disappear.

"Thank you." Elle started crying tears of happiness. "I don't know what I would do without you guys. I think I'm going to go sleep in the guest room. Nick said we are going to the ranch this weekend?"

"Of course you are, Elle." Harlynn smiled at Kate. "You are always welcomed at the ranch when we invite everyone there. Open invitation the second weekend of the month from now on."

"Wow, I'm completely touched and I know Nick will be also. I can't wait to see the wall hangings up when we get there, Kate. I'm very excited."

Kate watched as Nick came in the art studio looking disgruntled. He went to Elle, holding her while he closed his eyes. Kate and Harlynn left them alone. It was nice to know that other relationships struggled from day to day.

———

There was no time for their meeting at the loft since Levi wanted his mother. Laney wanted her mother, also. Kate sat in the playroom on the floor trying to wear the children out for the trip to the ranch. Laney was easy to wear out at this age while Levi was tough and his stamina was never ending as they played ball, then hide-n-seek and organized all the toys in the playroom. Harlynn was picking up Janey from school, which was very helpful. She smiled hearing him come down the hall whistling. This was their very crazy life and it was good.

"I told Stan, he and Janey should come up to the ranch if he wants. I think they will come tomorrow." Harlynn smiled as he came in the playroom knowing that would get him bonus points.

"Really? Thank you!" She picked up Laney to go change her before they left. "Can you get Levi ready, and then we are ready to go. Five minute warning."

"Come on little man, let's get your backpack." Harlynn smiled because Levi was running around in circles he was so excited.

"I want to ride my pony when we get there Dada! And I want to swim and find bugs and see you!" The little boy was elated at the prospect of being at the ranch with his father.

"We are going to have a good time, son." Harlynn promised him. There it was again, that look in his eyes that was the old Harlynn.

On the way to the ranch, Kate went through the FedEx envelopes from her assistant Ann. One envelope was full of messages as she glanced through them. She had a new Blackberry number that she was not giving out to anyone. All calls went through Ann except for immediate family and very, very close friends.

As she kept going over the messages Kate stopped. She stared at it then turned to Harlynn handing it to him.

"Why do you have a message from the White House?" Harlynn asked glancing at it then going back to traffic.

"You talk to the White House more than I do?"

"I will be on the call with you because it has to concern Moon Water."

"You seem mad," Kate questioned.

"Nope, I'm feeling ignored by you. I'm trying to figure out how I get back in your good graces to get attention from you." He looked in the rearview mirror and sighed. There was a caravan of black SUVs going down the highway behind them. He drove Kate and the kids with the nanny in the very back to check on the children. Harlynn didn't like someone driving him, plus it gave them a chance to talk.

"Come to bed early with me. The comments about drinking made me unhappy. The last thing I need is you going after me for anything including if I decide to drink more than normal. Thank God you didn't know me in college or you would have totally freaked out."

"Well, I had this epiphany that we shouldn't be drinking a lot around the children. And I'm trying to change how I deal with stress. I don't want you drinking because of Moon Water or me."

"I don't always feel like you're on my side." She admitted.

"I'm always on your side no matter what, Kateland." He glanced at her raising his eyebrows. "Why are you so sensitive about the alcohol issue? It's like I hit a nerve when I said I didn't like you drinking with lunch. Kate you are in the really big time, love. People are watching us all the time."

"I saw the picture of you and Levi in the paper this morning from the zoo. Why didn't you tell me?"

"I was hiding it. I thought you would be upset with me."

"It was a really cute picture of you two together. You need to get a digital copy of it. I want to blow it up for the house. And you will have to do one with Janey."

"Already have the digital and scheduling a day with Janey we can do it. I didn't think you would see it in the paper since you don't read the local one that often."

"I had about a hundred people text me over it Harlynn, be real, I know a ton of people in this town." He laughed. "You are my silly man some days."

"Blacky yelled at me for it. I told him I didn't care. I had this amazing experience with my son. Levi is the best medicine, if you want the truth."

"You seem different? Tell me what is going on in that head of yours."

"You were right. Stopping Dr. Brown helped me and I can't explain why. It's like I needed you to say, look Harlynn, there is nothing wrong with how you have lived your life or your success."

"We all have mistakes we have made in our personal lives. It didn't seem productive the path that Dr. Brown was taking you down."

"You were right Kateland, that's why I'm married to you. If you ever see me doing something that doesn't look right, I need you to be open and honest. It's going to take time for me to get back where I want to be."

"You can take as much time as you like, Babes." She closed her eyes wanting to sleep for a while before they got to the ranch.

———

When they walked in the house, Christa was there waiting for them. The house was stunning. Kate wasn't sure how Christa got it all done, but what Kate anticipated taking months had taken eight weeks to complete. It looked more like Kate and Harlynn now. Harlynn's father was even more prominent in the space than before. There was a stunning portrait of Paul framed when you walked in the front door. Kate had instructed Christa to give the picture to an artist she knew. The artist had done a portrait from it that was almost life size. The new couch was perfect as Kate sat on it feeling the navy suede that made the room more inviting. The color scheme of the whole house was now whites and grays, accented with blues and red, rustic but modern. It was everything she wanted was all Kate could think.

As Kate walked through the house she stuck her head in each room. The playroom along with the children's room was inviting. The children had beautiful wooden toys to play with and explore in a vibrant room done in red, white and blue with a giant Texas flag on one wall.

Kate stopped when she saw the wall hanging in her room that Elle had done. It was geometric pattern done in navy and white. The bedspread was that same beautiful navy. Depending on how you looked at it you saw different things like the sun or a flower or a horse. It was done by layering and it was amazing. It was the little things, like new towels or a boot rack to put the boots in when you came in the house. Or the pillows that were full of color. Everything flowed like Kate wanted it to flow.

"This house is more my father now than it ever has been, Kate. He would have loved what you have done with it. I'm so impressed with the changes," Harlynn whispered to her. "Thank you."

"Are you okay?" The look was back again. The pain was back as he thought of his father.

"Profoundly sad. It will pass. I think I'm going to jump in the shower before dinner."

—

Dinner was fun as everyone talked about the house and the incredible changes. Christa was praised by everyone at dinner. There was calmness in the house as though all your problems could be left outside the front door. Silence filled the room as the fire crackled in the fireplace.

"It was Kate." Christa confessed looking worried. "I was given twenty pages of notes and things started to arrive every day. I can't take credit for what she did or what she taught me. Most of the orders took place at three in the morning. Do you ever sleep?"

Kate felt several eyes turn toward with concern. Apparently Kate was the one to worry over. Harlynn gently reached over placing his arm around her. "That would be when Laney takes her bottle and can't go back to sleep. Kate is always good at multi-tasking."

Kate blushed not saying a word because she wasn't good at lying. After feeding Laney most nights she never went back to bed. Then she would start working and that was that.

—

It was only nine and Kate decided to go to sleep. She was tired from the drive and work. She wondered why she was so tired as she got ready for bed. Or maybe she was faking it to get away from everyone. She pulled out a book to read as she heard a knock on the door.

"Come in." She waited to see who it was, knowing it was Keaton. To her surprise it was Henry. He had been in New York for the last three days.

"Hi," he said coming in the room. He sat on the edge of the bed, excited to see her. "I missed you the last couple of days. I got your emails."

"I got yours too. How was New York?" It made Kate think of when she was a child and Henry came home from a business trip. She stayed with Henry a lot growing up. Those were good memories as she giggled.

"It was good. The house looks incredible, Kateland." He paused. "Thank you for calling me your father in that interview. You have no idea how good it feels to have you do that, Kate." Kate leaned over and gave him a hug.

"You are the best father anyone could have. What did you think of the interview?"

"You had complete control of the interview the whole time. The FDA is on overload with the emails and phone calls they are getting concerning drug trials for children. You made the world stop and take action. You always make me very proud."

Henry's eyes sparkled as she watched him, the man was truly happy, which made Kate happy. They sat there catching up until Harlynn walked in the room at ten.

"Hi, Henry! I didn't realize you had come in." He walked over as the two men embraced. "Thanks for coming up, I know that you have been busy."

"I'm never too busy for my family. I will let you two go to bed and see you in the morning." When the door closed behind Henry, Kate looked at Harlynn the way she did when she wanted him.

"Can I take a shower? I was outside by the fire and probably smell like smoke."

"I really did want to go to the loft with you today and I promise we will do that another time. Right now we are here and I promise not to make too much noise, but you better lock the door and maybe put on some music."

Kate sat there watching his every move from the door to the Bose stereo to taking off his clothes. She slowly undid her robe for him revealing a very sexy short see through night gown that fit like a second skin.

"That is very new because I would remember that one." He laid on the bed next to her pulling her closer to him. "I think we are going back to that schedule of making love every day, if that's okay with you?"

"Mister, I think that would be the best therapy that any doctor could prescribe. I know that when you touch me it makes everything bad go away and for a moment I feel safe."

"When I'm with you I don't feel lost and my confidence comes back along with that calmness." He closed his eyes. "I started reading the other letters my Dad wrote and they are beautiful, Kate," he whispered. "I didn't know he could write so poetically."

"I bet you learn a lot of things about your father in those letters. He told me to tell you he is always with you and he will be watching out for you." Harlynn buried his head in her neck as she held him. There were times he needed to be held by her, she reminded herself.

"Tomorrow I want to go back to the tepee. Will you come with me?"

"Yes," he told her sitting up. "I want to kiss you all night long."

"That would be what I need, Babes." Then he slowly took off her night gown and stared to kiss her neck and work his way down. Then he stopped watching her as she watched him back in the dark. "I'm sorry that I've been putting you through this hell."

"We will get through it, Harlynn." Then she slowly got up and kissed him pushing back in the pillows. She got on top of him then kissed him back as she wrapped her body around him.

Everything felt different in this room when they made love was all Kate could think as she lay in the darkness with Harlynn next to her. The room was cold as she moved closer to him.

"Are you awake?' Kate whispered to him.

"Completely." Harlynn smiled at her. "I can't stop thinking of you, and this house. Why is everything new and different with you, Kateland?"

"What do you mean?" Kate asked sitting up and pulling the sheets up close to her. "You know I have this thing with colors, remember in my other life I'm a well known artist. And I guess that I'm finally accepting that this is our life. This ranch is going to be part of our lives and the people around us are here to help us. And the children. We have these three children to teach about the world."

She reached over the bed to her side drawer and pulled out a bottle of her moon water she had made with Janey. The moon water was made with moon beams and could heal, only if you believed and prayed to St. Jude. She placed three drops over Harlynn's heart. "You are going to feel better in your heart going forward."

"When I close my eyes I can still feel my father in this house."

"What would you say to Paul if you could talk to him one more time?"

"I would tell him that he was the best father that I have ever known. I hope I can do that for my children. If I could just hear his voice, I don't know. It's not like we could change anything that happened and bring him back."

"Each day I'm going to try to write one letter to each of our children. To have those letters from your father is going to help you get through these days, and months and years to come." She kissed him.

"I already started doing it. I wrote a ten page letter to our daughter. If anything ever happens to me I want her to know that I love her." He pushed Kate's hair back.

Kate leaned over kissing Harlynn again. She couldn't believe this father he was becoming in front of her eyes. The reality was that he was finally slowing down to see this family and these friends he had in his life.

"I don't think we are going to get any sleep tonight."

"Yeah, I figured that out about two hours ago." She giggled, as he kissed her neck and she could feel his heart beating slowly.

~Chapter 22

The office seemed crowded as Kate put a list of topics on the wipe board and watched as everyone typed it down on their IPads. She looked around the room smiling. It was apparent she was not the only one who didn't sleep last night. Keat threw his eye drops at her and smiled back.

"Kate, do you mind if Blacky joins us?" Nick looked up from his Blackberry.

"That's a good idea. He needs to understand what is going on." A moment later Blacky appeared taking a seat with his IPad.

"Nick, why don't you start with an update on the meetings and what is going on with the FDA trial. The letter I got says we can start in four weeks with drug trials. What obstacles do you foresee?"

"I can only speak from the pure logistics of the project. I think if we want the medical side we better have a call with Danny later." Kate glanced at her watch.

"Why don't we skip you and text Danny? Let's get all the information at one time." She made a note to herself to always have Danny available for the calls going forward. "Keaton can you give me an update on the licensing agreement with Gene Code?"

"They want a discount." Keat replied. "It's not outrageous and there were some other minor issues."

"How much did they pay their CEO last year?" Kate smiled as Henry walked in and sat down.

"With stock, he probably cleared ten million," Keat said slowly.

"No discount. Tell him I will be glad to discuss it with him. If we give him a price break he will be bragging all over place. I know Ted and he is about as boastful as a CEO can be."

"It would be nice to have him on the list, though." Keaton countered. "They have the leading technology in diagnostics. If we get on one of those chips the revenue stream would be amazing. If our goal is to eventually be part of a chip or diagnostic test we need them."

"I'm not going to have Ted Mack state the terms of the deal. It has to work in our favor. See what else you can come up with." Kate looked up to see Harlynn in the room, which she didn't realize as their eyes met.

"Why don't you show me his proposal and I'll work with you on it, Keat. You're both right." Everyone in the room turned looking at Harlynn, it was very apparent hadn't slept last night either by the red puffy eyes.

"That would be perfect." Kate smiled at him for a second then turned to her father, asking Sam for an update on what he was finding at the Woodlands.

"I feel we are moving ahead too fast and I'm starting to see problems. I think we need to be very focused on what areas we want to venture in going forward. Blacky and I are still working on the security issues. I'm seeing some hefty orders come through so I've ask each group for a budget for the coming year. Even if we have deep pockets the research groups should not be wasteful. The inventories are not in check. I'm still working on it."

"Do you think part of the problem is this group of scientist is basically used to spending what they want?" Henry asked.

"There are some real damn pre-Madonnas in that place. I've dealt with them before and they need to understand that they don't own the place."

"Wow." Kate sat back thinking. "Let's plan on a walkthrough of the facility on Wednesday."

"That should work." He said as he nodded his head. "We need a more defined plan for the facility and the scientists need to understand they don't have the spending authority, I do."

Kate pulled out a stack of envelopes and handed them out. She watched as everyone sat back for a moment. It was the first distribution for the owners of Moon Water. She could have held on to the money to the end of the year instead she decided quarterly distributions would be better for all the countless hours everyone had worked. She watched as each person stared at the checks in awe shaking their heads. If Moon Water ceased to exist at that moment, no one in the room would have to work again, nor their children or grand children or great grand children.

"I want to thank everyone for making Moon Water possible and I hope that next time the checks will be bigger. Henry and Harlynn if you could stay a moment I would appreciate it. Everyone else can go back to sleep." It was six-thirty in the morning.

"Thank you." Keaton hugged his sister, and then Nick did the same.

"I'm going to make breakfast for everyone," Nick said going to the kitchen.

"I'm taking Levi out to feed the horses, and then we will be in for breakfast," Keat said following Nick.

Kate watched as Harlynn picked up the phone and dialed the number from the email he had gotten this morning.

"This is Harlynn Barrett. I have a call scheduled for seven-thirty."

Kate waited as her palms began to sweat as Harlynn put the call on speaker then waited as Blacky put a recording device next to the phone.

"This is the Secretary of Defense, Scott Campbell. Could the individuals on the phone identify themselves?"

"Kate Jones."

"Henry Grayden"

"Jack Black."

"Harlynn Barrett."

"Thank you for making time for the call today. Glad to see you are still around Jack."

"Thank you, sir." Blacky waited. "As you know we have had several security problems surrounding Moon Water and the safety of Harlynn and Kate."

"Yes. I have seen the reports from different intelligence agencies. From our information concerning Star Pharmaceutical the threats are almost all dimensioned. As long as you are overseeing their families and company security, I have complete confidence that they will remain safe. Also, I want you to know that we are here to help you in any way we can, Jack. I want to hear from you if there is anything we can do."

"Thank you sir. What can we do for you today?" Blacky asked as he stared at Harlynn.

"We are asking for Moon Water to assist the military in development of a drug to counter act a chemical weapon that our troops are being exposed to in the Middle East. Our best guess is that the weapon was designed by Iran. We need the technology that is owned in that room you are sitting in. We are willing to pay for the development of it and to pay any future licensing agreements. Name your price and I'll pay it."

This was not what Kate was expecting from the phone call. She had never envisioned Moon Water being used by the military. What if they decided to use the technology in a different way than they were saying? It was like Harlynn could read her mind as they listened.

"Sir, this is Harlynn Barrett, I have to ask you what guarantee can you give us that this technology won't be used to create any types of weapons? Moon Water has no intention of developing weapons that would kill people." Silence filled the phone line.

"I understand your concern, Harlynn and I'm listening to you. Right now our only concern is the safety of our soldiers. This biochemical agent is one of the most horrible things we have seen. We are asking for your help. You can oversee the development of it in Houston, if that's what it takes. We are interested in starting as soon as possible."

"I need to see the classified reports on what has been found, Scott," Blacky stated firmly. "You know where to send the material. We can talk after I have read through what you have gathered."

"We aren't ready to commit to anything. We are always open to helping protect our soldiers." Henry stated firmly. "I think I speak for everyone in this room."

"Thank you for your time," the Secretary said before hanging up.

They all sat in the room as it filled with silence over what this meant. Working with the government, creating a drug to protect the military? They had a true monopoly. The United States government was at their mercy.

"Blacky did you know they were going to ask us to do this?" Harlynn asked frustrated.

"I know several pieces of information that either I can't confirm or I'm not allowed to confirm. There will be more is all I can say. I'm not going to run to you with every report I get because ninety percent has no merit."

Kate looked at her phone seeing Danny was calling. She laughed because he had been avoiding her since he got sick at the interview. She put him on speaker.

"Hey stranger, how are you feeling?" Kate asked. "Are you better? We are all at the ranch and you should come?" Harlynn shook his head and smiled at Kate because she could get anyone to do what she wanted without them knowing it.

"Who's on the speaker with you?" Danny asked slowly.

"Henry, Harlynn and Blacky are in the room." She listened as they all said hello then the silence came back. She closed her eyes. "What's her blood count? You have been dodging me for two days." The room fell silent because this was her life of peaks and valley. She sure as hell didn't want to be in this valley.

"Kateland, I'm concerned. There is nothing conclusive to worry about and remember that Levi was sick with the sinus infection." He waited. "Her white count is higher than I like. There are a few other counts that are off. I saw her late last night and we are running everything as a precaution."

"How did she take it?" Harlynn asked.

"Like Janey always does. She looked me in the eye and told me it was nothing. Apparently God and she had another talk. It's not her time."

"Danny, why don't you come up when you get the results back? I will have a car pick you up at two and my plane will take you here." Henry strongly suggested.

"That sounds fine. Kate, can you please pick up?"

"Hey." Kate said as Henry watched her. Danny ran through all the numbers while she listened. It wasn't bad or good in her opinion.

"Kateland, you listen to me. We both know someday this cancer is going to come back and now I can say I have a way to treat it."

"I know. I will see you this afternoon. Thank you for calling me Danny. I know how it kills you."

"You better have a bed ready for me. I'm having some of your Patron and going to sleep. I can't remember the last time I slept more than three hours between the hospital and Moon Water. Thanks for the check, Kate. I don't know what else to say."

"We love you." She hung up the phone wishing everyone wasn't staring at her. Finally, she looked at Blacky, who looked like he might lose it at any moment, which she had never seen. Henry forced a smile for her as if to say, you can handle this, Kateland. Harlynn was completely crushed at the thought of anything wrong with one of his children.

"I think we should all hold hands and pray that God will keep her with us for as long as he is willing to." Kate managed to say. It was a hard way to start the day, but at least everyone was here for her was all Kate could think.

Claire appeared with Laney, handing her to Kate, almost like it was timed. Kate took her holding on to Laney as though she could never possible let go of her. Laney made everything better was all Kate could think as she giggled Kate's giggle in her tiny voice.

"I'm going to take Laney for a walk." Kate smiled at Harlynn through the pain and the memories. "Would you like to come?"

"Let me change and I will be back in five minutes." Harlynn stopped and kissed her as he walked by. "Remember what I told you? I will do everything I can to help her."

"I remember." She nodded.

"I need to go tell Nick and Keat what's going on." Blacky looked into her eyes. "We will all do whatever has to be done, Kateland. You have the support of everyone here. And we love you and we love Janey."

"I know. I just didn't see it coming this time." She stared into Laney's eyes. "Your Mama is so silly?"

Finally it was only Henry and Kate sitting in the office on the couch watching Laney. They sat there in silence. She needed to know that Henry was there for her no matter what was going on.

"You make me very proud, Kateland," Henry admitted. "The first thing you chose to do was ask for God's help. You could have cried or yelled or thrown the phone across the room. You prayed instead. I believe she will get through this, sweetheart."

"Maybe this is God's way of telling me I have to go forward with Moon Water. You know I've been waiving due to the fact people keep trying to kill us. I think this is God telling me I have a job to do and I better damn well do it."

"Yes. You are right, Kateland. We have the potential to do this and we are damn well going to do it." Henry held Laney up in the air like an airplane. "You are as beautiful as your mother. Why don't you and Harlynn go riding after lunch? Meg and I will watch the children?"

"We are going to search for the tepee. Don't tell anyone." She smiled.

"What tepee?" Henry asked cautiously. "Paul use to talk about this old Indian who lived out here in a tepee. You've been to the tepee?"

"When no one could find me I was in the tepee with the Chief."

"Is that the subject of your new paintings? The ranch and the tepee?"

"Yes. I know you want the last one for your office. You can have it."

"Thank you." He smiled at her. "What are you going to ask the Chief if you find him in the middle of nowhere in a tepee?"

"To heal Harlynn from his pain and to protect Janey."

"Be careful. Do you understand me?" Henry asked her as Laney gnawed on his finger.

"Harlynn is going to be with me. The Chief called Harlynn, Little Shark, and I'm the Dreamer."

"That makes perfect sense when you think about it." He covered Laney with kisses. "I think I might go for a run with Nick and Blacky."

"You should. Thank you for being here Henry and coming from New York. When is Meg coming?"

"In about thirty minutes and she baked you a surprise." She smiled getting up as Harlynn came in the room dressed in shorts and a t-shirt with sneakers on. His eyes looked a little puffier than before as he smiled at Kate and Henry with Laney. He left and came back with the camera taking several pictures.

"Let's roll because I have a new jogger for Laney." Harlynn took the child from Henry as she continued to giggle.

Henry reached over and cradled Kate in his arms for a good minute as Kate closed her eyes. He whispered all the things she needed to hear again. Kate liked that about Henry, he understood that she needed to hear things more than once to make them real. It was like his love was magic just like when she was a child. He knew how to heal her soul when it was aching.

It was a peaceful morning with clear blue sky as they sat by a small pond watching fish swim up to the surface. In the distance Kate could see Charlie. When she looked to her left she saw another body guard with the same sun glasses on.

"What are you thinking?" Harlynn asked as Laney watched the ducks. She loved ducks and it was fascinating to watch her expressions.

"My heart says she is fine. I can't stand to watch her go through another treatment of any kind. My brain says that statistical this is what usually happens. I have read every article and research paper on this type of cancer. It's not shocking intellectually if I could take the emotions out of it."

"Boy, it was like getting hit in the stomach for me. I can't stand it when Janey isn't here on the weekends. I can't stand anything happening to her, love. I just want to smell that strawberry shampoo you use in her hair."

"We have to keep our faith. We will find our way to keep her well and that's all there is too it." She leaned against him, closing her eyes.

"I hated when Danny told you about the blood tests. It made my heart ache to watch you suffer like that, Kate." He leaned over kissing her. "I had a wonderful time last night with you. Thank you."

"I will need a nap later because I'm not use to going without zero sleep. It was nice to have all your attention for that many hours. I felt like I was the most important person in your world."

"You are, Kateland. I'm glad you felt that way. Do you have any idea what it means the military wants us to assist in the development?"

"It means the government is going to be writing us a check with a lot of zeros."

"It takes Moon Water to a new level for everyone. I liked watching you in that meeting this morning. It reminded me of being at the law firm when you would challenge me in a meeting. I liked those days. They seem so simple compared to what is happening now."

"I can see your thoughts spinning behind those golden brown eyes."

"I'm ready to be part of Moon Water again. Not at the level I was at before. I want to be part of the meetings and take on a few things to see how I will do. I can't promise you anything except I will do my best. If there is anything going on with Janey I will do whatever I have to while you take care of her."

"Thank you." She leaned over kissing him. "Are you still going to do yoga with me?"

"Yes. I want us to do it together in the mornings. As I read these letters from my father it makes me realize how I need to be there for our children. When all of this started I kept thinking of what I wanted for me. I wanted to be the one out front and whose name was on the door at the law firm and the person on *Forbes*. I wanted to have all the answers and power."

"And now?" Kate asked slowly. "What do you want now, Harlynn. What's the most important accomplishment you would like to achieve in your life?"

"The only thing I truly want is you and to raise these children. I have to stop drinking because I don't want to end up like my father between the alcohol and smoking. Since meeting you I have gotten in better shape and I need to do more. I thank God for you all the time. I want to be the best husband and best father I can be. I'm not going to sacrifice our children's childhoods or our marriage."

"You make me very happy, mister. I only ask that whatever you do you take it slow. Like you told me in the beginning there will be good days and bad days."

"We have had enough bad days." He picked up Laney. "Let's head back and find your big brother, Laney."

"Well, your son got up at five this morning. He dressed himself, then came and got me. Don't say anything about the fact he has one brown boot and one blue boot. It was too cute, I couldn't tell him."

"Keaton told me what was going on last night by the fire. He is very nervous about this relationship. I don't like seeing him like this, Kate."

"I'm going to speak with Christa this morning, check on Elle and go to town with Sue so she will stop this crap."

"Do your best, Kate. Sue is in a hard place with her choices. It'll all work out in time."

"It's better. Thanks for coming with us to the pond."

"I don't want to be shut out anymore and I'm going to need you to get through my father dying. I really miss him."

"I'm here." She promised. "Nick is the one who told me we need to talk no matter what. Even if his parents have just had a fight, they still talk. If there is one marriage I want us to emulate it would Blacky's and Julia's marriage."

"They have such a connection you can see it when they are together. Even with both their careers they are seamless in getting through everything. Can you imagine what Julia has been through with what Blacky does?" Harlynn asked Kate as they came up to the house.

"She believes in him is how she can withstand what he does. I think Meg and Henry have a good marriage. I like the way Henry adores Meg no matter what he is doing. She has this voice that she uses that calms him down immediately. I've seen him leave a meeting to call Meg, just to hear her voice."

"I always wondered what he was doing when things would get heated and he stands up to go outside to make a call." Harlynn inhaled a deep breath. "Do you think Keaton and Christa will work out and get married? He is struggling being in this relationship with Christa."

"We didn't have very good role models, Harlynn. Keaton has a lot of anxiety when it comes to relationships thanks to our parents. A serious relationship or marriage scares the hell out of him."

"Are you going to talk to Christa?" Harlynn asked slowly as they saw Christa ahead going to the pool.

"Can you take both children and I will meet up with you in a little while?"

"Sure." He leaned over kissing her. "When Janey gets here I want to spend time with her."

"I think that would be nice because Stan and I need to talk. This has to be frightening for him. He doesn't have the support system I have with you and the family."

"I have tremendous respect for how hard Stan works to take care of Janey. And you? I wish I would have known you when you took on being part of Janey's life. Why did you do it, Kateland? You were twenty-five, a second year lawyer and you took on helping this child who was seriously ill?"

"When I would hold Janey there was this feeling of happiness that came over me. It was pure joy. It was a love that I had never felt before. I prayed about it for two days, and then I knew it was what I was supposed to do. Henry and Keaton understood immediately. They supported me along with Meg."

"I was surprised the first time I saw you with her. I was at the zoo with my nieces and I saw you with Janey. It was obvious that Janey was going through treatment. You were with Kenton that day."

"And what did you think?" Kate asked him smiling because he had never told her this story. "Why didn't you come over to say hello? You have been stalking me that far back?"

"Yes and I got what I wanted." He teased her. "It seemed like your time with your daughter. Plus, I was surprised that you had never mentioned it. I had Leezann ask Henry's assistant for the story. That's when I started going to the gala for the Pediatric Cancer Fund. Did you notice?"

"I thought you were doing it because of my father and Henry were your big clients. I remember thinking you didn't look happy with your wife."

"You think?" He laughed. "Why don't we have some breakfast? Afterwards you can talk to Christa." Harlynn suggested as he watched Laney smiling at him.

"I'm not really hungry." Kate got the look from Harlynn. "A protein smoothie?"

"Yes and pancakes with your favorite maple syrup."

"Okay, you are making me hungry now, Mr. Barrett."

—

Keaton and Nick both stared at Kate when she came in the kitchen. It was there in both their eyes because Keaton and Nick had been there when Janey went through all the treatments. The ups and downs for years came rushing back at the two men.

"We are here," Keaton whispered to her.

251

"Of course you and Nick are here." Kate pulled away smiling. "Look, we don't know anything yet for sure. Even if it's the worst we will figure it out. According to Danny, Janey was told that she will be fine."

"Who told her?" Nick asked already knowing the question.

"Casey and God." Kate smiled sitting down to eat. Casey was Janey's best friend who died from the same cancer two years ago. Casey would come to Janey in her dreams and tell her about meeting God. At times Casey would tell Janey things that were impossible for her to know. Like when Kate was pregnant with Levi, Janey already knew from Casey before Kate had told anyone.

"Well, that makes me feel better." Nick tried to smile. "Elle said to tell you she would try to get up before ten."

"She needs to rest and I completely understand," Kate said as she gave Laney a few Cheerios to play with. Everyone watched as she attempted to line them up like Levi use to do when he was this age.

"Wow," Keaton said slowly. "We need to start focusing on Laney apparently."

Laney laughed when she was done.

Harlynn got breakfast for Kate and her smoothie. It was like the old days when he would get up early before work to make sure she ate. Perhaps it was the way he gazed at her with Laney or the way when he walked by her he would run his hand gently across her back. There was this physical attraction between them that was defiant of everything in their world Kate realized. It was irrational and she knew they had no control over it.

Harlynn watched Kate as she drank her smoothie and then ate half of her breakfast. He gave her the look that meant, eat more please, because I don't want you passing out. Then he smiled at her with his eyes.

"You guys are doing that thing again where you have whole conversations without talking," Nick said getting up. "I haven't seen that in a long time. Let's go riding bro."

"I'll be there in a couple of minutes," Keaton said staring at Kate.

"Yes, I'm going to go out to the pool right now and talk with Christa. Don't worry." She smiled getting up from the table, then she stopped kissing Harlynn and he tasted like syrup. It made her think of the morning after they got married. They were in bed eating breakfast when he leaned over kissing her tasting like maple syrup. The memory was powerful as he watched her.

"The morning," he waited, "after our wedding." She nodded as she watched his eyes sparkle and she giggled.

"Text me when Janey gets here." Kate requested taking their plates off the table.

"I will." Harlynn watched Kate as she walked towards the door.

"I want that," Keaton said in a whisper. "I want to be loved the way you two love each other."

"You will," Kate called back to him. For all the times her brother had helped her with Harlynn, she would do the same for him.

Meg and Henry were coming down the path towards Kate as she walked to the pool. Kate could tell that Meg was very upset by the news concerning Janey. It made Kate sad, but then she felt good that Janey was so incredible loved.

"Where are you off to?" Henry asked her.

"Christa. Keat needs help with his love life." She stopped embracing Meg for two minutes. "Thank you for loving Janey and me."

"I think she will be fine," Meg whispered.

"We will figure it out like we always do."

"Yes we will." Henry patted her on the back. "Go help your brother."

———

Christa was sitting under an umbrella by the pool thumbing through decorating magazines with a big floppy hat on and sunglasses. She wore a sheer turquoise cover up with a black string bikini underneath. Again, Kate was sure she could be a model with those long legs and beautiful porcelain skin.

"I hope you're not working?" Kate sat down under the umbrella as a pitcher of mimosas came out to them with her favorite cream cheese cinnamon rolls that only Meg could make. Kate slowly poured two glasses and sat back wondering what Christa needed. She closed her eyes trying to find the words to explain her family and her brother.

"Look at this room?" She tore out the page handing it to Kateland. "Now imagine it with what's in black, but now navy and what's in white, we make a smoke gray?"

"With yellow pillows?" Kate inquired. "For Henry and Meg?" Christa nodded.

"And then we could carry it into his office with the same navy. And look at this strip." She flipped the pages in another magazine. "And then this desk? Contemporary, but rustic still?"

"Why don't we show Meg? I think its brilliant Christa." Kate waited. "How are things? Honestly?" Kate watched as Christa pushed aside the magazines and sat back thinking.

"It's like a fairy tale. I fly around the country with the most amazing job one could wish for in a life. I have met prince charming. The man who loves me is kind, smart, athletic and religious. He is thoughtful and loving always. My mother always told me there weren't men like him in the world."

"We seem to have more than our fair share of them on this ranch at the moment if you look around. Do you mind if I ask what you want or what is bothering you?"

"To be with Keaton and Keaton. If everything is going well then why can't we talk about our future together?"

"Because Keaton wants to take things slowly is not a reflection of the feelings he has for you, Christa. The caution is a byproduct of my parent's relationship and also Henry. Henry always told us to really think about the relationships we have with people. He wanted us to analyze if this was someone who we wanted in our lives for the next thirty years or more."

"I want to be with Keaton forever and I can't explain it. He is very funny and makes me laugh at myself. I like the way he talks to me. Everything is enchanting about him from his voice to the way he reaches over to hold my hand. He works incredible hard on Moon Water for you."

"He isn't working for me on Moon Water; he is doing it for himself. He owns ten percent of Moon Water, Christa. Do you have a problem with how close Keaton and I are because for Harlynn it was hard, and some days it still is difficult, I suppose. There is a tremendous love between them like two brothers would have. You have to throw Nick in with them."

"It's hard for me to understand how everyone can be so invasive. If I marry Keaton will I be required to spend every vacation and weekend with you and the people here? For an outsider it borders on crazy. You have people trying to kill you, Harlynn and your daughter."

"We are trying to change the world and help people, Christa." She told herself to calm down. "I would say that it's very important for us to get along for Keaton to marry you. I'm not trying to threaten you, I'm being honest. If Harlynn and Keat hated each other I wouldn't have married Harlynn." She sighed. "I think you are very interesting and kind, Christa. I respect who you are and your endless talents. I would be willing to bet money on you and Keat getting married. I'm not sure when."

"What if you do something I don't like?" Christa asked. "You are Kate Jones?"

"You send me an email or text or call me and we sit down and talk over tequila or maybe not. It depends on the time of day. If you treat Keaton with respect and love him, we will never have a problem from my point of view. Do you two get a honeymoon without us? Absolutely, for a little while. Will there be family vacations with all of us and weekends at the ranch and skiing trips and the adventure trips we take? Absolutely. Will you always have alone time? Yes. Do we want you to be part of this family? Yes and we hope you want to be part of it. It's crazy, stressful and sometimes there is a lot of drama. We all love each other. We would be there in a second for each other. It's nice Christa. There are not many people you can count on. You can count on the people in this house to be there for you just like they have been there for Harlynn. Do you have to tell them to back off every once in a while? Yes, they always mean well."

"I'm afraid of losing Keaton?" Christa admitted.

"I honestly don't think he would do that to you. It's really up to God when you think about it. If it's meant to work out it will. And I will tell you what Harlynn told me in the beginning, you will have good days and bad days. I do have one question. Do you love Keaton? I mean do you truly love him at this second?"

"Yes, I do love him. It was one of those loves that people talk about that I never understood. It was instant. He had my heart when he walked into the room with that towel around him.

"Do you think you can handle that Keaton and I are best friends. Everything I do I share with him, except you know sex. I don't discuss what I do with my husband with other people." She smiled.

"I think you are one of the coolest people I've ever met, Kateland. And I hope we can be close."

"Do you feel better? Keat's happiness is very important to me, Christa. I would do anything for my brother."

"I feel accepted by you, which is what I needed." Christa closed her eyes finishing her mimosa.

~Chapter 23

Sometime after lunch Harlynn came to Kate with a look in his eyes that sent chills down her spine. He was scared and furious in the same instance with a rage building. He said they needed to go for a ride and he had packed a backpack for them. Then he turned to Henry asking him to watch over the children. That was an hour ago as they continued across the open range with Harlynn stopping to look at a map he had and a compass. She waited. They proceeded for another thirty minutes then suddenly Harlynn stopped and got off his horse tying it to a tree.

"Why are we stopping? What are we doing Harlynn?" Kate asked baffled by her husband.

"Please get down?" he said in a soft voice that was smooth. She did as he requested and sat in the shade of the tree drinking from the klean kanteen he handed her that had Gatorade in.

"What did Janey tell you?" she used a very calm voice as Harlynn sat down next to her and laid back in the grass. She poured some water on a towel from the backpack and wiped the dirt and sweat offs his face.

"She told me things from her dreams that confuse me. She said that Casey had been spending time with my father. Paul loves being in heaven and he is happy there with Flynn."

"Who is Flynn?" Kate asked slowly as she watched him.

"Remember when I found out that Joan had the abortion? When I found the ultrasound pictures of the three and half month old boy who would have been my son? Dr. Brown told me I should name him and write him a letter explaining what happened. She told me to give that child the love through my words in that letter and I should write to him several times. I wrote to him four times and I called him Flynn. I have never told a living soul what I named him or what was in those letters."

Kate didn't know what to do or say as her heart raced. She could feel the pain he was in as she laid her head on his chest closing her eyes. They both watched as the clouds rolled by in the blue sky.

"My dad is taking care of Flynn in heaven. They go on long walks and my father tells him everything about me." He paused. "Casey said I was to ride to the tree where I played as a boy and the Chief would come to see us. The Chief will take us to my father."

Kate felt her eyes grow heavy as they waited in the hot Texas sun and just when she was about to fall asleep the Chief appeared before them. Kate slowly got up as Harlynn stood up blinking several times. Harlynn knelt bowing his head as the Chief made the sign of the cross over his head. When Harlynn stood up Kate watched as tears came down the Chief's face, but he never said a word. Harlynn had the same tears, and then slowly they began to walk into the huge bushes. The bushes were so thick with thorns, but the thorns didn't touch them. The bushes parted, letting them pass and closed behind them. Instead of the heat that Kate had felt on her face and scalp it was cool with the sound of water running.

Kate's feet began to ache until they came to the tepee. The enormous tepee stood in front of them. It was much taller than Kate had remembered and the designs on the tepee resembled the graphics Elle had made for their room. The blankets were there in front of them, the same blankets that were so soft and smelled of the breeze with bluebonnets in them.

"Little shark returns much bigger. He has been deeply missed." The Chief placed his hand over his heart. "Little shark still wanders with the Dreamer, I see."

Harlynn nodded his head as he stared into the flames. He was far away in his childhood memories as Kate felt her eyes growing heavy again. There was one cup as the chief poured water into it. The water tasted sweet like honey or maybe it was maple syrup. She started to shake from the cold as Harlynn put a blanket around her. The crackle of the fire became very loud was all Kate could think as she saw the Chief talking, but she couldn't understand him. She leaned against Harlynn as he put his arm around her, then her eyes closed as she went to sleep.

She dreamed of three graves on the ranch not far from the tree.

She watched as the Chief told them of these men who came at night to hurt them and their family. He would not allow that to happen to Little Shark and the Dreamer. They stood over the graves as the Chief handed him the wallets of the three men. The first wallet was Frank Waters, the second wallet was David Call and the finally one was Max Black. Harlynn looked at the photos and took the wallets placing them in his backpack.

When she woke up Paul was sitting next to Harlynn in the tepee. Kate reached out to touch him and it was him. She could feel the denim of his pants and the flesh of his skin as he touched her hand squeezing it, like he had done in the hospital. Again the crackle of the fire was loud as she watched the men talk with the Chief. It only seemed to be a minute when the Chief stood up letting them know it was time to go. He put a bracelet on her wrist, then one on Harlynn's wrist and made the sign of the cross again.

"Your souls are one," the Chief told them as Harlynn kissed her. She could feel his breath fill her lungs for a long time then she breathed back into his lungs. There was a wind that walked through her as she closed her eyes. All the badness left her that she had ever felt. Images of her mother trying to kill her were erased from her soul along with all the bad moments from the last two years. Her eyes grew heavy again as she felt like she might fall. Harlynn was next to her holding her hand. It was exhausting as her muscles grew more tired but a wind came again, bringing energy this time. An energy based on their love that was powerful.

"You will change the world," the Chief told them both.

Paul stood up with vigor embracing his son. Then he held Kate for a moment telling her that she was a good mother and he would be there to help her. He placed a red bracelet on her wrist and a red one on Harlynn's wrist then he walked out of the tepee. There was no sadness or pain.

"It is the process," the Chief told them as they all sat down again. She listened as the Chief asked Harlynn questions listening to what Harlynn would say. Then he would wait to answer as he pondered each word that Harlynn had chosen. Finally he told them to close their eyes and sleep.

—

The next time Kate opened her eyes Henry was shaking her to wake up as Harlynn opened his eyes at the same moment. The sun was setting as the darkness crept up on them. Everyone stared at one another not speaking for a moment. Kate looked at her wrist and saw the bracelets then she looked at Harlynn's wrist that had the same bracelets. It had happened.

"Are you okay?" Henry asked slowly as they both sat up. "When you didn't come back, Blacky sent out search teams looking for you. Harlynn looked at his watch visibly surprised by the time it read.

In the distance they could see cars and a commotion taking place as Blacky walked towards them. He had a look in his eyes Kate had never seen before. She stood up immediately as Harlynn got up taking a drink of water that Henry had for him.

"What happened while you two were out here?" Blacky asked frantically.

Kate stared at Harlynn for an explanation. Silence filled the space as Blacky waited for some sort of answer.

"Why?" Harlynn finally answered. "Apparently we got lost and fell asleep. I probably got disoriented. I haven't been out this far in ten years without one of the ranch hands."

"There are three dead men buried over there with their throats slit, Harlynn. One resembles my son Max who I haven't heard from in three weeks. Frank Waters is dead along with another individual. I have no idea who he might be."

Kate bent down picking up the back pack and taking out the wallets. She handed them to Blacky who took them but didn't ask her how she got them. He went through them and stopped on the last one. David Call.

"Didn't David Call used to work for you, Henry?" Blacky asked slowly as he looked back over his shoulder.

"Yes," Henry stated firmly. "What the hell is going on Jack? Why is one of your son's dead?"

"I'm not sure it's him because he doesn't have his St. Jude medal on." Blacky closed his eyes. "The last time I spoke to Max he told me he had important information to give me concerning Moon Water. A friend of his at the Department of Justice had given him a USB stick filled with documents. We have a pending disaster on our hands that has to be cleaned up."

"David had tried to steal the process for the Goo." Henry admitted. "He had worked for me for ten years. I fired him six months ago."

"Are we being set up by our government?" Harlynn yelled at Blacky.

"Yes," Blacky said quietly. "Is there anything else that you found?"

"No," Kate said firmly.

"No one says a word about this to anyone. It never happened, do you understand me?" Everyone nodded in agreement.

"I need to get everyone back to the house," Charlie instructed them quietly as he pointed to the jeep that was waiting for them. Kate looked around as though something was missing until she saw it. It was the blanket that had been around her earlier in the tepee. She picked it up as she avoided making eye contact with Harlynn.

—

Kate sat in silence the whole way back to the ranch house, even when they got back she didn't say a word to anyone. The only thing she wanted to do was see her children and go to bed. She could feel everyone stare as she came into the house going to the nursery. There before her was Laney, waiting for Kate.

"Kate?" Keaton came in the room. "What happened?"

"I don't know, Keaton. We got lost, then we fell asleep and I had these strange dreams."

"Are you sure they were dreams?" Keaton asked handing her a bottle for Laney as Levi came in the room hanging on her. He was smiling as he danced around the room making Laney giggle in her baby way. Next Janey came in escaping from Stan as he came running down the hallway. It was a complete overthrow of the adults in the house. No one seemed to mind the children taking charge.

Janey stopped walking over to Kateland looking at her bracelets.

She touched the beads counting them as she smiled at her mother.

"Do you know what this one means?" Kate asked softly

"Your souls are one?" Janey told her in a whisper.

"And the red one is protection for loved ones?" Kate whispered back to her.

"No, they are health. Good health for you and all you love. They will help me feel good." Janey smiled. "Did Paul give them to you?"

"Yes," Kate replied in a hush. "Keaton will read to you love bug." Keat picked her up and carried her out of the room.

"Levi, come with me little man?" Harlynn leaned over kissing Kate as he took Levi. "I love you." She watched as Laney drank her bottle. Then Kate slowly rocked her as her eyes closed while the baby fell into a deep sleep. Kate sat there in the dark unable to move as she waited for Harlynn to come back. She finally heard his footsteps coming down the hallway.

"You look tired. Have you been in here for the last hour?" Harlynn asked her in a whisper as he took Laney from her arms. "You need to go to sleep, Kateland?"

"I'm hungry," she admitted to herself. "I have to have dinner or you know what will happen."

"You could take a shower, and then we will eat," he whispered. "We are going to be fine, I promise."

"You are completely back?" Kate asked as they stood outside Laney's room.

"Yes, I am." He peered into her eyes.

"Did we have the same dreams out there?" Kate asked as Harlynn leaned against her in the hallway, holding her hands then kissed her.

"I remember when the Chief said our souls are one now and we kissed taking the air out of each other's lungs. It was like nothing I have ever experienced. I don't think it was a dream to be honest with you."

"It was like you became part of my anatomy when your breath went into my lungs," she admitted as he nodded at her. "I thought I was dreaming, but it was all real, I guess." She licked her lips that were parched from being in the elements for so many hours. "I couldn't always hear what you were saying because the fire was so loud."

"I know. Chief said there were things you should hear and things that you shouldn't hear, but that when I knew it was the right time I would tell you. They are good things about our life together." He gave her a slight smile and his eyes danced. "I think I needed to speak to my father again and hear about Flynn. I needed to know he was doing okay. He said to thank you for getting him to heaven."

"I can't wait to meet Flynn some day. We have this other child to pray for now." She leaned over and kissed Harlynn. "Fix me something good to eat, mister."

"I will," he stammered. "What should we do about Blacky?"

"I'm completely in shock. I mean Harlynn what the hell was going out there? Are all those men really dead? Are they who the wallets say they are and who put them there? Dead people keep showing up with their throat slit. Don't you think it's a problem?"

"Not if they were part of the people who want us dead."

"True." She turned walking towards their room with her head hung down. Kate searched her memories about Max Black. He was two years older than Nick. She had spent time with him over the years. He didn't look like Nick or Blacky. He had gone to law school and worked in Washington. He was very good with computers, but he was nothing like Nick. Max and Nick spoke often. What did Nick know?

She thought of all the times Nick had been there for her. Was Blacky going to tell him? She couldn't lie to Nick while she looked at him straight in the eyes.

As she soaked in the bath again her mind went back to all the images, smells and sounds. Her wrist still had the bracelets and she was hesitant to take them off. She could feel them still healing her in many ways.

When she was dressed again she felt stronger from the day. For weeks now she had prayed that Harlynn would be whole again and he was, in her mind. He had told her he was back, which brought relief to her mind and heart. As she brushed her hair in the mirror she noticed the dark circles were gone around her eyes. She put lip balm on her dry lips then a little makeup.

"You look different?" Keaton commented coming in their room.

"I feel different," Kate smiled at him with the love she felt for her brother.

"Thank you for talking to Christa this morning. I'm not sure what you said to her or how you made her understand me, but you did Kate." He paused. "I think I'm going to get her a nice engagement ring that tells her one day we will get married. She is going to live here half the week and in Houston with us depending on schedules. Plus, we will be here on the weekend a lot. I needed time to get use to all of this."

"Do you see her as the one you want to spend your life with Keaton?" Kate asked him in a voice that was hypnotic. "What do you see?"

"She is the one that I want to be with for the rest of my life. I had a dream we lived next door to you and Harlynn. There is nothing like listening to her sing to me, Kateland. There are so many things about her that make her this amazing individual. Do you like her?"

"I do. I can't explain it Keaton except she fits with us in a way I never envisioned. It will come together if you take it slow. I'm so happy for you Keaton." She waited. "Are you going to ask me what happened out there this afternoon?"

"Apparently you found the Chief again."

"We did." She took in a deep breath. "It was surreal, Keaton, is all I can say. It reminded me of my dreams."

"Your dreams are usually real, Kateland. Do you think we are safe? I'm worried about you and Harlynn." He searched her eyes for the truth. "You can't leave me and these children do you understand?"

"I do. We are going to make it through this and there will be lots of bumps. There are a lot of unanswered questions right now. People don't want us to produce a cure for this cancer that is cost-effective. We are going to do it."

"I'm more worried about you and Harlynn being safe. The rest of the world can take a hike."

"I'm hoping life will be better. We have so much to celebrate, dear brother."

"Our mother wants to come see Laney at the ranch, but I told her no."

"I don't want the memories here marred by her to be honest. I think the fact that Laney looks like me is going to send her over the edge, again. I don't know how to handle her, why don't you figure it out for me."

"I'll talk to Dad and get his input. I'm glad she has been in France for the last six weeks."

"How is Elle doing?" Kate asked as she pulled her hair up into a pony tail. "I was supposed to go to town with her today, but then we got lost."

"No, don't give me the line you got lost again because I know Harlynn. The man never gets lost no matter where he goes, Kateland. Tell me?"

"We talked to Paul? I touched his knee and felt his skin. It was amazing, Keaton, I can't explain it. As we sat around a fire, I watched Harlynn speaking with his father."

"Then what?" Keaton asked perplexed.

"The Chief married our souls together and this wind came through. It took away those feelings that I've always had. The loneliness was gone. The words our mother used on me as a child that were imprinted in my mind. I can't hear her voice in my head anymore. I can't hear all the awful things she said to me."

"What do you hear now?" Keat asked her curious because there were few people in the world that actually understood what Kate had endured throughout her childhood.

"I see the people who love me and hear good voices. I see good things and places."

"What are we going to do about Sue and Dad?" Keaton asked.

"The wedding shower is next week then I need a break from the drama to be honest. Harlynn has asked that we only have everyone here one weekend a month. You and Henry are always welcomed."

"Are you moving here?" Keat frowned. "I know this place is fantastic. You don't want to live out here all the time, do you?"

"No, I don't." She put on some of her pink frost lip gloss. "I will come with Harlynn a couple times a month. I'm hungry."

"Nick made your favorite lasagna for dinner with garlic bread. Harlynn is waiting for you."

Harlynn had a Patron waiting for her when she came in the dining area. The lights were low as she sat at the table with Meg and Henry. Harlynn watched her, but didn't say much as the others joined them. There was no tension in the room Kate noticed as she listened to what everyone had done during the afternoon mixed with market news. It was calm for that hour, which was nice.

~Chapter 24

Kate found Blacky by the fire outside with a bottle of Patron and a shot glass. It was unlike him to be reckless and to openly drink. She could see all the emotions spilling out of him and it made her profoundly sad as they sat there drinking.

She didn't say anything as he poured her another shot and handed it to her. She took it and drank it thinking she was absolutely not going to do that again tonight because she had to feed Laney in two hours. Again she watched the fire and thought of all the things that had happened.

"I don't think it was Max in that grave." Kate told him as Blacky stared at her.

"Why? I won't have confirmation until tomorrow," Blacky admitted. "There's no logic to any of it. We have conformation on the other two bodies."

"Max is too smart to end up in a grave, Blacky. Both your sons have been trained to be observant and calculating since they could walk. Max will contact you soon."

"I'm glad that mother fucker Waters is dead," he told her with a smile. "I don't know how any of us are alive except by the grace of God, Kateland."

"And you." Kate laughed.

"And where would my son or I be without you and the love of these people. I was so burned out. I was like Harlynn when you met him, almost dead on the inside and still smiling on the outside."

"I didn't know." Kate watched him as he had another shot. "I think that might need to be your last. I cannot carry your ass back to the house."

"No one knew, not even Julia. I was afraid if anyone found out, I guess." He swallowed. "Something happened when Levi was born and all the problems started. I felt like I was needed and part of Nick's life again. "

"That makes me very happy, Jack. Nick always talks about you, even though you may not realize it. He is ecstatic whenever there is an opportunity to see you. He wants you to be proud of him and to be loved by you."

"I love when I get to see everyone and spending time with the children. You would think they were my grandchildren. At the office people are always asking to see a picture of Levi."

"Well, I consider you part of this family. And pretty soon you will have your own granddaughter to dote over."

"It won't change how I feel about your three." He waited. "You are paying me too much, Kateland."

"Please." She took a deep breath. "How about five hundred a month?"

"Kateland, that's six million a year!" Blacky yelled at her.

"I would pay you twice as much if I had my way. I'm not going to cut your salary, Jack. Do something you've always wanted to do with it."

"I got Julia a beautiful outrageous rock of ring that you can see across the damn football field. Harlynn helped me get it through the person he uses. It's one of those things I always wanted to. When I gave it to her she was speechless. In all the years of knowing my beautiful wife she has never been speechless. I think next month I'll get her earrings and someday when this shit stops I'm taking her on a vacation to Hawaii."

"I think you need a new car for yourself, I'm thinking a Porsche. I think we should go car shopping when we get back to Houston."

"That sounds good to me." They both looked up when Nick appeared.

"What the hell are you two doing out here by yourselves?" He asked pissed off at being left out.

"Watching the stars," his father answered looking at Kate. "I'm getting very drunk and Kate is talking to me while I get very drunk."

"Do you have a number for Max?" Nick asked stunned. "He called me and left a message without a number."

"What did he say?" Kate asked because Blacky was tongue tied as he gazed at the fire.

"He said to tell Dad that I'm fine. And he was clean. What the hell did he do this time? He didn't get disbarred did he?"

"What time did he call?" Blacky asked slowly.

"About ten minutes ago." Blacky looked at him irritated. "I was with Elle."

"Yeah, I bet you were Nicky." Kate teased him as she got up. "Don't let him do anymore shots." She hung on Blacky for a moment and whispered in his ears. "I told you he was okay. You need to find your faith."

—

In another minute, Kate thought she might lose it because her head was pounding from the Patron she drank last night with Blacky or maybe it was Sue going on about how she felt left out, again. Kate smiled at Blacky who still had his sunglasses on as he tried to look serious until he saw Kate open her eyes wide and make her silly smile. He started laughing like no one had ever heard at the table. Then she reached across the table taking a sip of Blacky's orange juice.

"Tequila Sunrise. Yum."

"How do you have that affect on men?" Harlynn asked not amused by his wife's drinking behavior last night.

"Hypocrite! Do you want me to tell?" Now Harlynn was laughing as hard as Blacky as Kate made a face at him that said do you really want all these people at this table to know what we did last night.

Nick and Keaton half laughed because they knew if Kate wanted them to laugh she could make them do it in a middle of a meeting. Sue didn't think it was funny and her father just shook his head for a moment because he had spent a life time dealing with either Kate laughing or laughing at him or about something he or his ex-wife had done. It was just her way.

"Mama you gave away your giggles again?" Levi told her looking in her eyes. "You know I don't like when you give away those giggles."

"That's what is so nice about giggles, you can always get more," Kate told her son. "What do you want to do Levi?" Hopefully her son

268

would save her from these unfun people. She didn't feel like working or talking about a security threat today. She was going to spend the morning with her son and spoil him.

"Books! New Books. Please?" The large green eyes looked through her like they always did. Her son was as impossible to say no to as her husband.

"What kind of books would you like, Levi?"

"Planets and stars. The moon." He smiled with delight. "Big books."

"Looks like we are going to town to find you a few books, little man." Kate held the little boy close to her heart. "And we are going by ourselves, except the bodyguards." Kate frowned. "I'm escaping this joint for the morning."

She watched as Harlynn looked hurt by being excluded from going, but she decided to ignore him. They had two other children that he could spend the morning with Kate told him with her eyes. It had been a long time since she had her son to herself.

"Will you come home for lunch or we can meet you in town?" Harlynn waited for her answer as everyone watched her.

"That sounds good. Meet us in town at *Casa Blanca* at noon. Can you call and reserve the back room?" She smiled telling him he was still loved and not to worry, she was not rejecting him.

"I will call." Keat offered getting up from the table. "We could go to the River Walk after because Levi hasn't been there?"

"The River Walk with a stroller is not my idea of a good time," Nick commented, "but I'm sure we can manage." He smiled at Kate with the smile that said I need to speak with you about what the hell happened out there last night.

Kate watched as everyone left the table leaving her and Harlynn watching each other. There was a little tension in the air because Kate didn't give in to his wants and he didn't like it. She waited to see if Harlynn was really back or pretending.

"That hurt my feelings, Kateland," he told her not smiling. "What did you and Blacky talk about last night?"

"Life, pay cuts, his sons and how he hated his job before he came to work for us. It was a good talk, Harlynn. Are you going to be mad if I take Levi to town?"

"What if something happens to you?" he questioned her. "You just want to get the hell out of this place because people are getting on your nerves."

"I feel smothered, if the truth be known. I need time to figure out yesterday and what it meant? Or maybe I wish you were sitting around the fire with us last night getting smashed on Patron."

"Kate," he leaned forward so no one could hear what he was saying. "I almost died in that hospital because of what I took with alcohol, love. I didn't understand why every time I had a drink for the last two months I could hardly focus. I don't know when, maybe one day I will be able to have alcohol again, but not today. There is no way I'm going to lose you over booze."

"How about you come with us and let us go to the bookstore by ourselves?" He sort of smiled. "Okay, how about you let me pick out books with him first, then you can pick out books with him and we have to bring Laney."

"What about Janey and Stan?" Harlynn questioned her.

"Ask her if she wants to come. I think Meg was teaching her to embroider this morning then cooking with her."

"I like that Meg teachers her things like that." Harlynn admitted. "Our life is never going to be simple Kateland?"

"I know. I wanted to be the one to explore books with Levi today. There is this look he gets in his eyes of pure joy when he opens a new book."

"I want to get some new books to read to Laney and Janey wants to start reading Harry Potter. We need to get her a collection she can have in her room."

"Or do you think she should read C.S. Lewis first?"

"We can get both and let her pick." He smiled. "Are you mad?"

"No. Its sweet you want to protect me and its sweet you want to be with Levi, Laney and Janey. You need a lot of love right now to finish healing." She sighed. "When are you going to work on those letters your father left you?"

"I've read about fifty of them since we've been here. It's a daunting experience as I hear the words come off the pages. He told me that I need to slow down and not rush the process. It's not about reading them as fast as I can, rather understanding them."

"How should we protect them?" Kate asked him because she wasn't sure.

"I like your idea of putting them in a book of some sort. Then the children will have them to read. There is a whole box about the children, which surprised me."

"Good. I wrote Laney a letter yesterday telling her about her life and how she is loved. I'm trying to rotate who I write to."

"Why don't you go get ready and I will pack up the backpack for the children." Harlynn offered trying to be helpful. "Can you come over here first?" He watched as Kate came around the table and he pulled her into his chair with him. He kissed her. "I love you," he whispered.

She smiled as he kept kissing her then held on to her. It was unlike Harlynn to be open around other people and playful. It was refreshing after the last months to be his center of attention in a good way.

"And I love you, always," Kate told him as he kissed her again. Levi came in the room watching his parents laughing. Kate had never thought how this little boy saw his parents. They didn't show the affection they had for each other in front of him. They needed to start doing that so he could see how his parents loved each other.

"Go, go," Levi told them dragging his bag with him to keep him entertained in the car to town. It was forty-five minutes to San Antonio from the ranch or thirty depending on who was driving. Harlynn held on to Kate for a couple more minutes as Levi unpacked and packed the backpack.

—

In the book store Kate sat with Levi on the floor going through the books he had chosen. There were frog books, planet books and books about the moon. And of course there were books about cars and baseball. Then there was a book about inventions. She marveled at how he read different words and tried to sound out others. Out of the corner of her eye, Kate could see Harlynn playing with Laney and showing her different books, in their own little world of father and daughter.

It was incredibly peaceful to be among these books with no one watching them. She got up going to get a book on horses. Levi and Harlynn were looking at the books while Laney slept in Harlynn's arms. Charlie was standing guard over them pretending to read a *People Magazine.* Kate laughed at him as he ignored her trying to focus.

"This is for you?" Kate stepped back as a man in a baseball cap with bleached blond hair approached her. Those crystal blue eyes belonged to Blacky. It was Nick's brother, Max.

"Please give this to my father." He handed her a thick envelope.

"Wait. You have to call him Max." Kate pleaded with him.

"In a couple of days I will. Be very careful, Kateland."

Kate saw both Harlynn and Charlie stand up moving towards her. Harlynn handed Laney to Charlie going after Max. Levi watched his father following this man as Kateland picked him up. Immediately other bodyguards showed up picking up the books to pay for them and taking them to the car. For a moment it had been normal, but now it wasn't normal.

"My books!" Levi started yelling at Kate.

"Dan is getting them. We need to go." Kate kissed the child. "It's going to be fine Levi, I promise you." She forced a smile staring at Charlie.

"It was Max Black," Kate whispered to Charlie as she got in the car. "Find me Blacky."

"Who was out there in that field?" Charlie asked. "How could it be Max?"

"I looked him straight in the eye and it was Max. Do you know what is going on?"

"I have a few ideas we can discuss," Charlie whispered as Harlynn came out front with the bag of books. As soon as everyone was in the car they pulled out of the parking lot cutting through traffic. Finally, they pulled into a McDonald's as one of the bodyguards checked the car for a tracking device and another called Blacky.

Harlynn put out his hand for the envelope. A USB stick and a gold medallion of St. Jude were inside. Harlynn smiled because he had a medallion that was very similar that Kate had given him when they first started dating. She had told him that it was the saint of the impossible to help him.

"Blacky told him to find you and give you this. We are not being followed, Kateland," Harlynn whispered to her. "I gave Max all the cash and a credit card. He found evidence that the government is going after Moon Water that was given to him by a friend at the DOJ."

"What is the infraction?" Kate asked slowly.

"Insider trading by Henry and your father or we give up Moon Water?"

"Is it true?" Kate asked slowly. "Henry and Sam wouldn't do that, Harlynn."

"I know." He closed his eyes going over anything that would be a problem, and then he stopped, picking up his phone.

"Leezann, it's me. Is anyone there from the DOJ or FBI?"

"Go into the files in my office and pull three large files out on a small oil company called W. Right. Take my car at the office and start driving to the ranch. Take the extra Blackberry in my desk with you and call me from it when you are on I-10." He hung up the phone sitting back. Then he called Ed who had basically ate and slept since he got to the ranch.

"It's me and we have got one hell of a problem."

"Remember W.Right?"

"Yes. You got your laptop? Pull it all off the server. I don't know how long we have to track down these files. Leezann is bringing me the originals from my office." Even though it was Sunday there were lawyers working. "I'm sending Mark an email to stall for however long they can." Harlynn hung up the phone looking out the window.

"Tell me?" Kate asked as she watched their children sleeping.

"W.Right was a small drilling company that Henry learned about from the owner's son while playing golf. The son never told Henry that they had found a new way to extract oil from the shale in West Texas. Henry and Sam went out to see the company, and then decided to take it over. You cannot tell anyone because I could be disbarred, Kateland."

"I've never heard of this company or seen it on a tax return?" Kate was getting suspicious.

"You don't see all your father's tax returns." He waited. "Gems had just died and Henry didn't want the company going to his daughter, Jessica. Your father knew someday he would divorce your mother. They created an offshore account for the company."

"How much is it worth." Kate asked pissed off because Sam and Henry just might be going to jail.

"A billion or more. No money has ever come out of it. All revenue is turned back into the company. They are incorporated in the Cayman Islands and no one has taken a cent from the company or a paper clip. "

"It wasn't listed in the assets on the divorce nor did Jessica get part of it when her mother died. Jessica was entitled to part of that company."

"No. We got around Jessica by making the closing after Gems death. Your mother agreed to all assets in the United States. This is incorporated outside the United States. I didn't draw up the document, Kateland."

"I don't see how it could be insider trading when they didn't know about the discovery. This goes back over fifteen years." Kate stared at Harlynn.

"I need to go through the documents to see what the problem might be."

Kate could tell he was very worried, but trying not to let her see it. She would never let Henry be charged with insider trading and everyone knew it. If the government had a strong case then Moon Water would be shut down before she gave it to them.

—

Lunch was relaxing was all Kate could think as she looked around the table with all the children there. Janey had been telling her all about her morning with Meg. She had learned to make cinnamon rolls and embroidered a beautiful butterfly on a shirt for Laney. It made Kate smile to see Janey showering her sister with such passionate love.

"Are you going to tell me what the hell is going on?" Nick asked her with a smile taking Laney from her. "Can you believe we are going to have a little girl?" She watched as he lovingly glanced at Elle then back to Laney.

"We should go for a walk when we get back to the ranch." Kate glanced at his father letting him know that Blacky was watching them. "Why don't we do some more pictures in the bluebonnets?"

"We should do that." Nick gave Laney a bottle slowly rocking her as she smiled at him.

—

Kate watched as Harlynn, Henry and Sam along with Ed went into the office and closed the door. She was playing with Levi when Janey came in the room and got in her face.

"What's going on?" Kate asked with a smile. "Do you like your new books? I can't wait to start reading them with you, Janey."

"You are always playing with Levi and Laney!" She yelled at her, which everyone in the house heard. Next she lunged at Kateland as though she might hit her. Immediately Harlynn appeared to see what was going on as Janey turned around and hit Levi.

"Janey stop it." He picked her up while she was kicking her feet in the air. "We don't hit!" He told her sternly as she tried to hit Harlynn in the face.

"You only love Levi and Laney!" She burst into tears.

"Janey, who told you that nonsense?" Harlynn asked slowly. "You know that your mom and I love you. We love everyone the same, Janey. Why would you think your mom and I don't love you?"

She pulled out a post card from her pocket and handed it to him as he looked at it. He read it closing his eyes. Kate was trying to comfort Levi, who was bewildered by what happened. Harlynn handed the postcard to Kate from Disney World. It was crazy. It told Janey she was not part of the family. That's all it took to send her over the edge on top of going to do a bunch of blood test.

"Janey look at me?" He waited. "I love you forever, sweet heart. You are my daughter and no one will ever change that, honey." She buried her head in his neck hiding as Harlynn held her.

"You were mean to me?" Levi yelled at her wiping his tears away. "Janey, why were you mean to me?"

"I'm sorry," she apologized. "I didn't think you loved me."

"Yes we do." Kate promised her with a smile.

"Janey, why don't you go get your swimsuit and we'll go for a swim?" Harlynn whispered to her. "Then we are going to start reading one of your new books."

"Can my Dad come with us?"

"Sure." Harlynn smiled thinking it was very sweet she wanted both her father's together.

She turned towards Kate, looking down embarrassed. Kate sat down on the couch with Levi so she could sit with them.

"Do you love me?" Janey asked.

"Forever, no matter what, do you understand? It's a silly post card that doesn't mean anything. Where did you get it?"

"I found it in the mail," Janey explained to her.

"I need to give it to Blacky, okay?" Kate smiled. "Janey you are so loved and important to everyone in our family. Don't you remember how Meg spent the morning with you?"

"That lady at tennis told me that she loved me and that I was her daughter?"

"What was her name?" Kate asked.

"She didn't tell me. Why would she say that when you are my mom?"

"I will have to think on it." Kate waited. "Maybe she thought you were someone else?"

"Oh, I never thought of that, Mama. I thought she was the lady who left me when I was a baby."

"Well, if she was would you want to meet her?" Kate looked at Harlynn for help.

"No, I love my family and I promise not to hit Levi again."

"What do you think your punishment should be for hitting Levi?" Kate asked.

"No movies tonight?" Kate nodded in agreement.

"You know that you could really hurt Levi or Laney?" Harlynn reminded her.

"Yes, I'm sorry."

"Go swim with your Papa and Dad." Kate hugged her, and then Levi hugged her. Kate and Harlynn stared at each other until Janey left the room to go change.

"What is going on with her? What if that was Laney who she hit like that? Christ, I never thought in a million years I would see her go after Levi or you with such anger."

"It will be okay, Harlynn. She was due for a meltdown with all that is going on. I think having another girl in the family is hard on her. Remember she was the princess for a long time and now, while she loves Levi and Laney, they are competition. Plus, she doesn't feel well. If there is any evidence that Amy Rivers has done this her ass is in jail," Kate whispered to him. "No mercy. At least I got my answer if Janey wants to meet her."

Harlynn picked up Levi looking at his forehead where Janey smacked him. There was a red welt, but he would be okay. He held him then put him on his shoulders spinning him around as he giggled. Finally he put him down on the floor as the child stayed there laughing."

"They don't want me to know, do they?" Kate asked staring at Harlynn.

"I told them they either let you be involved or I won't work on it. I'm not going to let this come between us, Kateland." He leaned over kissing her. "When Leezann gets here with the files can you come get me?"

"Yes. Thank you Harlynn." She beamed with pride because Harlynn had stood up to Henry and her father along with Ed. It made her smile for a moment.

~Chapter 25

As Kate went through her emails she sighed thinking this was not fun. Two hundred emails on a daily bases took too much time. There were friends and family, work, and the others. The others were about her art or people who wanted her art and had found her email. Then there were the different charities that Kate and Harlynn supported in Houston. Ann was good about cutting down the emails, but it was still a lot.

"Why is everyone so uptight?" Sue asked sitting down at the kitchen table as Kate watched Laney wiggling across the floor.

"Well, because of the legalities of it you need to talk to Sam. It's a complicated matter that I don't have that much knowledge about, Sue. It's not that I don't want to tell you. I don't have any details to tell you. It all goes back to Moon Water."

"Do you think Sam will tell me? We never talk about his business or money?"

"What? Sue, you're his wife and you should know about the finances. You're smarter than that my best friend."

"He tells me not to worry, that I will never have to worry about financial security again. He is good to me. He basically says I can have anything. If I'm spending over ten grand I talk to him."

"You need to see the tax returns. You need to know where the money is if anything ever happened to him. Did you sign a prenuptial agreement?"

"No, he said he loved me and would always take care of me no matter what."

"Do you want me to help you with this, Sue?" Kate asked slowly.

"I don't know. Your father is under too much stress with Moon Water and worrying about you. Let's figure this out after we get through the wedding shower, Nick's wedding and when people stop trying to kill you guys."

"I don't mind talking to him if it comes to that, Sue. Things are going to get worse before they get better, but I believe we will make it through this and it is going to make us a better family."

"We will." She smiled. "Are you worried?"

"No. I stopped worrying a couple weeks ago. It's more like I'm cautious knowing that we have to go through the forest to get to the promise land of peace. It's our journey."

"How are you and Harlynn?" She smiled. "I'm asking for everyone who doesn't have the guts to ask. The list is very long at this point in time."

"It's good at times. I'm still adjusting to what is going on with him. Sometimes I am happy and less happy at other moments. Sex is great." She watched as Sue starting laughing, falling off her chair. "What else?"

"You look good in spite of all this shit going on and no one understands why you haven't fallen apart twice over. Did you really meet with the Chief?"

"It was this amazing sensual experience that even though I know it happened I don't know if I believe I was there. It was mystical."

"Really? That doesn't sound like you, Kate. You're so logical, except for your secret dreams."

"It was clearer then my dreams." She waited. "Hunter is coming home today from being shot. I can't believe that dog made it through three surgeries?"

"Even your dog is a super hero." Sue stopped smiling when they saw Blacky and Charlie walk into the room.

"Leezann is here." Blacky informed the two women calmly. "Dennis Kavel is with her. You didn't tell me you were expecting Dennis Kavel, Kateland?"

"I wasn't. I had a couple messages from him the last two days. We don't have a board meeting until next month. How did he end up with Leezann?"

"He ran into her in the parking garage at the firm. Dennis had flown to Houston to speak with you. He only wants to speak to you?"

"Must be important?' Kate got up from the table taking Laney with her kissing the baby on the head. "What is going on, now?" Kate whispered to herself.

—

Dennis Kavel was CEO of Wireless Email (WE), a multi-billion dollar company that Kateland sat on the board of for the last two years. Harlynn's firm did the legal work for WE and it was Kate's account. Kate had known Dennis before Harlynn and the crazy life she now owned. WE held the most exclusive patents for email and texting. They also had one of the most secure networks in the world.

For the first five minutes Dennis watched as Kate put Laney on the floor on her back and she rolled over. The baby stared at Dennis trying to figure him out because she didn't know his voice or his eyes. Laney was an eyes baby. When she looked in your eyes it was like she could read you. After a minute she giggled at Dennis and smiled her toothless smile.

Kate watched as Dennis sat there staring at her daughter and she wondered what he was thinking. The silence of the room was broken by raspberry lemonade being served along with baked brie cheese and sour dough bread.

"She is absolutely stunning, Kateland. Can we use her in a commercial?"

"That would be fun." She waited. "Dennis, we have been friends for a long time. Tell me why you are here and don't worry-there are few things in this world that could possibly shock me."

"You'll be shocked, I promise." He had a couple crackers sitting back and finished his drink. "I think I need some Scotch." Kate pointed to the bar as Henry bought in a bottle for Laney. She could see the alarm in Henry's eyes as he stared at Dennis.

"Do you mind if Henry stays?" Kate questioned as Dennis stammered for a few seconds.

"Of course Henry can stay." He paused. "Is Harlynn around?" Dennis asked quietly.

"He has Levi and Janey in the pool at the moment. Why don't we talk first?" Kate suggested thinking Harlynn was not going to like Dennis showing up with Leezann.

She watched as Laney closed her eyes while she drank the bottle exhausted from her busy day at the bookstore and going out for lunch.

Kate sat in the rocking chair rocking even when she was asleep.

"You are a board member of WE and as a result we do security sweeps for all the emails and texts on the servers throughout the world using the names of our executive officers and board members to insure their safety. Your name along with Harlynn and the children have come up in some very unexpected places."

"I assume this is legal?" Henry asked slowly.

"Completely," Dennis told him as Kate nodded her head. "There are people in high places who want you dead along with everyone in this house, Kateland."

"How high?" Harlynn asked standing in the doorway with his hair still wet and sticking up, looking like he had literally jumped out of the pool, which he had two minutes ago when Leezann came out to tell him who was in the house. Meg bought him a robe for him to put on, taking his towel. Then she took Laney from Kate, taking her to the nursery.

"The President of the United States ordered a hit on you Kateland along with your family."

"Oh, my God!" Harlynn's voice echoed through the house. "You can't be serious, Dennis?"

"Son of a bitch! I helped put that bastard in office!" Henry yelled.

"Can I see the print out?" Kate asked calmly as she watched Dennis open his briefcase. He handed a copy to everyone.

"I've made several copies of these emails and who is involved. If anything happens to us they automatically go to seven newspapers around the world." The room filled with silence.

"President Howard is very tied to healthcare and the pharmaceutical industry." Dennis told the room as they read through the emails. "Moon Water will prevent him from getting re-elected in November. Apparently several executives have told him if he doesn't take care of you then he is over."

"Who knows about these emails and texts?" Kate asked slowly going over them again. Part of her wanted to throw up, but the other part would be damned if she would allow this to happen.

"Pete and David, only the top people at WE. They have copies of what I've uncovered. It's been a busy forty-eight hours. I need to take a shower and sleep for a couple hours before we talk about how to handle this or if you need anything else from me. I have to catch a plane at mid-night. Again, I apologize for the intrusion on your weekend." He smiled at Kate. "Kate don't worry, I have other emails on the President if we need to use them."

"Here, let me show you to a room where you can shower and rest." Kate smiled because this man had just saved her life. He was risking everything to help her and the people who she loved. "I will bring you some clean clothes since you're about the size of Harlynn." She looked him up and down.

"When I saw your name Kateland, I lost it. I'm sorry for showing up the way I did, but I didn't think it was safe to have this discussion over the phone. No one knows I'm here visiting you."

"Thank you from all of my family. This is an opportunity to make the world a better place, Dennis. Don't apologize." She turned walking down the hallway to her room as she grabbed a basket filling it with everything from pajamas to a swimsuit to dental floss and everything in between. Then she sent a text to the chef to quickly make a light dinner for Dennis, his favorite pasta with marina sauce and grilled chicken with red wine.

In a way she felt relieved because now she knew the enemy. This individual who thought he was powerful enough to destroy her and her family. Everything seemed crystal clear to her as she put the basket on Dennis's bed and closed the door behind her. A great weight had been lifted from her because her mind was spinning on how to challenge this threat.

Blacky came at her in the hallway looking rather disgruntled. He had caught heavy heat, she imagined, from the people in the other room. She stopped putting her hands on her hips, tilting her head to the side watching him. He stood in front of her about six inches away.

"I got my ass chewed off by Henry and Harlynn," he told her slowly. Blacky was not use to getting his ass chewed off by anyone. He usually did the chewing. "I didn't know and I should have known. My gut told me it was from high up, but I didn't think it was this."

"Tell them to go to hell." She watched him. "We all had an idea there were major players in this. No one wanted to admit it Blacky and there are no dumbasses in this place. Do you think we are safe on this ranch?"

"We need to go back tomorrow. It's safer in the daylight than leaving at night. I have people all around here within twenty miles. We will know if something is coming and I have reinforcement if we need it. I called some favors in with the F.B.I. as backup. You and Harlynn are doing an interview tomorrow."

"I was thinking that was what we need to do. We could go hide on an island somewhere or we can face them. I mean interviews, pictures in the paper, and anything that gets our faces in the media. Then we have a meeting?"

"What kind of meeting?"

"We have a summit here at the ranch with the most important business leaders in the country and our handpicked officials."

"Then what?"

"Then we decide how we are getting rid of this President. Do we go public and destroy him, which might be bad for the country and economy or do we painfully force him out by letting him telling him we know he put out a contract on my family."

"A summit?" Blacky nodded. "Have you told anyone yet?"

"No. Should it come from you or maybe Harlynn?"

"I think it should be Harlynn's idea. I think you should give the President a dinner at your home as a fund raiser for his campaign bid." They stared at each other. "You are going to be busier than you like, Kateland. You are going to have open up your home and your life with these children. No more hiding."

"Double barrels. We hit them from every angle possible. And we hit them hard whether it's Harlynn or me."

"I will move the plan into action starting tonight. Don't go along with everything, do you understand me?"

"I can always be difficult."

"I thought you would be frightened or want to go into hiding?" Blacky whispered to her as he watched her facial expressions. "You always surprise me, Kate."

"It's this primal instinct is all I can tell you. I suppose it's like Harlynn wanting to be on this ranch. You just know what to do next without thinking."

"I'm going to call Julia."

"She needs a bodyguard, Blacky. Don't be dumb."

"I was worried about her last week and assigned one to her. She's going to be more pissed at me after I call her. The idea was that life would be safer now." He took a deep breath in. "I will see you back in the living room in twenty minutes."

"Tell Julia I said hello." They went their separate ways towards different places for the same reason.

—

When she walked into the room the Patron was sitting on the table, but she didn't want any. As she sat on the couch she picked up one of the transcripts with Blacky's initials on the top. This one started eight weeks ago and didn't have all the lines blacked out like the first one she read. Even as she read it her skin began to crawl. There were lots of details about her life in these pages. The guess whether Kate would take a leave absence because of having a baby? Was the baby healthy? Did Janey have cancer again? Was there anything that might distract her from Moon Water or delay a product from coming to market? There was one line that caught her attention. It simply said he is dead now, on the date of Paul's death. Had Paul been killed to distract Harlynn from Moon Water? She closed her eyes and prayed for a moment asking for God's guidance.

Then she closed the document as Levi came in the room smiling with Meg. He knew instantly that his mother needed him. He sat on her lap watching everyone intrigued by the different faces.

"How are you?" Kate whispered in his ear quietly as he giggled.

"I'm a cowboy?" He turned smiling at Kate who tried to cover her surprise. "Dada said when I'm big we are going to run the ranch together."

"That's swell." Kate glanced at Harlynn across the room while he was on his Blackberry checking to see if leaving in the morning was possible. He was trying to decide if it was better to drive or fly. Then there was the question of whether they would hit any storms. Her evil eye meant that Harlynn better not be brainwashing their son at the age of two. Or was it good that Levi would have that connection to the land like his father did? This land would always be part of Harlynn's blood.

"Would you like to paint, Levi? We could paint Laney's feet and make a picture?" Levi giggled at the prospect of painting his sister. "We have to use special paints that won't hurt the baby and we only paint her feet with Mama. Do you understand?"

"Yes." He smiled.

"I've got him." Meg smiled at Kate. "You work on whatever is up and don't worry about the children. Claire, Sue and I can take care of them.

"Thank you, Meg." She gave Levi one more hug. "Meg will give you a snack and help you change out of your swimming clothes, and then we will paint." Kate smiled at him warmly as he clung to her again. Everyone in the room stared in awe because this is what they would fight for going forward. They would fight for this little boy to have a life with his mother.

Blacky came in the room looking like he had just gotten chewed out again. He saw Kate reading his copy and gracefully walked over to her.

"I believe that's my copy?" he whispered to her trying to take it from her.

"Mine," Kate whispered back. "Your copy is much more intriguing Mr. Black. I think there might be one or two things that you forgot to mention."

"We'll talk later." Blacky didn't look happy with her. She didn't give a care and he knew it.

Slowly they sat down at the table as silence filled the room. For now it was only Blacky, Harlynn, Henry and Kate. The others had gone horseback riding, but would be back in the next hour.

"Let's start by deciding who gets to know?" Blacky suggested.

"I think only Keat and Nick need to know for the time being. We will tell Meg, Sam and Sue later, but let's try to keep it simple." Henry suggested quietly as everyone agreed. "We don't need everyone breaking down over this."

"What information do you have on who would take this job besides the killers that we've already met?" Harlynn spoke to Blacky directly with a touch of malice in his voice.

"From what my contacts tell me," Blacky began slowly. "No one will take the job. If the price goes up we will have a big problem because the next level of hit men won't make the mistakes these did." He waited. "I think the way to deter anyone else from becoming involved is to become very public figures. For the last two years there has been this sense of mystery surrounding everyone at this table. I think we have to take away the mystery and let the public meet you as the executives of Moon Water and as a family. There are always two of you in an interview except if Harlynn is commenting on a merger. I think we need to start tomorrow with Harlynn and Kate doing an interview about balancing work and a family together on the *View*."

"I have an offer to write a book about my father," Harlynn admitted. "I think I would like to do it if that works with your plan."

"Are you sure?" Blacky tried to act resistant and Kate tried not to laugh at him.

"What do you think, Kateland?" Harlynn asked her slowly; almost afraid of what she would say.

"I have no doubt it's the right thing for you to do at this point in your life and it would be an amazing tribute to your father." Henry nodded in agreement.

"I hope everyone is ready to be back on the party circuit for the next six months. Does anyone have any other ideas," Blacky asked as everyone stared at him.

"I think we need to start surrounding ourselves with the most powerful people in this country and develop a strategic alliance." Harlynn mandated.

"Go on?" Henry questioned.

"We need a plan. We need to figure out how to get this guy out of office." Harlynn continued. "What is it they say? Keep your friends close, but keep your enemies closer. I think we need to have a fund raiser at our house or Henry's house for the President?"

"Really?" Blacky questioned slowly. Everyone nodded in agreement as again Blacky tried to look baffled and annoyed.

"We need an alliance of power to take out the President because it has to be done. If you think about it we have the cards in our hands. We need to let this individual know that he is not going to win. He is not going to be re-elected and he will be lucky if he is not impeached." Harlynn stared at Blacky. "I don't want my family dead or to cause this country to go into a recession."

"Okay. Then we go forward. We do it slowly and methodically." Blacky added.

———

Kate was packing and cleaning since they were leaving first thing in the morning, even though it was mid-night. Sleep seemed futile as she tried to process what was happening to her life. It all seemed so impossible, but then she felt the back of her neck where she had been injured. Part of her wondered if it would ever stop or would their luck run out?

"Kate?" Harlynn watched her as she stared into his eyes knowing what he was thinking. "Come to bed. I'll help you in the morning." He smiled softly at her reaching out for her hand.

"I can't sleep," she explained. "My eyes are exhausted and my brain is racing. Harlynn, how did we get to this point? How did Moon Water become such a threat that people want to kill us?" She was dumbfounded by the life that they were leading.

"It's hard to change the world all at once. The important thing to remember is that we are doing well." He watched as she reached for his hand and he pulled her into their room, then closed the door and locked it. He turned to her and kissed her. "I think you are the most amazing person I have ever known in my life, Kateland." He kissed her again, with more of himself. "You are fearless and make everyone else fearless. Everyone in the room was very afraid today except you. You faced it and took a stand against it."

"I have you." She smiled kissing him, thinking that if she wasn't going to sleep she was going to be with Harlynn and stay up all night talking to him.

~Chapter 26

As Kate and Harlynn finished the last balancing pose in their yoga session the instructor put on music while they laid down in the darkness closing their eyes to meditate. It was Kate's favorite moment as every muscle in her body relaxed. She could feel the sweat dry on her arms as the instructor, Bev, covered them in a blanket and left the room. For the next thirty minutes they lay there in perfect silence until Kate slowly opened her eyes, revived from the session. She slowly got up as Harlynn moved his fingers and sat up. They sat across from each other bowing their heads acknowledging their session was over and their day would begin again.

It had been a month of parties, galas and being in the newspaper almost daily, whether in the local or national papers. The interviews were endless, and it was paying off in spades because it was a feeding frenzy. People wanted to be seen with them and slowly their plan was coming together. Harlynn was now on Fox Business Report at least twice a week. When people came in town they wanted to have dinner with Kate and Harlynn. The weekly dinner parties at their home were a coveted invitation. It was done with all of them working together. Meg was Kate's sounding board whether on what to wear or who was worth her time. Sue was organizing Kate's schedule along with Christa. They took care of shopping for her and the children. Sue approved all pictures that went in the paper and talked to all the media.

Keaton and Nick were also very much being seen as well and interfacing with CEO's because it helped make the family and business more visible. It was all orchestrated by Blacky and nothing happened without his approval. Blacky worked non-stop on the plan and their safety. Everyone held their breath that there was time to make it happen. They had several contingency plans if things went south; in a split second they were taken to planes going to secret locations. Bodyguards carried guns now and at times even local police and FBI agents helped them out.

"How are you?" Harlynn asked softly when they were finished.

"Good." She smiled thinking if I told you the truth you couldn't handled it. She told herself to do the next thing and not over analyze the day in front of her. She was planning on taking Janey shopping today and to get their nails done. Janey still wasn't feeling well, but there was nothing Dr. Danny could find wrong. All they could do was watch and wait for the next symptom if it came.

"You don't seem good?" he questioned in the same voice. "I need you to open up to me, Kateland." He took both her hands, gingerly.

It had been a month since they had sex, if one was counting. Harlynn had said he didn't feel like it one night and it had started a war between them. It became a game to Kate, because she could go for a lot longer than he could without having sex. She was running a lot, swimming and doing her yoga. The last three days she had rejected him seven times, if one was counting.

"Can I kiss you?" Harlynn asked her as he gazed into her eyes.

"No, I don't feel like kissing because that's a code word for I want sex."

"I'm sorry," he said staring at her in the darkness. "I'm sorry a month ago that you wanted to have sex and I didn't."

"You reminded me of my childhood, you were cruel." She got up leaving Harlynn in the meditation room by himself. There were times she wished she never let him see inside her. Now he knew why she was upset, even she wasn't sure how to fix it. It was like something in her brain turned off and she didn't care about sex anymore. Maybe it was the stress from the schedule she was forced to keep or maybe it was the stress from people wanting her dead.

When she came out of the shower Harlynn was waiting to go in. Keep moving was all she could think as she wrapped the thick white robe around her body. The robe consumed her like her thoughts did making her unable to render a conversation with Harlynn or anyone else.

He started to ask her a question and stopped with his mouth open wide. He was reconsidering each word, in an attempt to not make it worse. Kate kept moving without hesitation telling herself over and over again to do the next thing. While she was getting dressed she stopped with her black silk blouse on and makeup done. It was as though she couldn't step forward or backward, she was stuck. As she looked at the clothes that Sue had already laid out for her, she turned and went to the sitting area in their room. She curled up on the couch and sat there staring off into space. There was so much to do and so many places to be. What if she didn't make that breakfast or lunch or meeting or phone call? What would happen if she stopped parading around with this procession of individuals dressing her and planning her day? Were they all going to end up dead anyway? How does one stop the President of the United States of America from killing you?

"What's going on?" Harlynn sat down next to her and he knew by the look in her eyes. He was also not completely dressed either with his undershirt and gray slacks on. "Do you need for me to cancel things for the morning?"

"Yes," she said slowly. "I think I want to go back to bed for a couple of hours. This tiredness hit me or maybe it's this circus that has become our lives. I need some time to stop and think, Harlynn."

"Me too." He softly smiled at her and leaned back in the couch. "I could use a break from all this crap we have been doing also. I don't want to live our lives like this, Kateland. I think we need to speed up the plan of action and decide what we are going to do." There was extreme doubt in his eyes as he spoke.

She sat there on the couch listening as he made one call to Blacky that he needed to cancel everything until noon and he would let him know if he needed to cancel the day by ten for both he and Kateland." Then Harlynn paced as he sent several texts in order that no one would barge into their room.

"What about the children?" Kate asked realizing that she couldn't abandon the children.

"Claire is getting Janey and Levi ready for school. Keat is fixing breakfast and lunch. Meg is riding with them to school. Then Claire will have Laney for a little longer." Harlynn smiled with his eyes at her. "We are good. I'm going to get you some breakfast and will check on everyone."

Again she wondered how she had gotten to the point of needing a person to coordinate her schedule and pick out her clothes. At least it gave her time to be with the children. For some reason it seemed she had more time with the children amiss the chaos. Everyone knew not to bother her if she had one of the children with her. Moon Water was growing faster and the trials had started on the JR6.

Her Blackberry was vibrating away as she finally picked it up going through the emails that poured in the morning. She only went through the emails twice a day or she would make herself crazy. Now on top of work there were requests for dinner or lunch with people. They only went to a dinner party after the children were in bed and they had been read to.

She turned as Harlynn came in the room with breakfast and a stack of request from different people in the family. She smiled at the drawings by the children and Keaton.

"Who else?" Kate smiled as he pulled out two others from her pocket. One was from Blacky that said to call him when she had a chance and the other from Henry with a quote from the Bible. She waited thinking. "Why don't you go for a bike ride, Harlynn?"

"Maybe later." He smiled as he put the dish down in front of her. "I would rather have this time with you, even if it's for a couple of hours. I would like us to go away alone for a night?"

"I don't know if I can leave the children, what if something happened?" She watched as Harlynn sat back in the couch next to her.

"Kate we have to take care of our marriage and we aren't doing that right now. We are both being pulled in twenty different directions. If Blacky says its okay, will you do it for me?"

"Let me think on it." She took a couple bits of the pancakes and sat back. She wasn't hungry at all. Next she forced herself to drink half the protein shake.

"Do you think you are sick or is it stress?" Harlynn asked her as he watched her and the room filled with complete silence.

"Stress and lack of sleep I would guess. It's hard how late we have been staying out five nights a week. I'm not use to it, Harlynn."

"I'll see what we can do with the schedule, Kate. Let's cut back to three nights a week for going out?"

"That would be good." She smiled relieved to a degree because everyone was telling her how important it was to be at these events. Maybe she would paint after she rested this morning.

"Perhaps not drinking at all the parties would help you too?" Harlynn offered because that was how Kate got through the parties and talking to all the strangers who thought they were dear friends.

"Then how would I be charming and delightful?" She smiled. "Not everyone is like you, Babes. I think you like going out all the time and seeing all these individuals who you haven't seen since we got married."

"I'm a good actor." He responded back at her. "There are a few people who I've enjoyed seeing, but most of them don't really matter. They always want a favor or information about the markets or a deal. And they act like they care about me or you or the children, they don't."

"Has Blacky said anything?" Kate looked down not really wanting to know. This was what Blacky had meant when he said there would be days she didn't want to do this.

"The head of fundraising for the President called yesterday. Blacky is talking to him this morning. We are thinking of doing the summit at the ranch in two weeks. I think we have who we need to go forward. We are ahead of schedule."

"I wish we didn't have a schedule." Kate slowly raised her eyes at Harlynn. "It was the tone of your voice, the way you said it. It was harsh, Harlynn."

"I was overwhelmed and tired that night." He sat down on the couch next to her. "I was mad because I know you talked to Blacky about the plan before he sat down with us. I can tell the way you two look at each other at times."

"Like I've never been left out of a secret conversation between the two of you?"

"Kateland!" He protested.

"No! Harlynn, that's not the same! Do you know how many times I've been sound asleep and you wake me up to make love? Or how many times I'm exhausted from the children and I always make time for you?"

"I guess it never crossed my mind that you were unhappy with our sex life." He looked crushed as she said each word.

"Now you are putting words in my mouth. You don't understand what I'm trying to say at all. This relationship has to be about both of us!"

"What do I have to do to make up for what I did?" Harlynn asked her closing his eyes. "I told you I was very sorry for what I did, Kate. You know when we aren't working I can't focus, I can't sleep and I get scared."

"You have seemed fine for the last month?" Kate questioned.

"After you go to sleep I stay up reading or working, then around four, I sleep for a couple of hours until we get up." He licked his lips slowly. "I'm barely making it, Kate. When we don't talk or don't get along, my world starts to fall apart." There was desperation in his voice.

"You don't seem like you're falling apart," Kate whispered.

"That's because I'm not drinking. What can I do?"

"I miss you. I miss the way you hold me and kiss me. I want for things to be better between us."

"I don't understand what I did that made you think of your childhood? When you implied I made you feel like your mother did, I swear my heart stopped. That is the worst thing I think you've ever said to me."

"After the tepee I didn't feel those feelings from my mother. When you said you were tired and didn't feel like sex, it was like my brain went into this mode that you were going to hurt me again. I know it's irrational, but that's how it felt. I don't know if I'm being clear with you or if you can understand?"

"I snapped at you that day we came home from the ranch. I was exhausted and upset about you speaking to Blacky. I didn't know how to handle what we facing on top of losing my father. I know you can't stand all these parties and our picture in the paper."

"I think if they were in moderation it would be fine. We do need to go out and see people. We need to go out a little, but not this."

"We have had a tremendous amount of change and turmoil in our lives, love. We will have grown up time again someday. You're safety is all that I care about at the moment."

"You make me very happy." She smiled as he leaned over and kissed her,

"Don't shut me out because I can't take it." He smiled back. "I'm going to check on the children. Then I will be back with Laney because you know how she loves her Mama." He winked at her then left her alone to relax.

Two seconds later the door flew open to their room. She hadn't answered any of Keaton's emails or texts since five. She didn't even open her eyes as he stood in front of her.

"You have freaked out?" Keat demanded as she opened one eye to make sure it was him.

"No," she told him calmly. "Why?" She smiled at him pulling the soft blanket from the tepee over herself.

"Everyone thinks you freaked out, Kateland? You can't cancel an interview two hours before you are supposed to go on the air."

"But I did." She closed her eyes. "I need time to unwind Keaton. I'm going mock five with three kids and I'm sick of it."

"This is all because you two haven't had sex in forever," Keaton blurted out.

"Did Harlynn tell you that?" she questioned because if he did, then he for sure wasn't getting any for a lot longer.

"Harlynn doesn't discuss that with anyone. It's a guy thing, okay. I can tell you two are not connecting."

"It's hard to connect when you don't have any alone time, brother dearest, so scram if you understand me. I need sleep and to relax. You tell Blacky I want this done soon because I'm sick of all this shit." She closed her eyes trying to go back to sleep.

"Fine. I will tell him. You better not get us all killed!" She opened her eyes to see him smile at her. "I'm sick of all this shit, also. I want to go back to simple times, Kateland, but I don't know if that can ever happen again. Christa needs a raise?"

"Fine. Twenty percent. What else?"

"Mom is coming to visit."

"No. And double no, do you understand me!" Kate yelled at him.

"I will tell Blacky to let her know that you can't do it." He smiled again. "I love having Blacky deal with all the things we don't like to do."

"Let's go to lunch by ourselves today." She watched as he nodded his head at her.

"If you are out of bed by then?" he teased before he left the room.

Kate got up and changed into one of Harlynn's soft t-shirts and climbed into bed. She turned on the television watching the cooking channel, which would allow her brain to stop for a moment. She was almost asleep when Harlynn brought in Laney who gave her Mama some baby kisses and smiled at her. Laney curled up on her chest and closed her eyes as Kate rubbed her back slowly.

Harlynn came back to bed, gently taking the child and putting her in the bassinet in their room. Then he was there next to Kate with his arms around her as he whispered in her ear how much he needed her. The chatter stopped in her head as she fell asleep.

~Chapter 27

As Janey and Kate sat eating cupcakes at *Sprinkles* they watched the traffic go by on Westhiemer. Kate had managed to make the interview that was moved to the afternoon and taken Janey with her. The world was getting to see a face that this new drug would hopefully help someday. Kate had taken her to James Avery and they had matching heart necklaces now. Janey looked healthy to her, but at the same time there was something in her eyes that told Kate the world was not right. After Janey finished her pink strawberry cupcake with kiwi frosting she wiped her mouth and smiled at Kate for a moment. Kate watched as the smile faded and her eyes were full of worry.

"What is it, Janey?" Kate asked as she saw Charlie's face fill with concern through the window. They were interrupted as one of the cupcake girls brought their order to go. Kate had gotten cupcakes for the family and bodyguards.

"The cancer is back, Mama." She said in a matter of fact tone. "I think the Chief can cure me for a while. Casey told me to go as soon as I can."

"We'll go this weekend," Kate told herself not to cry. She couldn't let Janey see her panic with complete fear. "I'm curious why do you think its back, love bug?"

"I'm very tired all the time and my bones hurt like they use to hurt. I don't feel like eating anymore because of the pain. They have hurt for a long time, Mama. Danny knows, I can tell by the way he looks at me."

"Danny is keeping a watch on you because he loves you. What do I always tell you when life is hard?" Kate asked her with a forced smile.

"Talk to God. Casey told me in my dream I'll be fine if I go to the Chief. What do you think?"

"I think our dreams are very powerful. We need to find the right medicine for you so you won't be in pain because I don't want you to be in any pain. I'm not sure where it will come from, but you know that you have all these people who love you, Janey. The family will do everything they can to make you feel better."

"I know. We're going to win, you know. In two months all these things are going to go away and it will be just our family again. We will have a couple of the bodyguards to make sure we are safe. Charlie has to stay with us because he needs us."

"I think we need Charlie as much as he needs us. Maybe we should adopt Charlie?" She watched as Janey laughed this airy laugh that was beautiful. People turned to see who it was coming from. "You notice what is going on, don't you?" Kate asked her daughter. She didn't know what Janey knew.

"Blacky will never let these people hurt us. My Papa won't let anyone hurt the people who he loves." She finished her Dr. Pepper and waved at Charlie who waved back at her. "Can we go home?"

"I thought we would stop by the art store to get new paints for you."

"I have yours, Mama?" Janey had made a mess of Kate's paints to get her attention and it had worked.

"Mama needs to get new paints since someone created chaos in mine."

"Oh, it must have been Levi!" Janey now had acquired the hiccups from laughing as people smiled at her. Kate could feel her heart ache as her throat tightened. It was so unfair was all she could think.

—

When they got home Charlie carried Janey to her room since she was sound asleep. For two minutes Kate stood there watching her. All the articles and medical books played over in her head that the cancer always came back.

"Is she okay?" Charlie asked Kate as he watched her.

"She is sick again." Kate admitted. "I need to call Harlynn."

"I'll get Claire to come in with her while she sleeps." Charlie managed to say with his voice cracking.

Kate went into her office with Levi and Laney closing the door. They were both so happy to see her as Kate poured a basket of blocks on the floor. Laney immediately started to chew on a block with her big smile that had two teeth. Levi started to build an airport to show his father with all his concentration. Laney watched and listened to Levi as he explained the importance of a good foundation.

Slowly Kate picked up the phone calling Harlynn with her hand shaking. She knew he was in a meeting, but this was more important. It was Janey.

"What's up?" he answered the phone on the first ring.

"I need two minutes." Her voice wavered as she held back the tears desperately trying to be positive.

"Hold on." She could hear him as he excused himself from the meeting and went out of the room. "Okay? Tell me? What's wrong?"

"She told me she has cancer again, Harlynn." The tears came like a watershed as they hit her desk. "She is in a lot of pain and I didn't know it."

"I'm walking out the door." The phone went dead as she covered her eyes.

Levi crawled up in her lap as she held him. He was still sitting there when Harlynn came in the office.

"Where is she?" Harlynn asked slowly as he picked up Laney who was still gnawing on the block because all her teeth seemed to be coming in at the same moment. Harlynn let her gnaw on his finger as she smiled at him, glad to see her Dada. Levi just stayed with his mother trying to protect her from what was making her cry or maybe he knew.

"Sleeping upstairs. Claire is watching her. She wants to go see the Chief?"

"Then we'll fly there tonight as soon as Blacky can arrange security. I called Danny. He is in the Woodlands and will come by the house in an hour."

"I'm so frightened it's like I can't move." Kate told him as she watched Levi close his eyes. "She told me her bones hurt like they use to, Harlynn. I remember how she used to tell me that when she was little and she would go to sleep."

"Could she be growing? I remember when I was little my legs and arms ached when I was going through a growth spurt. It was extremely painful."

"Really?" Kate asked with hope because at this point she would believe anything.

"What else did she say?" He asked as Laney wiggled in his arms with her eye on Levi's airport. "No, you are not going to knock it down, Laney." Harlynn whispered to her as he grabbed a wooden rattle and gave it to her.

"Casey said the Chief could cure her for now. Did you tell her about the Chief?"

"Yes, but not what happened to us. I told her how he taught me about the land when I was little and stories about my childhood on the ranch."

"Can you leave town?" Kate asked concerned, knowing that Harlynn was trying to close a few deals for Moon Water and the law firm.

"One of our children needs us, that's all that matters. I don't have to explain myself to anyone. I'm going to tell Leezann to clear our schedules for the next week." He waited for Kate to nod her head.

"Don't use this against me. I want to go to that damn ranch. I want to get away from this city for a couple of days to regroup."

"Me too. You've been on my mind all day. Are you holding up?" Harlynn asked her still rocking Laney to sleep.

"Somewhat rattled, although there is an improvement from this morning. Thank you for coming home for us, Babes." She smiled. "I could use some alone time with you tonight at the ranch." Kate watched as Harlynn came over to her still holding their daughter and kissed her. It was one of those kisses that made her want him all the way down to her toes.

Harlynn went back to the rocking chair and kept rocking Laney, while he sent out a flurry of texts. He was an expert at texting while holding a child in his arms. When he was done he turned off his Blackberry and threw it on the floor. It was nice to have this quiet time with two of their children.

Five minutes later Blacky came into the office in a calm huff. He obviously was flustered since he didn't understand what was going on. He was in panic mood as he stood there staring at Kate.

"Where is Harlynn? He walked out of signing a multi-million dollar deal and no one knows where he is Kateland? Why would he do that? Shit. Nick is all over my ass to find him so he can figure out what to do. What happened with Janey today because Charlie said something was going on? The guy was almost in tears, which I have never seen in knowing him for the last twelve years. And why are we going to the ranch tonight?" Blacky apparently was on severe overload as he slowly regained his composure.

Kate pointed at Harlynn who kissed his daughters head, slowly he looked up at Blacky while he continued rocking. It was breathtaking to watch Harlynn with his daughter with the late afternoon sunlight coming through the window. It was the way he held her and looked at this child that could stop anyone in their tracks, including secret spy Jack Black. Literally he stopped in mid-step and didn't say a word.

"I will come see you when I'm done." Harlynn said in a quiet voice. "We are going to the ranch tonight. Janey . . . is in a lot of pain." Blacky nodded and left the room, quietly, and less frustrated. They all needed a break including Blacky.

For the next hour they sat there with the children sleeping in their arms, just talking. They needed to talk for a while with no one around them. It was a conversation about the mundane things in life instead of business or investments or family.

"I was thinking we should do a date night." Kate offered up to Harlynn. "We need time without everyone being there. Or we could go to the Four Seasons next weekend for a night. Keat said he would stay with the children."

"Really?" She watched as Harlynn smiled. He needed to know he was important and loved.

"And I promise not to be as difficult as I've been the last month. I wonder why you put up with me at times."

"I love you." He watched her with their son as an expression of awe came over him. "And I can be just as difficult, so it wasn't completely your fault."

"True. It was more your fault." Kate giggled. "I don't know what gets into my head at times, Harlynn. There are these voices that tell me that I'm not loveable and the world hates me. I told you in the beginning I was a little screwed up."

"I've missed hearing the way you giggle. I love that both our children have that giggle." He paused reflecting on his next choice of words. "You aren't screwed up in the least bit and I know a lot of screwed up people. Let's be honest here. The only person who hates you is your mother, Kateland. No one actually ever says she is a complete bitch with a lot of problems. She is, so don't worry about what she thinks. I remember Joan use to tell me I was a failure who would never be successful. It's easy to believe those words when you hear them over and over again. If you start hearing those voices I want you to come to me and I will tell you how I love you."

"I will." He had a way of making her feel whole like no one else could in the world.

—

Kate went through her messages as she made sure she had everything to go to the ranch. It was almost down to a science now that everything was there. The children had one bag for traveling and they each had a backpack. Everyone had a color: Janey was fuchsia, Levi was lime green and Laney was lavender. On the inside of each backpack was labeled what the contents should be. She had her briefcase and an overnight duffle and Harlynn had a backpack and his briefcase. It was a miracle, was all she could think, as everything was lined up ready to go. Eventually it would get fine tuned to only one backpack for each child and one briefcase for each adult.

There were three messages from Henry along with three emails, which meant she was going to be in trouble. She picked up the phone realizing she hadn't called him all day.

"Are you okay?" were the first words out of his mouth. It sounded like he was in traffic, probably coming back from the airport. He had been in Jackson Hole seeing his daughter, Jessica.

"You know, Henry, I'm maintaining. How was Jessica?" Kate asked redirecting. She didn't want to explain herself and wondered if Henry would understand.

"The arthritis is in her left elbow and very painful. She needs to have surgery in a month from what the doctor said. Do you think you could call her tonight? You always seem to help get her through these tough moments."

"I'll call her on the way to the ranch. I should have known it was bad since she hasn't emailed me back this week. How are you, Henry?"

"I'm tired and worried about you, sweetheart. It's been a bad day if you want the truth. Are we invited to the ranch?" He asked awkwardly. "If you don't want your old man there, I understand. Was I supposed to take a hint from you by not returning my phone calls today?"

"Henry?" Kate was stunned because she had hurt his feelings. "I don't know what to say. I'm sorry I didn't call you today."

"What's wrong, Kate?" He asked waiting as silence filled the phone.

"I had a bad day too. Keaton was supposed to call you to tell you about the ranch. Janey told me she is in a lot of pain and thinks the cancer is back. Her white count is slowly climbing."

"Damn!" Silence filled the phone. "Why are you taking her to the ranch? Shouldn't she be at Texas Children's or M.D. Anderson? You know all I have to do is make a call." Henry asked trying to piece the puzzle together. When Kate finished telling him there was silence on the line again. "Kateland, you taught me a long time ago with your dreams that there are ways we communicate with God that I don't understand. I will stand by your side, sweetheart."

"You have no idea how much that means me to me, Henry. I know that there are times I don't understand my dreams or what happened in the tepee. God is there in that tepee and in the Chief."

"How are you and Harlynn doing?" he asked because he had heard about this morning. "Have you thought about calling Father Steve?"

"We are doing much better since my breakdown this morning. I realized there are times he needs my attention and I need to make time for our relationship. So you better be prepared to take your grandchildren one night a week."

"Gladly. Marriage is something you have to work at everyday, sweetheart."

"We are doing fine. As soon as I called him he walked out of his meeting and came home."

"Good. If he hadn't, I would chew his ass out again." Henry paused listening to Kate giggle at him because she knew it was true. "I will see you in an hour."

"Hey Henry?"

"Yes, sweetheart."

"I love you. I know I don't always tell you. You are one of the most important people in my life. In the future if we are going to the ranch you are always included. I will send you a text next time. I'm sure Keaton just got busy and forgot."

"I wish you could know how much I love you, Kateland. I'm so grateful for your love and your family. I will see you soon."

Kate hung up the phone feeling better than she had in a long time. She felt her heart rate slow down for the first time in weeks. From the moment she woke up until she went to bed at night her heart would race with an adrenaline flow she had never experienced. The feeling of fighting for her existence was gone. Even if he was the President of the United States, he couldn't wipe out her family and all the people she knew.

Or was it simple. Did they shoot down the plane everyone was on and it looked like an accident? Maybe they should drive to the ranch on second thought, just to be safe. She sent Harlynn and Blacky a text. They both agreed instantly with no questions. Everyone was apparently thinking the same thing.

Kate was dressing the children in their pajamas so they wouldn't have to change them when they got to the ranch. Harlynn laughed at how all three children had matching pajamas, all lime green and white stripped.

"Don't laugh too hard because you have a pair also." Kate smiled at him.

"Only if you wear yours first."

"The problem would be, I don't like to wear any clothes when I sleep with you," she whispered in his ear as she carried Laney out to the car.

"And you definitely won't be on this trip," he whispered back, quickly kissing her.

"No kissing." Levi blurted out. "You get germs when girls touch you!"

"Who told you that?" Keaton gathered him to put him in the car.

"My teacher told the girls not to kiss me. Germs!" Levi stated in his own way with his big green eyes. "You will get sick!"

"What girls are kissing you, little man?" Keaton asked him looking him in the eye. "Did you kiss them first?" He tickled him in a way only Uncle Keat could.

"No way!" Levi began to giggle, just like his mother, which meant for the next fifteen minutes he would keep giggling and hopefully wouldn't throw up his dinner.

"Thanks Keaton," Harlynn said walking by. "If he throws up you are cleaning out the car."

"No way. We have people to do that crap," he told Harlynn with a smile as he helped put everything in the cars and went to find Christa.

"We are leaving in two minutes," Harlynn yelled because once the children were in the car seats it was time to roll.

Kate got in the car next to him in the front seat and handed him his Oakley sunglasses. For the next thirty minutes the sun would be setting in their eyes and on top of that they were hitting thunder storms. She watched as Henry pulled up behind them in their suburban followed by two more for Blacky and the others. Julia was in town so hopefully Blacky would get his groove back. The caravan was small with only four SUVs today. It always took her breath away now when they went somewhere. Then she watched as two state troopers pulled up, which was a new thing. Apparently they would have their own escort tonight.

Blacky walked up to the car as Harlynn put down his window. He looked worried to Kate as he leaned in. "The President is at his ranch this weekend and is thinking of making a visit to come see us." Blacky took off his sunglasses. "This makes me nervous. It means the Secret Service will be all over the ranch."

"Tell them Janey isn't feeling well. We will let him know tomorrow," Kate responded to Blacky's requests. She didn't know if she could come face to face with this man after reading the emails and text. She needed to see what Dennis had to say and make sure that nothing else had come across on the servers.

"We have to give him something, Kateland." Blacky stammered.

"We understand," Harlynn tried to maintain the peace since everyone was beyond tired. "Kate will text you in ten minutes." Harlynn rolled up his window as they started down the road.

"We have to play him, Kateland. If we don't meet with him it's going to look bad and look like we're not sincere about his re-election campaign. You think I want to meet with that s.o.b.? I loathe the man."

"Outside. I mean I don't give a damn if he has to go pee in the woods."

"Noon for a swim and cookout?" Harlynn offered.

"Fine. I'll text Blacky. I sure as hell hope no one is reading what we text back and forth." They probably had better encryption than the President of the United States if the truth be known.

Kate turned and glanced at the three children because they were already asleep ten minutes down the road. She was about to turn off the movie for the children when she noticed Charlie, the bodyguard was in the very back along with Claire. They were sitting close together, which was odd. Kate spied on them as she watched them whispering. She saw Charlie take Claire's hand very casually. Then Claire leaned over and kissed him.

"What's up?" Harlynn asked looking in the rearview mirror. "Didn't see that one coming," he whispered to her, smiling.

"What do you think? Is that okay?" she asked wondering if there was a work place issue.

"Charlie helped save my life, Kateland. If he wants the nanny, he gets her. I'll speak to Blacky so they have the same schedule. At least they can see each other on their time off."

"You are too romantic, Babes. Who would have thought my bodyguard and our nanny hitting it off?" Kate giggled.

"We are fortunate that we have such good people watching out for us. Tell me more about what we were discussing earlier today. I think it's good we are figuring out a way to deal with what is bothering you, Kate."

"I know that we are going to have issues and not agree on everything. I have to handle it better and talk to you. I shut you completely out for the last month. I'm sorry I did that to you, Harlynn."

"I'm sorry that I didn't handle it better. You know I can be a jerk at times. I wanted you to cave in first, which was childish."

"I'm trying to unlearn these mechanisms I created to protect myself from my mother. You help, most of the time."

"What do mean when you say unlearn?" Harlynn asked her with confusion.

"I'm still getting use to the fact that you love me, unconditionally. Logically I know that you do, but it doesn't take much for me to regress back into this other person who is defensive and hyper sensitive. I have to be very mindful of what I let go on in my head. I think I'm doing well, considering all that has transpired in the last six months."

"I think you are doing amazingly well with all of the changes, Kate." He waited a moment. "What do you think of what Janey said? Danny said her white count was higher than last week. He will do a bone scan next week. Do you think he doesn't want to admit what is going on with Janey?"

"I don't want to admit it. It brings back a flood of terrible memories."

"I need you to promise me that we handle whatever happens together and no more shutting me out." He stared at her waiting for an answer. "Full disclosure?"

"Yes, I promise we will be in this together." Kate stared out the window. "When do you want to ride out to the tepee?"

"Tomorrow, at sunrise. Henry and Blacky want to come with us to meet the Chief? I'm okay with them being there, if you are okay."

"I would really like them to be there for support. Thank you for letting them come with us. You have no idea how happy you make me, mister."

"I like hearing that I did something right for a change." He watched as she giggled at him and he tried not to laugh.

"You do a lot of things right, Harlynn."

"God knows I'm trying."

As they drove in the thunder storm there was thunder booming and lightning that lit up the sky. It was a horrible storm as she watched Harlynn completely focused on the road. She wondered how this was all going to work out in the next twenty-four hours. She had decided she wasn't going to wait. It was time.

~Chapter 28

When Kate came in the house she noticed the orchids that were in the living room and kitchen. Her favorite chef was there making dinner, somehow. Everything was already prepared in order that she could relax with her family. Kate smiled as she put Laney in her crib and Harlynn carried Levi to the other side of the room to his bed. Keaton had taken Janey to her room next door. All the children seemed at peace and perfectly at home.

Harlynn wrapped his arms around Kate holding her as she closed her eyes leaning into him. She was emotionally exhausted she concluded as she felt him kiss her. They stood there watching the two children. Kate finally checked the room and put out their clothes for tomorrow. Then she turned on the night lights as Harlynn gently took her hand, squeezing it. It was the old Harlynn, but he was worried like the rest of them.

"Let's go have a late dinner before we turn in. That was not a fun drive in the rain getting here tonight." He waited. "I know you are worried, Kate."

"I'm good. Thank you for having the house ready for me when we got here. I want Meg and Henry to relax this weekend. I don't want Meg feeling like she has to orchestrate every meal."

"I called Christa and everything happened quickly. She is capable of a lot more than I had ever anticipated. What's going on with her and Keat?"

"Keaton will always be cautious about his relationships. I keep praying for him to know in his heart what he needs. I have complete faith in my big brother and his choices. I want him to be truly happy if they get married."

"Are you truly happy?" Harlynn watched her face as she answered him.

"I'm truly happy in this marriage and having a family with you.

I'm truly happy that we are surrounded with all the people who love us. I want this to end this weekend, Harlynn. I don't want to wait any longer to see if someone else will come after us."

"Do you want me to do it or you?" he asked quietly.

"Whoever has the first opportunity is what I would say. I invited Dennis Kavel to come to the ranch for lunch tomorrow." She watched as Harlynn laughed at her shaking his head.

"I invited Walter Reed and a couple others. It looks like we were thinking of the same plan."

"Let's go eat before I pass out, mister." She leaned up on her tippy toes kissing him. "I want to go to bed with you after dinner, do you understand me."

"Yes." He kissed her again. "You know that what we are going to do will change history?"

"I know that I will not allow anyone to hurt my family and if it means that we change history, Harlynn, then we change it for the better."

They made their way to the dining room where everyone was waiting for them, famished. There was little talking as everyone drank their wine, taking in the people who were next to them, or across from them. There were only two things they were thinking: please God don't let there be anything wrong with Janey and how much they hated the man who was President of the United States because he would have everyone in the room dead if he could.

—

As Kate sat in the kitchen going over menus with the chef for the next two days Meg came in. Kate could see the smile fade as she watched her start getting out the flour to make the dough for her cinnamon and cream cheese rolls for breakfast.

"No. You are not staying up for the next two hours cooking, Meg." Kate told her as Fred smiled. "Fred is making crepes in the morning and muffins, along with a quiche."

"I will see you in the morning, Ms. Kate," Fred said as he left the kitchen to the two women.

"Would you like some wine?" Kate offered Meg. "Then you will tell me what's bothering you. I'm sorry for the last minute trip to the ranch. I hope it didn't interfere with anything you had planned."

"Are you kidding? You got me out of going to a gala and two dinner parties." She batted her eyelashes. "You can't imagine how grateful I am at this moment. I get Henry to myself for three days."

"I can see it in your eyes, Meg."

They sat on the barstools in silence nibbling on the plate of chocolate chip cookies that were still warm. Kate wondered what Meg knew or didn't know. Henry didn't like her to know everything going on because it would be upsetting, which Kate thought was bullshit. Meg was perfectly capable of dealing with whatever came at her.

"Janey. I keep thinking of her," Meg whispered to her as though she didn't want anyone to hear her. "And Henry won't tell me what is going on. He can't sleep or eat and he won't tell me. I asked him what was happening at dinner. It was this love that encased the room tonight. At the same time there was this very ominous feeling that I've never felt in my entire life. I might need some of Nick's weed."

"I have it if you want it." Kate didn't smile as she looked down. "The person who wants me and everyone in this house dead is coming to visit tomorrow for lunch."

"President Howard?" Meg eyes filled with tears that were made from fear and anger. She immediately became overwhelmed as the immense danger they were facing registered with her.

"That's why we've been so public for the last four weeks in hopes of keeping them at bay and buying time. Did you really think I wanted to go to all those parties and interviews?" Kate giggled for a moment because it was easier than admitting the truth: at any moment someone might shoot her or her husband or her children. She told herself to just breathe to get through the next moment and the moment after that.

"I don't know how you get out of bed in the morning, Kateland. How do you manage with all these stresses put upon you? No wonder everyone looks like complete hell."

"There is a lot of good that has come out of this Meg. Harlynn and I are stronger than ever together. Blacky and Nick are very close again. I really feel like you are my mother, Meg. And Henry, I couldn't love him anymore than I do at this moment. There is such closeness with all the people and children in this house."

"I've seen it. I've seen this love that has come out of nowhere. Everything use to be about business and it is still, but there is this bond that has come about and it's beautiful. A friend of mine was watching the interview you did with Harlynn last month. She said you could see the love between you both and she is right."

"I hope you know how much I love you, Meg. I tried to tell Henry this afternoon because I want him to know." She leaned closer to Meg.

"He told me," she whispered. "And it meant the world to him, Kateland. You and Henry have a very special relationship. It's been nice seeing you two grow closer over this last year. And you will always be the daughter that God gave me. I have to admit that Henry and I have reached this different level in our relationship. He loves coming to the ranch."

"Can you understand why Henry didn't want to tell you?" Kate asked.

"Yes. I'm not going to tell him I know because than he will worry more. He would probably send me home in fear of what I'll do when I see President Howard. What a bastard. Do you know everything we have done to get him in office?"

"I know and I'm sorry, Meg."

"It's not you, Kateland, its pure greed for power and money." Meg had a look in her eyes that would kill.

"Harlynn is waiting on me. It might be one of those sleepless nights at the ranch." Kate confessed as Meg laughed with her.

"Good. This place is the absolute best place to have sex." Meg stood up. "I guess I'll go find Henry." She was up to no good.

"There's a bottle of champagne in the refrigerator if you want it?" Kate offered as Meg nodded her head. The two women embraced each other. Kate felt calm as she walked back to her bedroom.

—

Harlynn was in bed feeding Laney a bottle as he admired her. Laney turned to Kate smiling at her, then went back to gazing into her father's eyes as he spoke to her in his enchanting voice that could seduce any woman. There was something about seeing Harlynn with the baby against his bare chest that made her stare. She could see everything that had happened in the last ten months at once. What had made him not get on the plane that day, she would always wonder. As she walked by the bed she stopped to kiss him.

"Hi," she felt his damp hair and noticed he had on his black silk pajama bottoms. "Would you like me to take her?"

"No. Blacky can wait another ten minutes. I told him I was feeding her since I wasn't sure what you were up to." He watched as Laney put her hands around her bottle as if to say I can do this, watch me. "I ran a bath for you, it should still be warm." He glanced up at Kate with his school boy eyes.

"Thank you." Kate kissed him again. "Can we not do this again?"

"Absolutely. I don't know what got into me, Kate," he whispered to her as Laney started to close her eyes. "No you don't Lane, you've got to burp." He held her up as he patted her on the back.

"I'm going to take my bath. You can put her in the bassinet in our room."

"Blacky wants to talk to me because there is a new threat. He sounded freaked out when he called. I think the stress is getting to him, Kate. Do you think he could have sleep deprivation?"

"We pay him a lot of money to not sleep, worry and freak out for us. I will wait fifteen minutes for you. In forty-eight hours this is going to be over with, Babes."

"I don't know if it will ever be over. We just have to go on with our lives and not get stuck again. We need to focus on our family and finding drugs that will help fight diseases like Janey's. I guess I should put on a pair of jeans before I go out there."

"I'll get them for you." She went in the closet grabbing his favorite jeans, a shirt and some running shoes. When she opened the drawer for his shirt she had seen his guns there with the safety locks on. It was so strange that they had to live with guns like this.

She watched as he gently placed Laney on the center of the bed while he began to change. She lay next to Laney watching this child fall into a deep slumber as her own eyes grew heavy. Harlynn finished dressing going back into the vanity. He put more water in her bath to make sure it would be warm.

"Don't you dare fall asleep on me! I got Laney. Go take your bath."

"I will." She said as she slowly got up. Out of the corner of her eye she could see that he had one of the guns on him and he seemed worried now. He paused putting on his watch and checking his Blackberry again.

Kate went into the bathroom to find a warm bath drawn with rose petals in it and a lavender candle burning next to the bathtub, her favorite. He was so sneaky at times. There was a beautiful night gown for her the color of the golden flecks in Harlynn's eyes. She would have never chosen that color for herself. As she held it against her skin it made her glow. He had picked it out, she realized. He had done these things for her. She wasn't sure how or when he had found the time to think of her.

As she sat in the bath with the lights off and the candle's flame dancing on the wall she suddenly saw a figure approaching through the opaque glass at the end of the vanity, twenty feet away. She quickly pinched the flame out of the candle as she saw a man holding up a gun and for the life of her she could only think of Laney. Laney was asleep in the other room under the large bay window and someone with a gun was only feet away! Her heart was pounding to the point it echoed in her eardrums.

Methodically Kate got out of the bathtub grabbing a robe and moving stealth like in the darkness to the closet for safety. She had to get to Laney was her only focus and the others? Was someone in the house? Had they been there the whole time she wondered? Quickly she threw her favorite pink warm up and put on running shoes. It was something she had been taught in one of the self-defense classes Blacky made her take. Don't let yourself be physically vulnerable. Immediately she went for Harlynn's other gun: she moved silently, taking it out and removing the safety lock on it. It felt heavy and cold in her hand as she waited, watching the reflection of the figure in the mirror. Part of her wanted to shoot the bastard, but Laney was so close. She managed to get her Blackberry off the counter. There where fifteen texts telling her to stay where she was in the bathroom. The children were fine. They had found two men on the property.

Kate typed back what was going on and told them about the man outside her window standing there waiting, with a gun. This was not how she was planning to spend her evening. She asked if Laney was safe. Had Harlynn put her in the nursery?

She watched the figure as he shifted his weight from one leg to another. Turning slowly to look over his shoulder every once in a while. She could see the red lazar of his gun moving around the room as she stayed completely still in the closet on her stomach. Then another text came from Harlynn he was coming to get her. There was one lone bullet fired as the gunman fell to the ground and Harlynn grabbed her taking her out of the closet through the bedroom and down the hallway to the others. Everyone was in less than their pajamas as Kate, Meg and Christa looked at each other. Kate was glad she had put on the warm up on instead of being butt naked and wet.

"Well, I guess you had more time to get dressed than the rest of us," Christa said quietly as she held Laney sleeping in her arms. "I think someday I want one of these." She watched the child who was unaware of anything going on.

"We have a rule you have to wait until you get married," Meg said in her kindest voice with a little edge. "Levi you are getting heavy, my little man." He went back to sleep in Meg's arms, also unaware of what was happening. Janey was curled up on the couch with her Mr. Rabbit. Kate put her gun on one of the shelves as the three women sat in the dark, watching the people outside. At least three men stood in front of the door with machine guns and another three crouched down by the window. In the distance there was gunfire, but no one even flinched. Kate kept thinking why and how would someone know exactly where their bedroom was in this house with all the remodeling that had been done in the last two years?

"Christa have you shared the plans of the ranch with anyone in the last month?"

"I declined a request from a magazine four weeks ago. Why?" Christa waited as Kate was pacing much the way Harlynn would.

"Emma?" Kate finally guessed. "Emma would give out the plans because she is a complete idiot." Kate took in a deep breath as she heard the commotion coming towards the house. She could see Harlynn running towards the door with blood on his shirt.

"Kate." Harlynn watched her. "Keat got stabbed. You need to

come with me."

"How? Where is he?" Kate swallowed thinking it couldn't be that bad, could it? She turned to Christa who was crying. Claire came in taking Laney from her, as Meg put Levi down on the couch and went to Christa.

"Come with me, now," Harlynn told her taking Kate's hand. "Christa, I will come back and get you as soon as I can." As they walked she could see Harlynn fighting back the tears. "The guy came out of nowhere and jumped them. He was with Blacky by the outside of the stables. We called for life flight and an ambulance. They are twenty minutes out, thank God Julia is here. He lost a lot of blood, Kateland. He is fading in and out. He is on the verge of going into shock and he is bleeding. I'm sorry. "

"Wait? Are you telling me he is going to die?" Kateland stopped. "No, Harlynn! He can't die do you understand me!"

"He only wants to see you." He held her hand tight. "You cannot freak out on him."

There in one of the cabins, Keat was lying on his side as Julia pressed the compress against his back. She took it off as Kate stared at it. It was just under his rib cage on the right side as blood poured out of him. Kate cringed as Julia stuck her finger in the hole for five seconds and Keaton's eyes water with pure pain. She put another compress on it and held it with all her weight. Everyone held their breath waiting.

She watched as Blacky brought in two large black duffle bags of medical supplies. It was like a triage room as surgical clothes were placed all over. Blacky put gloves on and held the compress as Julia put her gloves on. Next antiseptic spray was sprayed all over Keaton's back. Julia called out drug names as Blacky filled the syringes placing them on a tray. Packets of sterile instruments were opened with lightening speed. Charlie appeared with two I.V. bags.

"Keaton stay with me," Julia yelled him as she looked at her watch. "Look I have to start sewing this up, we can't wait. There is no damage to your diaphragm or major arteries. Blacky and Harlynn are going to roll you over to your stomach. You'll feel something very cold and some pricks. I'm giving you a big dose of morphine. I can't lie; this is going to hurt like you can't believe, Keat. I'm sorry, but I don't have a choice." She motioned for Harlynn and Blacky to try to keep him still.

"Where's Kate?" Keat managed to say with barely any voice left.

"I'm here." She walked around the bed looking into his eyes. He was scared. "Hey, I'm here." She took his hand holding on to it. "Talk to me?"

"I think I'm gonna pass out," he told her slowly. "This really fucking hurts. Fuck!"

"Close your eyes and hold my hand. I know you, Keaton, and you will be fine because you have to! Do you understand me? Where would I be without you? Where would Levi be without you? And Nick? And Henry?"

"Tell Christa I love her. Give her the ring in my drawer, okay. And take care of her, Kate."

"You are going to give her that ring! Do you understand me Keaton?" She watched Julia's hands working diligently as Blacky handed what she would point at. She worked with such concentration and perfection. Her hands moved in the exact motion as she pulled the sutures tight and sweat poured from Keaton.

"Hang in there, Keaton. I almost have the bleeding stopped. I know you can hang in there with me." She took a deep breath waiting and watching. "I got it."

"What's his blood pressure?" Julia asked as Blacky took it.

"Ninety over fifty?"

"Roll him to his side." She took the stethoscope and listened to his heart. "Keaton I'm going to start an I.V. and get some fluids into you. Where is the helicopter?"

Harlynn looked at his Blackberry reading the latest update. "Ten minutes." He bit his lip.

"Cover him with blankets. When that shot wears off he is going to be in tremendous pain. I'll go with him to the hospital." Julia took his blood pressure one more time and stared at Blacky.

"Hey Keat?" Kate spoke to him in a voice that was calming and hypnotic. "Where do you want to go on your honeymoon?" Somehow she able to block out everything in the room like it was only them sitting with a bottle of Patron listening to some music.

"Bora Bora. Then you guys can come after a couple of days. Sort of like when we crashed your honeymoon and just showed up. I will never forget that look on his face. I'm sure Harlynn was thinking what the fuck?"

"I see you have a nice buzz from the morphine. I remember Harlynn walking around mumbling something like 'who the fuck crashes someone's honeymoon'. I think Janey and Levi will love Bora Bora. Tell me what you feel?"

"I feel cold. Pain. It's getting worse. I want more fucking drugs. Please, Kate!"

Kate looked at Julia for help as she shook her head no. Blacky nodded at her to keep talking as he and Harlynn tried to clean up the bloody mess because everyone could hear Charlie trying to get Christa under control. Henry paced in the background yelling on his phone to get helicopter here.

"Look, my son just got stabbed!" Henry yelled in the phone. "You find me a damn helicopter now and you make sure you have the best damn surgeon when we get to the hospital." Then he threw the phone against the wall. Everyone was losing it.

"I can't believe you got stabbed? I guess it's better than getting shot? I think getting shot would hurt like shit." She watched as Keat closed his eyes for a moment. "Why didn't you kung fu them after taking all those classes?" Kate watched as Keat tried not to laugh along with everyone else in the room. "Do you know how pissed Nick is going to be that he wasn't here? This is my idea; we blame Nick for not being here. It is so his fault for not being here."

"He is on his way to surprise you." Keat closed his eyes. "He heard about Janey and he got in his car. He called me from the road doing a least a hundred." Kate looked up at Blacky as he pulled out his Blackberry calling Nick.

"Tell me how you're feeling now?" Kate asked as Julia listened to his heart again and took his blood pressure with a smile.

"I feel like I'm gonna be sick. Don't be pissed if I puke all over you."

"It's okay if you do. I have puked on you a couple dozen times in my life."

"More like projectile vomit." He nodded at her. "You're the best sister in the world, Kitty Kat. I won the lottery." His words drifted off.

"Well, you are pretty damn amazing," Kate whispered as she wiped away her tears. Then Kate looked up as she heard the commotion. Nick was standing there with the Chief.

"I found someone outside who wants to see you, Keaton. He said the Dreamers other half needed the bleeding to stop when I got out of my car."

Kate could see that calm panic in Nick's eyes as he looked at the wound and blood all over the place. She wondered if she was dreaming now as she watched the Chief. How would he know?

Nick went over to him taking his other hand. He leaned over and whispered something in his ear as Keat smiled. The Chief came over and placed his hands on his feet. Immediately Kate and Nick felt this energy come through Keaton's hand as he began. It was warm and moved throughout each of their bodies. Kate closed her eyes and prayed for her brother. The Chief stood there for ten minutes making a slight humming sound with his eyes closed.

When Kate opened her eyes she could see more sweat pouring off Keaton's body and then he opened his eyes blinking several times. He sat up slowly with a look of confusion in his eyes. When Julia took the gauze off the wound it looked as though it was healing. The stitches and dried blood were still there and the wound was closing instead of a gaping hole sewed together. The room was completely silent as everyone's jaw hung open.

"Thank you." Keat told the Chief as the Chief nodded at him with the smallest smile.

"You are the Good brother. Do well in this life that has been given back to you." He looked around the room. "Where is the Princess?" He asked Harlynn. "The one who's bones ache."

"I'll take you to her." Kate got up slowly, kissing her brother. "I'll be right back. Don't go anywhere."

She watched as Julia stared at the wound puzzled. She gently poked at it then she looked at Blacky completely stunned. Next she took his blood pressure and pulse with a broad smile across her face.

"The chopper is about to land." Blacky told him.

"I'll go with you." Nick offered to his mother. Julia started to turn pale as it sank what had just happened. "Let's get you out of these clothes." He grabbed some clothes from the closet. "You need to get the blood off you before Christa sees you, man. What the hell did you do? Getting stabbed when I'm not here to take care of your ass?"

"He saved your old man's life, is what he did, son. Thank you, Keaton." Everyone in the room stopped, absorbing the words that Blacky had spoken. "I've met a lot of brave people in my life. You are one of the bravest." Blacky turned leaving the room in silence.

—

Janey was sound asleep as the Chief placed his hands on her feet with Kate and Harlynn each holding one hand. Again Kate felt the warm sensation going through her body, but it was different this time. At one point Janey opened her eyes and smiled at her and Harlynn. It seemed to take much longer with Janey. Kate felt tears of sadness running down her cheeks, she didn't know why. It was like the sadness ran out of her and as she looked up at Harlynn she saw the same sadness and tears.

—

Later, when the chaos of the evening had stopped, the house was quiet as everyone sat in the living room waiting to be briefed by Blacky. There was one empty bottle of Patron as Julia set another one down. Everyone in the room had at least three shots. Julia had given Christa a sedative after she freaked out upon seeing the room. Kate thought it was a sign of weakness because they had cleaned up the room. There was a little blood on the floors, bedspread and wall, but it was nothing compared to earlier. Harlynn told her to be nice and not say a word.

Kate watched as Blacky stood talking to Julia in the hallway before he came in the living room. She watched as Julia broke down in tears as he cradled her. The sobbing echoed through the room as Blacky walked her to their room and closed the door. To see Julia crumble like that brought tears to everyone's eyes. Two minutes later Blacky appeared in the room looking shaken. He sat down in front of the Patron and took two shots. No one said a word as he stood up.

"After tomorrow I think we can safely say there will be no more attacks." Blacky began. "We had ten people come on the property. We have seven of them in custody and three causalities." He looked around the room swallowing. "I had a call from Keaton and Nick. Keaton, thanks to the grace of God, Julia and the Chief is going to be fine. They should be landing here in ten minutes. We probably need to keep the Chief under wraps because I don't think anyone wants to explain what they saw happen in this house tonight." Everyone nodded in agreement.

"How did they get the plans to the ranch?" Kate asked.

"The plans we found on one of them are from Paul's home office as you had guessed. Harlynn's sister gave them to a person posing for a magazine. It is the same person who had contacted Christa a month ago for the same fraudulent magazine. We will take care of that problem later."

"What was the objective of the plan?" Kate asked already knowing the plan.

"There wanted to kill everyone in this house. Mostly they wanted me and you dead." Blacky said calmly. "We have the evidence to take down the President even without the texts from WE. We know who is exactly behind the plan. I don't know if the President will show tomorrow. It doesn't matter because he can't and won't escape what he has done."

"Did you know they were coming, Blacky?" Harlynn asked quietly.

"We expected trouble. There were no sources on how many but yes, we had a hunch that there would be one more attempt. They were able to get here before we could due to the weather. As we know this was an unscheduled, last minute visit. In the future I need twenty-four hours notice before we go somewhere or we don't go. We are very lucky no one in this room is dead."

"What is going to happen to those men you caught?" Henry asked staring off in the distance trying to comprehend what had happened along with everyone else in the house.

"We will hold them until everything that needs to be resolved is resolved. I have the assistance of people I trust to take care of it. All the plans have been in place for a while. Technically they are being held by the government and I have been contracted to oversee their care."

"Thank you for what you did tonight." Harlynn told him in a somber tone. "You saved everyone in this house tonight from being killed."

"You need to thank Keaton because he was the real hero tonight. He saw the attack coming and jumped in front of me. I'm not that young, anymore." Blacky swallowed. "I would have been dead."

Silence filled the room as Blacky pushed back the tears. It was Henry who stood up and went to embrace him. "We all love you Jack. Don't ever forget that as long as you live." Blacky tried to regain his composure.

"There is one matter that we need to talk about before I go take care of my wife. Christa's brother, Jeff Grant, is alive and has contacted me. He has important evidence to support what we have found. He was put in the government protection program due to his work in the Middle East. Let's say for simplicity, he has been monitoring our problem because of Christa and Keat being involved. He is coming out to protect his sister and this family. He is an outstanding individual and I think you will all enjoy getting to know him."

"What time is the President coming tomorrow? If the bastard decides to come." Harlynn asked.

"He will be here around one o'clock. Secret Service will be here at four A.M. I don't think they will be in the house. They will be in the two cabins closest to the pool house."

—

It was two by the time Kate made it to bed. When Keat got home she stayed up with him and they both cried. Tomorrow he was going to give Christa the engagement ring. He told her that things were very clear now. It was clear what he wanted in his life. Kate smiled when he asked Henry if he had gotten him the house next door to her. Henry smiled back and nodded his head.

Kate slide on the golden colored nightgown that fit like a glove. The silk was smooth was all Kate could think as she came to bed with Harlynn feeding Laney again. It was almost like the last couple of hours hadn't happened at all. She watched him as he held the child next to his chest and looked up at her.

Laney drank her bottle then burped as soon as she sat up. She grabbed Harlynn's face and kissed him.

"I love you baby girl. You need to go back to sleep," he whispered to her as she blinked at him. "Your Mama needs some loving and your Dada needs loving too." He watched as she laughed at him before she closed her eyes. He sat there holding her while she got herself to sleep listening to his heart beat and holding on to his fingers.

"Will you put her in the bassinette?" Harlynn asked Kate as she gently reached over. "I want to go check in with Keat and Blacky in case they need anything."

"Please do. Make sure you come back here quickly, do you understand me?"

"Yes." He leaned over kissing her as her toes tingled. "Do you like the night gown?" He ran his hands over her back.

"Yes." She looked into his eyes seeing the golden flecks that matched what she was wearing. "I will be here. Keaton. It scared the hell out of me tonight."

"Me too." Harlynn confessed.

"I saw those tears in your eyes." She waited as she watched Laney stretch her tiny arms. "I'm afraid some day that our luck is going to run out."

"We have God on our side. I'll be back in a moment."

Kate closed her eyes feeling the tears come back down her face as she fell asleep.

~Chapter 29

Kate was already up with Laney when Levi came in the room bouncing on the bed while Harlynn tried to sleep ten more minutes. He was feeling the effect of the tequila after not drinking for several months. He grabbed Levi tickling him as the child screamed with delight.

"What are you doing, little man?" Harlynn asked his son hugging him tight.

"Time to ride!" Levi yelled at his father.

"What else?" Harlynn asked him peering into his green eyes.

"Men with dark glasses and guns." Levi told him in a whisper. "Blacky is very, very mad."

"I understand. Some men are bad." Harlynn told him softly. "Blacky will get the bad guys and take them to jail."

"Bad." The little boy nodded his head thinking.

Kate stood there with Laney chewing on her finger thinking it was that simple. There were good cowboys and bad cowboys on the ranch last night. The good cowboys won last night, but did they always win, Kate wondered? Did good always triumph evil? They were about to find out in a matter of hours.

"I'm going to get Uncle Keat! He needs to get up and ride with me!" The two year old screamed at the top of his lungs taking off before he could be stopped. Kate was hoping that they had clothes on.

"Is Claire around?" Harlynn asked as he gazed at her. "I missed you last night. I need some time with you."

"I'll be back in a moment to take care of you." Kate smiled at him because she understood what he needed. He wanted to lie in bed and talk about the last twenty-four hours. He had to get his mind clear for the day in front of them.

Keat was in the nursery helping Levi put on his jeans and boots that matched. He looked better to her as she watched him with her son, grateful for that moment. Again she wondered what had happened last night and how it had changed all of them. Never, for one second, would she take for granite her brother. She would cherish what they have together, knowing it was a true gift from God.

"Now go eat. Meg has your breakfast ready." Keaton told Levi with a smile. He stopped, giving Levi a hug, as Levi smiled. "I love you, little man."

"And I love you more. You are my hero." Levi kissed him, and then ran off.

Kate watched as his brother wiped away a few tears and laughed to himself. She went to him and hung on him for a good five minutes. They sat there on the floor thinking of what might have happened.

"How do you feel?" Kate asked him in a hush.

"Better. It hurts, but not like when it happened. I thought I was going to die. I remember pieces of last night. You'll have to tell me later over a lot of Patron. I couldn't let that guy take down Blacky like that, Kate. Do you understand why I did it?"

"I do." She swallowed. "Henry went crazy last night like I have never seen him before, Keat. He was screaming on the phone to get the helicopter here. At one point he said his son had been stabbed."

"Really?" Keat sat back thinking. "What did the Chief do? I remembered he touched my feet and I felt this sensation that was powerful and warm. It was like electricity going through my body." He watched as Kate shrugged her shoulders.

"I prayed. I held your hand and prayed. I don't know Keaton." She hugged her knees rocking back and forth. "Do you think this will ever stop?"

"We have to apply force and it will stop. Do you understand me, Kateland?"

"Yes." She waited. "I checked on Janey and she is still sleeping."

"She is going to be fine, Kate." He took a deep breath. "I gave Christa the ring this morning and she was blown away. I don't know when we will get married. She is the one for my heart. And I want to thank you baby sister because you kept us together when I had doubted myself. I don't know how to thank you. See, you think I'm the one always saving you, but you have saved my butt so many times I can't count them anymore. Always know how I love you."

"I do. You know I love you, Keaton." She swallowed. "I think we should all go to Hawaii for two weeks starting Tuesday. Everyone goes."

"I would like that, Kate." He leaned over and hugged her for a moment. "Go see your man. I'm not supposed to tell you this. Your husband was a complete stud last night out there. I don't think Nick or I will be picking on him anymore."

"Shit." Kate whispered shaking her head as she felt her heart race again.

"I never thought I could love Harlynn the way I do. He and Nick are my brothers."

"Yeah, you scared the hell out of everyone last night. He cried. Everyone did. You saved Blacky from getting killed from what he said."

"I'm not hero. Blacky has kept us all alive for a long time."

"True. You've been my hero since I can remember."

"Thanks." He blushed with profound embarrassment. "I'm going to take Levi out for a ride on his pony. I will see you later."

—

Harlynn was still in bed with Janey next to him. She was dressed with her pink ropers on and there was energy in her voice and a smile that made Kate almost cry as she watched her telling Harlynn everything she wanted to do. And she talked about the Chief. She told him about last night and how it felt to have all the cancer gone from her body. Harlynn leaned over and pulled her over to his chest and held her.

"You make me so incredible happy, Janey. We will go and thank the Chief one day."

"I would like him to teach me about the land, like he taught you Papa." Her eyes sparkled.

"Go eat your breakfast. Mama and I will be out soon."

"Meg and I are baking cupcakes for the party this afternoon. Pink cupcakes. Do you think the President will eat pink cupcakes?"

"I'm not sharing your cupcakes with the President!" He tickled her then watched as she scampered out of the room, just like Levi. He leaned back in the pillows closing his eyes with a smile on his face as

Kate closed the door to their room.

Then it was Kate who was laying on his chest as he ran his fingers through her hair listening to his heart beat. She remembered the first time that she ever put her head on his chest as she closed her eyes.

"Are you keeping it together?" he asked her.

"I keep telling myself to do the next thing. God is watching over us and keeping us safe." She felt him lean over and kiss her head as he held her tight. "Have you seen the Chief do that before?"

"When I was thirteen I got bit by a rattle snake and he found me. He took me to the tepee and healed me. I would have died if he hadn't found me."

"Why didn't your father go to him?" Kate wondered out loud.

"Dad, didn't believe until you showed him, Kate. There are only certain times that the Chief can help." Harlynn waited. "Janey looks one hundred percent better today."

"She does. Thank you. Thank you for this life Harlynn because there is so much good."

"Yes, Kate, there is so much good in our lives. You have given me all the things I have ever wanted in my life."

"I wish we could stay in this bed all day long and not move." She confessed. "I just want to hear your voice and what you're thinking."

"I'm thinking I need to take a shower with you. It'll help me get ready for what we have to do today." He kissed her again.

"I'm petrified that one day that they are going to kill us, Harlynn. I can't admit that to anyone except you."

"Every morning I wake up I ask God to protect us. That's why we have Blacky and bodyguards who care and love us. I know that last night was frightening for you. The idea of Keaton being gone from our lives haunts me like the plane crash. I have to believe after today that the President will back off."

"Will the drug companies back off?" Kate asked.

"Most of the companies are implicated in the hiring of the hit man. Blacky said that Christa's brother Jeff was able to gather all the information to convict them. There are going to be a lot of new CEO positions in the drug industry. We're not giving up or backing down. We know who the enemy is Kateland and that makes all the difference." For the next ten minutes they stayed there until finally Harlynn pulled Kate out of bed with him.

—

When Kate made it out of the vanity, trying to stretch out the process as long as possible, she had a hell of a surprise waiting for her. Not only was Harlynn's sister there, but her mother, in person. She froze as she saw her mother holding her daughter and then she was furious.

Harlynn was pacing the room as Blacky stood with his arms crossed. Henry was fixing a mimosa and brought it over to Kate. Meg walked over gracefully taking the baby from Kate's mother to give her a bottle.

"I wouldn't want her to spit up all over you." Meg said with a smile.

"Kateland always did that until she was two years old. It was horrible. It ruined my whole wardrobe."

"It's called acid reflux and a child doesn't have any control over it." Harlynn said between his teeth since this was more than he could handle on top of last night.

"How thoughtful of you to surprise us, mother." Kate commented with no inflection in her voice. She sat down as Harlynn bought her over breakfast. Kate and her mother didn't have a good relationship going back to the time she was born. It wasn't a secret.

"We returned from our honeymoon, yesterday. Ann said you were here at this ranch in the middle of nowhere. I wanted to see your daughter."

"Her name is Lane." Kate told her between eating the crepe and strawberries. "I thought we talked about not showing up without calling. I didn't have a call from you? How would you know where the ranch might be in the middle of nowhere?"

"I called Harlynn's sister and she said she was going to the ranch. I told her I would be glad to come see my grandchildren."

"Bullshit." Kate said as she sat there eating. "Laney was born almost three months ago and I haven't a word from you. What do you want, mother?"

"Where did you come up with that name, Kateland? There are a million names to choose from and you pick Lane or Laney? You are going to call her Laney?"

"Lane is my middle name. She was named after me. Do you have a problem with that Jackie?" Henry said as he finished his mimosa. "Why are you here, Jackie? We know why you're here, Emma."

"I didn't know who I was giving the plans to when they called," Emma blurted out.

"I find that hard to believe," Harlynn told her quietly. "Jackie, what do you think of your granddaughter?"

"She looks exactly like Kateland. I was hoping she would look like you Harlynn, like Levi does." Kate glared at her mother. "Really, hopefully she isn't like Kate in every way. That would be tragic, now wouldn't it? The world doesn't need another Kateland Bass Jones."

"Mother you are being a bitch," Keaton said coming in the room. "Kate is beautiful, even though you would never admit it. Kate is brilliant and accomplished, even though you always tried to destroy her. What do you want because you have about ten seconds before I throw you out of this house? I will not listen to this shit today."

"You tell your father I want the rest of the money from the offshore account."

"It's not yours," Henry told her firmly. "You have no claim to it. You agreed to only domestic assets."

"I have a right to that money! I will take you and Sam to court, you tricked me. I had a lawyer call me that I have a right to it."

"Go ahead," Henry told her with hate. "I promise you I will ruin you and your new husband. I will run you out of Houston so fast you won't know what happened, Jackie. I have put up with you for the last thirty-six years, but I don't have to anymore because you're no longer married to Sam. You can go to hell for all I care. You should go to hell for what you put Keat and Kate through. If you want I can explain everything to everyone right now." Henry told her slowly as he finished his drink.

"You can't kick me out of Kate and Keaton's lives. It's not your choice Henry Grayden!"

"I just did," Henry told her. "And I can, because I raised those two. I'm the only person who cared about them for the last thirty-four years and you don't have a say who is in this family!'"

"There is a driver who can take you back to Houston." Harlynn told her as he picked up Kate's plate. "Today is not the day that we are going to figure this out. We will speak to you at a later time."

"You're telling me to leave?" Kate's mother asked with surprise.

"Yes." Harlynn told her standing up and waiting to walk her to the door.

"I'll have my lawyers call you, Harlynn. I have a right to see my grandchildren."

"I look forward to hearing from them." He replied with a kind voice and a smile. "Have a safe trip home."

As the door closed Harlynn turned around glaring at his sister. He walked over sitting down on the couch as Kate watched him. He didn't want to do this today, but apparently had been left no choice.

"You almost got everyone killed last night!" Harlynn yelled at his sister. "Why the hell would you give out the plans to this ranch that doesn't even belong to you? Do you know I have the authority in the Will to keep all the money if I want to?"

"No you don't!" Emma yelled back.

"Yes, he does," Henry told her quietly. "Your father gave him complete discretion in distribution of all assets. I would advise you not to push too hard, Emma."

"Now tell me any other stupid things you have done. I will cut you off so fast you have no idea. The only thing Dad said I had to do was make sure Mom was taken care." Harlynn was on the verge of losing his temper.

"A reporter wanted to know if I had a recent picture of the children. It was a month ago," Emma told him. "He said he was working on a book about you. He wanted all sorts of information on you."

"What did you tell him Emma?" Blacky asked quickly. "People are trying to kill Harlynn and his family, Emma. I need anything you have on this person: email, phone number or a name." She opened her purse and pulled out a clump of emails handing them to Blacky.

"I'm sorry. I didn't know what was going on," she told Harlynn. "Harlynn, you have to believe me."

"You should have called me, Emma," he told her as he looked at the emails after Blacky had gone through them. "You're going to have to have a bodyguard for you and the girls for a while. You are not to discuss this with anyone except Dave. I don't want mom knowing what is going on. We already have someone who follows her everywhere and the house keeper is an undercover agent. We will talk more about this when things calm down. I need you to go back to Houston with Kate's mom."

"I really like what you have done to the ranch, Kate," Emma told her as she got up. "I'm sorry for what I said about Janey. I know that my dad loved her like all the other grandchildren."

"Thank you. We will call you, I promise." Kate told her as she stood next to Harlynn. Harlynn walked her sister out to the car that was waiting to take her back to Houston.

The room was silent as everyone waited for Harlynn to come back. Harlynn needed Emma in his life and maybe this was the first step in long chain of steps to follow. Just maybe Emma realized also that she needed Harlynn more than the money that had been left to her by their father.

When Harlynn came back in the house he looked relieved. Kate wasn't quite sure if it was because her mother and Emma were gone or because he was speaking with his sister again. It might have been all of the above as Kate watched him. She wondered if he knew that he felt better. They had ten minutes before Christa's brother, Jeff Grant, showed up.

"What needs to be done?" Kate asked as Blacky gave them each a read out from the people that had been captured and a schedule for the day. "How is Christa's going to handle seeing her brother after being told he had been killed?"

"What?" Keaton looked at Nick who had the same expression. "Christa has always thought he is alive. Oh, my God."

"I've seen it before. I imagine from what I know about Christa she will be grateful to have him back. The questions will be what he decides to do next."

"What do you mean?" Keaton asked slowly.

"There is at least a million dollars offered for his head. He broke up one of the most important terrorist cells in Pakistan a year ago. It would have been worse than 9/11 if they succeeded with their plans."

Blacky waited. "We will see what we can do for him. I think you can say we have leverage." Black said with complete confidence.

"How are we going to handle dealing with the President?" Henry asked. "I think we need some sort of a plan."

"We do it today. I have a book of everything together. There are ten copies that have been given to certain people for our safety. Each of you has a copy of the notebook in your room under your beds in a black box to ensure your safety going forward. Make sure you keep it safe."

"I want to confront him," Kateland said slowly. "I want to ask him why he wants me dead."

"We'll be there supporting you, sweetheart." Henry told her as Harlynn nodded. "You know what I have always told you."

"Don't take any shit from anyone," Keaton and Kateland said together as everyone laughed. The laughter was broken by a knocking at the door as everyone looked at Blacky.

They watched as Blacky got up with confidence going to the door. He waited a moment before he opened it, and then stepped outside.

"I think I need to go get Christa from the pool." Keat announced to the group with trepidation.

"What are you going to say to her?" Kate asked.

"I don't know, exactly." He got up from the couch going outside to the pool.

Harlynn sat down with Kate, as Meg gave her Laney, who was rubbing her eyes as she blinked. The child didn't like to sleep, was all Kate could think, as she held her and watched her squirm. Then Laney reached out for Harlynn.

"Da-da." She said perfectly clear with a smile. "Dada."

"Yes, that's my girl." Harlynn said taking her from Kate as everyone sat in silence because it was almost perfect the way she said it. In an instant all the terrible violence from last night was erased. Smiles crept across the faces in the room. The purpose of their battle, the months of fighting for their existence was symbolized by Laney, Levi and Janey. Laney had reminded them with the simple utterance of her first word.

"I can't believe it," Nick whispered. "She is ahead of Levi."

"You better believe it because she is named after me." Henry smiled, unashamed.

Kate watched as Christa came in the house wearing a tunic over her turquoise bathing suit. She had a smile on her face in spite of last night. The rock on her hand had a lot to do with the smile, Kate imagined.

It was good that she hadn't seen Keaton with all the blood, was all Kate could think since the images still haunted her. Keaton looked tired today though no one would ever know that less than twenty-four hours ago there was blood spewing from his back from a stab wound. It was a mystery of sorts if Kate focused on it. How did the Chief know exactly when to show up?

"I know everyone here, Keaton," she batted her long eye lashes at him.

"Be patient," Keaton told her as they sat down next to Harlynn, who was still admiring his daughter as she slept. Nick was pacing much the way his father did when he was under stress. Henry and Meg looked at each other trying to decide whether to leave or stay.

"When is the last time you talked to your brother, Jeff?" Henry asked slowly.

"Nine months ago. It was a strange conversation. He told me that he would always be watching out for me. He said he had a very difficult mission ahead of him and he was worried."

"Did he say anything else?" Nick asked quietly.

"Just the regular stuff: I miss you, I love you and be very careful who I was dating. He wanted me to live my dream of writing music. And he did say one thing; nothing will appear as it truly should be. The very last thing he said was to always believe in him." Blacky opened the door slowly. The room filled with silence as Christa stood up as her brother came in the living room.

Kate watched as Jeff stared at his sister while the tears ran down her face because she was unable to move or speak. When she opened her mouth nothing came out, so finally she closed it.

"Go see him, it's him, I promise." Keat told her as she slowly she moved towards him and finally her brother reached for her. They both cried as did everyone in the room.

"I think we should give them time to talk." Kate suggested as everyone slowly got up and went their separate ways. It was one of the most emotional moments she had ever witnessed in her life. Christa and her brother looked very similar in facial features with different coloring. Jeff had dark olive skin and jet black hair. They had the same almond shaped green eyes with dark thick lashes that made it look like they both wore mascara. They had pouty beautiful lips with flawless smiles.

"Keaton, could you stay?" Jeff asked still holding on to his sister. "I would like to meet and get to know the man who is going to marry my sister. And you must be, Kateland? Thank you for being kind and generous to my sister."

"We are excited to have her be part of our family, Jeff. That would mean you also. We will talk later. Are you staying with us tonight?"

"If you have room for me I would love to stay and spend time with everyone."

"Done. This is Laney and she needs to nap in her crib because basically someone holds her almost all day long. And this is Harlynn, my husband." Kate watched as they shook hands for a moment.

"We will come back in a little while to catch up. We are glad to have you here with us Jeff." Harlynn stared in awe at the brother and sister.

Levi sat in Nick's arms watching a movie while Kate read with Janey. Harlynn, Blacky and Henry were meeting with the Secret Service to go over the visit with the President this afternoon. Meg was in charge of the flowers and food along with Christa. Kate smiled when Keaton came in the room wanting attention.

"How is Christa doing?" Kate asked as Janey decided she wanted to be with Levi watching the movie. Nick came over and joined them.

"She is good. I think I might have been pissed. She accepted that he didn't have a choice. He seems like a good guy to have for a brother–in–law. When is Elle getting here?" Keat asked Nick. "How is she feeling?"

"Now that the morning sickness is gone, she is doing fine. She decided she wanted to stay in Houston for this one. She said she was afraid what might come out of her mouth when the President got here, especially with her hormones."

"What are you going to say to him, Kate?" Keat asked her.

"I don't know exactly. I want him to know that I know what he did. I want him to know that we will go public. I want him to resign."

"Maybe you should wait until he brings up his re-election and the support he needs from everyone." Nick offered. "I can't believe we are talking about how we are going to oust the President of the United States."

"I've been praying for the right moment and words when the time comes. I have to believe that this is my path and there is a reason I have been put in this position." She sat back in the couch as the three of them just waited. They were waiting for the next thing to happen.

—

As Kate got ready for the President's visit, Harlynn came in the vanity to change. The silence was thick between them as Kate put her makeup on and brushed her teeth. It was the third time she had brushed her teeth. She had also changed her clothes five times and still couldn't pick her shoes. Perhaps she would wear the blue dress with a pair of red cowboy boots.

"You are beautiful, Kate." Harlynn told her as he slowly buttoned up his shirt. He didn't have time to jump in the shower because the President was actually only five minutes away.

"Thank you." It was a deep blue linen halter dress that made her eyes greener with the contrast of the blue. It fit her body moving with each curve and it was short.

"I'll do this, if you want me to. I don't want you to feel like you are alone in this because Henry and I are here. Nick and Keat are here too." Harlynn stood behind her watching her in the mirror.

"Do you think we could do it together? I don't know if I'll be able to actually say the words when it comes time or maybe I will. I don't know." She could feel his body brush against her.

"Are you nervous?" Harlynn untied the straps around her neck letting the dress slowly slide down to her waist. He moved her hair to one side kissing her neck.

"No. Basically I want to look President Howard right in the eye and tell him we know you ordered the hit on us and the children. " She felt his fingers gently touch her nipples as she closed her eyes. His hands moved gingerly across her body with the lightest touch.

"We will make this good, again." He promised kissing her back.

"You always make the bad, good." Kate smiled in the mirror at Harlynn. "I really don't know what I would do without you, Babes."

"You won't ever have to know." He kept kissing her on the back of her neck until she turned around and kissed him back as he pulled off her dress and the red lace thong. She saw the look in Harlynn's eyes that said you have what I need right now.

"It was the dress, wasn't it?" Kate whispered in his ear as she undid the buttons on his shirt. Then she bent down picking up the dress, so it wouldn't be wrinkled to meet the President.

"It was you. The way you stand up for us and our children. It was the dress, partly." He whispered back to her. "I need that calm feeling you always give me when we make love. We don't have a lot of time, if you know what I mean."

"You can make up for it tonight." She closed her eyes and felt him touch her in a way that only he could.

"I will," he whispered closing his eyes.

They were going to be late to meet the President of the United States.

~Chapter 30

Kate decided on the red cowboy boots with the short halter dress, which made Harlynn laugh because never in a million years would he have guessed she would wear her boots with a short dress. He watched as she put her hair up in a high pony tail and retouched her makeup. Finally she picked up her sunglasses.

"You look like a model. I always said you could be in magazines," he told her as he kissed her getting lip gloss on his lips. "Yum, cherry frost, one of my most favorites."

"Let's go." She smiled as she put Harlynn's straw cowboy hat on him, it made her giggle. "You gonna tuck in your shirt mister or should I do it for you?"

"We would never get out of here." He smiled back at her taking her hand.

—

As they made the walk from the house out to the pool she lost count of the Secret Service people and the bodyguards, all with big guns. A small war could be staged in a matter of fifty yards. She felt Harlynn grip her hand as she squeezed his back glancing up at him.

Everyone was there who was supposed to be there. Henry and Meg were talking to the President and his campaign manager. Christa and Keaton were talking to her brother. Blacky and Julia were talking to Dennis Kavel. Walter Reed was speaking to the CEO of one of the largest oil companies, Steve Patrick. Her father Sam and Sue had arrived as promised. And there were others there, as Kate glanced around the get together. Everyone turned slowly when Kate and Harlynn joined them.

"I think I'll get us each a Patron with soda." Harlynn offered eyeing the crowd.

"That would be a swell idea, mister." Kate watched as Keaton immediately came over.

"Man, what are you trying to do, seduce the President. You look gorgeous."

"The Commander and Chief will have no idea what he is up against. I don't want him to know until the words roll off my tongue." She raised her eyebrows. "How late are we?" Kate asked as she watched everyone trying to decide who should come over to her.

"It's all good." Keat smiled. "I like that you weren't here when the President arrived. I wish I would have thought of that one. You should be nervous, but you are glowing, Kateland."

"Yeah, we just had really great unexpected sex," Kate told her brother as he choked on his beer. She gave him a moment as he caught his breath and everyone stopped starring. "Did you think of when you might be marrying Christa? The ring is gorgeous."

"Don't do that to me, okay," Keat pleaded with her as a waiter brought him over a napkin and another beer. "I'm switching to Patron because this is going to be one long night. Shit, I hate when it goes up in my sinuses. Only you can make me do that. You are so cruel at times. Remember I almost died last night?" He smiled as she laughed at him. "I want to get married in Deer Valley in October. Just like your wedding."

"You don't get to plan the wedding. Christa does." Kate reminded him as Harlynn returned with her drink.

"I guess I have to go say hello to the President. I need you to come over in five minutes. Promise?" Harlynn searched her eyes as he handed them each a drink. "Try not to choke on this one, Keaton."

"Yes, I will be there." Kate made a grimace because this is why they were doing this. She watched as he walked over shaking the hand of the President and getting their picture taken. Kate dug the toe of her boot into the soft grass.

"Cover it up," Keat told her between his teeth, looking away. "It was her idea to get married in Deer Valley. She had seen a write up on your wedding in the papers. I like following in your footsteps, Kitty Kat. It means a lot to me that we will get married in the same church."

Nick joined them trying to be very casual about what was happening. He gave Kate a long hug.

"Very nice dress and I love the boots. You are as much a weekend cowboy as Harlynn." He teased her. "You seem good."

"I am." Kate promised Nick with one of her smiles that said I will win.

"Good. Harlynn has that very calm look in his eyes, which everyone knows there is only one way her gets there. I hope I have that kind of marriage with Elle."

"Me too." Keat added looking over at Christa with her brother. "I think I might get drunk?"

"I was thinking the same thing. Not just a little drunk, rather, midnight rodeo drunk, brother Keat." Nick added as Blacky walked up behind him.

"No and double no, do you two understand me?" Blacky stated firmly as Keat and Nick blinked several times at him like they didn't understand. "I think you rattled the President of the United States when you two showed up late, Kateland."

"Really?" Kate smiled like she didn't care and Blacky knew it. "We were doing yoga." This time Nick choked on his drink because he was laughing since he knew what kind of yoga she was referencing. He causally walked away to see with his mother and Keaton went to see Christa. It was her with Blacky, which she needed.

"Kateland?" Blacky tried not to smile, but he couldn't help it. "You are definitely winning this round, let's keep it that way." He paused as a waiter bought him over a sparkling water. "Tonight I want a bottle of your Patron, do you understand me?"

"Only if I get to drink it with you. I heard your brilliant wife has been offered a position at three different hospitals in the medical center in Houston."

"We are looking forward to living in Houston. I put an offer on the house next to Nick. I haven't told him."

"You'll have your own compound a block away from us. I think that is wonderful and I know that Elle and Nick are going to be happy. It's nice to see how close Elle and Julia are getting."

"It makes me very happy. I want to thank you. I know that you have a lot to do with all the good things that are happening in my life."

"You're welcome Blacky. How is Max doing? Is he safe?" Kate

asked slowly.

"Yes. I think when this is over he will stay with us and perhaps help me out at Moon Water until he decides what he wants to do."

"I'm very happy to hear Max will be with us." Kate became quiet. "Am I doing the right thing?"

"Definitely. If you and Harlynn don't want to do it, Henry and I will do it." He put his arm around her as he saw the tears in her eyes form for a split second.

"Short tears." She admitted. "If I stop and think of all that has happened, including last night, it gets to me. I'm thinking when things calm down we all need to take a trip to Hawaii next week. Tuesday. Can you make that happen?"

"Yes. Julia will be thrilled to spend time in Hawaii with the family." His eyes quickly moved around the party. "You need to go help out your husband. He is getting that very angry look in his eyes, which is not a good sign. I will come over in two minutes." Blacky nodded to Harlynn.

Kate slowly walked over to Harlynn putting her hand on the small of his back to let him know she was there. Again pictures were taken as Kate and Harlynn forced smiles for the camera.

"It's been a while since you and Harlynn came to the White House?" President Howard began the conversation, "You should come for a visit next month or anytime for that matter."

"That would be lovely, Mr. President. With the resent attempts on our lives I think it will have to wait until everything is resolved." Kate smiled finishing her tequila and signaling to Keat she would like another one.

"I told Harlynn not to call me the President, Kateland and I'm telling you the same. I want everyone to call me Roger when we are at a gathering like this. These people here will ensure my re-election in the Fall. I want to thank you for all your support. I hope we can count on you and Harlynn for the next six months. It's going to be a tough race."

Kate looked at Harlynn as he nodded his head at her with pure rage in his eyes. She smiled as Keaton handed her a drink and excused himself. From the corner of her eye she could see Henry watching and waiting. Everyone at the party knew what was about to happen.

"When is the last time we had a meeting about your re-election?" Kate pretended like she was thinking. "It must have been in November?"

"I think that's right." The waiter brought over a Scotch for the President.

"A lot has changed for us over the last seven months, Roger." Her voice was like silk as she said each word.

"I can only imagine with three children and this empire you have created. You have the world begging at your feet, including the United States government. I told the Secretary of Defense you would come through for us." He paused. "Is there something I can do for you, Kateland? All you have to ask." The President glanced over at his campaign manager who immediately appeared at his side.

At that moment Meg brought over Laney dressed in a blue print dress that matched her mother's blue dress. Kate took the child as the President stared at her. Then Levi came over to his father wrapping himself around his leg laughing as Nick swept him up as he walked by.

"Your children are stunning, Kateland. Where is Janey?"

"She will be out later, she is resting."

"Is she doing all right?" The President asked cautiously. "I realize she has been the catalyst for the new cure you have found."

"Actually, she is doing well." Harlynn told him taking Laney from Kate as she squealed with delight. "Thank you for your concern about our children."

"What is on your mind, Kateland? I'm willing to set up a separate track for your drug testing at the FDA if we need to." The President offered as his campaign manager Bob Fields nodded his head.

"Whatever you need?" Bob reiterated with the President.

"Wouldn't that be a conflict with your support for the health care industry and more specifically the pharmaceutical companies who got you elected?"

"There's no conflict." The President reassured her. "I'm not sure where you're getting your information from, Kateland."

"Well." She glanced at Henry to come over, "I have been given information that has upset me, Roger."

"I'm sure if someone has upset you that it will be taken care of, Kateland." The President finished his Scotch as another one appeared. "Tell us what the information is and we will take care of it. We need you for this election, Kateland."

"Did I ever tell you that Kateland and her brother are my Godchildren," Henry asked the President like a proud father as he joined them. "In fact, by all accounts she is my daughter and I would do anything for her. Isn't that right, Harlynn?"

"Yes." Harlynn said as Meg took Laney because she was wiggling. "Henry Grayden is the closest thing Kate has to a father and I consider him part of my family."

"I'm getting a negative feeling." The President said quietly. "Let's get straight to the point and save time."

"The point would be, Roger, I know that you put a contract out on me, Harlynn and my children. I have the proof that you did it and all the people that are involved. All seven CEO's and everyone in your staff that helped set it up. Your choice is not to run or to be impeached."

"That's ridiculous. You can't prove it." Bob stated firmly. "How could you make such an outrageous accusation?"

At that point Blacky appeared handing the black notebook to the President. "We can prove it. As well as the seven members left of the people you sent here last night to kill us. As well as Jeff Grant who will testify. And if anything happens to the people who are here today or anyone remotely related to them it all will go straight to the press, Mr. President."

"And you think I'm not going to fight this?" Mr. President responded.

"Then you will be the first sitting President to ever go to jail for attempted murder." Harlynn told him without mixing works. "We have the texts Roger. Didn't you realize that Kate is one of the board members of WE? Have you met Dennis Kavel, the CEO of WE, who is standing fifteen feet from you? Did you know every text and email you ever sent is on WE's server?"

"Does anyone else here know what's in the notebook?" The President asked as perspiration rolled down his face. As each moment passed he became paler with the realization of what was happening to him.

"Everyone here knows," Blacky told him quietly.

"You can't do this," Bob stated firmly.

"How much money do you want?" the President asked.

"Look at who you're talking to, Roger. The people standing in front of you are worth billions. We are not for sale in any way, shape or form." Harlynn told him in disgust.

"You can't put out contracts on people and their children because they make a better widget! Why, would be my question? Why do you want me dead or Harlynn or my beautiful, innocent children?" Kate asked with such force that every person stopped and stared.

"You are the most powerful person in the world and you don't even know it. You are going to change the world. At the age of thirty you have the power that will shape the world for the next hundred years. This drug is only the beginning of what you will do. I didn't have a choice."

"Are you willing to stop it?" Blacky asked him. "Are you willing to stop it or get impeached?"

"You would do that, Jack?" The President asked him.

"Yes. Every person here is willing to make sure it happens, even if they have to die."

"And you will not run again." Henry added to the demands. "You can keep the money you have in your war chest. In the very near future you will announce you are not running due to heart problems."

"How much time?" Roger managed to ask.

"You have two weeks." Kateland told him. "And you will do everything in your power to protect my family and company going forward while you are in office. You will tell the officers of those companies they are to resign immediately or they go to jail." Kate turned and walked away.

She walked over to her daughter and took her from Meg. Next she went and sat down on a lounge chair by the pool watching Laney, wondering if she would get to see her grow up. She wiped away the tears that were pure fear, wishing someone could make them go away.

Keat sat down on the other side of Laney as the child looked up at her uncle and squealed with joy. He waited for several minutes before he spoke.

"You're not alone in this, Kateland." He said as he peered into her eyes. "I know this life is very different from what you want, but I believe everything happens for a reason."

"The President of the United States admitted he had hired people to kill us. How do we stop this from happening again, Keaton?"

"We pick the next President of the United States." He smiled. "The people who are going to have dinner with us tonight have the ability to make that happen."

"Keaton, this is crazy," she whispered.

"If it keeps us all alive, that's what we have to do."

"Tell me he isn't staying for dinner?" Kate asked as her brother as she giggled.

"No, he decided to go back to his ranch. He wasn't feeling well. At least that is what the Presidential news release will say."

"Do you mind taking Laney for a while? I need to go thank Dennis Kavel for saving our lives."

"That would be a good idea. Although, I think Jeff Grant would have done it."

"True. You gave her a beautiful ring." Kate told him quietly. "I want you to be happy, Keaton."

"I'm completely happy. Now I have two people to buy jewelry for is the only thing that's different." He watched as his sister tried not to cry. "I have someone to share my feelings and help me get through life besides you. I think Christa understands how close we are, hopefully."

"It's like Harlynn. He gets a little jealous, but it's okay. Christa is going to get mad some days and it will work out. I have faith it will all work out."

"It feels like it will. I'm taking this child back to her nanny since she is looking tired. Did you know that your bodyguard and nanny are shacking up?"

"Yes," Kate giggled. "You want to go to Hawaii next week for some r and r?"

"Only if you promise to surf with Nick and me."

"I promise." Kate got up to mingle with her guest and somehow managed to pretend she wasn't scared out of her mind. She had changed history today and now she had to move forward.

—

It was late, as she sat by the fire outside gazing into the flames. She glanced at her Blackberry seeing a text from Harlynn saying she needed to come to bed. She could hear Blacky on the phone in the background because his phone had not stopped ringing. They had agreed he would handle 'the problem' as it was now called.

"He wants the two weeks," Blacky said sitting down. "Do you think he will do it?"

"I don't know." Kate took another sip of her tequila thinking maybe she should give it up. "Is that true what he said about me being one of the most powerful people in the world?"

"Yes. From the reports that I've read, Moon Water has the potential to change life as we know it. Think about how much of our economy is based on healthcare, Kateland? Those dollars can be used to build a new economy."

"When we get back from Hawaii I would like to see all of those reports. I need a few weeks to clear my head."

"I understand. Jeff Grant is coming to work for us, if that's okay with you." Blacky smiled as Kate nodded her head. "Apparently Dr. Carr is coming on vacation with us so Elle can come with us."

"Good. I want Elle and Nick to be with us." Kate paused as she stood up. "Thank you Blacky because I don't know where the hell I would be without you." He gave Kate a long hug.

"I could say the same to you, Kateland. Go to sleep and I'm going to find my wife who is probably drinking with Meg. Now those two together are a handful."

"Do you want to talk about last night? You look like you need to talk."

Blacky sat back down drinking another shot. He stared into the fire, struggling before he spoke. His eyes went from soft to hard and she wondered if he was reliving last night. Finally, he turned towards Kate as he nodded his head.

"Keat saved me. I'm not supposed to tell you this. Harlynn saved Keaton and I afterwards or we would both be dead. It was a well laid out trap, almost like they knew we would be there." Kate watched as

343

Blacky's eyes welled over. "Your husband, being the man he is, didn't want you know what he had done. I broke my word to him, which is something I don't do. I thought it was more important you know."

"I won't tell him." Kate felt the tears come down her face once again. "It was that close?"

"Yes. Harlynn isn't someone you want to mess with when he is angry. There was such a rage that came over him when he saw what was happening, it was stunning. Your husband has abilities that few people I know in my world have, Kate. It could be from being an athlete all his life or seeing someone injuring Keaton. I don't know. I do know you shouldn't be concerned about the safety of you or the children if he is there. Harlynn can handle it."

"The man is full of surprises." She winked at him. "I noticed your wife was not herself today."

"It frightened Julia to the point she asked me to resign." He waited. "I think bringing on Jeff Grant will be good support for me, Burt and Charlie."

"Let me know what you decide." Kate tried to breathe telling herself it would be okay.

"Kate, I'm not going to leave you. There were a few times I was stabbed or shot, a long time ago. Julia was never there when it happened and never saw me until I was basically recovered. She usually would see the scar and ask what happened."

"I would have killed you." Kate admitted, having another shot of tequila.

"She almost did one time." He took another shot. "It frightened her because it was Keaton, and she loves Keaton like he is one of hers. This is what I do, just like Henry or Harlynn. We do what we do and it's never going to change. Leopard's never change their spots. I would never ask her to stop being a surgeon. Julia and I will be fine, so please don't worry."

"I love you both. She is an amazing individual, Blacky. I don't know how she did what she did last night." Blacky proudly smiled and nodded his head.

"We are doing what we have to do to ensure the integrity of this country. Go see Harlynn. Thank you for letting me spill my guts to you."

—

As Kate came in the house she saw Nick, Jeff and Keaton in the living room telling stories while Christa, Meg and Julia where in the kitchen discussing the next wedding. Kate wondered where Henry was as she went down the hallway to his room knocking on the door.

"Come in," he said from his office as he looked up, "hi, sweetheart." She walked over and gave him a hug. "Your husband just left two minutes ago."

"Why didn't you come out to the fire?" Kate asked because she didn't understand,

"You needed some time with Blacky to talk, plus, I needed to get Harlynn calmed down. It's a little easier now that he will take a drink, if you know what I mean."

"Tell me what you are thinking?"

"You made me proud because you didn't take anyone's shit." He smiled. "You did better than I could have done. I wanted to kill the man. I don't care if he is the President, the bastard."

"I'm still trying to figure out what he was trying to tell me."

"I think you need to take one day at time until we see how everything goes. I will be here by your side, always."

"Thank you, Henry." She gave him one more hug. "I need to go find my husband and thank him."

"He could use that, Kateland." He was trying to let her know that this was hard on everyone, but especially Harlynn.

—

Harlynn was already showered and laying in bed watching the news. He turned off the television once Kate came in the door. She walked past him going to take a shower. She needed to feel that water on her face. It felt as though the water was washing away the last six months. She needed to put all of it behind her and relax. There would be no more crazy days. Her days were going to flow. There would be the children, Harlynn and family, then came Moon Water.

The white plush robe felt good as she brushed her teeth. She wanted to sleep in late if that was remotely possible. Images of Janey bouncing all over the house today made her calm inside. That's what mattered to her.

"You did it." Harlynn smiled with his eyes at her.

"We did it. I can't wait to take Levi to Hawaii and hear him laugh at the waves."

"I was told that you are this amazing surfer?" Harlynn told her undoing her robe and kissing her stomach.

"Henry taught me to surf when I was five."

"I've only been surfing a couple times so I may need some help." Harlynn admitted as he looked up at her. "You. I need you."

And Kate knew exactly what he was trying to say to her without all the words. He appreciated that she would face the President and stand up for them. He appreciated Moon Water even thought it made her crazy at times. Most of all he appreciated how she had given him this family and how she loved him.

"Thank you for being here. Life is good."

"Yes, it's perfect now."

—

Two weeks later there was an ocean breeze coming in their bungalow as the sound of the waves broke on the shore only to repeat a moment later in perfect rhythm. She opened her eyes to Harlynn watching her with breakfast waiting. He had already gone running on the beach and swam with the children.

"I like your hair all curly like this." He confessed laying next to her. Harlynn reached for his phone as it rang.

"Put on the television. We are hitting the waves in thirty minutes. Tell Kate to get a move on." Henry hung up the phone.

Kate and Harlynn sat in bed as Claire brought Laney in to see them. Claire had just given her a bath after her morning swim with her father. She had the same curly hair as her mother as she wiggled into her mother's arm and rested her head on her chest. She only wanted to be held by her Mama.

"Hi Laney girl," Kate whispered as she kissed her.

Harlynn found the remote, and then turned on the news. Every station had the same breaking news. President Howard has been found to have a heart valve problem and will not run for re-election in November.

"There has been an undercurrent to impeach President Howard for his relationship to the seven CEOs in the pharmaceutical industry that tried to destroy Moon Water and kill Harlynn Barrett. Now this turn of events is strange. Last month the President was fine during his physical."

Harlynn turned off the television as they sat there watching their daughter for several minutes.

"Do you think it's over?" Kate asked searching his eyes.

"My hope is that we are very close to getting our lives back," he whispered.

—

As they sat with their surf boards resting on the beach Kate leaned over to Harlynn and kissed him. He leaned over kissing her back on their private beach. She could hear Levi and Janey playing chase in the waves with Keaton.

"I want to go to the ranch when we get back."

"Are you teasing me?" Harlynn smiled.

"I miss it. I want to take some time to figure out our lives. And I know that you love that ranch. It'll always be part of you, Harlynn." Kate confessed. "You are my weekend cowboy."

"Yep." Harlynn confessed back to her. "I am."

CPSIA information can be obtained at www.ICGtesting.com
Printed in the USA
LVOW132135281112

309260LV00001B/7/P